I0690933

Retribution

J.L. CAMPBELL

Retribution Copyright © J.L. Campbell

Published by The Writers' Suite

All rights reserved. No portion of this book may be reproduced, stored in a retrieval system, or transmitted in any form or by any means—electronic, photocopy, recording, scanning or other—except for brief quotations in reviews or articles, without written consent from the publisher.

Publisher's Note: This novel is a work of fiction. Names, characters, places and incidents are either products of the author's imagination or used fictitiously. All characters are fictional, and any similarity to people living or dead is purely coincidental.

License Note: This eBook is licensed for your personal enjoyment only. This eBook may not be re-sold or given away to other people. If you would like to share this book with another person, please purchase an additional copy for each person you share it with. If you're reading this and did not purchase it, or it was not purchased for your use only, then you should purchase your own copy. Thank you for respecting the author's work.

ISBN Ebook: 978-976-8307-01-9

Trade Paperback ISBN: 978-976-95586-4-9

Dedication

To my family for putting up with me, although I'm missing in story land half the time and to the reviewers at The Next Big Writer, in particular, Dagny and Diana Hockley, who championed Justine and Xavier's story and kept me writing.

− 9 −

Saturday, January 15

Justine

Proverb: Trouble nuh set like rain.
Meaning: Unlike approaching bad weather, trouble doesn't give any warning before it descends.

Guitar in hand, Justine pushed the door open with her hip and pivoted inside Rapporté. Her daughter, Yolanda, insisted this place was Kingston's best outlet for musical instruments, which was how they came to purchase the guitar. According to her, they sold the coolest equipment and gave the best service.

The wind chimes jingled in a pleasing melody, which summoned the attendant from somewhere in the back of the shop. When the salesclerk spotted Justine, her shoulders drooped and her mouth puckered. Then she straightened her body and smiled, an insincere curling of the lips.

Poor woman, Justine thought, I understand how she feels. Fourteen-year-old Yolanda would try the patience of a saint. She had behaved like a spoiled three-year-old last week after the shop owner adjusted the strings on the guitar, and she hadn't stopped complaining since. Justine put on her best smile and approached the counter.

The woman grimaced as though she'd sucked on a lime. "Good afternoon. What can I do for you this time?"

Laying the guitar on the counter, Justine said. "Hi, it's nothing major. My daughter says the tuners are wound too tight. Can you fix them, please?"

The woman drew a breath, which escaped just short of a sigh, and picked up the guitar. "I'll be right back."

The saloon-style door swung shut behind her, and her footsteps hammered a path on the wooden floor of the passage.

Justine walked to the plate-glass window to check on the children. She'd parked the Camry a little way down the curb, as the spot immediately in front of the store was occupied.

She didn't see a lot of movement inside the car, and hoped Yolanda and Emile could share the same space for a few more minutes without starting a fight. The front passenger door opened. So much for that, Justine thought as Yolanda got out and crossed the sidewalk. Justine met her at the front door, prepared for the usual moaning about Emile's behavior. "What's wrong?"

"Nothing," Yolanda said, "I just wanna know what's happening."

"The saleswoman took it around the back. I should be out of here in a few minutes."

Yolanda's face fell into disgruntled lines. "As long as they get it right," she said.

"Not to worry, I'm sure they'll manage to fix it to your standard," Justine said, ashamed as the words left her mouth. She really shouldn't let Yolanda provoke her to pettiness.

Yolanda flounced away, muttering.

Justine looked at her watch before strolling to the counter. Five minutes. She leaned against the aluminum and glass showcase, and let her gaze roam the shop floor. A set of drums occupied one corner and several guitars hung in display cases around the room. Wind instruments, some of which Justine couldn't identify, demanded her attention. She walked over to examine a brass trombone and put out a hand, but didn't make contact. Just in time, she remembered one of her mantras to her children—look, but don't touch. A chill snaked up her spine and she glanced toward the car, tilting her head. The children were okay.

She frowned and lifted the hair off her neck; its thickness was making her uncomfortable. The heat was too much for a day in January, she thought, raising a hand to test the air, but the air conditioner was working fine, blowing cold air. She peered at the car again and threw a glance over her shoulder, toward the back of the store. Couldn't they hurry up and finish?

Measured footsteps alerted Justine to the woman's return. If her pace was anything to go by, she was no longer annoyed. The treads ceased, but the attendant remained silent. Justine rubbed the back of her neck, hot and ill at ease again. She pressed her handbag close and turned to face the woman.

For a second, Justine thought she was having one of the nightmares that had plagued her for years. Her blood turned to icy sludge, seeping from the top of her head to the bottom of her feet. She swallowed, tried to make her voice work, but nothing happened. She had to be wrapped up in bed, asleep. But no, the shiver taking hold of her body was real.

In front of her stood Xavier McKellop, the man for whom she had almost left her husband. His impressive height still sucked the breath from her lungs. He hadn't gained any weight and apart from lines marking his forehead and bracketing his mouth, he looked the same.

But something was missing.

Despite her silent pleas to her body, Justine's stomach pitched and heaved as though she'd vomit. She swallowed and forced herself to breathe slow and easy. She wouldn't fall apart. She'd act her forty-three years, even if she died trying, but it would be easier if she got her tongue and brain to work together.

Xavier stared, taking in the casual beige pantsuit with matching wedge-heeled sandals and handbag. His scrutiny made Justine grateful for the care she'd given her body over the years.

"Seems you're quite a demanding customer." He laid the guitar on the glass and inclined his head toward the instrument. "One of the tuners was stuck. This should do it."

So he was going to behave as if he didn't know her. She could handle that, if the ice now encasing her would melt and allow her to move, but she was also convinced that if she so much as shifted, she'd shatter into millions of pieces that would be impossible to put back together.

She had pictured this sequence of events hundreds of times, but nothing she imagined could have prepared her for this meeting. She got her feet to move, and picked up the guitar, wanting to sprint out of the shop. Instead, she commanded herself to work toward a dignified exit. "Thank you."

Now that she was over her initial shock, Justine allowed herself what she intended to be a detailed body sweep. That didn't happen. She put a hand to her mouth to stifle a moan, but her anguished cry fell between them.

Xavier's gorgeous locks were gone.

Her jumping nerves sent her reaching for the hair pulled together at the back of her neck. Since their separation, all she had done to her hair was process, treat, and trim. Now she acknowledged why she had refused to cut it. Xavier had loved her hair, and used to bury his face in it when they made love.

She licked her lips and dragged her mind away from what she used to do with him on Tuesday and Friday evenings of years past. The door chime played its airy tune, while Justine scrabbled to collect her senses in the silence that had grown chilly. A small hand slid into hers, shooting panic through her veins.

"Mommy, can you come now? Yolanda's slapping me. Can we drop her off somewhere and never pick her up again?"

Cold air from the room flowed into Justine's mouth. She snapped her lips shut, grabbed Emile's arm and propelled him toward the door.

He resisted her, whining. "Mommy, you're squeezing my arm!"

"Justine!"

She didn't respond to the accusation in Xavier's voice. Instead, she shoved Emile gently. "Go sit in the car, I'm coming now."

"Okay, but I'm gonna stay outside 'til you come."

He dashed out the door, tall and sturdy for his six and a half years; a near replica of his father.

She watched Emile leave, while her thoughts scattered, leaving her mind blank. What was she going to say to Xavier, whose shock and anger carried to her when he called her name? She didn't have the courage to face him, so she stood motionless.

A prolonged creak from the floorboards warned her that he had left the sales desk. He stopped a few feet away, as still as a cactus. She felt his presence, but didn't move. Unable to look away, Justine stared at her children through the plate glass. Yolanda sat sideways in the front passenger seat, with her feet on the walkway. Emile leaned against the car, eyebrows pulled into a frown while he dragged the toe of his sneaker across the concrete sidewalk. Leaning forward, Yolanda said something, before slapping at him. Emile jumped out of her reach and stuck out his tongue.

Yolanda struck out at Emile a second time, but didn't land a blow. A man going past them said something to Yolanda, after which Emile made a face at her. She glared at him, swung her legs inside the car and slammed the door.

Justine didn't doubt that Xavier's eyes were glued to Emile. She risked looking at Xavier. A tic pulsed above his cheek. He blinked hard and continued to observe Emile. From where Justine stood, she heard Xavier's deep intake of air. Staring straight ahead, she hoped that by some miracle the man beside her wouldn't see what was obvious.

Xavier walked around her and stopped inches away. She refused to look anywhere above his neck, which moved as he swallowed. The russet skin was lighter where the opening of his shirt revealed his chest. A slight shake of the head grounded her and she clutched the guitar as though it was a lifeline.

Xavier sighed, and his breath washed over her, reminding her of things she had forced herself to forget. Hands in his pockets, he moved a few feet away to stand near the plate glass. She assumed he was still looking at Emile, who stood facing them, while he examined something on the sidewalk.

Slowly, Xavier walked out of sight and then came back to where she stood, rooted to the floor. His mouth opened and as though choosing his words with care, he hesitated before he asked, "Why?"

She studied the red and blue pinstripes on his shirt, fascinated by the raised stitches on the white material.

"I couldn't—"

"You couldn't what?"

His voice was a whip, cracking against her skin.

In their time together, she had never heard him speak in anger. It shocked her. His even temper was one of the qualities she had most admired about him.

He glowered, lips drawn tight, and it was as if the easygoing side of him had never existed. "How the hell could you do something like this?"

Movement outside the window distracted her; Emile was coming back. Willing her voice not to waver, she said, "I have to go."

A vice clamped her arm. Xavier spoke in her ear. "You owe me an explanation."

She couldn't think of anything to say. Her thoughts became a beehive, humming between her ears and her legs threatened to leave her without support. Summoning her strength and willpower, Justine twisted out of Xavier's grip and met Emile in the doorway.

Shaking like a sapling at the mercy of a storm, Justine grabbed her son's hand, and threw hurried words over her shoulder. "I can't talk. Not now."

Xavier's intense scrutiny doubled her body heat, but Justine kept moving. If she stopped, who knew what he might do. The door opened behind her, the musical notes from the wind chimes now reduced to a jangling noise.

"Justine!"

Emile planted his feet on the sidewalk. "That man is calling you, Mommy."

"Come on, we have to go," Justine said, pulling him along.

"Mommy, you're squeezing my arm again."

Justine pretended not to hear Xavier, while Emile continued to complain that she was roughing him up. She pushed him into the back of the car, trotted to the driver's side, and peeled away from the sidewalk, minus the seat belt.

***

Justine sat at the dining table, staring out the window, where the Frangipani's yellow-white blooms stirred in the evening breeze. The elongated leaves drooped as though exhausted. Pretty much how I feel.

She cupped a hand to her cheek, thinking how well the showy blossoms and sagging leaves mirrored her life; a study in contrasts.

Emile and Yolanda were busy eating Stewed Peas, a family favorite. Their longtime household helper, Miss Pauline, had the weekend off and although the children were used to a light Saturday evening meal in her absence, Justine had prepared the filling stew to keep them happy.

Every so often, Emile smiled at her, echoing the affection with which she looked at him. She stole a glance at Yolanda, who for once, didn't look at her with open hostility.

Life would be wonderful if Justine could find a way for them to get along, but their truces never lasted long. Her latest efforts at peacemaking had landed her back on Xavier's radar.

Since they got home, Justine had avoided thinking about how she'd deal with that situation.

Yolanda lifted her head and put on a smile intended to charm Justine. "Mom, can I have another couple of picks for the guitar?"

"What happened to the ones you got when we bought it?"

"One of them broke." She pushed a forkful of rice around her plate before mumbling, "And I lost the other."

"You have to be more careful," Justine said, panic-stricken at the thought of going anywhere near Xavier.

"Emile is the one who broke it."

"And I suppose you're going to blame him for losing the other one."

"Well, he won't stop messing around my things."

"If you'd put your things out of his reach, then maybe—"

"You blame me for everything!"

Emile slurped from his straw, distracting Justine. "Emile, stop that."

"Sorry."

Urging herself to be patient, Justine continued, "All I'm trying to tell you is that you should take better care of your things."

"How can I, when he's always interfering with my stuff? I won't ask for anything else if you're going to make such a big deal over it."

"Just stop right there," Justine said, irritated by the shrill edge to her daughter's voice. "First, the tuners weren't right. Then, they clashed with the fret board. I don't remember what it was after that and now you want something I bought already.

"I can't believe you think I'm unreasonable because I refuse to continue going back and forth over a stupid guitar. You could have asked me to get the pick this morning."

"But I didn't remember."

Justine stared Yolanda down. "Too bad. I'm not buying anything. I'm tired of your attitude and your tantrums. Act your age. Maybe then, I'll think about going out of my way for you. If you need that pick so much, you can buy it next Saturday on your time."

Yolanda's mouth formed an O.

Behind her drinking glass, Justine hid a satisfied smile. For the first time in years, she'd told Yolanda exactly what she thought of her behavior. It was way past time to rein her in. God knew she was happy Yolanda hadn't fallen in with a bad crowd, but her demands were too much to cope with, and they had gotten worse since she turned fourteen.

Yolanda's brows drew together as she prepared to spew her anger, but Justine held up one hand. "Be very careful what you say to me. If I don't like what you say, or how you say it, you'll regret it."

Yolanda sank back, hugged herself, and pouted. The minutes wound by, and the only sound in the room came from Emile's fork scraping the plate. He knew better than to say anything and risk one or the other of them snapping at him.

Imitating the tone she used when she wanted something, Yolanda said, "Come on, Mom. You know how much this means to me. I need to practice. How am I gonna do that if everything's not exactly right?"

"At the rate you're going, you'll never be satisfied."

"Mom!"

The stretching of 'Mom' to three syllables was something Yolanda used to do as an eight year old. Before that, Justine was Yolanda's adored 'Mommy', who could do no wrong. Justine missed those days when her daughter had been a sweet, uncomplicated child, much like Emile. She'd be fifteen in a few months and Justine dreaded the battles that lay before them.

Yolanda moaned, raised her hands, and let them fall to the tabletop. "I'm gonna go bananas if everything isn't right and—"

"You said that with whatever-that-thing-was you used to play, and you said that with the keyboard and now—"

"But I'm really into the guitar. If I wasn't, I'd have given it up long ago."

Justine laid both hands on the table. "All right. I get it. You have a point. But like I said, you'll have to buy whatever you need at your convenience."

Yolanda heaved the air out of her lungs and nodded. "Okay."

Justine studied Yolanda with a neutral expression in place. The neck of her humongous tee-shirt slid off one shoulder, revealing the merino underneath. She'd bunched her hair into a rat's nest, and her striking face had crumpled into a frown. Justine saw herself reflected as she'd been many years ago. Why hadn't she put her foot down before now?

She couldn't find a good answer.

With her fingertips, she pressed the spot between her brows, hoping the faint headache wouldn't get worse.

A clatter came from Emile's side of the table. The knife and fork had fallen from his hands and bits of beef, pig's tail and rice littered the placemat.

"It's Landy's fault," he said, "she pinched me."

"Landy, why—"

Yolanda glared at Justine. "Of course, you're going to take his side. Again."

Fighting weariness and worry, Justine propped her elbow on the table and cupped her forehead. "Actually, I was going to ask you to help him clean up."

"Oh." Yolanda slouched, fiddling with the placemat.

Justine pushed aside the meal she hadn't touched and got to her feet. "I'm going to lie down. Try not to kill each other, okay?"

Emile and Yolanda mumbled together, their eyes cast down. Justine had never disappeared during dinnertime, but she couldn't sit there a moment longer, pretending everything was fine. The constant fighting had worn through her defenses.

And there was Xavier.

She wanted to weep until she ran out of tears. It wouldn't solve anything, but might relieve the tension that had been stiffening her neck and squeezing her throat each time her mind rested on him.

Since Emile's birth, the fear of having his true paternity revealed had paralyzed Justine, and after keeping him a secret for so long, she'd been caught out because of her willful daughter and a damn guitar.

Writing her thoughts down would have helped Justine sift through this crisis, but she'd stopped keeping a diary a few years after Emile was born. A couple of near misses with her husband and the radical changes to Yolanda's personality made it risky to express her feelings on paper. She'd resigned herself to keeping her secrets inside where nobody but herself could expose them.

Her stomach grumbled, reminding her it was empty, but she didn't have the energy for eating. The confrontation to come with Xavier demanded all her attention. His eyes had given away his intention. He'd come looking for her and make sure she paid for what she'd done.

– 2 –

Two weeks later, Saturday, January 29

Xavier

Proverb: Mi come ya (here) fi drink milk, mi nuh come ya fi count cow.
Meaning: It's best to conduct important business in a straightforward way.

Thanks to the customer log, it was easy to find Justine's telephone number. Xavier let a week pass before contacting her, thinking seven days would give her enough time to think about how she had wronged him. When he called the first two times, she did her best to avoid setting a date to meet him, but he ignored her ready-made excuses.

Now she sat across from him, hands folded in her lap, refusing to meet his eyes. The bottled water remained untouched, sweat gathering on the plastic container. He sipped black coffee, which tasted awful, but he needed its added bitterness to do what he planned.

With a clink, he placed the cup on its matching saucer and looked around the café, making Justine wait. The tiny tables, delicate glassware, and frilly curtains made him conscious of his size. No doubt, that's why she chose to meet him in this airy-fairy place. *Pandora's Box*. Even the name was flighty, he thought, but fitting in their situation.

Justine continued to study her hands, as though she would find the answers to her problems engraved on her skin. She reminded him of a child who'd been caught doing something wrong and didn't want to admit guilt or face punishment.

He felt himself softening and quashed the remembered tenderness between them that tried to edge past his defenses.

"What the hell were you thinking?" he asked.

She started, and her white shirt opened to reveal a black tank top. Xavier blanked his expression and met her eyes. Though a sheen of perspiration appeared on her forehead, she gave no hint that she was disturbed. His instincts told him she had to be terrified since she didn't know what he wanted.

He wasn't sure he knew either, but that didn't stop his attack. "Or should I ask whether you stopped to think about anybody but yourself?"

Justine's shoulders lifted and she ducked her head, as though expecting a blow.

"That boy. My son. What is his name?"

She whispered something indistinct.

Xavier leaned forward. "I didn't hear that."

She spoke again, this time louder. "Emile."

He caught his budding smile in time. The fact that she gave Emile his middle name pleased him, but he suspected he'd get mad again in a minute. "What is his last name?"

She shot him a panic-stricken glance before she answered. "Charles."

Xavier's next words exploded from his mouth. "You gave my son your husband's last name?"

Her quick sweep of the café reminded him where they were and confirmed why she chose to meet him here. She thought she'd be safe.

The customers around them continued their conversations, their movements relaxed. A tinkle of laughter rose somewhere to his left.

Didn't these people have anything better to do than sit around in the middle of the day gossiping and drinking tea?

The tables were so positioned that others could hear their business if they spoke at full voice; not that Xavier cared. Justine thought she was altogether too smart. Xavier scowled at the elderly man sitting at the next table. With a jerk of the head, the man shifted his gaze to the newspaper in front of him.

Damn inquisitive.

Justine drew herself up and her eyes shone, the first spark of fire since she sat down. "What was I supposed to do?"

Xavier sipped more coffee, holding in a grimace. Over the rim, he studied Justine. She hadn't changed much and was still a head turner, her skin flawless, her hair thick and glossy, but her eyes puzzled him. He couldn't analyze what they were telling him, but he'd figure that out later. Right now, he needed to focus on her question and the reason for their meeting.

"*The right thing, Justine.* That's what you should have done. Instead, you chose to be selfish and took the coward's way out. Didn't it—?"

Her fist landed on the table and set the bottle wobbling. She whispered, leaning toward him. "Don't you dare judge me. You weren't around when I had to deal with the fact that I almost lost my daughter while I was in bed with you!"

Heat curled in his belly and shot out of his mouth. "That was your choice. You wanted to be a martyr. You didn't have to do it alone."

Her breath came in short puffs, lifting her shoulders. "And you don't know what it feels like to be married and have to live with the knowledge that the baby in your belly doesn't belong to your husband."

"And that gave you the right not to tell me about my son?"

She wrung the cap off the water, gulped twice, and slammed the container down. "What would you have done about him?" she asked. "Taken him home to Annette?"

"You're being ridiculous, and—"

Hand to her throat, Justine spat words at him. "I made the best choice I could have at the time."

He raised his brows and cocked his head to the side. "And I'm supposed to be satisfied with that?"

"What else could I have done?" Justine shouted.

The customers in the coffee bar went still. The only sound relieving the lull was the cash register's chatter. Head lowered, Justine picked at something in her lap. Another moment passed before the other customers forgot them and restarted their conversation.

Xavier didn't give a shit. He suspected Justine was blinking back tears, but reminded himself to stay focused. *Remember what she did to you.*

"I want to see my son. I want to talk to him. I need to spend time with him."

She grabbed his wrist, squeezing hard. Tears hung on her lashes. "I...don't do this. Please...I..."

He removed his hand from her grip, ignoring the heat seeping into his face. He didn't need to be reminded of what her touch did to him. "I don't care how you explain this to your husband. You figure it out."

"But Milton is..." She sighed. "Why d'you want to do this. Why can't we just keep things the way they are now? Why d'you have to stir things up?"

A bark of laughter escaped him. Had she lost her mind? "We're not talking about a pet. This boy is my son, who you chose to hide to suit your purposes." Reckless with frustration, Xavier spoke before he thought. "Milton obviously couldn't give you a son, so you soothed his ego with mine."

She choked on the insult, which in turn shamed him. He felt as if he'd kicked a puppy. He knew better than to say something like that, even if it was the truth. However, he refused to apologize. He didn't owe her any kindness. If anything, she owed him a whole lot more than an apology.

Justine pulled her handbag off the back of the chair and dropped it in her lap, still glaring at him. "That's not true!"

"Why else would you pass off my son as your husband's child?"

"For a quiet and peaceful life!"

She dragged a handful of tissue out of the bag and blew her nose. With watery eyes, she studied him. He stared back at her, refusing to change course. He smiled, but the gesture had nothing to do with amusement. "Milton must be blind or stupid to believe that boy belongs to him. So much for your *quiet and peaceful life*."

She hunched over the table, but he continued to punish her. "Maybe it suits you to think Milton is a fool, like the fool you took me for, but he probably knows what you did. You just refuse to acknowledge that he knows."

She blew into the tissue again and shoved the wadded paper into her handbag. "There's no need for you to act like this."

His forehead throbbed and he struggled not to smash his fists on the table. When he was sure the top of his head hadn't exploded, Xavier spoke again. "Woman, don't force me to be rude to you. All I'm prepared to do is give you time to think about how you're going to arrange for me to meet my son."

She pressed her lips together, as though holding back curse words. After a defiant stare meant to convey what she thought of him, Justine pulled her shoulders back. "Listen, my—Emile has a comfortable life, which you're going to disrupt for no good reason. You can't take him home...and what if you don't like him?"

"Justine, stop." He raised a hand. "You're being silly."

The man beside them shot Xavier a look, which said he should be ashamed of his behavior.

If only you knew, Xavier thought.

From his wallet, Xavier pulled a business card and placed it in front of Justine. Then, he got to his feet. "Don't make me wait too long."

He walked away, his mind in an uproar. During their year together, they hadn't exchanged a harsh word. *But difficult circumstances call for drastic measures.* By keeping his son's birth a secret, Justine had robbed him of something precious. It didn't matter that he was married; he had a right to know and had no choice but to claim his son.

Justine must have gone mad to make that sort of decision, which forced him to question his judgment. He couldn't have known her as well as he thought.

What kind of woman would do what she had done to him?

She had led him on, making him believe she'd have left Milton for him. He should have known better, but got obsessed with her, and the need to be loved. Like an idiot, he'd ignored all the signs that told him she never would have turned her life upside down to start over with him.

Xavier had regretted his stupidity countless times, and dreaded reliving the pain of Justine's rejection, but he knew one thing for sure; come hell or high water, she'd give him what was due to him.

– 3 –

Justine

Proverb: Bull horn never too heavy fi him head
Meaning: Our troubles are such that we can bear them, even if no one else can.

Justine sat in a stifling fog brought on by panic. She had to think, but her brain wouldn't cooperate.

The sun added to her discomfort. A bead of sweat trickled down her neck and ran between her breasts. She pressed a hand to her chest, as much to calm herself as to dry her damp skin. Droplets of perspiration formed at her hairline, increasing her misery. She blotted her forehead with the back of her hand, while beating back troubling thoughts.

To still the unending questions, she got out of the car, slamming the door. She crossed the driveway in a few steps, slipped through the grille and stepped inside Dionne's verandah. A doorstop held the front door open, as always. No matter how bad crime got on the island, Dionne insisted she wouldn't be held prisoner in her home. At least she had the good sense to hang the open padlock on the grille so she could hear whenever someone came through it.

From a patio chair, a pair of dolls kept watch over the garden. For a few moments, they took Justine's mind off her problems. She should have life so easy.

With a couple of hours to herself before she picked up Emile from football practice, she'd called Dionne and she, in turn, had called Kyra to come over.

"Anybody home?" Justine asked on entering the uncluttered living area.

"In the kitchen," Dionne called.

"Hey." Justine collapsed at the table and hung her bag over the back of the chair. The familiar kitchen reflected Justine's, with its buttercup yellow walls and frilly curtains. The colorful magnetic stickers on the refrigerator were a reminder that children lived in the house. The windows, flung wide open, caught the afternoon sunlight and splashed it into every corner of the room. Dionne, Kyra and she had worked out many problems in the octagon-shaped room over the last five years, since Dionne moved house, and the ritual continued.

Kyra was already there, shoes cast off beneath the table. She cupped her chin in one hand and pushed the hair off her forehead with the other. Her cheerful expression vanished when she met Justine's eyes. "You look like hell. I guess things didn't go well."

Justine rifled through her handbag, found a pack of tissues, and blew her nose. Her lips trembled, but she willed herself not to cry. She'd gotten past the stage where crying provided a satisfactory outlet. She was strong, independent, and could handle her business without falling apart. She had survived countless challenges alone for seven years. She wouldn't allow a run-in with Xavier to get the best of her.

Dionne covered a pot on the stove, and came to sit with them. She rewound her bun, secured it with a scrunchy and then rubbed her palm over Justine's arm. "What did he say?"

Tiny pieces of tissue fell between Justine's fingers like a flurry in a snow globe. "That I was selfish to do what I did. That I was ridiculous and silly."

"Come on, Jay, he didn't say that."

Her face went hot at the remembered insults and her gaffe to do with whether he'd like Emile. "Yes, he did say those things. And he said I gave Milton his son to soothe his ego."

She shredded more tissue before finishing her thought. "That he wanted time with Emile."

Dionne folded her hands on the table, her narrow face reflecting concern. "I can't say I'm surprised."

Justine continued ripping the paper, but waited for Dionne's analysis.

"Put yourself in his position, Jay. You cut the man off seven and a half years ago to be exact, and one day he sees this boy, by accident. I'd have been shocked if he said anything different."

"You're siding with him?" Kyra asked.

"Of course not, but you know I'm always fair."

Kyra tapped the tabletop with her nails. "Most Jamaican men would be relieved at not having responsibility for another child."

"Clearly, Xavier's not one of them," Dionne said, while patting Justine's hand. "And who said he wanted responsibility anyway?"

Irritated by Dionne's touch, Justine pulled her arm away. They were trying to help, but they couldn't know what she was going through. It bugged her that they would even think Xavier had any rights to her child.

"I've taken care of my children since Milton passed," she said. "I don't need Xavier McKellop taking any *responsibility* for my son."

"Emile is his son too," Dionne reminded her gently.

Justine avoided looking at her. She could count on Dionne to be sensible despite how much the truth hurt. Justine scraped at the pile of tissue on the cherry wood table and took deep breaths. Her mind skated in circles while she gathered the tissue in her palm. Her fingers jerked and her hands opened, scattering white flakes over the polished wooden surface. She gave in to panic. "What am I gonna do? What if he wants to take Emile away?"

Kyra gripped Justine's shoulder. "Calm down, Jay. You're running ahead of yourself."

Dionne left them and took something out of the cupboard before going to the stove. She came back with a steaming cup, which she set before Justine. "Drink this, and let me think."

She returned to the stove and stirred the simmering soup, a staple at her house on Saturday afternoons. The aroma of escallion, pimento, thyme and chicken floated to Justine. As delicious as it smelled, Justine didn't see how she could eat anything after that disastrous meeting with Xavier. Her throat felt as though it was swollen, making it hard to breathe or swallow.

Dionne flung the metal spoon into the sink, startling Justine. Then she sat, adjusting the strap on her tank top. "Okay, let's approach this rationally."

Justine folded her fingers together and raised them to cover her trembling lips.

"Xavier would be in shock over this, okay?"

Justine nodded, but muttered through her fingers. "He had two weeks to get over it."

Kyra rolled her eyes, and chuckled. "You're something else, you know that?"

Dionne rapped the table with her knuckles to get their attention. "Like I was saying, you shocked the man with about a thousand volts of electricity. Of course, he'd want to know more about his son. D'you know if he had any more children?"

"How am I supposed to know that?" Justine snapped.

"I don't know why I asked. Whether or not he has other children, he'll want to spend time with Emile."

"And what am I going to tell Emile?"

"Don't worry about it just yet. Surely you can make up some excuse for now. Tell him Xavier's a business associate or something. The man you were in love with wouldn't shove the truth down a six year old's throat."

But that was the trouble. Xavier was no longer the same person. The man she had loved never raised his voice, unless he was singing to her in that soothing baritone of his, nor would he ever call her names. Today, he had done all that. She shook her head and the weight of her ponytail settled on her shoulder. She wanted to cry again. "He's not the same man."

Dionne cupped her cheek and spoke gently. "What d'you mean?"

Tracing the patterns in the wood, Justine gathered her thoughts before she spoke. "He's hard. Bitter. Cruel. The Xavier McKellop I loved is gone."

No one said anything for a while. Then, Dionne touched Justine's arm. "Other than saying he wanted to meet Emile, did Xavier ask for anything?"

Justine shook her head, stirring bits of tissue with one finger. Dionne prodded her shoulder, until Justine stared at her with wet eyes.

Dionne's eyes were also moist. "Then why you running yourself to a wreck over this? Remember long ago, we agreed we'd take things day by day and that together, we could face anything?"

"Uh-huh."

"Then stop wasting your eye-water and worrying yourself to death about something that might never happen."

"I'll stop when you stop wasting yours."

They all laughed while Justine and Dionne dried their eyes. Since Dionne had her last child—Fiona, who was a few months older than Emile—she had gone from brash and pushy to compassionate and protective.

Justine picked through the scattered tissue. "I can't help it. What if he—?"

"Sometimes, I think you have a copyright on worrying," Kyra said before Justine could finish. "What you worried about now?"

"What if he wants to take Emile away from me? What then?"

Kyra rolled her eyes again. "Come on, Justine. Listen to yourself. Which Jamaican man you know going to want to a raise a child by himself? The man only ask to meet him son and look how far you gone. Stop worrying. No court in Jamaica is going to award a child to a man who didn't know he had a son 'til a couple of weeks ago."

"I can't help it. You didn't see how he acted. Full of hate. At one point, I thought he was going to hit me."

Dionne laughed. "Come on, Justine. Music Man wouldn't hurt a fly."

"You weren't there today. You didn't see how he treated me."

Leaning her head to one side, Kyra studied Justine. "Trust me, I understand what he's going through. Remember I didn't meet my father until I was fifteen and when we did meet, we had so much catching up to do."

"I remember," Dionne said. "For weeks, all we could hear was Daddy this and Daddy that."

"D'you want to deprive Emile of the chance to connect with his father?" Dionne got to her feet. "Think about it, Jay. You know he has serious daddy issues."

That was the last thing Justine wanted to think about. She had too much at stake to disrupt their lives. Yolanda was already uncontrollable. How would Justine explain her relationship with Xavier? And what plausible story could she give Emile, when she'd drilled it into his head that his daddy had gone to heaven before he was born?

She shook her head. Somehow, she had to find a way to change Xavier's mind. He had to see the wisdom of leaving things as they stood. What would he gain from disrupting his life?

You're a fool, Justine. You disrupted his life years ago by doing what you did to him.

She ignored that thought and sipped chamomile tea.

As of this minute, she didn't have a plan, but resolved to do anything to prevent Xavier from destroying her family's stability.

– 4 –

Saturday, January 29, 2:30 PM

Justine

Proverb: If yuh 'fraid fi eye, yuh never nyam (eat) head.
Meaning: If you think too much of other people's opinion, you'll never succeed.

Seated in the concrete stands, Justine twisted her hands together while Emile ran across the field. Practice ended at three o' clock, but she'd left Dionne's house early for no other reason than to watch Emile play. He ran backward, waving at her. She returned his salute, acknowledging another of his growth spurts. The hem of his shorts rode higher on his thighs than in the previous month.

She closed her eyes, listening to the leaves of the Plum tree beating against each other. The sun caressed her skin where it came through the foliage. As if protecting herself, Justine wrapped her arms around her waist. Though she sat in the open air, the heat of Xavier's hostility still burned.

What would she do if he demanded more than a talk with Emile?

A wave of excited voices disturbed her and she followed the movement of arms and legs protruding from a squirming heap of boys. She craned her neck, heart racing, hoping Emile wasn't at the bottom of the pile. She relaxed when she spotted him standing by the goalpost.

Coach Black blew the whistle and the boys gathered around him. After refueling with a drink poured from the team igloo, Emile raced toward her and hurled himself on the bench. "Time to go, Mommy. Tutenstein will be on soon."

"D'you ever watch anything but cartoons?" She gathered his water bottle and towel and then zipped them into his bag, recalling similar conversations with Yolanda years ago.

"They're innerestin'."

He raced her to the car, shot into the passenger seat, and turned the radio to a station playing rap music. Before she drove off, Justine turned it down.

"Mom!" Emile's head bopped in time to the repetitive beat.

Tapping the wheel, Justine pulled away from the field. "D'you want to stop for some wings or something?"

Emile grinned. "Of course."

In the drive-through line at KFC, Justine thought about how to introduce Xavier to Emile, without the child getting suspicious. She'd have to be inventive, because her son was as bright as Yolanda was at his age.

While she inched along behind another customer, Justine wondered why she was even thinking about an introduction when she'd already decided there was no way she would let Xavier have anything to do with Emile.

She glanced at him while she waited. He had Xavier's wide forehead and toffee-colored skin. Sometimes, when Emile looked at her, Justine saw his father reflected in his eyes. She held back a chuckle. There were also times she stared at Emile, only to have him tell her she was creeping him out. He couldn't know she saw Xavier when she looked at him.

"I'm looking at you like that 'cause I love you," she'd say.

Trying not to giggle, he'd reply, "Just don't do it when we go out. And remember, no kissing."

She paid for the food, her mind still wrapped around Xavier, hoping he wouldn't press for anything more, at least not for a while. Maybe if she prayed hard enough he'd hold off with his demands. Despite all the things she'd done, God had never let her down.

Justine dragged her teeth over her bottom lip, while thinking. Emile reasoned as though he was older, but if the truth came out, what explanation would she give for keeping him and his father apart? He would never understand the fears that beset her years ago, each time she thought about what the neighbors would say if they knew the child she carried didn't belong to her husband.

Although Milton had passed before Emile's birth, that wouldn't have mattered. If people knew the truth, she'd have lost her reputation. Even now, she sometimes caught Milton's mother looking at Emile with curiosity in her gaze, which was one of the reasons Justine avoided going to her house.

She curled her lips. Men got away with fathering children with different women, but women were held to much higher standards. Sighing, she reminded herself that what she had done was unforgiveable, which brought her back to all the reasons why she couldn't tell Emile that Xavier was his daddy.

To Dionne and Kyra, her way of thinking might sound irrational and desperate, but she was all Emile had, and couldn't afford to have anything come between them. How would she live with herself if he grew to hate her? If Emile found out the truth, somehow, she'd have to make him understand that everything she had done was for his benefit.

A horn blew behind her, forcing her mind into the present. She edged forward, collected Emile's meal and left the drive through. He raided the paper bag, blew on the French fries and popped a couple into his mouth. When he stopped chewing, he smiled while licking his fingers. "Thanks, Mommy. You're super cool. Can we come again next week?"

"Maybe."

Though she smiled in return, her thoughts continued churning. Would Emile still look at her with adoration if he knew about Xavier? She stared straight ahead, reminding herself to take things as they came. Not that that ever worked in situations like these. Even as she told herself that ninety-nine percent of the things she worried about never happened, a new concern weighed her down.

How had depriving Emile of a father made his life better?

– 5 –

Saturday, February 12, 1:30 PM

Xavier

Proverb: Di more yuh look, di less yuh see.

Meaning: Sometimes it seems the more you find out, the less you know about a given situation.

Xavier walked through the entryway into the yard, frowning. No sign of Justine, but her car was in the parking lot. He strolled down the cement walkway, scanning the area. To his left, Justine stood in the garden. From this angle, she looked as if she belonged in a painting. She stood motionless, as though she had bloomed among the ginger lilies.

Her raised hand shielded her eyes, while she peered at something he couldn't see. In her other hand, she carried a canvas bag. The breeze picked up, lifting her hair and pressing the loose dress against breasts, belly and thighs. He dragged his eyes from where they had strayed as his crotch tightened, reacting to her as though time hadn't intervened.

If he closed his eyes, he could picture her, hair undone, eyelids trembling, flesh clenching around him. He bit down on his lip and shuffled his feet on the concrete to ground himself before approaching her. Her back was to him now and she turned in a half circle and put up both hands to form a frame.

What was she doing?

She shifted another few degrees and caught him in her line of sight. She went still and let her hands float down to her sides, but before the shades dropped over her eyes and shut him out, he saw the appreciation in her gaze. Justine used to have a thing about his height and size.

He drew himself up, pasted on a half smile, and nodded. She mimicked his gesture, but her eyes shifted to something behind him, to the right. He willed himself not to turn, but guessed Emile was somewhere close.

She pointed to a gazebo. "D'you mind sitting over there?"

"That's fine," he said walking beside her.

Justine put space between them, walking at the edge of the concrete despite the leaves brushing her white dress. When they sat in the shade of the wooden structure, Xavier let his eyes rove the grounds, trying to catch sight of Emile.

No such luck.

A nerve danced under his eye and he hoped Justine wasn't playing games with him. She probably wouldn't say anything about Emile if he didn't ask.

Piped music flowed from somewhere above them, distracting him. He drew a breath to speak and changed his mind when Emile appeared. He ran toward them, legs churning and a huge smile splitting his face. He took the wooden steps two at a time, stopping when he noticed Xavier. "Hi," he said.

"Hi, Emile."

Emile wrinkled his brows the way Justine did when she was concentrating hard. He was probably wondering how Xavier knew him. Emile's brow cleared and he said, "You're the man from the store where we went to fix Yolanda's guitar."

Xavier nodded and allowed himself to smile. The child's memory was excellent.

Justine held out a hand toward her son, and Xavier suspected it was an attempt to end the conversation.

"What's that you have there?" she asked.

After a glance at Xavier, Emile moved to her side and opened his fist.

Justine let out a tiny yelp and steered Emile to the railing. "Let it go."

"But I just caught it."

"You can't keep it. You're gonna eat. Go wash your hands."

A green blur leaped from Emile's palm. Xavier figured it was a grasshopper. Good boy, he thought. My son's no sissy.

Justine made a disgusted face. "Where did you find that huge thing anyway?"

"Near Auntie Elaine's office."

Xavier wondered who Auntie Elaine was to Justine, but doubted he'd find out. Emile thundered down the wooden steps at Justine's urging, and ran off, pulling up the waist of his jeans as he went. One corner of Xavier's mouth lifted. He was the same as a boy, never walked anywhere when he could run.

Xavier followed Emile's progress into the main building of the rustic restaurant and garden, wondering again what had possessed Justine. Even now she was holding out on him. It was two weeks since he'd seen her. Two weeks during which he wanted to pick up the phone and curse her out for not letting him see his son.

Only God knew why she'd continue to punish him after withholding this precious knowledge for so many years. At the point when he decided he couldn't wait any longer to see Emile, she'd called, trying to worm her way out of another meeting. Patience wasn't his strong suit these days, so again, he railroaded her into setting a date.

Emile ran up the steps and slid into one of the wrought iron chairs, breathing hard. Justine handed him a menu, which he studied with a serious expression. It was clear they'd done this before. Xavier tried not to stare while the boy decided what he wanted to eat and then told Justine. After that, Emile closed the menu and set to kicking the table leg. Justine wrapped her fingers around his arm. "No, Emile."

Xavier telegraphed a message to Justine, which she ignored. Seemed she had no plans to introduce them properly. He caught the looks the boy threw him across the table. Emile would have many questions for Justine after the three of them parted company. Another intense eye lock with Justine yielded nothing but more silence. Apart from being conniving and dishonest, Justine had also lost her mind. Narrowing his eyes, Xavier made his decision.

"Emile," he said, "my name is Xavier. Xavier McKellop. I'm your mother's friend."

Emile shot a look at Justine, before fixing his gaze on Xavier. "Mommy said you do business together."

A likely story. Xavier hid the sour grin trying to take hold of his face. "When did she tell you that?"

Today, when we were driving over here."

"Did she tell you that I knew her a long time ago, before you were born?"

Emile's eyes popped wide and he propped his chin on both fists. "Really?"

"Yeah, we used to be good friends."

Emile stole a glance at Justine before asking, "So you knew her when she was young?"

Xavier couldn't help the laughter that escaped. "I don't think she's what I'd call old right now."

"'Course she is. She's all of—"

The waiter interrupted them to take their order. Xavier now had some time to study the woman Justine had become. She spoke to the waiter, her words barely loud enough for him to hear.

For a forty-three-year-old woman, her face was youthful. He didn't see any laughter lines and she had no crow's feet, which told him she didn't venture out in the sun often. She also didn't do much laughing. The back of her hands were smooth, her ring finger bare. Had something happened in her marriage? She avoided his eyes, which didn't give him a chance to study what he saw there. At a guess, he'd say sadness and resignation. But over what?

When she looked at Emile, everything changed. She grew animated and indulgence oozed from her. He could only imagine how she had spoiled the boy, not that he acted like it, but it didn't take much to see where her heart was—right where Xavier thought he'd been ages ago.

Curiosity took him unawares and he wanted to know everything he'd missed in the intervening years. Emile was talkative, so the right questions would provide the answers he needed.

He didn't care if Justine was married. That made her off-limits, which worked for him because his gut told him she'd do even more damage if he opened himself to her a second time. He was now as close as he could come to being happy. He needed nothing to add to his wellbeing except a relationship with his son, which might prove ticklish to manage. While he was getting to know Emile, Xavier would find out whatever he needed to know about Justine's situation.

He wasn't sure how much time passed before the waiter came back, but Xavier was conscious of the murmur of conversation between Justine and Emile. The waiter laid the plates down, and Xavier's stomach grumbled. He'd skipped breakfast and hadn't realized how hungry he was. He picked up his fork to find Justine and Emile waiting for him so they could start lunch.

"Sorry," he said.

Emile lowered his head for a few seconds, saying grace, before he attacked a mound of chicken and fries. Justine ate a few mouthfuls of batter-fried fish fillet and occupied herself pushing the vegetables around the plate. She stared beyond Xavier at the garden, but each time he swallowed a chunk of the club sandwich, she tensed.

What did she think he was going to do? Tell the boy he was his father, without preparing him? Surely, she knew him better than that? He waited a few more seconds then decided that since she didn't plan to do anything for them to get better acquainted, he had to do it himself.

"So Emile, tell me some of the stuff you like to do."

"Running, riding my bicycle, swimming, watching TV, drumming." He took his mother to task with a frown. "But Mommy won't let me have any drums. She can't handle the noise with both drums and a guitar."

Xavier put aside the question he wanted to ask and let his smile spread from within to without. "I teach kids music."

Emile sat forward, both hands on the table, eyes open to capacity. "Really?"

Xavier nodded, ignoring the ice chips flowing off Justine.

"Cooooool!" Emile's head snapped toward Justine. "Mom, can I have lessons?"

"I, uh...I'll think about it."

Emile slouched, folded his arms, and pouted. "You let Yolanda get lessons, so why can't I have some too?"

" You don't stick with anything for long."

"Mom!" The word stretched into three syllables. "You know I like the drums. Kevin's father got him a set and the only time I get to practice is at his house. Why can't I—?"

"That's enough." Justine said. A look passed between mother and son, after which Emile pushed back his chair from the table, scrunched down further in the seat and blinked hard a few times.

"It wouldn't cost you," Xavier said.

"That's not the point," she snapped.

"What *is* the point, Justine?"

She concentrated on something over his shoulder. "I don't want..."

You don't want me to spend any more time with my son than you see fit to give me, Xavier thought.

Xavier flashed a glance at Emile, who stared in his lap, bottom lip pooched out.

"You owe me," Xavier whispered, leaning forward.

"I don't owe you anything," she hissed back.

Xavier licked his lips and prayed for patience. "This can be easy or nasty. Your choice."

She squished her brows together and fisted her hand against her cheek to block Emile's view of her mouth. "If you think I'm gonna leave my son alone with you, you're making a sad mistake."

"What am I gonna do?" Xavier spoke through clamped teeth and an aching jaw. "Tell him what you should have told him long ago?"

Their whispered conversation stirred Emile's interest and he straightened in the seat, head angled in their direction. His square-cut hairline, yellow-brown skin, the shape of his mouth and his sturdy frame all cemented in Xavier's mind the fact that he was this boy's father. Justine's soulful eyes stared at him out of the boy's face, willing him to do battle.

"Emile," she said, "would you go tell Auntie Elaine to send a waiter?"

Xavier was sure Emile sighed before he said okay and ran off. Determined not to waste any time, Xavier told Justine what was on him mind. "Let's get one thing straight, I'm not up for any games, okay? I'll respect your wishes not to tell Emile the truth immediately, but he needs to know I'm his father."

"D'you know how hard it will be for him to understand something like this?"

"You should have thought of that before you chose to lie."

Justine pressed her lips together and looked as though she wanted to hit him. "I didn't lie!"

"You lied by omission. You cheated me, Justine, and you're cheating that boy of a relationship with his father."

She opened her mouth and closed it seconds later, as if she'd forgotten what she planned to say.

"Listen." He touched her hand that lay on the table.

She pulled her hand into a fist, staring at the tablecloth.

He sighed, rubbing his forehead. "You have to deal with this. I'm not going to disappear. Matter of fact, I don't care what you do, as long as I get to see Emile."

She winced, as though he'd hit her, but said nothing. He quashed the sympathy stirring inside him. She was selfish and thoughtless. Why should he care about her feelings?

"Giving him lessons is the most natural way I can think of spending time with him. You can come if you want. Doesn't matter to me. We need to talk about money."

She clasped her hands together, as if praying. "I don't need your money. I'll take care of my son myself."

His phone vibrated at his waist. He removed it from the holder and peered at the display. Annette wanted to talk to him again. He rarely answered her calls, but she'd found a way around that. She'd started texting him about the disciplinary problems she now had with their daughter, Kelleigh.

Justine went silent. He'd missed half of what she said. Another sigh left him. If he lived to be a hundred, he'd never understand women. During their time together, Annette had never needed him. Now that their marriage was all but over, she talked to him more regularly than when they lived in the same house. He deleted the text and replaced the phone in its case. He'd call later.

Emile bounded up the steps and sat, his displeasure forgotten. Xavier listened while Emile argued with his mother about where he planned to put another soda, willing her to let the boy live a little. He believed parents had better results with kids when they presented a unified front, so he stayed quiet.

She gave in and ordered Emile a small soft drink, which the waiter returned with inside a minute. Xavier ate another mouthful of the sandwich, but noted that Justine's appetite had disappeared. She heaped the fish and vegetables in small piles, while her other hand worried the ends of her hair.

He felt sorry for her. Only God knew why, because as sure as faith, she wouldn't move on his suggestion for another few weeks. He'd missed the first six years of Emile's life and didn't plan to miss any more.

Xavier wiped his mouth, and directed his words at Emile. "Your mother has agreed you can have lessons. We start next Saturday afternoon, two o' clock sharp."

"Cool!" Emile's delight was all the reward Xavier needed.

"He has football practice," Justine said, scowling at Xavier.

A patient expression sat on Emile's face. "Remember it was at two o' clock last week because coach had something in the morning. We go at ten o' clock again on Saturday."

"I forgot," Justine said.

Another cock-and-bull story, Xavier thought. She was simply trying to avoid them being together. He had the impression that Justine handled all of Emile's extracurricular activities, which meant her situation had gotten worse. She used to complain that Milton was too preoccupied to spend time with her, and Xavier understood that neglect was one of the reasons she'd been susceptible to an affair.

He sat forward and tested the waters with a question. "So your dad takes you to football practice?"

Justine drew a sharp breath. Emile's mouth drooped, and he swirled the straw around the glass of Kola Champagne. "I don't have a daddy."

Xavier wasn't sure he understood. Justine had gone still, her mouth half-open and eyes pulled wide. Xavier was intrigued and couldn't have prevented himself from asking the next question if his life depended on him staying silent.

"What d'you mean? Doesn't your daddy live at home?"

Slowly, Emile moved his head from side to side. "Mommy said he died before I was born."

Xavier frowned, still at a loss. Was it possible Justine had told the boy Milton wasn't his father? He had to be sure. "Who lives at home, Emile?"

The boy counted off people on his fingers. "Mommy, Yolanda and me. Oh, and Miss Pauline, but this is her weekend off, so she went home yesterday evening."

Justine grabbed the edges of the table, cleared her throat, and tried to speak. No words came out. She tried again, and this time she squeaked the boy's name.

Shooting a glare at Justine to keep her quiet, Xavier asked another question. "Where is your father, Emile?"

The child stopped short of rolling his eyes. "I told you, Daddy never lived at home. Mommy said he went to heaven before I came."

The air left Xavier's lungs in a rush, as if sucked away by an unseen force. He struggled to form words that would make sense, but his brain had turned into a wad of cotton.

– 6 –

Saturday, February 19, 11:30 AM

Justine

Proverb: Yuh haffi learn fi dance a yard before you can dance abroad.

Meaning: If you practice good habits in your own surroundings, you won't embarrass yourself in public.

The alarm on her phone went off, reminding Justine that she needed to get moving. Football practice would end soon and she had to get Emile home, fed, and off to Xavier's studio for his lesson at two o'clock.

After silencing the alarm and grabbing her handbag from the bedroom, she slipped into the car and started the engine, weighed down by a creeping lethargy. She pulled away from the sidewalk, barely able to keep the car moving in a straight line. Her palms stuck to the wheel and she flexed her fingers, cursing her overactive glands.

Although she had escaped Xavier for a week, a deeper conversation was inevitable. The thought forced her to grip the wheel tighter.

So he'd found out Milton was dead. That didn't change anything. She could no more go back to Xavier than she could take money from him for Emile's care.

The air spilled from her lips in a slow gust. She had spent so much time fretting that she might one day run into Xavier; Kingston wasn't a big enough city to avoid him totally, but somehow she'd been lucky. More to the point, she had stayed away from the places where she might have seen him. She'd avoided going to church for months after their breakup, since it was there that she first met him. She also stopped going anywhere that featured a live band, for fear that he'd be playing. Eventually, she also beat the urge to hide every time she spotted a tall man wearing locks.

After she refused to see him and months had passed, Xavier realized she was serious about not wanting to continue their affair and stopped trying to contact her. She helped the process along by changing her cell number and cutting out instant messaging. She closed all her social networking accounts and didn't open new ones. Shutting down the e-mail address he knew was a drastic step, but it suited her purpose.

Over time, she'd accepted her husband's death and settled into life without him. Milton had succumbed to cancer a month before Emile's birth, which gave her some measure of relief. She'd dreaded having to make up a story for Milton as to why their son didn't resemble him at all. That thought awakened her guilt.

A horn blasted behind her, and without checking, she drove into the road. Too late, she saw the red light. Luck was on her side as the person with the right-of-way honked his horn, but waited until she was out of the intersection before moving.

Worry had eaten at her this past week, and continued to weigh on her spirit. She had to get her anxiety in check before it started affecting her health.

She parked the car in the lot next to the football field, and got out to find a seat in the stands. A few other parents were scattered on the concrete benches.

The boys stood in line and at the shrill sound of the coach's whistle, they each moved the ball assigned to them down the field. Justine's watch confirmed she had fifteen minutes to wait. She hunched on the bench while Emile took his turn dribbling the ball. Involuntarily, she smiled. Although the boys were all the same age, Emile was the tallest in the group. Like his father, he stood out in any gathering. She had reassured him early on that being tall carried advantages and that he shouldn't allow other children to make him feel uncomfortable with how God made him.

"Hey, Justine."

Another mother waved on her way past. Justine returned the greeting, letting her gaze rest on Emile. Her mind went back to the problem that refused to be suspended since she ran into Xavier five weeks ago.

She would lose face with Emile if she told him Xavier was his father. Emile would be ecstatic and have a thousand questions, for which she had no answers. She couldn't bear the thought of him losing faith in her and he would when he found out his father was alive.

The fact that she had cheated on her husband was something she'd have to face again as a front-burner issue after so many years. Emile would want to know how he belonged to both men, but Yolanda was another matter. Justine's shoulders drooped at the prospect of battling Yolanda over a situation that should have stayed in the past.

God never gives us more than we can bear, Justine reminded herself and straightened her spine. She'd deal with that problem when she got to it. For now, she'd concentrate on getting through the time she'd be forced to spend in Xavier's company.

Emile shot across the grass toward her, a smile on his face. She'd sat next to his things to wait. From the side pocket of his duffle bag, she pulled out the water bottle. "How was practice?"

"All right. We had fun."

He dropped onto the seat beside her, guzzling water, his head tilted backward. She rubbed his hair, making a note to take him to the barber soon. Emile bowed to escape her hand. The sunlight flowing through the branches of the Plum tree dappled his skin and forced him to squint. He glanced at the other children. "Mom!"

His tone and fleeting disapproval brought Xavier to mind; not the man she once knew, but the hostile person he'd become.

She lifted the duffle. "We have to get moving if we're gonna be on time later."

They strolled to the car and got in, discussing all the things Emile thought he couldn't live without.

"Now remember, you don't have a lot of time for television when we get home," she said.

"It's only twelve-thirty, so—"

"And before you know it, it will be two o' clock."

"I'll shower and *then* watch television."

Justine shook her head. "No. You'll shower, get something to eat and by then it'll be time to leave. We don't wanna be late."

More to the point, she didn't want Xavier to come looking for her, and she sensed he would. How she was going to handle being in his space for an hour she didn't know. The knot of anxiety in her stomach refused to go away, but she was determined not to fall apart. She had to act normal for Emile's sake and get through what she was sure would be an ordeal.

She drew up in the driveway, got out and herded Emile into the house. He detoured toward the kitchen instead of going to the shower. Yolanda sat at the table eating Banana Chips and reading a book. "Hi, Mom."

Justine mumbled a greeting and got a drink of water. She dropped her bag on a chair before sitting. Emile hung on to the back of the seat. "Mommy, can I have—"

With both hands, Justine massaged her forehead. "Whatever it is, the answer is no. Go bathe, and I'll fix you something to eat in the meantime."

He slouched away, carrying the weight of his grievance on his shoulders. Yolanda waited until he left before she spoke. "Mom, about the guitar. I wonder—"

Justine didn't let Yolanda finish. "The same goes for you. Whatever you want, the answer is no. Whatever is wrong with that guitar, you'll have to live with."

"But, Mom, all I was going to say—"

"The answer is no."

"Maybe if you'd listen to what I want before you say no—"

"I'm sure you're going to have another unreasonable request. I'm used to that by now."

"All I was going to ask is whether I could have lessons with Emile's new teacher."

The thought of it made Justine sweat. "Absolutely not. You *have* a teacher, in case you've forgotten."

"The lessons are boring 'cause he's like a hundred. Plus, his mouth smells like the toilet at school."

Justine went to the sink to rinse the glass. She kept her back to Yolanda to hide her amusement. When she had a grip on her laughter, she returned to sit at the table. "How come you've never said anything before? Now Emile's getting lessons, you suddenly want to change teachers."

Yolanda glared at Justine through her bangs. "There was a sign in the store. I saw it the last time I went in. I just forgot to ask you. I'm gonna die if I have to endure Mr. Coombs's stinky breath forever."

"You die over the simplest things. We'll see."

Justine had no intention of letting Yolanda have lessons with Xavier. She saw too much.

Yolanda got to her feet, her shoulders heaving. "You're so unfair. Emile can't even play the drums properly."

"Which is why he needs lessons. You've had lessons on the clarinet, the keyboard, and other things that I can't even pronounce."

Yolanda planted her hands on her hips. "I was just finding my instrument."

"Yes, and meantime, I had to *find* money each time you wanted to learn something new. Don't tell me you envy your brother?"

"I didn't say that."

"That's the way it sounds."

"Never mind." Yolanda flapped her arm. "I'll talk to you about this when you're in a better mood."

Justine let her breath out, amused despite her annoyance. Yolanda had repeated the same words Justine used on her all too often. Getting to her feet, Yolanda gathered the snack bag and cup and went to the bin. Her restrained movements told Justine her daughter was trying not to be petulant. At least she was making an effort, which was more than she'd done in a long time. But of course, she wanted something.

Justine had the same thought she'd been having all too frequently. If not for Yolanda, she wouldn't be in her present pickle. Fact was, Xavier was back in her life and she still needed a strategy to handle their enforced contact.

***

Justine slid Yolanda a glance, where she hunched in the passenger seat. Why did she have to be so miserable to live with? She'd resurrected the argument over the guitar lessons, and was running Justine's nerves to a wreck.

"But don't you see?" Yolanda spread her hands wide. "It'd be easier for you to collect both of us in one place."

"Are you forgetting you come home on your own?"

"Well, it'd be easier if I had lessons on a Saturday."

Justine exited the car and motioned for Emile to get out. His sneakers hit the sidewalk and without waiting for her, he bounced toward the door, oblivious of the glare and heat of the sun.

"Emile, please wait." Justine stooped to talk to Yolanda, who was fiddling with the air-conditioning dial. "Stay here 'til I come back."

Inside the shop, Emile was bent over, peering into the display case. At Justine's approach, the woman behind the counter put on a bogus smile. Justine was too relieved at getting out of the searing heat and into the air-conditioning to be concerned about the shop attendant's attitude.

"Good afternoon," Justine said. "I'm here to see Mr. McKellop."

The attendant's face twisted in a scowl. "Can I say what it's about?"

"A lesson."

"I'll let him know."

She picked up the phone, turned toward the wall and spoke into the instrument. When she faced Justine, her mouth was crimped in a tight circle. She opened the counter. "He'll see you now. Second door on the right."

"Thanks."

Who put a burr in her panties, Justine wondered as she pushed the swing door and took Emile's hand to stop him from running ahead of her. After rapping on the door, she waited for Xavier's response. When it came, his voice was muffled.

Pulling her shoulders back, Justine ignored the heat seeping over her skin and sauntered into the room. Immediately, Emile twisted his wrist, trying to escape her grasp. A drum set, keyboard and guitar were set up in three corners of the room. No doubt, Emile was dying to lay hands on them.

Xavier had both hands on the guitar, as though he'd just repositioned it. He faced her, the soft fabric of his worn jeans clinging to his thighs. She forced her gaze to safer ground, but the navy tee-shirt hugging his chest only reminded her of what lay beneath the cotton material. The drag on her arm brought her attention back to Emile.

"Don't touch anything," she said, before releasing his hand.

"I'm just gonna look." Emile smiled at Xavier. "Hello."

"Hi, Emile. You ready to get going?"

At Emile's nod, Xavier pointed to the drum set. "Sit over there."

"Remember not to touch anything unless you're told," Justine said.

The door opened behind her and Justine turned sideways. Yolanda stood sulking in the doorway. Justine's spirit sank further. She refrained from taking Yolanda to task over her bad manners, since that would only bring more aggravation.

Yolanda scanned the room and walked to the guitar. When she stretched to touch it, Justine intervened. "I just told Emile not to touch anything."

Yolanda turned her head. "I wouldn't do anything to wreck it. It's awesome." She spoke to Xavier. "You actually let people use this?"

He nodded. "Sure."

Yolanda's eyebrows rose, and her mouth opened. Justine groaned. Yolanda was slipping into wheedling mode. Justine didn't see what was so special about the instrument, but clearly her daughter did. The wood resembled cedar and the sides appeared to be made of mahogany. Justine shrugged to loosen the tension at the back of her neck. Why couldn't Yolanda ever do as instructed?

"Can I?" Yolanda asked.

"Certainly." Xavier lifted the guitar from its stand and handed it to Yolanda. She took it gently, as though it was something to be treasured. Eyes shining, she looked up at Xavier. "Can I play it?"

At a nod from him, she breathed deeply, positioned her fingers and plucked the strings. It wasn't the harsh sounds Justine was used to hearing from the electric guitar, but a mellow tune, which she recognized as Marley's Redemption Songs. She stared at her daughter, wondering what had come over her.

Yolanda exchanged a look with Xavier, who nodded in approval. Justine listened, awestruck while her daughter played through to the ending notes.

"That was beautiful," she whispered when Yolanda finished.

"Young lady, you have some talent on you," Xavier said when she handed him the instrument.

"Only Mom doesn't want to admit it."

Justine felt the need to defend herself. "You've never played anything like that at home. It's always loud and maddening." She looked at her watch. "Emile has an hour and we're cutting into the time. I'll drop you off and come back here."

"Can't I stay?" Yolanda asked, sliding her hands into the pockets of her jeans.

"Didn't you insist that you'd die if you didn't get to visit Jeanelle this afternoon?" Justine narrowed her eyes. "Is that boy, Tariq, going to be over there?"

Yolanda studied her sneakers, but didn't respond. A rumble came from the drum and Justine remembered they were in the middle of Xavier's classroom.

"We should go," she said, touching Yolanda's arm.

Yolanda pulled away, stepping out of her reach. "So explain to me again why I can't have lessons?"

Sighing, Justine shifted her handbag. "Do we have to do this here?"

"Yes. How come Emile always gets the best deal?"

"You're just being difficult. Mr. Coombs was perfectly all right until you heard Emile was starting his lessons."

Yolanda hissed air through her teeth and put both hands on her hips. "I told you already, he's positively dead, has bad breath and he smells frowsy."

Justine let her gaze travel to Xavier, who had to be horrified.

He turned his head away, hiding a smile.

Glaring at him, Justine said, "That didn't bother you last week."

Despite where they were, Yolanda's voice climbed higher. "I never told you 'cause you never listen to me."

Softly, Justine spoke. "This is not the place for this discussion."

"Excuse me." Emile spoke in an accent drawn from one of his cartoon programs and put up a finger. "Can the two of you go now, please? I want to start my lesson."

Justine grabbed Yolanda's arm and moved her toward the door. "Come on. We can talk about this in the car."

"Don't bother! You're only going to tell me no anyway." She flounced out of the room, and let the door slam.

Heat wrapped around Justine's neck. She wanted to melt into a puddle and slide across the floor, away from Xavier. "I'll be back in a bit," she mumbled to Emile.

He seemed torn between exhilaration, and sympathy for her, but happiness won and he waved, stick in hand. "Bye, Mommy!"

He could sound a little less happy to be rid of me.

Xavier crossed to the door and held it open. To her surprise, he spoke as she walked by him. "I understand. Kelleigh behaves the same way."

Justine curved her lips in a smile that didn't reach her insides. "Yeah, they only grow more difficult as the years pass."

"Don't worry. She'll get past it," he said.

When she looked up, he was smiling. Her lips lifted in response. This time, her smile was genuine.

She let her breath out when he closed the door behind her. Despite the argument to come with Yolanda, Justine felt as though a burden had left her shoulders.

− 7 −

Saturday, February 19, 2:20 PM

Justine

Proverb: Pretty rose got macka jook (thorns that hurt).
Meaning: Every seemingly good situation carries disadvantages.

Justine pulled away from the sidewalk, hoping to drop off Yolanda without another spat. Yolanda's friendship with Tariq bothered Justine. At sixteen, he was more than a year older than Yolanda and even though they didn't seem overly close, Justine continued to worry.

Yolanda pretended to be knowledgeable about the ways of the world, but she wasn't. She was just a girl growing into her skin and her sexuality, like so many others. Justine had always taken her to and from school, so Yolanda had no spare time to learn all the things she was still too young to experience. Unless she was being exposed at school, but there was little Justine could do about that.

Yolanda had angled her body away from Justine while she stared out the window. Her folded arms and deep frown told Justine she'd be mad for a while to come. Not that things had been any different for ages.

Justine longed to go back to the time when her little girl was just that—a sweet child, who adored her mother and did everything to please her.

Justine made a sound in her throat. Those days were long gone, perhaps never to return. She prayed that wouldn't be the case with Emile, which brought her back to their situation. How was she going to tell her son his father wasn't dead? Maybe Xavier could find a way to do it that wouldn't be upsetting, but that didn't comfort her.

Yolanda touched Justine's arm, disrupting her thoughts. "What do I have to do to convince you to make me change teachers? Mr. McKellop is really cool. Mr. Coombs would never let me touch any of his instruments like that. And I don't feel I'm progressing as I should."

The intensity and maturity behind Yolanda's words struck a chord with Justine.

"I know I haven't given you any reason to think I deserve the things you do for me, but I appreciate everything," Yolanda said.

Justine smiled at the line of traffic ahead. "Landy, are you buttering me up 'cause you want those lessons so bad?"

Her daughter grinned back. "Kinda-sorta, but I did mean everything I said. Now, can I have those lessons? Please, pretty please."

Justine focused on the road, thinking. Yolanda had played the guitar beautifully, and she did sound as if she genuinely wanted to learn more. Justine would be spending time at Xavier's business place, whether she liked it or not, so it wouldn't be a hardship for Yolanda to use the same facility.

Yolanda was inquisitive, but in her excitement over lessons with Xavier, would she have time to note the similarities between man and boy? Maybe not. At worst, she'd accuse Justine and they'd have a knockdown, drag-out fight over it. That scenario couldn't be any worse than the fights they'd had already, and the lessons would keep Yolanda happy for a while.

She tapped Yolanda's leg. "I guess it's okay."

Yolanda tried to hug Justine, but the seatbelt restrained her. The sweet smile she wore reminded Justine of the days when Yolanda was her only child.

"You're the best, Mom!"

"Yeah, until we quarrel over something else," Justine muttered.

"Even then, Mom, I love you!" she sang.

Justine shook her head. What had she been thinking all this time? There was nothing like a little discipline to keep teenagers focused. Since Yolanda was in such a good mood, Justine tackled one of her biggest worries. "Tariq, is he your boyfriend?"

"No. He's into the guitar, plays in a band."

Rather than reassuring Justine, that explanation made her more uncomfortable. "He goes to your school, right?"

Yolanda nodded. "Yeah, he's a year ahead of me, but he's really cool. Plays like a dream."

"Be careful, okay?"

"Why would you say that?"

"Boys will be boys, even if they aren't in a relationship with you. I'm just asking you to stay on your guard, okay?"

"Tariq isn't like that."

"Fine, but I'm just saying."

A group of young people had already gathered at Jeanelle's house. Justine had no idea what they did on a Saturday afternoon apart from studying, but the girl's parents seemed attentive, so Justine kept her worries in proportion. If Yolanda said she wasn't involved with that boy, then she'd take her at her word.

***

Justine told herself to get over the sourpuss at the counter. She fiddled with her bag strap, wondering whether the attendant was extra bitchy because of her run-ins with Yolanda or if her grumpiness was habitual. Or maybe she saw the resemblance between Emile and Xavier.

Justine pushed that thought away. She'd spent enough of her life feeding her fear, guilt and regret.

Inside the studio, Emile played a repetitive set of beats, his forehead furrowed and the tip of his tongue licking one side of his mouth. Justine pursed her lips to suppress a smile over his show of concentration and approached Xavier, where he sat at the desk flipping through a file.

"Uh..." she hesitated, realizing she didn't know how to address him. He'd called her by her first name, but somehow she felt presumptuous calling him by his. Besides, she wasn't sure he wouldn't insult her if she addressed him as she had in the past.

"Would you consider giving Yolanda lessons too? Seems she's taken with you."

Too late, she realized how her words sounded.

Xavier let his gaze move up to her face, then he smiled. She blinked and her body temperature shot up by a few notches. She stepped back, hoping she wouldn't start sweating the way she used to in the early days before she got to know him.

"Somebody has a case of sour grapes."

She cut her eyes at him. "Nothing like that. Just that she wouldn't stop begging. I'll pay for those lessons, of course."

"Fine. It's three thousand dollars an hour or I can give you a special price for ten lessons."

That was more than she paid Mr. Coombs, but if Yolanda wanted it so bad, the least Justine could do was meet her halfway.

"Should I bring her at the same time as Emile?"

"Yeah." He inclined his head to the right. "I have another room down the hall that she can use. I don't think she'll need as much supervision as Emile."

"Thanks." She squeezed out a half smile.

Come, Emile," she called. "Time to go."

She rushed away gripping Emile's hand, but was mindful that he had to keep up with her. Used to be, she was relaxed in Xavier's presence, now she was as tense as a rope in a game of tug-of-war. At the counter, she wrote a check to cover Yolanda's lessons and left the saleswoman scowling.

On the way to pick up Yolanda, Emile chattered while Justine listened with half an ear.

"...and he showed me the different ways to grip the drumstick. He said the most popular are the French, matched, and traditional way."

"Okay."

"Then he showed me how to count time properly using something called a metro—metronome."

"Mmm-hmm."

"And he said I could learn to play any instrument I want."

"That's pretty cool."

"Yeah, I think so too."

The wind blew through the car, cooling Justine's skin, but her thoughts ran all over the place. Emile continued to talk about his lesson, and she responded with encouraging murmurs. Her interest piqued when Emile began talking about Xavier, the man. "He has a daughter and she's nearly the same age as Yolanda."

Although the information wasn't new to her, Justine wanted to find out everything Emile knew. "Really?"

"Yeah, but he doesn't have a son yet. He said if he could have one, he'd want him to be like me."

Justine flashed Emile a quick look. "What else did he say?"

"He said we'd be spending more time together, outside the music room." Emile sounded as if nothing better had ever happened to him.

Justine's heart tripped and she had to swallow a few times to avoid choking. Was Xavier mad? How dare he tell her son any such thing? If she didn't know what she knew, she'd think he was a damn pervert.

You're forgetting he's Xavier's son too.

She ignored that fact.

He had to be losing his marbles if he thought she'd allow him to take her son anywhere without her. She'd rather die than give him the chance to fill Emile's head with things she didn't want him knowing.

The next time she saw Xavier, she'd sort him out properly. That's if he didn't demand the impossible of her first.

– 8 –

Sunday, February 20

Xavier

Proverbs: What dog see, him bark all night. Ram goat see, it nuh trouble him.
Meaning: Situations affect people differently.

Xavier lowered the newspaper to his lap and picked up the phone. Annette again. He braced himself for another round of aggravation. Kelleigh was always her excuse. Not that he didn't know what a monster his child had become. Too much indulgence and too little discipline did that to children. He ignored the voice that reminded him there was a reason Kelleigh had two parents.

He flipped the phone open. "Yes, Annette."

"Why don't you ever return my calls? I can't manage Kelleigh alone. You need to come over and talk to your daughter. She's driving me mad."

He wondered what he was supposed to say.

"She's out of control and you aren't here to help. Promise me you'll come and talk to her."

"What did she do this time?"

"She sneaked out last night and I didn't know she was gone until this morning."

"When was the last time you saw her?"

"Before bedtime. Are you implying I should be checking up on her in the middle of the night?"

"But didn't you say she's done this before?"

"Yes, but—"

"You need to keep a closer eye on her. What have you said to her?"

"Doesn't matter. She's not listening to me."

"Yeah, because Kelleigh knows who's in charge. You talk at her all the time, but don't follow through on discipline."

"What d'you expect me to do? You're off living your life and I'm left to fend for myself."

While she ranted, Xavier's thoughts took him down another road. Why did Annette expect any other result? She was the most self-contained woman he knew. Justine ran a close second, but had been much freer with her affection.

The older his marriage to Annette grew, the more she withdrew into herself. She'd gotten a degree and was now pursuing a Master's in the Social Sciences, and during that time their family and marriage had fallen apart.

He'd grown away from her because he had no evidence that she wanted or needed him, not the way that Justine did. With Justine, he'd felt like he had something she couldn't get from any other man and that also made him love her. Too bad he'd had to wake up to the reality that Justine preferred being a martyr to being with him.

Annette's tone sharpened and he shifted on the sofa and tuned back in to her tirade. "So you're gonna make me go through this alone, or will I see you later?"

Wondering why he was even going to bother, for he already knew the outcome of any family meeting, Xavier gave in. "Yeah, sure. I'll be there around five."

Sunday afternoon, and he'd be driving back and forth, when he should be at home with them. What a long way they'd come from the early days when he believed his marriage to Annette would have lasted. Justine had been a wonderful interlude and he had hoped to have a second go at marriage with someone who understood him. That was a pipe dream, from which he'd been slapped awake.

After Justine left him, he resigned himself to making do with Annette and their sterile home life. It wasn't that he didn't love her. He did, but it was hard being around her when it was clear he had no real purpose in her life. Annette had no clue what marriage was about, and to think they'd had a dozen counseling sessions before their wedding, as prescribed by the church.

He continued reading the sports pages, but couldn't concentrate. For weeks, he avoided dwelling on Emile and Justine, telling himself he preferred to live in the present. The truth was it would hurt a hell of a lot to drag himself through what was best forgotten, but he seemed incapable of helping himself, so he closed his eyes and gave in to the memories that insisted on being relived.

After Justine left him, he continued taking Kelleigh to tennis lessons at the facility Justine managed. When he finally accepted Justine's rejection and the thought of seeing her got too painful, he found another tennis coach, despite Kelleigh's objections. Distance didn't cure his ache for Justine, but as time went by, he missed her less. He'd always maintained that life was what he made of it, but for the first time in his forty-six years, he now accepted that life wasn't always fair.

The townhouse he now called home was where he used to meet Justine. A few months after she dumped him, his friend had sold him the place and migrated to Florida. It wasn't until lately that Xavier realized Justine didn't fill his days or the townhouse anymore.

Now that he had finally settled into acceptance, she was back to turn him upside down, and he found himself powerless to ignore the emotions he thought he'd overcome. What was worse, and a huge blow to his ego, was that Milton had died.

If Milton was out of the way, what reason did Justine have to give up their relationship? Did guilt lead her to believe they shouldn't have anything to do with each other? She bloody well knew he'd committed to leaving Annette and would have married her after his divorce. So what could she have been thinking to erase him from her life like some damn mistake? Small wonder she hadn't aborted Emile.

He rolled his head from side to side to negate that thought. The Justine he knew had carried loads of guilt over their affair. She'd never have considered an abortion. Justine was a good Catholic, steeped in morality and ridden with remorse over the smallest of things. No matter the mood she was in, her conscience bothered her during the times they were together. He'd been surprised that she stayed with him for as long as she had.

For all the hours he'd spent analyzing their love affair, he still didn't understand her actions.

After admitting her love and planning a future with him, Justine had cast him aside like garbage, leaving him gutted.

***

Kelleigh sat across from Xavier, defiance in the set of her mouth. He hadn't seen her in more than a week, but every time he did, he worried. Petulant described her perfectly.

Kelleigh unfolded her arms and shifted to make herself more comfortable. Frowning, Xavier clasped his fingers together to avoid reaching over the table and yanking at her blouse. The tank top she wore was much too skimpy.

Annette sat to his left, seemingly un-perplexed by all the flesh Kelleigh had on display. Xavier wanted to shake Annette out of her stupor. Kelleigh was growing at the pace of a weed, without guidance because her mother was too busy being the high-profile social worker and consultant. What would people think if they knew the expert they saw on television doling out advice didn't have the first clue how to run her home?

He gazed around the kitchen where he had spent many evenings on his laptop chatting with Justine on instant messenger. In the two years since he'd moved out, Annette hadn't bothered to have the walls repainted, but that wasn't his problem. He let his gaze settle on Kelleigh. "Your mother tells me you're sneaking out at night."

She stared at him, as if daring him to say more.

"I don't know what it is you're doing on the streets, but decent girls don't run around at night."

"*Decent girls* are overrated," she said.

"And being a slut is all that?"

She glared at him. "Don't call me that!"

"Well, if you dress like one and behave like one..."

Kelleigh spun in her seat, eyes turned on her mother. "How can you let him talk to me like that?"

Annette didn't respond. The kettle pealed, breaking the momentary silence. Still not speaking, Annette moved to the stove, turned the burner off and made a cup of tea. Xavier watched her, wondering if the routine of making tea was a way to avoid what was happening in her kitchen—if only for a few moments.

Xavier focused on Kelleigh, reaching for an explanation that wouldn't make him sound like a tyrant. "In case you forgot, we live in Jamaica. It's not the safe little island paradise it used to be. We're simply concerned about you."

Kelleigh rolled her eyes as if his words weren't worth considering.

When Annette sat, Kelleigh continued her attack. "You called him over here to help you gang up on me, plus you're letting him insult me."

Annette sipped from the cup before responding. "I didn't call him over to 'gang up on you' as you put it, but since you won't listen to me—"

"Why the hell should I listen to you? You don't—"

"Watch your mouth," Xavier heard himself shout.

His daughter stared at him, as if he'd done something obscene. He'd never raised his voice to her before. She recovered quickly and sassed him, eyes narrowed as though daring him to do his worst. "You can't tell me what to do."

Xavier wanted to wring her neck. When had she become this rotten bit of fluff? She'd always been demanding, but until recently she'd stayed respectful. As he examined Kelleigh, he admitted that since his disaster with Justine, he hadn't paid much attention to anything but traveling to different islands with the band and establishing his business, as if that would have cured all that ailed him.

In forcing himself to stay occupied, he'd missed seeing the negative changes developing in his daughter. He was halfway to waking up, but feared he might be too late to curb Kelleigh's bad temper and willfulness.

"You might think you're a woman, but all you are is a spoiled child," he said through his teeth. "Don't you dare speak to me like that again, or so help me, your ass is gonna be grass and I'll be the Weed Whacker."

She lowered her gaze to the tabletop.

"D'you understand me?"

She refused to answer.

He slammed his palm on the wooden surface.

She jumped and her eyes shot to his.

"You got that, Miss Thang?"

She ground her teeth together, face set as if she wanted to kill him. Then, she sniffed and nodded.

"Now," he continued, "you're going to treat your mother with some respect. You do what she tells you, and if I hear about you sneaking out again, I'm going to chain you in the house myself. You're way out of line and it's time someone took you in hand. You're excused."

She dragged the chair across the tiles and stood. After she rammed the chair under the table, she avoided looking at him and shuffled down the passage. When her bedroom door closed, he told Annette what was on his mind. "You need to pay more attention to Kell. If you don't keep an eye on her, next thing you know she'll be having sex, that's if she hasn't already."

Annette's hand fluttered upward to fiddle with the pendant on her necklace. She blinked at him, eyes large in her face, full lips forming an O.

"That's impossible. She couldn't—"

"What d'you think she's out doing at night? Annette, get real. Kelleigh is growing up right before your eyes. Did you notice what she had on? Her jeans don't cover her ass and her tits are hanging out of her blouse. She already thinks she's a woman, and you're in denial."

"How can you say that?"

"If you can ask me that, you're even sillier than I thought. You're so absorbed in your career, you can't see shit."

"If that's the way you feel, then—"

"Don't worry, I'm leaving, but trust me, you need to get hold of that child, otherwise you'll be bringing up a grandchild soon. One I won't be helping you raise."

He pushed away from the table. "You need to think about what you want for your only child. I'll do my best to support you and keep her in line, but I suggest you pull your finger out of your ass and pay attention before our child becomes a statistic."

Annette said nothing, but folded her hands around the empty cup. He left her, taking a detour on the way out of the house.

Her response to his knock on the door was curt. "What?"

He opened the door on chaos. Heaps of clothing covered the bed, chairs, even the floor. He frowned, and prepared to remark on the mess, but reminded himself her mother had to do her part. Kelleigh had cleared a space on the bed, and lay on her belly reading a book. He met her defiance head-on.

"I'll be calling to talk to you in the evenings. Make sure you're here and that you've done your assignments. I know your grades are slipping."

He examined the room again. "I wasn't going to say anything, but you're my child and I'd be failing you as a parent if I stay silent." He took in the piles of rubble. "You're only fifteen, but you should know that no man likes a nasty woman, and anybody who's lazy is just a step away from being nasty."

Tears filled her eyes, but he pretended not to see them. Though he wanted to comfort her, he couldn't find the words, and hoped she'd realize he wasn't being mean for the sake of it, but was trying to do his best as a parent.

He went back to the kitchen where Annette still sat at the table, reading a textbook. He hoped something he said would get through to her. Their situation was a repeat of what he'd seen with Justine the previous day when she and Yolanda were fighting. The difference though, was that Justine had tried to rein in her daughter.

This brought him back to his unexplained need to make Justine suffer. It was a given that he couldn't walk away from Emile, but with the challenges he faced raising Kelleigh, was he crazy to get in a fight with Justine, knowing the additional problems that a relationship with his son would bring to his life?

– *9* –

Justine

Proverb: Bush have ears and wall have eyes.
Meaning: Be careful how you disclose sensitive information that can filter to those you don't want to know your business.

Though Xavier gave no indication he knew she was in the room, Justine struggled to relax. Why was she allowing him to unnerve her? She was her own woman, confident, strong and way past the age where any man should make her uneasy.

To add to her discomfort, Xavier had his arm around Emile, guiding his movements as a father would. But what could she do about it? He was now firmly entrenched in their lives. All she heard these days from her children was Mr. McKay this and Mr. McKay that. If they talked about him any more than they were already doing, he'd soon be up for sainthood.

She shifted, and he raised his head. For a moment, he looked at her the way he used to, when he loved her.

Where had that thought come from?

Positioned as he was behind Emile, Xavier made her breath stop. This picture of father and son was something she'd never thought to see, and here they were, in close proximity.

The muscles on Xavier's arms shifted as he demonstrated the timing to Emile. His large hands engulfed their son's smaller pair. She remembered too well what those hands could do to the secret places on her body. Her mouth opened slightly and stayed that way, while her breathing refused to steady.

Xavier moved his head, as if to see her better, eyes as dark as the black tee-shirt he wore. His intense study interrupted her daydream. She flushed hot with embarrassment. The knowing light in his eyes confirmed he could still read her mind and knew exactly where her thoughts lay. She broke their eye lock, grateful when a hand slid around her neck.

Yolanda hugged her from behind. "Hey, Moms, you're early."

"Mmm-hmm, can't leave you two to run the place to a wreck."

"As if we'd do anything like that." She looked to Xavier for confirmation. "We respect your stuff, don't we, Mr. McKay?"

"Yeah, you're my keenest students."

Yolanda's hand slid off Justine's shoulder and she cocked her head, staring at Xavier and her brother. She looked hard at Justine, but didn't say anything.

Justine guessed what might have caused that reaction. Only the blind couldn't see the resemblance between Xavier and Emile. Hopefully, Yolanda was still innocent enough to have missed the bit of live drama set before her eyes. Justine tugged at her gold pendant and willed herself to relax. If she kept anticipating trouble, it would certainly find her.

"Uh, kids, I'm ready to go. Can you give me a moment alone with Mr. McKellop, please?"

Taking as long as they could about it, Emile and Yolanda gathered their things and left with the car key. The door hadn't closed completely, but far enough so they could have some privacy.

Justine rehearsed the words she wanted to say to Xavier. She had spent the last hour wrapping her brain around an idea she wanted to convey to him.

Xavier sat in the seat Emile had vacated moments ago. While he watched her, he tapped a beat on the snare drums, and what Emile called high hat cymbals, with a pair of percussion sticks.

She wished he'd get out from the behind the drums. It made her uncomfortable to be isolated, as if she was on display in the middle of the room. Suddenly, she regretted the care she'd taken with her hair and the choice of an ankle-length sundress that complemented her figure. What had she been thinking, trying to dress to impress a man who hated her?

To add to her discomfort, he was deliberately making her wait.

"Can we talk?" she asked, masking her irritation.

Abruptly, he got up and walked to where she stood. "What d'you want to talk about?"

Justine backed away, clutching her handbag in front of her. Over the past few weeks, she had thought about making a doctor's appointment to check whether she was approaching early menopause. But her blood only hovered near boiling point when she was with Xavier. She prayed her sweat glands wouldn't let her down and dragged her mind back to the matter at hand. "I want to make a proposal."

Xavier's eyebrows shot up and his head tipped to the side.

She put up both hands, conscious of how he might interpret her words. "I didn't mean that like it sounds. I...I wanted to suggest something to you."

He waited, bottom lip sucked into his mouth. She fastened her eyes on his, though fearing she'd melt into a steaming puddle at his feet. She could do this. She just needed to keep her mind on her goal.

But her attention wouldn't stop wandering. Hairs sprouted along his jaw line, and she traced the shadow along his cheek where a full beard would grow in, if he allowed it to.

He cleared his throat, which sent another tide of heat flowing into her face. His cocked eyebrow sent words jetting from her throat. "I was thinking that since you're still, uh, married, maybe it wouldn't be such a bad thing if you moved slowly with Emile. I know the damage something like this can do to a marriage."

Xavier's eyebrows drew closer together and his eyes turned black. She swore the blood crept up his neck and darkened his face, but still, he said nothing.

Menopause definitely had to be attacking her, because ice crystals filled her legs and flooded upward to chill her body, but she couldn't stop now. She was fighting for her child. "I mean, I wouldn't want to break up your home. Your wife—"

"Is none of your business," he said.

She inhaled, an abrupt sound, which gave away her shock. Surely, she hadn't heard him right. But no, he carried on lashing her with cruel words, some of which escaped her.

"...how dare you? Who the hell d'you think you are?"

He walked out of eyeshot, and something crashed to the desk behind her. She jerked and turned to face him.

"You just don't get it, do you?" Xavier now stood behind the desk, his eyes boring into her flesh. "As far as you're concerned, you've done nothing wrong, and you expect me to go away, so you can have your tidy little life back. Wake up, Justine. It ain't gonna happen."

She moved closer, prepared to make him see reason. Seconds crawled by and she tried a few times before she got her voice to work. "All I'm trying to do is save your family from the heartache this situation will cause."

He sat and laid both hands on the desk. "My family is also none of your concern, and the only person you're trying to *save* is yourself. I put my life in your hands once and you fucked it up, so mind your own damn business."

He turned his head away, as if he couldn't bear to look at her.

"Get out."

Justine gripped the edge of the desk to keep herself from stumbling. She must have heard wrong.

Something bumped the door, and Justine spun toward it, but nothing happened. Maybe a draft from the air-conditioner, or the front door opening, had caused it to move. She forgot the interruption and looked at Xavier.

He spoke louder this time. "I said, get out."

When she didn't move, he shot to his feet. The chair crashed into the wall behind him, sending a trophy from the shelf toppling to the floor. He ignored it, marched around the desk and grabbed her arm. Urging her forward, he pushed the door open and escorted her to the end of the passage. Behind the swing door, he gripped her upper arms and spoke into her ear in a furious whisper. "You've done enough to ruin my life. Don't make it any worse. I'll talk to you when you're in a more rational frame of mind."

He stalked away and slammed the door to the studio.

Justine lifted her chin and shoulders and walked into the storefront. The witch at the counter looked at her as if to say she was responsible for the racket in the back of the shop. Justine didn't give her the time of day.

She sauntered to the Camry, checked that the children were strapped in, and drove away as though she didn't have a care in the world. Why give that woman the satisfaction of knowing Xavier had just shredded her insides and left her feeling as though the world had collapsed around her? She still felt the pressure where he'd grabbed her arms, and wondered what the hell he'd been smoking. The old Xavier never would have manhandled her like that.

She drew up to the stoplight, mind still inside *Rapporté*. A boy approached the window with a bottle of soapy water and a worn-out squeegee. "Miss, mi can clean yuh glass?"

On a normal day, Justine would have wound the window up on approaching the stoplight, but her run-in with Xavier had her thoughts all over the place. She stared into the boy's earnest eyes, somehow knowing he wouldn't try to grab anything.

From the ashtray, she got some coins and gave them to him, waving him away when he attempted to lift the wiper blades. "It's okay. You don't have to do that."

"T'anks, Miss," he said, before moving to the next car in line.

Justine watched him, wondering about his parents, as she did each time a child accosted her on the street for money.

Yolanda accused her from the passenger seat. "I thought you said it wasn't wise to give street boys money."

"It isn't, but he caught me off guard and he looks like he really needs it."

In the rearview mirror she watched him hurrying to clean a windscreen before the light changed. "He's so small to be out here."

"You should take your own advice," Yolanda said, watching the stoplight. She started to say something else, but changed her mind.

"Yes, I should."

Yolanda's brows lifted and she stared hard at Justine before tracing the pattern on the leg of her jeans as if it was her most important task of the day.

Emile sat forward and held on to her seat. "So, Mommy, did Mr. McKay tell you what I did today?"

Justine made encouraging noises, which was enough for Emile. His chatter was white noise that went over her head and for once, Justine didn't mind Yolanda's silence.

***

As was customary on a Saturday when Miss Pauline was away, Justine made a snack and reminded the children she wouldn't be cooking dinner. Though she complained, Yolanda agreed to make more sandwiches if they were hungry later in the evening.

Filled with Corned Beef sandwiches and longing for adventure, Emile wandered outside to play in the backyard, carrying a plastic sword and pirate hat. Yolanda sat at the table working her way through a slice of hardough bread.

While Justine wiped the counter, the space between her shoulder blades prickled. She couldn't be sure, but thought Yolanda was studying her, as if saddling up for something big. Justine wiped her brow with the back of her arm, thinking that writers knew exactly what they were talking about when they described air as being thick with tension. She had the urge to turn around and see if Yolanda was staring, but didn't.

Yolanda wouldn't admit to what she was doing. She'd turned baiting Justine into an art form.

Justine joined Yolanda at the table, her mind going back to the years when they used to sit like this on a Saturday morning and catch up on everything they hadn't discussed during the weekdays.

It was a relief to be on a not-so-rocky footing with Yolanda. Their standoffs exhausted Justine, who didn't know what to do to make things better, but Yolanda thrived on their arguments. Sometimes, the fighting wore on Justine so much that it was easier to close her eyes to Yolanda's attitude problems and avoid conflict. Even now, her eyes glittered with something close to malice.

Despite the obvious signs, Justine hoped they could get through the evening without an argument and then strained silence with Yolanda slamming her way around the house.

She sipped from her glass, put it down and stared at Justine. "Emile told me you knew Mr. McKay before he was born. You guys go way back, huh?"

Justine jerked her head in a nod, while having a flashback of Yolanda studying Emile and Xavier earlier in the day. Surely she couldn't have made that connection. *You're seeing complication where none exists*, Justine told herself.

"How far back?" Yolanda asked.

Her open expression didn't fool Justine for a second. Her question was leading somewhere. Fighting to sound casual and ignore her knotted stomach, Justine asked, "Why d'you want to know?"

Yolanda leaned toward her, elbows on the table. "Emile looks just like him."

Forcing herself not to blink or show any reaction, Justine scrambled for something to say. "I'm sure it's your imagination."

After all this time, she should have been prepared with an explanation that sounded a lot less lame.

Shaking her head, Yolanda drew a circle on the tabletop. "Nope. Their skin is the same color. Their forehead, nose and mouth look the same, and when they stand close to each other, Emile is a smaller version of that man."

Justine's belly plunged in a tailspin. For a moment her mind blanked out and then settled. *She thinks exactly the way I would. She's observant enough to be a writer too.* Hands on the table, Justine commanded her tongue to untie itself. She picked what she thought were noncommittal words. "Why would that be important?"

Yolanda smiled, a gesture filled with sadness. When she looked at Justine again, the corners of her mouth puckered in a sneer.

Justine's throat closed and she waited for Yolanda to land what she would consider a killing blow.

"I heard you talking to Mr. McKellop today." Yolanda spat his name as though it was poison on her tongue. "So I know what the two of you did."

Shaking her head from side to side, Justine willed her mind to settle. She smoothed a hand over her hair, ignoring the sweat chilling the space above her lip, while her stomach heaved and swelled. She should be giving Yolanda hell over eavesdropping; instead, the situation was slipping out of her control. Ashamed, and feeling like a fool, Justine muttered, "It was a long time ago."

Nostrils flared, Yolanda shouted, "This means you cheated on Daddy."

Stealing a glance at the window, Justine said, "Keep your voice down."

Yolanda jumped from her seat. "You keep hounding me about Tariq and being careful, but you can't give any advice, 'cause you're no better."

A sour taste invaded the back of Justine's mouth; she was about to lose her dinner. She pressed a hand to her stomach. "I'm still your mother, so watch what you say to me."

Yolanda hung over the table, using her hands to support her weight. "You may be my mother, but you're also a slut!"

Whack.

Justine's hand twanged and throbbed.

Yolanda's face reddened, tears filled her eyes, and she screamed. "Slut!"

Justine slapped her other cheek. "Shut up! You don't know what you're talking about."

Yolanda screamed the insult louder.

Flinging the chair back without a care where it fell, Justine got to her feet and rushed to the other side of the table. Grabbing Yolanda by the arm, Justine shoved her down the passage. "Go to your room, and don't come out 'til I tell you!"

Sobbing, Yolanda stumbled past Emile with a hand pressed to her cheek.

How had he appeared so quickly?

"What happened, Mommy?"

The door slammed and within a moment, glass shattered inside Yolanda's room.

When Emile cringed, Justine kissed his forehead and slipped a hand over his shoulder. "Just the usual, hon. Go back outside and play."

He frowned, unconvinced. "Sis gone mad again, huh?"

Justine swept a hand across her cheek, smearing her tears, too miserable to correct Emile's speech. "Guess so."

He stared up at her, serious under his pirate hat. "Why you crying?"

"You know it makes me sad when we quarrel."

"But why you had to hit her?"

Justine righted the chair before responding. "She said something rude."

"She's rude all the time."

He abandoned his sword on the counter, got a glass and opened the refrigerator, while Justine put her head in her hands and slumped against the tabletop. She moved when Emile's feet appeared in her line of sight. Raising her head, she asked, "What's up?"

"Maybe we need a daddy."

Though she couldn't have felt less like laughing, Justine chuckled. "What d'you mean by that?"

He sat close to her, cupping his cheeks, fingernails lined with dirt. Since he was going back outside, she didn't send him to wash his hands. Instead, she pulled his hands away from his face.

"Well," he said, "Kevin's sister is crazy like Landy, but when she gets mad Kevin's mommy tells her she's gonna let her father fix her business when he comes home. Maybe if we had a daddy, he'd fix Landy's business."

Justine rubbed his head. "Hon, it's not as easy as it sounds. First, Mommy would have to find someone she likes and then she'd have to make sure he gets along with you and your sister."

Emile sucked his bottom lip and studied the table. The clock counted out the seconds in the intervening silence.

"I know!" Emile beamed at her. "We could get Mr. McKay to be our daddy."

Justine's chest ached and she wanted to weep, but that wouldn't change what had happened so long ago. She didn't recognize her voice when she spoke. "It doesn't work like that, Emile."

"Why not, since he only has one daughter?"

She touched his cheek and raised a smile. "I'll explain it another time, Babes. Go find some gold or capture some pirates."

"Okay," he said, adjusting his hat. He grabbed the sword and ran out the door, letting it slam behind him. Drained of energy, she couldn't yell her usual warning that one day the panes of glass would fall out if he didn't stop banging the door.

Through the window, she watched him battle the potted Crown of Thorns, but was too disheartened to warn him about the spines. She'd told him often enough anyway.

She kneaded her forehead, fighting the depression trying to take root in her bones. She thought she'd had it licked, but it had slithered back, threatening to reclaim neutral ground she'd fought for and won. She knew the signs well. Her mouth and shoulders pulled down. Her throat was blocked by the phantom boulder doing its best to fall into her stomach and weigh her down.

Her eyes ached and her energy was lower than when she first sat. *Too many damn issues to deal with all at once.*

Xavier wanted her to tell Emile he had a father, which would reduce her carefully ordered life to shambles.

Yolanda despised her.

Emile thought a father would solve all their problems.

Justine had dreaded this day for what felt like forever. Dionne and Kyra had warned her often enough to prepare to deal with the consequences of her choice to raise Emile alone. As time passed and she felt safe in her deception, another worry replaced the fear of what Xavier would do if he found out about Emile.

Not only did she fret over Emile's wellbeing, in her heart she agonized that one day she'd lose him because he was a child of adultery. So many times, she'd gone backward and forward through David's experience in the Bible. He'd lost his son born of an adulterous relationship and if he was a man after God's heart, what right did she have to think Emile wouldn't be taken from her?

Part of her unease had to do with the fact that she had never confessed, but there was no way she could tell her pastor what she'd done. On a rational level, she understood that God forgave those who repented and believed in His forgiveness, but her conscience refused to let go of the guilt that woke with her every day, and over which she still did penance. Dionne and Kyra said her religion controlled her life, but Justine understood the enormity of the sin she'd committed.

She sighed and didn't try to stop the tears determined to flood from her body. If there was anything to be thankful for, it was that Miss Pauline had the weekend off and hadn't witnessed their drama. Only God knew what she'd think about Yolanda's revelation.

So many problems to work through. Sinking further into despair, Justine admitted she'd backed herself into a corner, with no clue what to do or which way to go.

– 10 –

Friday, March 4, 7:00 PM

Xavier

Proverb: Bend di tree when it young.
Meaning: Train your children properly when they are young.

Kelleigh shrank under Xavier's stare. He allowed the hush in the kitchen to continue until Annette and Kelleigh fidgeted in their seats. He spoke then. "This is the first and last time I'm going to any police station to get bail for you."

His gaze shifted to Annette. "The next time they lock her up, don't call me. D'you even know that your daughter is a fishwife? That she curses? D'you know whose company she's keeping? No, because you're too—"

He caught himself before he chewed Annette over in front of Kelleigh.

"Miss Thang."

Kelleigh's head snapped up and fire sparked in her eyes. She hated it when he called her names.

"Put this in your pipe and smoke it. The next time you get into any trouble. I don't care how small it is, I'm taking you from your mother and putting you in a place of safety. You will not subject me to any more embarrassment, cursing like a sailor and behaving as if you belong to careless parents from some ghetto in downtown Kingston."

Annette protested, waving her hands about. "Isn't that too harsh, consid—"

"Considering what?" Xavier snapped, forgetting his intention not to tell Annette exactly what he thought of her. "You can't even see what's happening in your own house."

He pointed at Kelleigh. "Better to put her someplace where somebody will have control over her, which you don't have."

"I'm doing the best I can." Annette flipped hair over her shoulder, full of attitude. "Am I supposed to know where she is every hour of the day?" she continued, cutting her eyes at him.

"Other parents have an idea where their children are, Annette, and who they're with."

He stared at Kelleigh, who crossed her arms beneath her breasts, which should have been better covered. Her belly-button peeked at him across the table. Didn't Annette see that Kelleigh had too much out in the open? She was racing toward adulthood and only the Lord knew what she was doing while nobody was watching her. Talking to her on the phone daily could only provide so much guidance and no more. She needed supervision. Fear of him would make her hesitate, but might not prevent her walking into disaster. That's if she wasn't setting herself up already. Awkwardness tied his tongue, but he had to know what was going on with her. He cleared his throat and clasped his hands on the tabletop. "Kelleigh, are you having sex?"

Annette stuttered, and then went silent at a glare from him while Kelleigh fiddled with the button on her jeans as if her father hadn't spoken.

Annoyance over having to ask such a question made his voice louder than he intended. "I asked you a question!"

She whispered.

"*What?*"

Tears ran down her cheeks, while she continued to stare in her lap.

"Look at me when I'm talking to you."

He hated treating her as though she was a little girl, but someone had to remind Kelleigh that she wasn't yet a woman. She met his eyes, blinked and more tears chased down her cheeks. He read the truth and slumped in relief.

"No, Daddy," she whispered.

"Good. Don't get any ideas. At fifteen, you're not ready for sex."

She sobbed, got off the chair and ran down the passage. He let her go only because he needed to talk to her mother.

Xavier wished he could find a way to get through to Annette, but doubted any miracles were in their immediate future. "I spoke to you about this same thing last week," he said. "Can you at least buy her some decent clothes?"

"What she has on is what kids are wearing these days."

"I don't care what other kids are wearing," he said, massaging his forehead. "This is *my* daughter we're talking about. Why does she have everything hanging out? Don't you talk to her about placing value on herself? Would you want to know she's giving it up to anybody who asks?"

Annette scowled. "Didn't she say she's not having sex?"

"She isn't now, but that means nothing. Ten chances to one, if she gets pregnant, you won't know until it's too late. Jesus, woman, can't you spare some time for your child? If you don't, who will? Have you even talked to her about sex?"

Annette gaped at him bug-eyed, and he stared at the ceiling. What kind of woman didn't talk to her teenager about life and sex?

Exhaustion washed over him and it took him a few seconds to stand. Despite his frustration, he squeezed Annette's shoulder on his way out of the kitchen. He asked himself how he could have married such a self-absorbed woman, but couldn't answer the question.

When he sat inside his truck, he smiled; a self-deprecating gesture. Seemed he had a thing for that type of woman. Justine was another good example of what not to look for in a woman, but he had been too blind and obsessed to see what was obvious from the start of their affair.

He'd see Justine tomorrow and no doubt, she'd have another shit-load of selfish ideas designed to keep him away from Emile.

She'd have to come good if she thought he was going to sit back and allow her to jerk him around like a kite on a string.

* * *

Saturday, March 5, 3:30 PM

Friday evening's encounter with Annette and Kelleigh followed Xavier into Saturday morning. His mood reflected the gray clouds hanging low in the sky.

For the first time, his session with Yolanda hadn't gone well. Instead of sticking to the scales he wanted her to practice, she kept playing some morose tune, which annoyed the shit out of him. She seemed determined to disobey him, and coming off yesterday evening's episode with Kelleigh, he wasn't in the mood to take crap from another teenage prima donna.

"If you can't follow my instructions, the door is over there," he said, when he'd had enough.

She glowered at him, grabbed her bag and left in a snit. Justine hadn't asked any questions when she got there and found Yolanda missing. He imagined a phone call from Yolanda would have alerted Justine to her whereabouts. How well he now understood what Justine was going through, but somehow he figured she would have had better results than he was seeing in his family.

He'd thought her a responsible parent during the year they had sneaked around with each other. Justine was racked by guilt whenever she couldn't be home with Yolanda, who made repeated phone calls in the evenings to track her mother's movements. On the weekends, although Justine had to work, she made time to be with her daughter, unlike Annette, who was always too busy. He'd ended up carving time from his schedule for Kelleigh's extracurricular activities.

Justine didn't impress him now. She'd become a wimp, a faint shadow of the woman he'd loved. The new Justine was willing to throw a veneer of normality over her problems, thinking that would solve them.

While in the studio, he avoided looking at her, not because she disgusted him, but because over the past weeks, he'd felt himself relaxing toward her. That wouldn't do. He needed to keep her at a distance and remember his pain when she cut him out of her life.

When she dropped off Emile earlier in the day, Xavier had let her know they needed to take some decisions. She'd suggested they go to her friend's place again, which he figured was a way to keep him off balance. She probably thought the studio gave him an advantage.

When she returned for Emile, he followed her here, hoping to break some new ground. His patience wasn't what it used to be, but he also didn't want to terrify her.

She'd left her hair loose and a bang brushed her eyebrows. The soft cloud around her head made him want to touch her, but he fisted his hands on his thighs waiting for the urge to pass.

She dropped the napkin on the table and stared at his chin.

The determined set of her face wiped away any sympathy he'd been harboring. "I don't know why I let you talk me into coming to this place again," he said. "Talking around the problem isn't helping. We could have done this just as easily at my shop."

Justine's mouth swelled in a pout. "I just don't see why you need to spend any more time with him than you do now."

Xavier bit down on the thoughts that longed to escape his mouth. He'd seen the effect his words had on her, deserving though she was.

To cool his anger, he let their surroundings distract him; the garden was manicured into submission, not a leaf or blade of grass out of place. He brought his attention back to her and sat straighter. "You think you're so smart, but I see what you're doing."

She fiddled with the thin gold watch she wore. "What's that supposed to mean?"

"It means you want to keep me in a position where you can supervise my time with Emile. I'm getting tired of it. You hang around for at least half of each lesson, thinking I don't understand what you're doing."

Justine shoved cold French Fries around the plate, then she stabbed at a fry and the fork clattered on the stoneware. "How am I supposed to tell Emile you're his father? What explanation can I give him?"

"You've asked me that already, and I can't help you. I don't believe you ever intend to tell him."

He ignored her gasp and refused to let her interrupt him. "My advice to you is to get over yourself. Your problem is that you don't want Emile to think badly of you. That's why you're hiding behind him."

She spoke through her teeth, cutting him with her eyes. "I am not hiding behind him."

He sighed and laid his hands on either side of the empty plate. "It's not enough for me to see my son in a classroom setting or at some outdoor restaurant. There are things I want to do with him, things you deprived me of with your lying and secrecy."

She continued to stare at him as though he was persecuting her. At the edge of the lawn, Emile watched the goldfish, his body splayed over the rocks surrounding the pond. The sun had emerged during the afternoon, lightening the atmosphere. A cool breeze rippled the water's surface. Emile's enjoyment lifted Xavier's spirit, but his mood turned somber when he faced Justine.

"I'm fed up with your delaying tactics. You've had enough time to work out a suitable arrangement. One hour on a Saturday afternoon isn't enough."

Her hand trembled as she brushed hair off her face.

Concern made him forget about minding his own business. "Something else bothering you?"

She sipped coconut water before she answered. "You could say that."

Though he didn't care about her troubles, curiosity prompted him to find out what was making her anxious. "What's the problem?"

"Yolanda guessed. She heard us on Saturday after I asked them to wait for me outside."

That explained the girl's bad behavior.

"She's been giving me some attitude too," he said. "Now that she knows, isn't it wise to tell Emile before she does?"

Justine looked at him as if he had blasphemed. "She wouldn't dare."

He shook his head. Did Justine live on the same planet he did? "She has a hair-trigger temper, and she doesn't think before she speaks. What makes you think she won't?"

"'Cause she knows I'd kill her."

He laughed. "There is that then. I wish you luck with that one, but seriously, you should tell him before he finds out by accident."

She passed both hands over her face. "I know...I just don't know how to do it."

"Would you like me to tell him?"

Her eyes opened wide and she screeched. "No!"

Emile looked at them over his shoulder, forcing Justine to wave at him, indicating everything was okay.

"I'll find a way," she said, stirring the cold fries.

"Better to do it sooner, rather than later."

She nodded, and stared toward the pond. If he didn't know better, he'd believe she was trying not to cry. Something he didn't want to put a name to, stirred inside him. He wanted to pull Justine on his lap, stroke her hair, and cuddle her, the way he used to when she worried about her troubles. Problem was, their situation had way more complications than a hug could cure.

"Tell you what," he said. "We can do it together. The worst has happened. Yolanda knows. If you come up with a way that works, we can tackle the problem together."

Her fingertip slid back and forth on the place mat. She sucked her lip into her mouth and furrowed her brow. When she was through thinking, she nodded. "Okay. I'll figure out the best way to do it and call you."

He smiled and patted her hand. "That works for me."

She brushed the hair away from her face and returned his smile.

She was beautiful.

– 99 –

Justine

Proverb: Yuh likkle, but yuh tallawah (powerful).
Meaning: Ordinary people (including children) can have a powerful impact.

"Would the two of you give me a break?" Justine spun her hair into a bun and secured it with a scrunchy. "I haven't worked things out in my mind yet."

Dionne wriggled her toes, stretched her legs and then lay on the sofa. "I'm not even going to consider that bit of rubbish. You've had how many weeks now? Six? Seven? Even you can't take that long to make up your mind."

"It's not your child he's trying to steal," Justine mumbled, aware that she was being bitchy.

"Nobody's trying to steal your child, Justine. Your problem is that you think too much. He ain't going away, so you better learn how to cope with him being in Emile's life."

Justine stared at the television, unwilling to admit she was procrastinating and that she did have the irrational desire for Xavier to disappear and leave her life the way it was before he turned it upside-down.

"The trouble is, Xavier's dragging you out of your comfort zone and you dunno how to deal with it. You've been existing since you ditched him and now he's shaken your world." Quick as lightning, a grin escaped. "Kinda like the way he rocked your world in the past."

Justine rolled her eyes; however, there was more than a grain of truth to what Dionne said.

"True dat," Kyra said, wandering back into her living room. She sat and broke off a bit of Bread Pudding from the slab on the saucer she carried. Closing her eyes, she chewed the dessert. Dionne snagged a piece and delicately licked her thumb and index finger. Justine had declined to have any, knowing Kyra had probably doused the pudding with a generous helping of rum.

As they had for many years, Dionne, Justine and Kyra spent time together at least two Saturday afternoons each month and backed that up with phone calls. In Justine's eyes, they hadn't aged much, but that was because she saw them often enough not to notice the changes. Dionne had kept her slim figure, and Kyra's low-cut hair and apple cheeks gave her a youthful appearance. Kyra's querulous tone cut into Justine's thoughts.

"Your body is here and you do all you need to do for Yolanda and Emile, but you really not living."

Justine sighed, smoothing her hair. "I'm very much alive, thank you. I just don't need the shit Xavier's stirring."

"Shit you heaped up because you didn't tell him about his son," Dionne said.

"You're a fine one to talk. You, the keeper of dreadful secrets."

"Be that as it may," Dionne said, "this is totally different."

Dionne looked away, and Justine felt a twinge of discomfort. She shouldn't have brought that up. Years before, Dionne's lover had raped her in a fit of spite when she tried to break off their affair. She'd kept the details to herself for a while and only shared what had happened just before her baby's birth, when she was scared and tormented over whether the baby belonged to her husband or her boyfriend. Since then, she'd remained faithful to Clayton.

Justine's frustration at being cornered was not a good enough reason for her to blurt something Dionne had tried to forget. Justine fiddled with the cushion on her lap. "Yeah, it is different. I had no reason to remind you about that. Sorry, girlfriend."

"No worries. You know I can take it. But you might not be able to take what I'm gonna tell you." Dionne swung her feet to the floor and sat up while Justine hugged a cushion.

"What's that?" Justine asked.

"You're gonna deny it, but part of the problem is that if you let Xavier into Emile's life, you're gonna have to share his love."

Shaking her head, Justine said. "No way. That's not it."

Dionne held up her hands. "Hear me out. You are the only parent Emile has known until now. Since the lessons started, you've complained bitterly how everything is Mr. McKay this and Mr. McKay that. You need to listen to yourself sometimes. You're jealous."

"That's not it. What gets me is that Xavier expects that I can just spring this news on Emile. I don't want to do that. Who knows how it will affect him."

Kyra rolled her eyes and shared a belly laugh with Dionne. Justine cautioned herself not to get upset with them. They knew her too well and her last statement did border on the ridiculous. Emile would be delighted to have a daddy, however he got one. He'd whined about his lack of a father more times than she could count.

"The only person this will affect is you," Kyra said. "Emile will be so happy, him goin' walk and tell even a cow howdy, so that ain't gonna fly, Jay."

Justine laughed despite the urge to hit both of them. Yes, she was the tiniest bit jealous, but she wasn't about to admit that.

She studied the frilly, layered curtains that Kyra had never grown out of and let her gaze rest on the matching floral sofa. Denton, her husband, was a saint and allowed Kyra to spend outrageous amounts redecorating every so often. Smiling, Justine reminded herself that Kyra was a homemaker at heart.

"What I want to know," Kyra said, "is how things are going with Xavier, other than the fact that you want to kill him for being alive?"

Justine's humor disappeared. "What exactly you mean by that?"

"Since I have to spell it out, any prospects for getting back together?"

Justine's throat closed and her heart pumped faster than it should, considering she hadn't moved. For a second, hope swept through her. Then reality reasserted itself. "He's still married."

"Him say so?" Kyra asked.

The living room had grown hot, or was it the thought of Xavier's marital status that made Justine uncomfortable? She fanned herself with a glossy brochure she lifted from the center table. "I assume he is. I wouldn't know anyway. He told me to mind my own business."

Dionne frowned at her. "You sure this is the same man who would have given up everything for you?"

Justine wondered the same thing, but shied away from going down that road. She wasn't sure how to cope with Xavier's harsh words and unreadable stares. She didn't deserve that sort of treatment. Didn't he understand that she was trying to preserve his family and her sanity when she'd told him good-bye? So, she hadn't told him to his face, but he had to know where her mind was at; he knew her that well.

Over the years she wondered what life would have been like if she had followed her dream, left Milton and gone to live with Xavier, but it was hard to form mental pictures because she couldn't fathom how they would have been happy together under a cloud of wrongdoing.

Why did Xavier have to turn up now, when she'd gotten used to shutting down the part of her that remembered every touch of his hand, the feel of his skin kissing hers in the heat of passion, the huskiness in his voice when he was about to have an orgasm, the musk he carried after sex? She'd done enough penance to atone for cheating on Milton, and for sinning against Xavier's wife, but sometimes when she looked at Emile, she wondered if she'd have to make an even bigger sacrifice. With each new dawn, she prayed her spirit would tell her she was forgiven for her transgressions.

That day and conviction hadn't come yet.

* * *

Saturday, March 5, 6:30 PM

Yolanda plunked the plate on the place mat and sat across from Justine. The ham sandwiches danced across the stoneware and ice cubes tinkled in the tumbler of lemonade she slammed on the coaster.

Justine massaged her temples, tired of the standoff, and defeated by the tension between them. Since Yolanda had started lessons with Xavier, the hostility had lessened. Now they were back to their old standoff, and Justine feared Yolanda would never forgive her. Not that Yolanda had a right to be listening outside closed doors. Hadn't she raised her to know better? It had to be more than curiosity that led Yolanda to do something so outrageous.

When Justine looked at her, Yolanda's gaze slid away. She chewed, eyes fixed on the plate, hands in her lap.

Without planning her words, Justine spoke. "It wasn't something I did willfully, and your father never knew."

Yolanda continued to chew as though Justine hadn't said a word.

"We had problems that—"

Staring across the room as if she was alone, Yolanda said, "I don't want to hear."

"We never worked out and it led to...what happened."

Eyes glinting, Yolanda spat an accusation. "All you're going to do is make excuses, say it was all Daddy's fault, but I know it wasn't."

"You're free to believe what you want, but think about what your father was like a while before he died and tell me you still think I'm a monster."

"Whatever. You're just trying to throw blame."

The dismissal stung, however, Justine saw the uncertainty in Yolanda's eyes before she made a show of pushing the hair off her forehead and sipping lemonade.

Justine said nothing, but her thoughts traveled back to the days when Milton started keeping secrets. His personality had changed over time and he'd gone from being even-tempered to snapping at Yolanda over the simplest things. Several times, they'd had run-ins over his treatment of their daughter. Surely, Yolanda couldn't have forgotten those times.

Maybe she prefers not to remember.

In the deepening silence, Yolanda tore bits of crust off the bread and threw them aside. The seriousness of her expression was at odds with the simple task she had set herself.

A sigh worked its way past Justine's lips. Every time she had one thing licked, another jumped up to bite her. When would something go her way? She shook off the self-pity trying to take hold. She wasn't worse off than anybody else. Since Emile's birth, her life had taken a smooth path. She'd cared for him and Yolanda, and discovered a talent for writing, which led to freelance assignments, including a weekly lifestyle newspaper column.

Justine made enough money to work from home and even did some event planning when the occasion arose. Best of all, she maintained a wonderful relationship with her friends. All these blessings were things she took for granted, which made the current upheaval almost more than she could bear.

She still hadn't decided how to tell Emile about his father and worse, she was at war with herself and Yolanda.

Yolanda shattered her thoughts, yelling, "This is your fault. You spoil everything! You probably killed Daddy. You ruined my life and now you've ruined the one thing I enjoy."

Justine ran her fingers into her hair, massaging her scalp. Staring at the table, she wondered how much more of Yolanda's abuse she could take before she snapped and did something else she'd regret.

The chair legs scraped the floor, Yolanda rose and rushed out of the kitchen. Seconds after she left, Emile yelped. "Ow!"

Justine's eyes snapped open and she rushed to where he stood in the doorway to the passage, one hand clasping the back of his head and the other cupping his nose.

Justine dragged Emile's hand away from his face. "What's wrong, hon?"

"Landy's elbow hit me and I lick my head on the wall."

His watery, pain-filled eyes made Justine's heart ache. Gently, she ran her hands over the back of his head. To her relief, he wasn't bleeding and there was no swelling.

"Let's get you something sweet to drink," Justine said, hauling him toward a chair. She had no idea what a sweet drink was supposed to do, but Justine's mother swore by that remedy whenever Justine had banged her head as a child.

She left Emile sitting at the table and told him she'd be back in a few minutes. A quick walk down the passage took her to Yolanda's door. She knocked once and swung it open. Yolanda lay on her side, facing the window, legs curled up, headphones in place.

She glared over her shoulder. "What d'you—oh."

Justine ensured she shut the door. "Take those things out of your ears."

Yolanda pressed her lips together in a show of defiance, but complied.

While she spoke, Justine walked toward the bed. "I don't care what mood you're in or what's happening. You need to be more careful around Emile. You could have hurt him badly when you hit him."

Yolanda got on both elbows. Her shoulders lifted and her mouth opened.

Hand raised, palm outward, Justine stopped her. "You might think you have every right in the world to be mad, but I really don't care." Justine continued, ignoring Yolanda's outraged silence. "Fact is, the next time you do something stupid and hurt Emile, I'm going to deal with you properly."

Without waiting for a reaction, Justine left the room, letting the door slam shut. It was about time she gave Yolanda some of what she'd dished out for so long.

Miss Pauline stood at the end of the passage, her forehead creased under the bandana she always wore. Justine had forgotten she was in the house.

"Everything all right, Miss Justine?"

"Same old, same old," Justine said.

Miss Pauline smiled, exposing the gold tip in her top dentures. "Never mind, mi dear. One day she will get past this stage."

"Yeah, hopefully sooner than later."

"You need help wid anyt'ing, ma'am?"

Shaking her head, Justine waved Miss Pauline away and went back to the kitchen where she slid into the chair opposite Emile.

"What's wrong with Landy now?" he asked after a few gulps of Flavor Aid.

"She's upset with me."

"Again?" Both of his eyebrows rose to question Justine. "Gee, she's always mad at you."

"It does feel that way."

"Maybe she really needs a daddy like Mr. McKay."

Justine's curiosity stirred. This was the second time he'd raised a daddy conversation that involved Xavier. "Why d'you say that?"

He spread his hands. "Well, she's always acting crazy and that's what daddies are for, to help with a problem child."

Justine chuckled, cupping his cheek in a brief caress. There wasn't a day when he didn't amaze her. Where had he heard that term?

"And," he continued, "Mr. McKellop can make her behave.

"Really?"

Justine sat forward, elbow on the table, chin in hand.

Emile leaned toward her, in danger of knocking over the tumbler. Justine moved it out of his way. "Yeah, he just gives her a look and she's quiet. Or he tells her this."

Emile deepened his voice and put on a frown. "If you can't behave, the door's over there."

He grinned, exposing shaky milk teeth. "Last time she had a fit, he told her to sit down and shut up."

"Really. Are you sure?" Justine wasn't certain how she felt about Xavier being rude to her child, but acknowledged that Yolanda could be overbearing.

Emile looked at the ceiling as though doubting her sanity. "Of course, and that's what she did. She got quiet and started banging on the guitar. Then he said 'if you can't respect my instruments, I won't let you touch them.'"

Justine didn't know what to say. Emile continued to fill the silence. "See, I told you he'd be a good daddy. Him would sort her out fast."

She frowned at him. "Stop speaking like that."

"Mr. McKay says it's okay."

"Liar," Justine mock glared at him. "He didn't."

"Yeah, he says it's fine if I'm with my friends."

"There you go, but you're not with your friends now, so faggedit."

They laughed, and Emile finished his drink. She could picture him and Xavier talking. No doubt, Xavier would appreciate his intelligence. He'd always believed in letting children speak their minds, which brought her to the reason he'd have to be firm with Yolanda. Who was she kidding? Her daughter was spoiled and rude, thanks to Justine's apathy. With Milton's death, she'd thought it best to let Yolanda have some slack. The trouble was, Justine had never reclaimed parental authority, resulting in the disrespect and indiscipline she was now reaping.

Emile pushed the glass back and forth, then scratched his ear. He always did that when he was thinking.

"What's on your mind, hon?"

"You sure you won't get mad?"

"Come on, don't I always encourage you to share everything with me?"

He nodded, lacing his fingers together.

"Kevin and his dad do things with each other all the time." His speech took on an apologetic tone. "But there's stuff mommies can't do, like football and basketball."

She nodded. "I understand, but what's the point?"

"Last week, when Yolanda went to the bathroom, I asked Mr. McKay if he'd be my dad."

Justine leaned closer to Emile, not wanting to miss his next words. Why hadn't Xavier discussed this conversation with her?

"And what did he say?"

"He said I had to ask you first."

She was going to kill that man. Why was he dragging her around in circles when he knew perfectly well what her son's reaction would be to any daddy conversation?

"I know you, Emile. What did he say after you pestered him?"

Emile beamed at her. "That he was already my daddy."

– 12 –

Saturday, March 12

Xavier

Proverb: Nanny goat never scratch him back 'til him see wall.
Meaning: Use each opportunity when it presents itself.

Emile shouted, and then laughed loudly. Justine's head snapped toward him, and she reacted that way each time Emile made any kind of noise. If Xavier didn't know better, he'd think Justine expected disaster to fall on the boy at any moment.

She spun the bottle of fruit juice, staring across the bed of grass. Hair blew across her face and the wind lifted her skirt. She held down her dress with one hand, while she kept an eye on Emile, who played with another boy a few feet away. They had left the zoo moments ago and now sat in the botanical gardens.

Xavier's gaze slid toward her again. While she watched Emile, he studied her from her floating hair—which he wanted to touch—to her slippered feet. Her drooping mouth reminded him of her periods of moroseness in the days of old when she worried about Milton. His chest constricted and he couldn't breathe.

Milton was dead, but somehow he'd forgotten that. It wasn't something he wanted to think about. If he dwelled on it, he would start wanting things he'd put behind him long ago—like a steady relationship. He'd been there and done that. His music was enough. He'd made it enough.

The sensation of her legs clamping his sides crept up on him, and he banished the matching image. The stirring between his thighs warned him that he was drifting into dangerous territory. He needed a diversion. With a last glance at the smooth skin on her arms, he broached the subject that had taken up most of his time in the last few weeks.

"Can I take it that you're going to use this opportunity to tell Emile?"

She turned to face him, her displeasure plain. "Based on what he said, it seems you've already told him you're his father."

"I meant I was already doing stuff with him that a father does with his child, like answering his questions, explaining stuff to him."

"Like what?"

He refused to let her rude tone bother him. "Like how come he doesn't have a daddy."

Her eyes and mouth opened wider, which amused Xavier.

"Don't worry. I didn't tell him anything you wouldn't."

She fiddled with the flap of the handbag on her lap, while she cast worried glances in Emile's direction.

Forgetting he wanted to keep his distance, Xavier slid a hand over hers. "What are you so afraid of?"

She shook her head and continued playing with the flap on the zip.

Xavier guessed what was bothering Justine. Her changing expressions as she kept Emile under her gaze confirmed his hunch. He wasn't sure she would admit what she was feeling, but he put his thoughts into words. "I think you're still worried that your son might not adore you as much as he does now when he discovers what you've kept from him."

Her lips parted, but he prevented her from saying anything by placing a finger over her lips. "You should give Emile more credit. He'll understand if you explain this to him in his terms."

For a few moments she stared into his eyes, as though in a trance. Then she cleared her throat and focused on their joined hands. "I'm not sure how to do that."

With his other hand, he lifted her chin. "We can do this together. That's the point of my being here and there's no better time than the present."

He wasn't sure, but thought a film of moisture washed her eyes. She blinked and lifted her shoulders. "Okay, fine. Just give me a minute."

The urge to kiss her forehead, as he used to do with Kelleigh, came over him, and he felt himself leaning toward her. Instead, he got to his feet. "I'll get Emile."

She nodded, but didn't look at him. The set of her brows gave away her distress, but he had come too far to turn back now. The decision to tell Emile was the right one.

Out in the open, the sun warmed his skin, reminding him how good it was to be in the present. The combined excitement and contentment reminded him how he'd felt each time he was due to see Justine. She never spoke of her feelings for him, but he saw the love and guilt whenever she opened herself to him. She'd pretend their connection didn't mean the world to her, but the way she touched him and the sadness that blanketed her at times, told him how much she loved him and agonized over their situation.

The loss he'd endured wanted to intrude on this moment, but he shook it off; nothing would spoil his growing connection with his son. This was the sort of place he could spend time with Emile. He'd teach him how to fly a kite and, since he liked to run, Emile could do so until he exhausted himself, without Justine fussing over him.

He called Emile, and he came running, but not before he waved good-bye to the boy he'd befriended. Emile slowed before he ran into Xavier, who bent over, hands on knees to speak to him. "Your mommy sent me to get you."

Emile kicked his head back, and asked, "Why?"

"We wanted to talk to you."

"About what?"

Xavier squeezed his hand. "Your mom and I will tell you in a minute."

Under the Blue Mahoe tree, Emile sat next to his mother. Justine's arm went around his shoulder and she cradled him to her side. Stroking his cheek, she spoke. "Um, Emile, you know how I tell you sometimes that things happen that we can't talk about or explain until the time is right?"

He nodded and moved over when Xavier sat on his other side.

"Well, this is one of those times." She took a deep breath and wiped her cheek. "Uh...I..."

She flashed Xavier a look so filled with panic, he thought she'd give up on telling Emile the truth. She exhaled through her mouth and kissed Emile's forehead. He squirmed and turned his head away. Xavier maintained a serious expression, knowing Emile was embarrassed over Justine's gesture.

She tried again. "What I'm trying to tell you is that you'll be spending more time with Mr. McKellop."

Xavier tried to make eye contact, but she avoided raising her head. His fingers curled into his palm and a pulse beat hard in his forehead. Why couldn't she just tell Emile the facts? He wanted to wring her neck, until Emile's words cut the fog of his anger.

"Mommy, why you crying?"

Justine shook her head. "I'm not."

Emile squinted at her. "How come you always tell us not to lie and now you're telling an untruth?"

She walked away from them, leaving her bag. Emile watched her go before swiveling to face Xavier. Frowning, he asked, "You know what's wrong with Mommy?"

She's a coward and hell-bent on driving me out of my goddamn mind.

Since he couldn't say that, Xavier improvised. "I think she might be feeling sad."

"Why?"

"She's trying to work out some stuff in her head."

From the corners of his eyes, Xavier spied Justine by a stand of red ginger lilies, hugging herself. He understood what she was feeling, but couldn't help his impatience. How much longer before she got up the nerve to do what she should have done already?

Xavier patted Emile's back and got up. "Wait here."

He crossed the grass, wondering how to avoid unleashing a string of curse words at Justine. She turned, trembling when he stood beside her. He ignored the wind flowing past his ears and the shrill cry of a nearby bird.

She placed a hand over her mouth. "I'm sorry. I just can't find a way to tell him."

Speaking through his aching jaw, he said, "The longer you drag this out, the more it's gonna wear on your nerves."

She pushed strands of hair off her forehead, her hand shaking. She let it drop to her side. "I know, but—"

Xavier rubbed the nerve dancing under his eye, before thrusting both hands into his pockets, disappointment heavy in his stomach. "You're obviously falling apart, but I won't wait forever. I'm frigging tired of this."

She snuffled, turning her head aside. "Then why don't you go away and leave us alone?"

For a few seconds, he couldn't see anything past the white-hot fury gripping him. Did she really say that? Hadn't they got past that point already? He wanted to slap the spinelessness out of her. Instead, he exhaled slowly. "Isn't it better to tell him, than for him to find out on his own? You're going to delay this until—"

She turned wet eyes on him. "How d'you plan to explain Emile to your wife and daughter?"

"Didn't I tell you not to worry about that?"

"It concerns me because it will affect Emile."

He expected another flimsy excuse, but couldn't help his response. "How?"

"Next thing I know, you'll want to take him to your house and I don't know if I approve."

"Justine, you're just avoiding the issue. I don't want to pressure you, when you clearly don't want to face this situation, but I'm warning you—"

"Don't threaten me," she snapped. "I'll deal with it in my own time."

He spoke into her face, gripping both her arms. "No way. You either tell him, or I will."

Her lips trembled, she blinked and more tears squeezed their way out of her eyes. "Let me go," she said.

He released her arms, but a cauldron of heat bubbled in his chest. Rage poured spite into his words. "You've spent enough time pretending you're a decent woman, when you're nothing but a user. If—"

His head jarred and snapped sideways. Blood flowed into his mouth where his teeth cut the inside of his lip. Justine had some nerve to think she could hit him and get away with it. His hands fisted and he drew in a breath, searching for the right combination of words to flatten her.

Emile intruded on the periphery of his vision.

Xavier swallowed blood while trying to stem the heat radiating through his body. "Don't ever do that again."

He looked down to where Emile stood, studying them. Hands on his sides, Emile asked, "Why you do that? And why Mommy hit you?"

Afraid he would blurt something he shouldn't, Xavier stooped to Emile's height. He ran his tongue over his teeth to clear away more blood. "Why don't you ask her?" he said.

Without looking at Justine, Xavier walked away.

– 13 –

Friday, March 18

Justine

Proverb: Every man honest 'til di day him get ketch (catch).
Meaning: You never know what someone is capable of until they are exposed.

Justine squinted in the fading light and tapped the horn. Didn't Yolanda say they were over here for some sort of study group? What kind of studying went on without books? And where were the adults who owned the house?

Justine pressed the horn longer this time. The gaggle of young people on the lawn stirred and turned in her direction. She waved at Yolanda, who pretended not to see her. After Justine leaned on the horn for several more beats, Yolanda grabbed her knapsack and marched toward the gate.

She flung herself into the seat and slammed the door, rocking the car. Justine pulled away from the curb, ignoring Yolanda's attempt to upset her. She had other important concerns.

"Who's that boy trying to suck the skin off your face? Isn't Tariq supposed to be your boyfriend?"

"He wasn't 'sucking any skin off my face' as you put it, and no, Tariq is not my boyfriend. How many times do I have to explain that he's just a friend?"

"Well, you and your friends seem extra close. I've told you already how boys treat girls who are easy. And where's your uniform?"

"In my bag and for your information, I don't have a relationship," Yolanda said, her tone sullen. "I suppose that makes you happy."

"You can't handle that anyway."

"What you mean? Some of my friends already have boyfriends and—"

Discomfited, Justine studied Yolanda. She hadn't been paying enough attention to her daughter's blossoming body and hormones. Her jeans clung to her legs and her shirt was skintight. Too revealing for a girl not yet fifteen. Justine made a note to get her some roomier clothes. Meanwhile, she'd find out exactly what was up. "Are you sexually active?"

Yolanda shot her a glare. "What?"

"Don't pretend you didn't hear me. I asked if you're having sex."

"That's none of your business."

Justine swung out of her lane and pulled up at the curb. She angled her body to meet Yolanda head on.

"It's my business if you're living in my house. Now, don't make me have to slap it out of you. Are you having intercourse with any of those boys?"

Folding her arms, Yolanda flung her back against the seat. "No, I'm not. I still don't see how—"

Sighing, Justine gripped the wheel, and leaned forward. "Look, I realize you're angry with me. Seems you've been that way for years now. All I want to know is that you're being careful. I wouldn't want you to make a mistake that's preventable."

Yolanda stared through the windscreen, giving no hint that she heard anything Justine said. Then she flexed her fingers and curled her lips in a nasty imitation of a smile. "Why should I take advice from you when you can't run your life? Wasn't my little brother a preventable mistake?"

The air rushed from Justine's lungs, leaving her speechless. When she got her vocal cords to work, Justine kept her tone steady despite feeling she'd been sucker punched. "I don't know what's happened to you, and maybe it's my fault, but I can't figure out when you turned into the spiteful creature you've become. You need to check yourself, Yolanda."

"It's all your fault," Yolanda screeched. "You don't care about me. You never did. The only thing you care about is Emile."

The love songs on the radio and the honking vehicles penetrated the cloud surrounding Justine. When she could think, she squeezed her voice past the pain in her throat. "How can you say that? What have you ever wanted that I haven't given you?"

"You," Yolanda howled. "You don't treat me the way you treat Emile. Everything you do is for him. Football practice, swimming lessons..." She hiccupped, bowed and let her hair fall around her face.

Justine leaned her head against the seat and closed her eyes, blindsided by the continuing accusations. "You never want to do anything," she said. "You stopped going to dance classes, you lost interest in every instrument you started learning to play, you—"

"Because you weren't interested! Because you didn't care! Nothing was fun anymore." She stopped screaming to swipe the back of one hand across her eyes and nose. "It didn't feel the way it used to. Since Emile—"

Sitting up, Justine said, "Don't blame this on Emile. Your father died, and—"

"Don't try to blame Daddy's death for the fact that you hate me."

Justine's insides were squeezed in a vise. "How can you say something like that? You know it's not true!"

Tears rained down Yolanda's cheeks, and Justine barely understood her daughter's words through her sobs. "If it isn't true, why did you hit me because of that man?"

Before Justine could react, Yolanda unstrapped herself, leaped out of the car and ran into the street. Cars veered and horns blared as she cut a path across the road. Terror tied Justine to the driver's seat as she watched Yolanda run, ignoring the vehicles.

A car braked, shredding Justine's nerves further. Hand to her mouth, she sighed when Yolanda reached the sidewalk. After throwing a glance over her shoulder, she walked into the plaza, head down, hands in her pockets.

Justine forced herself to take deep breaths and contain her anxiety. Yolanda would be fine. In her present mood, there was no reasoning with her. An hour would give her time to cool off and come home. Thank goodness she'd given in and gotten Yolanda a cell phone. If she landed in trouble, she'd call.

***

Justine sank in the sofa, rubbing her pounding temples. She'd relieved Miss Pauline, paid her and sent her home. She'd had the previous weekend off, but Justine wanted her out of the house. Although she considered Miss Pauline part of the family, Justine believed in keeping some things private. She was probably fooling herself, because at the rate Yolanda kept yelling and going on bad, Miss Pauline had to know all their business.

For the last half hour, Emile occupied the sofa in the living room, tranquilized by cartoons. Too exhausted to do anything, Justine sat in the office she'd converted into her own space when Milton died. The Lord knew she not only needed somewhere to work, but a place to clear her mind, away from the children's sharp eyes. Milton had spent a lot of time closeted in here with his problems and now she found herself traveling the same route.

That thought sent Justine tumbling back seven years.

She'd come close to financial ruin when Milton spent all their savings and after months of trying to find out why he'd withdrawn from her, Justine discovered that he was being blackmailed over a homosexual relationship. It had been twice as distressing to learn that his lover was Kyra's leech of a boyfriend. As she did each time the memories surfaced, Justine channeled her mind in another direction.

The mortgage on the house was paid off through her sweat, tears and personal savings. She also had money put aside for the children's education. Her writing, along with what she made from functions, kept those funds topped up and covered the family's expenses. Those things were what mattered.

In the dark, she stared at the slats on the wall drawn by the light from the street. The muted sounds from the television reassured her that her son was fine for the moment, but what to do about her daughter? She'd hate for Yolanda to turn out like so many other girls in Jamaica, pregnant with no prospects or hope for the future.

A car pulled up to the sidewalk. Justine stumbled out of her seat and pushed the drape aside. Yolanda got out of a silver Honda and a shrill female voice yelled good-bye. Yolanda waved at the cluster of bodies inside the vehicle before opening the gate.

The set of her shoulders told Justine she was still angry. Yolanda came toward the house, taking jerky steps. Justine thought about picking up the argument where they had left off, but what was the point? Better to wait until Yolanda was ready to listen, because nothing Justine said now was likely to reach her.

Justine sat, legs curled against her body. Maybe it was time to admit she didn't know what she was doing and ask for help.

* * *

Saturday, March 19, 4:30 PM

Justine's stomach vibrated in time with the ringing phone. She jerked awake and put it to her ear, holding back a yawn. She'd come home earlier, worn out by the setup she'd done at the restaurant where the anniversary party would be held later in the evening. Thankfully, the couple knew her situation and was okay with Justine being on call if they needed anything.

"Justine?"

At the sound of Xavier's voice, a shiver chased over Justine's flesh, bringing her voice down to a whisper. "Yes?"

"Emile's my last student today, so I'm gonna take him home and save you the trip over here."

A pulse fluttered in Justine's throat and she had a hard time forcing out her next words. "Uh...I...okay."

Reluctantly, she gave him directions.

"See you soon," he said.

She thought he was smiling, but wouldn't swear on it. Maybe her mind was playing tricks on her. He should still be pissed about her thumping him in the mouth. She'd had lots of time to think about that and still wondered what had made her do it. By nature, she wasn't violent, but so much had happened lately she could be forgiven for acting out of character. Most likely, frustration was the reason she hit him, plus he had no right to grab her like that.

She groaned and pushed a hand through her hair. She'd just made another mistake. She didn't want Xavier knowing where she lived or spending any time in or around her home. Once he invaded her space that would be it; she'd start seeing him there and she didn't need that.

The muted slamming of metal against the stovetop reminded her that Yolanda hadn't gone to her lesson. She'd stayed in her room making discordant notes that belonged in a heavy-metal band. When she wasn't grating on Justine's nerves, she played mournful tunes that made Justine want to weep.

Xavier hadn't remarked on Yolanda's absence when Justine dropped off Emile, but the lifting of his eyebrows in a questioning arch made her uncomfortable. Thankfully, Emile had chatted enough to distract Xavier. She'd rushed away from the shop and made another stop at a floral outlet to pick up the arrangement for the anniversary party. After that, she came home to Yolanda's disapproving silence.

Justine tried not to allow Yolanda's behavior to affect her too much, but it galled her that they couldn't get along. Guilt tried to drag her down, but Justine moved to the desk and pushed the switch on her computer. Maybe she'd write something. She needed to anyway, if she hoped to stay on top of the series of lifestyle articles she kept lined up for submission to the newspaper.

It took her a while to get going, but once her thoughts started flowing, her words took on a life of their own, pouring out of her like a geyser. Forty-five minutes later, she stood by the window, rubbing the back of her neck. She'd edit the article later.

Xavier's silver Tundra pulled up to the curb, sending an involuntary smile across her face. Emile had unlocked the seatbelt and opened the door, while Xavier got out on the other side. He locked the vehicle, while studying the house.

His black tee-shirt and jeans reminded her why she'd found him irresistible. The man was downright sexy. His wide chest and soft locks...that brought her back to reality. The locks that had so fascinated her were gone, like their ill-fated affair. She turned away from the window, her limbs dragging as if they didn't belong to her.

When she opened the front door, Emile clung to the grille, two feet off the ground, trying to open the top latch.

"Get down. How many times do I have to tell you not to do that?"

He jumped to the cement. "But Mommy, I know how to open it."

Justine opened the grille and stood blocking the entrance. Panic fluttered in her throat. *Please, let him go away.*

Emile gripped Xavier's hand and attempted to get past her. The half smile Xavier wore told her he was perfectly aware she didn't want him in her house. Emile's demand intruded on her dread. "'Scuse me. Mommy, can you move?"

Justine could either stand there and inhale Xavier's scent, or step aside. She chose the latter. He smelled of aftershave and something musky. One side of his mouth curved, then resettled into a line. Emile dragged him past her and entered the living room. She closed the grille and rushed inside to where Xavier stood waiting.

She motioned for him to sit on the sofa. "D'you want anything to drink?"

His gaze slid up her jeans, over her tee-shirt and stopped where her hair hung in silky waves on her shoulders. Where had Emile run off to? She didn't want to be alone with Xavier, who had the power to heat her blood simply by being in the same room.

He smiled, which set her blood racing. "Yeah."

Perplexed, Justine stuck her thumbs in the back pockets of her jeans. Did he have amnesia? Didn't he remember what she'd done to him? He couldn't pretend that didn't happen. "Fruit juice or soda?"

Why ask him that? He never drank carbonated drinks. But that was then.

"Fruit juice," he said.

She left, forcing herself not to dash out of the living room like a frightened mouse. She flung ice into a glass, splashed in some June Plum juice and grabbed a coaster and napkin on the way back to him.

Xavier sprawled on her sofa, reminding her of another time and place. Did he know the effect he had on her when he sat like that, reminding her of his power and stamina? Their eyes met and she answered her question. Of course, he did. Seemed he'd changed tactic, which hinted that he wanted something, but what?

The ice tinkled, reminding her to hand him the glass of pale-green liquid.

He put it on the side table and moved closer to Emile, who insisted he pay attention to the Xbox controller clutched in his fists.

Justine prayed Xavier would get bored and leave soon. The last thing she needed was more interaction with him. Already, she wanted to veer off course and curl against his side—though he hated her. That mental slap in the face grounded her in the present and she settled in the adjacent sofa.

A racket from the kitchen forced Justine out of her dream world. When had Yolanda gone past them? Of course, she'd come to investigate and do her best to embarrass her mother. Justine turned her head when Yolanda's slippers slapped the tiles, moving toward the living room.

"You left the fridge open."

Justine took her time before answering. "You do realize we have a guest?'

Yolanda hissed air through her teeth.

For a few seconds, Justine stared at her, lips parted, eyes wide. Then shame settled over her. Instead of jumping up and slapping Yolanda as she wanted to do, Justine measured her words through the heat crawling up her neck. "Since you have no manners or breeding, let me remind you that your teacher is sitting over there."

Yolanda rolled her eyes and dropped both hands on her hips. "I just came in to tell you—"

"You didn't come in here to tell me anything. You came to embarrass me. Now that you're satisfied, go to your room until you can behave like a civilized person."

Yolanda opened her mouth, drew in a breath, but Justine got her words in first. "Make sure you can handle the consequences of whatever you say."

Yolanda spun away and flounced out of the room. As usual, the bedroom door slammed in her wake. The cement would start falling off the walls in clumps if she kept up her crusade to destroy the doors.

Justine gripped the arms of the sofa and moved to get up.

Xavier shook his head. "Don't. Talking to her now will only make things worse. She'll think you're picking on her."

Justine sank back and closed her eyes. "How d'you know?"

"She's almost the same age as Kelleigh. My—we're going through the same thing."

That reminded Justine of his marital status, which left lead in her belly. She wanted him out of her house now.

The glass of juice stood untouched. As though Justine's looking at it prompted his memory, Xavier lifted it to his lips and eyed her over the rim.

"She just need a good lick," Emile mumbled before getting up and leaving the room. Justine watched him go, wanting to stroke his skin as she used to do when he was younger, but he'd have a fit if she tried anything like that in front of Xavier.

Having replaced the glass, Xavier rested both elbows on his knees and folded his fingers together. "I suppose only patience is gonna work with her. Guess she's in the throes of whatever girls go through these days." He chuckled. "Were you that complicated?"

Justine shook her head. "My mother would have smacked the complication right out of me."

He laughed; a rich sound that sent a jolt of delight through her chest to spread into her stomach and warm her whole body. A door opened and she suspected Emile had gone into his sister's room to talk. He was like that. Though he hated when Yolanda acted out, he always tried to coax her out of her bad mood. Half the time, he was successful.

"These days, girls are way different than I remem—"

A crash interrupted Xavier's words. Justine leaned outward and checked the passage. The door opened again. Yolanda screamed, and Emile backed into the passage. He met Justine's eyes, his chin wobbling, eyes flooded with tears. He blinked and they rolled down his cheeks.

Emile never cried. He was her stoic little man, holding things in, thinking he needed to be strong for both Yolanda and her. Wiping his eyes, he walked toward Justine minus his usual energy.

What had Yolanda done to him? Justine got up, ready to forget Xavier's advice and give her rotten daughter a taste of hell.

"Is true, Mommy?" Emile asked, dragging the back of one hand across his eyes.

A sour taste flooded Justine's mouth. Nausea squeezed her stomach. Something bad was coming. She whispered, "What?"

Emile gulped and wiped his eyes again. "Yolanda said you did a bad sin." He wiggled his finger to include Justine and Xavier. "That the two of you did it."

He sobbed, wringing his hands. "Mommy, is true I'm a terrible mistake?"

– 94 –

Friday, March 19, 5:30 PM

Xavier

Proverb: Chew family bickle (victuals), but nuh bite family story.

Meaning: If you have to get involved in another family's business, don't take sides.

The weight of his anger dropped and swelled in Xavier's stomach. For one moment, he wanted to kill Yolanda, but good sense asserted itself. She was hurting and the most natural thing in the world was to lash out. Pity she felt the need to attack the people closest to her. Nobody should be made to feel unwanted and that's how Emile must feel. *Poor little guy.*

He sat in Justine's lap, shoulders heaving. He was too big to fit comfortably, but Xavier understood Emile's need for comfort. Justine cuddled him as if her closeness could erase his pain.

If she'd done what he asked and told Emile what he needed to know, this drama and hurt could have been avoided, but she chose to be a coward. Justine's glare made him realize she was reading his thoughts.

"It would have prevented all of this," he said.

"Yolanda knows better," Justine said in a tearful voice.

Xavier shook his head. "She's young, impulsive. Her mouth ran away with her. Believe me, I understand."

"Well, I don't."

"What's done can't be undone. Now you have some work to do."

"Hon, go blow your nose," she said to Emile.

He scrubbed at his tears before asking Xavier. "You going away?"

Xavier shook his head and followed Emile's progress down the corridor. When he turned his attention to Justine, she sat as still as a statue, probably hoping the problem would go away. Well, he had news for her; things would only get more complicated from this point onward.

"He'll have questions," Xavier warned.

She stared at his shirt as if he hadn't spoken. Xavier sighed; he was in this by himself. "Never mind," he said. "Just follow my lead."

She still didn't say anything, which made him wonder about her mental state.

Emile returned and sank in one corner of the sofa. He twisted his fingers together, looking from Xavier to Justine. In a low voice, he said, "Mommy, why Landy behave like that and why she tell me that?"

Justine shrugged. "She's not happy, and sometimes she can't control the things she says."

Emile opened both hands wide. "But why she not happy?"

Before she answered, Justine leaned forward and stroked his brow. Flashing Xavier a look, she said. "She thinks I love you more than her."

"Is true?"

"I love both of you the same."

"So why she so mean?"

Justine clasped her hands and went silent for so long that Xavier thought she was praying. She sighed and rubbed her eyes like someone coming out of sleep. "Part of the reason is because her dad died when she was younger, and she hasn't gotten over it."

Emile straightened and peered at his mother. "I thought you said my daddy went to heaven. If he did, how come Yolanda said Mr. McKay's my daddy?"

Justine eyes went liquid and her neck moved as she swallowed. Then she did what Xavier expected.

Nothing.

A beautiful piece of artwork. That's what she represented, sitting there as if her blood had turned to salt in her veins. Only her darting eyes let him know she was trying to find words to explain her lapse. Sighing again, Xavier patted the cushion beside him. "Emile, come sit over here."

Slowly, Emile got up and did what Xavier asked, pushing away the Xbox controller. Across the room, the television screen was frozen on the image of a racing car. Xavier turned sideways in the seat. Now that it was time to tell Emile the truth, he was nervous.

Come on, you're dealing with a child, he told himself, licking his lips to give himself space to handpick his words. "Um, sometimes it's hard for adults to explain things to children so they understand." His gaze flicked to Justine. "And sometimes, adults think it's best not to give kids more information than they need. Or they wait until their children are old enough to know certain facts. Get me?"

Emile nodded, but continued to frown.

"I think that's why your mommy didn't tell you about me being your daddy."

Squinting, Emile tried to process the information.

"She wasn't sure how to tell you, so she was waiting for the right time. See, we lost touch with each other and didn't talk for many years. So I didn't know about you either."

Emile scratched his forehead, eyebrows still crumpled. "Really?"

"Yeah, I only found out just before you did."

"So this means you're really my daddy?"

Xavier nodded, unable to banish the smile from his lips. "Yeah, and I'm happy because I never had a son before."

Emile grinned. "And I never had a dad before."

"I guess we both have to get used to that then."

"Yeah. Does that mean you're going to come and live with us?"

Xavier caught Justine's panicked cry and motioned for her to be quiet. "Things don't work like that, son."

"Then can I come home with you?"

This time Justine found her voice. "Emile, you can't ask questions like that."

"Why not? If he's my daddy I can ask him anything."

That's my boy, Xavier thought. "Tell you what. Maybe later you can get to spend some time at my house."

Justine's tight mouth and cutting look said she wasn't pleased. Who cared what she thought anyway? He might have a challenge explaining Emile's sudden appearance to his family, but it was going to be well worth it. He snapped back to reality when Emile prodded his leg. "Can I do that soon?"

Xavier couldn't contain his laughter. "There's no hurry, Emile. I'll be your daddy forever."

"Are you sure? If I'm a mistake you might go away again and forget me."

"Emile, I don't care what Yolanda said. You're not a mistake." Xavier slipped a hand around him, thinking Yolanda needed a belt applied to her backside. "Trust me, there's no way I could forget you."

"It can happen, 'cause Mommy forgot about you." Emile turned his head toward Justine, giving her a look loaded with reproach. "Or she told an untruth."

– 15 –

Saturday, March 19, 7:45 PM

Justine

Proverb: Hard ears pickney bun (burn) inna sunhot.
Meaning: Children (or adults) will suffer if they refuse to take good advice.

Hours slipped by before Emile allowed Xavier to leave. Emile had many questions that needed answers, but Justine asked for a ceasefire. She settled him with a snack in front of the television, knowing he shouldn't have anything more to eat for the night but she figured after the shock he'd had, he was entitled. Though she wasn't sure what was happening in his mind, she knew he was thinking because he scratched his ear every so often.

Justine approached Yolanda's room, determined to lay down some new rules. She couldn't continue to let a fourteen year old dictate terms to her.

She rapped at the door, and entered when Yolanda did not respond. She lay on the bed, headphones over her ears, reading a novel. Her feet waved in the air while her fingers plucked at the pages of the book, giving away her restlessness.

"I need to talk to you," Justine said.

Yolanda stared at the novel, pretending she was alone. Justine wanted to yank it away, but restrained herself by folding her arms. She cleared her throat and repeated her words, this time with more force. Yolanda sat up, dragged the headphones off and folded her legs Indian style, looking everywhere else but at her mother.

Justine pulled out the chair at the computer table and sat, facing Yolanda. "I know you have plenty of resentment bottled up, but I didn't think you were vicious or spiteful. As of today, I have to rethink that."

In the silence, she studied her daughter. But for youth and the resentment distorting Yolanda's features, Justine could have been in front of a mirror. She couldn't pinpoint when Yolanda's feelings for her had changed or when she'd stopped being respectful. What concerned Justine most was her inability to do anything about the anger Yolanda wore like a favorite garment.

"I don't know why you'd choose to hurt your brother," Justine continued. "I expected better from you, but clearly, I was hoping for too much. I'm not going to punish you. I'm going to let you do that yourself."

Justine left the room satisfied. Though they were at war so often, Justine knew her daughter. Yolanda would die before she admitted that she felt awful inside, and her conscience wouldn't stop bugging her until she made up with Emile. Not that Emile would hold a grudge. Too bad, Yolanda didn't feel the same way.

The extent of her jealousy of Emile had floored Justine, who'd always assumed that theirs was the usual situation where the older sibling thought the younger a nuisance.

Why hadn't Yolanda ever expressed any bitterness before she found out about the connection between Emile and Xavier? As she had with Emile, Justine encouraged open communication with Yolanda because so many pitfalls lurked for unsuspecting teenagers. So far they'd been lucky, but Justine couldn't avoid worrying. How could she offer guidance if her child wouldn't listen, and Justine didn't have the first clue about how to win her back.

Outside the door, Justine stopped. A thump came from the other side of the wood. Yolanda had thrown something at the door. Justine went back to the living room, where Emile seemed absorbed by a dancing band of cartoon characters. She slid onto the seat beside him and touched his hand. "You all right, Pops?"

He nodded, but waited a few seconds before looking at her. "Are you really sure Mr. McKay's my daddy?"

"Hon, you asked us that a hundred times already."

"Since you lost him, maybe he's the wrong daddy."

Stroking his back, she reminded herself to be patient. He'd had this daddy fixation for a long time. At one point, he'd wanted to know why the priest couldn't be his daddy, since the people in their church community called him Father.

"To lose touch just means that we didn't see or talk to each other for a while."

"But how d'you *know* he's my daddy? Does it have to do with the sin Landy talked about?"

Again, Justine wished Yolanda had thought before spewing her anger in Emile's direction. "Yes and no. Yolanda shouldn't have said that to you. It wasn't like that."

"Kemar at school just had a baby sister. He said she came out of his mommy's tummy. Did Mr. McKay put me in yours?"

"Uh, yes. Something like that."

"How come he did it, instead of my daddy that went to heaven?"

To give herself time to think, Justine let her tongue swipe her lips. Emile slanted his head to one side while his crumpled brows questioned her.

"Well, at one time we loved each other. Er…making babies is something people do when they're in love." Even to her ears that explanation was past lame.

He let it pass, but the thundercloud covering his brow did not bode well for her peace of mind.

"I still don't understand how you could forget he's my daddy or how you lose somebody."

"It's kinda hard to explain, but things happen. People change addresses and telephone numbers sometimes."

"So you gonna try not to lose him this time?" he said with an edge to his voice she hadn't heard before.

She cupped his cheek. "Of course I won't lose him. Now that he knows about you, he's going to stay around. He already told you that."

Emile stared at the television for a while before he spoke again. "I really wish we get to live in the same house."

He grinned, a gesture that made her sad and delighted at the same time. She'd do anything to keep him happy, but some things were beyond her power.

"That would be really cool." He grabbed one of her hands, squeezing it. "Just make Landy behave so he won't go away."

She hugged him. "I doubt even she could do that."

"But she's weirder every day."

Justine hid a smile, but wondered if she shouldn't seek counseling for Yolanda. It wasn't the first time the thought had occurred to her and it could only do Yolanda good.

Movement just inside the range of her vision stopped Justine's next words. Yolanda sauntered past them toward the kitchen. Something about her struck Justine as odd, but she couldn't say what. She concentrated hard, seeing Yolanda in her mind's eye.

Her daughter was wearing street clothes, and a familiar scent lingered in the air. Chloe. Justine had bought a bottle of it for Yolanda the last time they went shopping.

Justine rushed into the kitchen, but the room was empty. She tested the door leading to the backyard. The lock was open, but the key was missing from the key holder. Hurrying back through the living room, she stifled curse words. What the hell was Yolanda thinking?

By the time Justine opened the front door, a car tore away from the sidewalk. Justine raced to the phone and took it into the kitchen so Emile wouldn't hear her conversation. She rang Yolanda's cell number, which was a waste of time. Wanting to smash something, Justine fought to clear her head. Heat spiraled through her veins as she searched for some way to show Yolanda who was in charge.

She bolted the door, wanting to vent, but knowing she couldn't. Since Yolanda had decided she was an independent woman, let her figure out how to get back inside the house.

Justine rang the cellular number again. No answer. A headache blasted its way across her forehead as she dialed the police.

The officer who answered sounded bored and barely concerned by Justine's explanation for her call. "D'you have the number for any of her friends' parents, ma'am?"

"Yes."

"You might want to call them. Did you see the license plate number on the car she left in?"

"No."

"Check in with the parents and call us if you don't find her, okay?"

Her throat swelled and instead of giving vent to her feelings, Justine whispered, "Okay."

She curled in one corner of the sofa, tempted to feel sorry for herself, but admitting she was at fault for Yolanda's behavior. She wasn't too far gone to rescue, but it would be a long road back from the rebelliousness now ingrained in her. Her grades were slipping and Justine wondered what it would take for Yolanda to start excelling again.

Maybe if she'd had a father figure when she hit her teens she would have been easier to handle. Emile was fatherless—up to now—yet he hadn't given her this many challenges. She hugged her knees, hot tears smarting behind her eyes. She didn't have time for that now. She needed to find Yolanda before she did something stupid out of spite. Justine slipped into the kitchen to contact the parents whose telephone numbers she had in her address book.

Half-a-dozen calls later, Justine gave in to worry. None of Yolanda's friends or their parents had seen her and if they knew where she went, they weren't saying.

Losing her patience, Justine snapped at Emile, who asked once too often where Yolanda had gone. Eventually, she gave him a story to cover Yolanda's absence and sent him to bed. She walked the living room floor, arms folded around her body. What would she do if anything happened to Yolanda? These days, it didn't take much for people to lose their temper and hurt others.

The regular night noises—chirping crickets and accompanying croaks from young toads—were at odds with the weight on Justine's spirit.

She settled on the sofa and tried Yolanda's phone again. This time, someone answered, or at least punched a button because Justine heard music and talking in the background. Yolanda giggled, while a male roared with laughter. Justine yelled into the phone, but no one answered. Glasses clinked together and music flooded through the phone speaker. Where was Yolanda? Justine pressed the phone to her ear as if that would keep her connected to Yolanda. The phone went silent, shooting desperation through Justine's veins and nausea into her stomach.

Justine wanted to get in the car and roar away, but didn't know where to search. She'd neglected to ring the police after the other calls. Anxiety had fogged her brain. She tried again and got the same officer.

"It's Mrs. Charles. I haven't found my daughter. Nobody's seen her. Can you do something, please?"

"You'll have to make a report at the station, ma'am."

"Listen, I have a six year old asleep here. There's no way I can leave him to make a report. Can't you send someone over here?"

He thought about that for what Justine thought were endless minutes. A muffled conversation took place while she waited.

"Someone will come shortly," he said.

"Thank you."

She gave him her address and went to sit on the verandah to stare into the street, seeing nothing. Though saddened by the way it had come about, Justine was glad that a new search-and-rescue system for missing children was in force on the island. Parents could now make a report the moment a child disappeared, which would mobilize the police straight away instead of waiting for a twenty-four hour period to expire.

Half an hour later, a marked white Toyota Corolla rolled up to the sidewalk, and a squat man in uniform got out. An officer with a beer belly joined him on the sidewalk. After she beckoned to them, one officer opened the gate and they came down the cement path a lot slower than she would have liked. She led them inside, where she shoved a head shot of Yolanda into the stout officer's hand.

"You're sure she's not with one of her friends?" He asked from the edge of the sofa.

"Not any of her close friends. I called everybody I could think of; nobody's seen her tonight."

"You told the officer she left without permission?"

"Yes, she sneaked out, and she's not answering her phone."

"Did you have a quarrel?"

"Yes, but that's nothing new. We quarrel all the time. Yolanda knows she's not allowed out at night." Tears stung her eyes again. "She's almost fifteen."

"I know how it is," he said. "I have a sixteen-year old who thinks she knows everything."

"Please do what you can to find her. I don't know what I'd do if—"

The second officer interrupted. "Give us a list of numbers you have for her friends. We'll make some checks. The worst thing you can do is to start imagining all sorts of terrible things. Stay close to the phone. We'll do all we can to find her."

"Thank you."

The words were inadequate, but what else could she say?

She closed the door when the car left, determined not to wear herself out worrying, but that feat wasn't easy to accomplish. Each time she beat a path from the kitchen to the living room, she imagined worse scenarios. Jamaica wasn't what it used to be, and despite what Yolanda thought, she was sheltered. Justine had only allowed Yolanda to use the public transport system recently because she had begged to ride the bus with her friends.

Justine said a prayer and sat on the settee, staring at the television. Every time she had an emergency that concerned Yolanda, she remembered the last night she made love with Xavier. While she was in his bed, Yolanda had suffered a severe asthma attack. Neither

Milton nor their household helper could reach Justine because she had turned off her phone.

Stuffing a cushion behind her head, Justine locked away that memory. She'd thought about all the possible consequences over the years. Yolanda didn't die and Justine had done the honorable thing and given up her affair with Xavier. Now was not the time to torture herself about the past.

Dionne and Kyra kept saying she liked being a martyr. While the thought hurt, she had to admit that she did prefer to suffer alone. A normal person would rally friends for support in a situation like this. She chose to bear her problems by herself.

A problem shared is a problem halved, Dionne liked to say, but what was the point in spreading her worry? She'd wait, and if Yolanda wasn't home by the end of the night, she'd let her friends know. Of course, they would have a thing or two to say to her about not telling them immediately, but for now, she wouldn't burden them.

***

A continuous banging woke Justine. She cocked her head and winced when her neck muscles twinged. The racket was coming from the kitchen. A glance at the clock confirmed that it was after midnight. She flung her feet to the floor and ran to the back door. She'd left the light on for Yolanda, but for safety's sake, drew the window curtain slowly and peered outside. Yolanda stood on the step, her back to the door. She stomped around, using her palms to chafe her arms.

With unsteady hands, Justine unbolted the door and yanked it open. Her fury fled in seconds. Black smears from smudged eyeliner surrounded Yolanda's eyes. Her lips trembled and she continued to shake. When she moved her arms away from her waist, her blouse fell open. The buttons were missing.

Fighting panic, Justine drew her inside, then shut and bolted the door. With both hands on Yolanda's shoulders she asked, "What happened to you?"

Yolanda sniffed, used the inside of her wrist to blot her tears, and lowered her head. Lifting her chin, Justine peered into her eyes. "Tell me. Did somebody hurt you?"

Yolanda nodded, sending Justine further into panic mode. Should she call the police? No. Hear what had happened first. She forced Yolanda into one of the dining table chairs and topped up the kettle. She didn't ask any more questions, but stayed close, squeezing Yolanda's shoulder and rubbing her back.

Yolanda rested her head on her folded hands, sniffling every few minutes. Justine murmured the same words for minutes on end. "It'll be all right. Everything's gonna be okay."

When the water heated, she made a cup of Milo, sweetened with condensed milk and topped with grated nutmeg, just as Yolanda liked it. She drank it slowly, while Justine cautioned herself to be patient.

Yolanda focused on the bottom of the cup, as though she wasn't ready to face her mother.

When she couldn't wait any longer, Justine covered Yolanda's hands with her own. "You have to tell me what happened."

Yolanda mumbled into her chest. "I went to Kim's house and then we went to see another friend, Jerrod. He took us to a party. He introduced me to his friend, Marcus, and we were hanging out. When we were in the car coming back, he started to...he said—"

"Shh. Shh. Slow down, hon."

"We were in the back seat and he said it was time for me to..." She glanced up at Justine and back at their hands. She swallowed, then continued, "show him some love. I tried to fight him off, but he ripped my shirt and tried to...you know."

Despite the decision to sit still and listen, Justine gave in to impatience. "Did he rape you?"

Shaking her head, Yolanda released an untidy mass of hair on her shoulders. Justine clasped her by the sides of her face. "Are you sure?"

Yolanda nodded. "Yes, Mommy. He tried to get my pants off, but I gave him a fight and jammed him in his you know what."

"Did Kim get home all right?"

"Yeah, I called Tariq and he and his older brother came for us. Those guys left us on the side of Red Hills Road."

Justine fought hard not to jump up and hover. "What kind of friend is that boy, Jerrod? I don't want to say I told you so, but you have to be more careful of the company you keep, okay?"

When Yolanda nodded, tears seeped from her eyes. Justine got up and touched her lips to Yolanda's forehead, leaving baby kisses as in the past when she was much younger. Justine hugged her tight, grateful that nothing worse had happened. Losing her innocence to rape would have been devastating.

Yolanda squeezed Justine's waist while she stroked her hair. Thinking she should let the police know things were okay, Justine pulled away. "We should call the police about this boy. He did try to rape you."

Yolanda shook her head. "I don't want to think about it anymore."

"But what if he tries that with you again?"

"He won't, 'cause I'm gonna stay away from him. He's not one of the guys from the band. He's a friend of another friend."

"Fine, if you say so."

But Justine had plans; she'd tell the police what she knew and let them handle the situation. Even a warning would be better than letting the boy get off without a reality check.

Justine left the cup in the sink, and motioned for Yolanda to get up. Together, they walked down the passage to Yolanda's room. "You want to shower?"

Yolanda nodded, and Justine left her to it. From the living room, Justine called the police and notified them of Yolanda's return, along with what she knew of the run-in. At the end of the conversation, she wished the officer good night and told him thanks for his help.

On the way back to Yolanda's door, Justine whispered grateful prayers for her safe return. Though the door was open, she knocked.

"Come!"

Yolanda sat in front of the mirror wearing a tee-shirt and sweatpants. A towel covered her shoulders and her hair was wet.

"You washed your hair at this time of night?"

"I just had to. I dunno why."

Justine understood the need to try to wash away the experience, even if the gesture was only symbolic. She picked up the blow dryer, fitted it with the comb attachment, and set to drying her daughter's hair. Yolanda nodded, half asleep, while Justine combed through her hair. She applied Olive Oil Moisturizer, wrapped Yolanda's hair, and sent her to bed.

She lay with the sheet tucked under her armpits, looking the way she had when she was Emile's age. Justine sat on the edge of the bed. Faintly, she smiled. "Can I trust you not to run off again?"

Nodding slowly, Yolanda spoke. "You can count on me. Once was enough. Thank God for Tariq."

With the back of her hand, Justine stroked Yolanda's forehead. "You know we still have some stuff to sort out, right?"

Yolanda ran her palms back and forth on the blanket and avoided looking at Justine. "Yeah, I know."

After Justine turned out the light and opened the door, Yolanda stopped her with a hesitant call.

"Yeah?" Justine answered.

"You know I don't hate you, right?"

Justine shrugged. "I guess."

"I really don't, but I do have some stuff I also want to talk about with you, 'kay?"

Drooping with exhaustion, Justine rubbed the back of her neck. At least, she had time to prepare herself. "Yes, hon, we do need to talk."

– 96 –

Sunday, March 20

Xavier

Proverb: Man who nuh done cross river mustn't cuss alligator long mouth.
Meaning: Avoid antagonizing someone who can obstruct you.

Xavier sighed and let the latest copy of *Guitarist* fall to his chest. He couldn't keep his mind off Justine. It wasn't as if she'd given him any encouragement, but that didn't stop his fixation. She struck him as defenseless, battered by her daughter and her circumstances, but she wouldn't like the thought of him wanting to protect her. She reminded him of a lost child, trying to make do on her own, but somewhere inside the old spark lived. It flickered to life whenever he challenged her.

The rays from the afternoon sun slanted across his body where he lay on the sofa. He lifted the magazine and stared at the words on the page, but his thoughts strayed again.

How was Justine coping with Emile? He didn't seem hard to manage, but would have lots more questions Justine might not want to answer. Xavier couldn't see her patiently fielding the hundred and one questions her son would have. She'd probably distract him with something or other.

Xavier considered the adjustments he'd need to make in his life. Would Justine let Emile spend weekends with him? She was so possessive, he could forget that for a while, but maybe she'd let him take Emile on day trips. She had to know Emile would be safe with him. After all, Annette used to trust him to transport Kelleigh to tennis lessons and anywhere he cared to take her. Back then, he spent a lot of time chatting with Justine in her office while Kelleigh was on the court with her coach. That's how he'd come to know Justine so well.

She'd been reluctant to engage him and eventually, she'd come straight out and asked him what he wanted from her. Funny, he couldn't remember what he said, but they went on to exchange a kiss that was the first step to the best relationship he ever had.

He had first seen her in church, where he sometimes filled in for the regular musician. After their eyes met the first time, he had difficulty keeping his off her. The time and place was all wrong and he had no right to look at her, but he couldn't help staring. She wasn't beautiful enough to cause a stir in a crowd, but there was something wholesome and magnetic about her. Maybe it was her shiny head of hair, or her eyes that held a touch of sadness, or perhaps the fact that her shyness was refreshing. She'd never sought his attention; instead she tried hard not to look at him. Before they met, he wondered what kind of person she was and what her life was like. In short, he couldn't keep his thoughts off her.

Just like you can't now.

Another sigh left him. More and more he doubted his ability to stay strong. During the first few weeks after Justine reappeared, he'd been militant about not getting mixed up with her again. She had ripped through his life like a hurricane, torn up his insides and left him blowing in the wind like a shell some molting insect had discarded.

He couldn't blame her for the deterioration of his marriage. That had been brewing for years, but after Justine, he insulated his heart and avoided any entanglement.

The phone vibrated against his hip. He got it out, knowing nobody but Annette would be calling him now. What bit of drama was she bringing this time? He sat up and put the phone to his ear. "Yeah, Annette."

"Something's wrong with Kelleigh. I don't know what."

"Have you asked what's troubling her?"

"No. She's just not herself."

He told himself to be patient. Annette never noticed anything, but there was always a first time for everything. "Wouldn't you get to the root of the problem faster if you talked to her?"

"Yes, but there's also something else I needed to talk to you about. Something important."

"Shoot."

"No, not on the phone. We have to do this face to face."

"Why?"

"I'll meet you somewhere," she said.

His eyebrows rose. It had to be important for her to want to leave home to meet him. She had never made that sort of effort when they were a couple. She wanted something from him, but what? After searching his mind, he suspected what she was up to, but couldn't believe Annette would try something like that with him.

"How about The View?"

"Fine. Say in half-an-hour?"

"What about Kelleigh? Where is she?"

"Here."

"You're taking her with you?"

"No."

"After all her antics, you're willing to leave her alone at home?"

"But—"

"I'll come to you," he said.

"I was looking forward to getting out of the house."

She sounded annoyed, but he could live with that. "See you in a few."

Twenty minutes later, he pulled up to the house, switched off the engine and let himself relax. The yard—carpeted with zoysia grass and dotted with Chinese Fan Palms—had always been restful. Pity he'd had to leave it, but it was either that or lose his mind in stages living with Annette. The grass was ragged, which probably meant Annette had forgotten to get the gardener to come in. Only last month he'd had to remind her that the lawn needed to be cut. Who was he kidding? His soon-to-be-ex-wife paid attention only when it suited her.

He put aside what was no longer his business. The sooner he got inside, the faster he'd go back home.

Annette was draped over the sofa, reading a book. When had she started wearing lipstick at home? Her hair was spread on her shoulders, the way he liked it. The dress was new, so were the slippers, but he'd moved out a while now, so who knew? She patted the seat beside her, inviting him to sit.

"Where's Kelleigh?"

"Sulking in her bedroom. Where else would she be?"

"I'll check on her and then we can talk."

She all but rolled her eyes, but he didn't care. Kelleigh was his concern. Annette could take care of herself.

The music hit him before he knocked the door. "Come in," Kelleigh yelled.

Her waving feet met him, and she looked at him over her shoulder and then sat up. After she pulled her tank top down and her pants up, she smiled, an uncertain gesture. "Hi, Dad."

"Hi, yourself," he said, and sat beside her. He moved the crush of books away from them while he scanned the room. Seemed she was trying to keep it clean. That pleased him.

"You okay?"

She nodded. "I guess."

"Things all right between you and your mother?"

"Yeah, when she remembers I live here."

What to say to the obvious truth? "Uh, you know you can spend time with me whenever you want, right?"

She curled both hands into fists and drew them close to her body. "That sounds so cool and it'd be a change from here."

Her enthusiasm put a smile on his face. Why hadn't he thought about putting some space between mother and daughter before? "You can come over on Friday night and spend the weekend if you like."

She squeezed his arm, an affectionate gesture that took him back to when they used to spend their Saturdays together while Annette was studying and needed them out of the way.

She leaned outward to meet his eyes. "You really mean that, Daddy?"

"'Course."

Hugging his waist, she said, "Okay, then pick me up at six."

He patted her shoulder and kissed her temple. "'Kay, baby."

She pulled her knees up to her chest, hugged them, and propped her chin on top. "Make sure you have ice cream and if you don't have any board games, get some. I'm gonna beat you 'til you beg for mercy."

He chuckled, enjoying her feistiness. "Anything you say, Ms. Thang."

This time, the name didn't offend her. They were the father and daughter of old.

In the living room, he dropped into the seat across from Annette. "What you wanted to talk about?"

"I wondered what you were doing so long."

"You forget I don't live here anymore?"

"That's not my fault."

"I know. Now, what d'you want from me?"

"I was thinking how difficult Kelleigh's been since you left home—"

"Hold up. She didn't start acting up yesterday. We both have long hours and allowed things to get out of hand."

"Well, she's behaving worse since you left."

He sat forward and linked his fingers. "You make it sound like I made the decision to separate without talking it over with you."

She shrugged. "I let you go because it seemed to be what you wanted."

Was this woman for real? Now she was blaming her lack of interest on him.

"Let's get back on point. You wanted to talk to me about something. What is it?'

She scratched the back of her neck, fiddled with her skirt and then smoothed her hair. He hoped she wasn't up to what he suspected and wanted to tell her to get a move on when she started fidgeting all over again. After wetting her lips, she spoke. "I was thinking that since our separation is affecting Kelleigh this much, maybe we should stay together."

The silence that greeted her rushed sentence dragged on. It wasn't that he didn't know what to say, but he couldn't believe she said what he heard. He ran a hand over his hair, gathering his thoughts. "We've been there and we know it won't work. I'm too detached from our marriage and you're too absorbed in your life."

"We could try—"

"We tried for seventeen years. What else d'you need to convince you we're through?"

"Maybe if I cut back my hours—"

"It would only be for a while, and it would make you unhappy."

"What the hell d'you know about my happiness? It's not as if you put any effort into making our marriage work."

Speechless, he stared at her. Where had that come from? Trying not to descend further into an argument, he was careful with his words. "Have you forgotten the many evenings you were off doing your own thing while Kell and I stayed home?"

"I was trying to better myself."

"And have you forgotten your permanent headache and the fact that you were always too tired for sex?"

"So that's your excuse for cheating on me?"

His gut turned over, but he reminded himself that fidelity didn't matter anymore. "Huh?"

"You heard me, Xavier McKellop, so don't pretend you didn't. I know you were seeing some woman."

And she never said a thing. That's how much she cared. Maybe if she'd paid a little more attention to him, he wouldn't have had time to fall for Justine. He sighed, a new habit he'd developed since she'd taken over his life again. Annette glowered, and he wondered why he was wasting his time. "Let's get this clear, I cheated on you for my own reasons, but bear in mind you weren't giving me anything I needed."

"You're a grown man. What on earth could you possibly need?"

"The same things your daughter needs that you're too selfish to give her. Attention. Affection. Companionship. Obviously, that's too much to ask of you."

Her voice rose and she spread her hands. "You never said you needed those things."

He shook his head. 'You're clueless, you know that? I shouldn't have to tell you. This is basic stuff for a man and woman."

When she didn't respond, he met her eyes, hoping she'd understand he wasn't going to consider her request. "I think you might want to revise that reconciliation you had in mind. If you didn't know what I needed for so many years, how d'you plan to supply what's necessary now?"

Her eyes blazed, and she stood. "You know what? Get out of my house."

"Our house, Annette. I haven't given it to you yet."

He paused on the way to the door. "By the way, I'm picking up Kell on Friday evening. She's spending the weekend with me."

Annette drew herself up and spoke through clenched teeth. "You didn't ask my permission."

"I don't need to, she's my daughter too. I'm doing you the courtesy of telling you now."

"Well, you should have discussed it with me first."

He rubbed his forehead. "This is silly. I'm telling you now, okay?"

Akimbo, Annette said, "You can forget it. She's not going anywhere."

Heat sizzled behind his eyeballs and he let a few seconds go by before he spoke. "I'm sorry I didn't ask you first, but I'm picking up Kelleigh on Friday evening and that's final."

Annette stood in front of him, her chest almost touching his. "First you ruin our marriage, and now you plan to take my daughter too?"

He stared into her eyes, his anger fanned into a higher flame. Stop this childish bickering, he told himself, but his mouth opened and his good intentions disappeared. "I thought you'd be glad to get rid of her for a while, since you're so wrapped up in yourself."

"The only way you're taking her is over my dead body," she whispered.

He'd always been the peacemaker, but this time he refused to oblige her by giving in to her demands. "Push me and that might very well be the case."

Her eyes went wide and she opened her mouth, but didn't respond. Since they'd known each other, this was the first time he'd said anything to her that could be interpreted as a threat.

Disgusted with himself, Xavier left the house and sat in his truck, gripping the wheel. When had he started threatening women? He'd done the same thing to Justine a week ago. This time though, he had to be careful. Annette could take spitefulness to unknown levels, and he didn't want Kelleigh to suffer for his sins.

– 17 –

Sunday, March 20

Justine

Proverb: When yuh go a fireside and see food, eat half and lef (leave) half.
Meaning: In important conversations, don't reveal everything you know.

Yolanda sat on the grass, back against the Mango tree, strumming her guitar. The wind, shade and music lulled Justine. She laid the book on her belly and closed her eyes. She could use a nap. The late-night activities had sapped her energy, so she hadn't gone to Mass. She'd gotten up early to prepare a special breakfast for Yolanda, and after a meal of Escoveitched fish and Bammies, they'd lazed the morning away.

The three of them had fixed dinner and now as the sun prepared to dip behind the mountains, they relaxed as they once did before their home became a war zone. When he got tired of their non-activity, Emile wandered inside to camp on the sofa, watching cartoons.

Aware that they had issues to sift through, Justine sucked her lip into her mouth and thought about the questions Yolanda might ask and what she'd say in response. As the final chords faded, Justine opened her eyes. "Did I tell you I'm proud of you for sticking with the lessons?"

"Nope."

"Well, I am, okay? Glad you finally found something you like."

"Last time I spent the weekend at Grandma's, she threatened to send me home early if, to quote her, I didn't stop making noise at her head."

"You know she's just talking, she loves having you over."

Justine reminded herself that she needed to call Milton's mother. They'd never been close, but Justine checked in with Hermine Charles every so often, although she'd been uncomfortable around her since Emile's birth.

"Yeah, I know." She glanced at the house and then focused on Justine. "I was thinking now would be a good time to ask those questions we talked about."

Justine's stomach quivered and her hands stiffened where they lay on the book. "Sure, go ahead. I assume you want to talk about my relationship with Mr. McKellop."

"I know it was before Daddy died, 'cause Emile came only a few months after." She laid the guitar in her lap. "What happened?"

How much to tell her? Mature as she was, Yolanda was still a child and could understand the circumstances only up to a point. Justine stared into the leafy canopy above. "It wasn't something we planned to do. First, we were friends. But we both had marital problems, which we couldn't resolve, and things went where we didn't want them to."

"So, did you know where he was all this time?"

Justine shook her head. "We stopped seeing each other before Emile came."

"If Daddy hadn't died, would you have left him?"

"Maybe." Justine fiddled with the book on her chest, letting the pages flutter. Why was it so hard to face the fact that even if Yolanda hadn't taken ill when she did, Justine never would have left Milton? Or so she'd always told herself.

Yolanda frowned up at her. "What would have made you go?"

"Like I said, we were having problems. Your father didn't believe in talking about his troubles, and I believe in communication, so things broke down between us."

"How come I didn't notice?" Yolanda asked, her eyes fixed on Justine.

"Sometimes, your father was a little harsh with you, but you wouldn't remember."

"Oh yeah, I do."

Her admission surprised Justine. "Really?"

Yolanda stroked the side of the guitar, and her voice dipped. "I remember one evening when you came home late and I wanted to stay up, but he wouldn't let me. He was really angry and hit me that time."

"How come you never said anything?"

Shrugging, Yolanda continued to sweep her fingers along the side of the guitar. "I dunno. I was always so glad when we were together that I didn't want to spoil things by telling you about that."

Justine stroked the hair away from Yolanda's face. "You always were strong willed, so I bet you pushed Milton to the limit."

A quick movement of Yolanda's eyebrows and the shifting of her gaze, confirmed the truth in Justine's words.

"So tell me, did Daddy know about Mr. McKay?"

Shaking her head, Justine sat up and closed the book. "I never wanted to hurt your father. I still cared about him, you know?"

Yolanda nodded, pulled a blade of grass, and put it in her mouth. "Did you love him?" she asked.

"Who?"

"Mr. McKay."

Should she lie or tell the truth? Justine closed her eyes to clear her mind and avoid the open curiosity on Yolanda's face. Within seconds, she made a decision. Subterfuge had cost her enough pain to last the rest of her life. "Yes, I did."

"So why did you break up?"

Justine smoothed Yolanda's hair again, thinking how much she had missed their closeness. "I loved you too much to wreck our home."

"So you stayed because of me?" Yolanda spat out the grass, frowning.

Justine nodded. "You wouldn't have understood what was happening, plus by then I found out your father was dying."

"So why didn't you get back with Mr. McKay after Dad died?"

"He had a family too."

"Where are they?"

Justine shrugged. She knew nothing of Xavier's present situation and maybe nothing had changed. Come to think of it, the only person he'd mentioned was Kelleigh. Not that she was going to get her hopes stirred up. The last thing she needed was a bitter man to make life miserable. She ignored the whisper that said she was the one who'd made him bitter.

She turned her head. Yolanda still waited for an answer. "I don't know."

Whether by accident or design, Yolanda's fingers plucked the strings, resulting in a sharp twang. "So you gonna get back with him?"

"No."

"Why not?"

Though Yolanda caressed the guitar with an open expression in place, Justine knew her daughter would hang on to every word she said.

"Things have changed. We're different people."

Yolanda wriggled her eyebrows and put up both thumbs. "For an old guy, he's hot."

Justine rolled her eyes. "You young people are so disrespectful. The way you talk, anybody would believe he's at least a hundred."

"Not exactly, but at my age, he'd seem pretty close. Imagine if I were Emile."

"Speaking of which—"

"Uh, oh."

"We didn't talk about your little chat with Emile." She faced Yolanda, letting the hem of her dress fall around her ankles. When she spoke again, her voice was gentle. "Why did you do that?'

Yolanda stared into the hedge. "Well, I was feeling down, and he wouldn't stop bugging me. I just wanted him to hurt like I was hurting."

"And you really wanted to make him suffer like that?"

"I didn't mean to, but he was going on and on about Mr. McKay and I couldn't take it anymore. I just blew."

Justine folded her hands on her knees. "You're getting older and responsibility comes with age. You can't just say what you like because you're hurting."

Yolanda rubbed at something on the guitar that Justine couldn't see. "I'm really sorry about that, Mom, but I'd say I made things easier."

Puzzled, Justine leaned closer to Yolanda. "What d'you mean?"

"I saved you the trouble of telling Emile about his father."

The evening had grown cooler and a lull fell on the garden. "I didn't plan to tell him."

The shock on Yolanda's face confirmed that Justine had spoken. She hadn't meant to voice her thoughts, nor had she been honest enough to admit to herself that she'd had no intention of telling Emile about his father.

Xavier was right.

Yolanda's eyes went wide in the approaching darkness. "But why not?"

"It wouldn't have made a difference now would it?"

Yolanda spread her hands wide. "But not telling him would be like robbing him. I think it's cool that he has a dad." Her voice turned wistful. "I'd really love to have Dad back."

She swished a hand across the grass and raised her head. "Is this gonna change things?"

Before she finished the question, Justine shook her head. "Emile may spend more time with Xavier, but that's it. Nothing's gonna change. We'll be the Charles trio, like before."

Hope shone from Yolanda's eyes and it was clear she wanted to believe Justine. Was she fooling herself, hoping Xavier wouldn't make any demands that might impact on her family too much?

While she stroked Yolanda's cheek, Justine couldn't help the sadness seeping over her. Even if it was possible for her to find love again, she wouldn't reach for happiness at the expense of her children.

***

Justine pulled herself up against the bed head and cradled the phone to her ear. "Can you be real for a moment here, Dionne? I'm not looking for a lover. Besides, the man is probably still married."

"You don't know that. You're just hoping he's married so you can go back to hibernating."

"I'm not hibernating, I'm just not into men right now."

"What's new? You haven't been *into men* since you split with that mouth-watering piece of manhood. I'll bet he's even sexier now that he has some age on him. "

Justine held back a smile before saying, "I didn't notice."

Dionne laughter sounded more like a bray. "Girl, you're the best. Only you would try to get me to believe you don't have the hots for Music Man. You need to be honest with yourself, if nobody else."

"Look, the last thing I need is to have a man complicating my life. I've learned to be happy with what I have and I'm sticking to that."

"You mean the empty space in your bed? Woman, get real. You're also the only smaddy who'd try to tell me she doesn't need some sex."

"It's overrated."

"Not the kind you used to have with that man."

Struggling not to smile, Justine said, "Don't remind me."

"What, your body parts are waking up?"

Justine chuckled, despite the heat crawling into her cheeks. "My body parts are fine. I just wish he hadn't come back."

"Yeah, that would have made life simple, and you could have gone on pretending to be dead."

"I haven't been pretending to be dead." She spread her hands, forgetting that Dionne couldn't see her. "I've just been taking care of my children."

"At the expense of your well-being."

"I'm making money and my children are fine. I have everything I need."

"Except a good man."

"That, I can live without."

"You can continue fooling yourself, but you ain't fooling me. Sex isn't the evil thing you're making it out to be. You like it as much as the next person, but insist on punishing yourself for something that almost happened. Not something that did."

Sighing, Justine eased down on her back. "No, Landy didn't die, but it changed everything for me. I should—"

"Yeah, you should have been at home, but you weren't. What have you achieved by dragging yourself over the coals for so long? I'll tell you what. Nothing!" She exhaled heavily, becoming too passionate as usual. "You could have had that man and some happiness in your life. And to think Milton was busy living it up with Warren, while you were whipping yourself for loving somebody else."

"You forget Milton wasn't exactly in that situation for the thrill of it."

"Whatever. Point is, you need to get a life."

Justine stared at the ceiling, reliving her fright over having missed a dozen calls from home during that last interlude with Xavier. Though she reminded herself that Yolanda hadn't succumbed to the asthma attack, dread and remorse from that night settled over her and she rubbed her neck, willing the muscles to unknot.

In her shame, she abandoned Xavier and sunk into a black place, where neither life nor the sun could reach her. She had clawed her way back to her current existence and didn't need anyone complicating her life. No matter how much her body awakened her at night, humming from the memories of Xavier's long-ago touch. No matter that she spent too much time thinking about what was now lost. Besides, there was his wife and child. If there was no other deterrent, the thought of breaking up his family was enough to kill any urges she had to continue their liaison.

Dionne's annoyed tone centered her in the bedroom.

"Are you even hearing me?"

"Sorry, I didn't hear a word you just said."

"I was just asking when you're gonna admit you still love that man, and aren't you gonna try to win him back?"

"I got over him a long time ago. Let's just leave it at that."

"Really? You're such a liar. You never stopped loving Music Man, but remember you're gonna hate yourself if you allow him to escape again."

"Yeah, whatever."

Justine hung up the phone, but her mind wouldn't stop turning over the possibilities Dionne had suggested.

– 18 –

Friday, March 25

Xavier

Proverb: Back never know di value o' ole shut (old shirt) 'til ole shut tear off.
Meaning: We don't appreciate people in our lives until they're no longer available.

Tired and irritable, Xavier dropped on the sofa across from Annette. He'd just finished a lesson with a teenager whose mother refused to recognize that her daughter had no skill or love for making music.

The floral fabric of the sofa was rough against his palm, reminding him of all the reasons why Annette and he didn't get along. He'd told her the damn thing was too coarse for relaxing in, but she always had to get her own way. Not that it mattered anymore. He wanted to be out of the house within fifteen minutes. Just the angle at which she held her head told him she was spoiling for a fight.

"Why are you here?" she asked, laying a monster of a textbook on the cushion beside her. On the television screen, a couple was attached by the lips. Annette stared at the set, pretending he wasn't in the room. Another of her mind games.

"I told you I was coming to get Kelleigh. Don't be difficult over this. You know she's looking forward to it."

"What she's looking forward to is getting out of the house." She poked her mouth out, like a three-year-old. "You put her up to this."

He shuffled his feet and hitched up his jeans, giving himself time to speak without snapping at her. "You know I don't play those games. Where is she anyway?"

"In her room."

Annette flounced past him to turn off the television while the credits ran upward on the screen, then stomped by him a second time and flopped onto the sofa, reminding him of Kelleigh when she got in a snit. Her crossed arms supported her breasts. "When you bringing her back?"

"Sunday evening."

"And what am I supposed to do over here by myself?"

Did she know how childish she sounded?

"The same thing you do when she's in the house and you're doing your own thing. I'm sure you'll survive."

She got ready to launch another assault, but Kelleigh hurried into the room, duffle slung over her shoulder. "Dad, why didn't you let me know you were here?"

"It didn't take you long to find out, did it?"

She flung a quick look at her mother, but didn't respond to her jab. "Can we go now?"

"My, you're in a hurry to leave," Annette said.

Kelleigh shifted from one foot to the next, clutching the bag strap, but stayed quiet. Xavier sensed she was doing her best not to backchat her mother, knowing where he stood on that sort of behavior. Her eyes begged him to get moving. He got up and told Annette he'd see her on Sunday.

When he let Kelleigh into the truck, he waited a moment before starting the engine, ridding himself of negative energy from his tangle with Annette.

"You bring your homework?" he asked.

She shook her head. "Got it out of the way already. I want the whole weekend to myself."

"Smart move."

He patted her arm and concentrated on backing out of the yard. On the drive to the townhouse, he listened to Kelleigh's complaints about school. The moment he parked the truck, Kelleigh hopped out to wait by the front door, pushing Angel's Trumpet and Schefflera leaves out of the way. "Man, you have a lot of bush around this place."

Justine had loved the Angel's Trumpets, but his daughter had no such appreciation for Mother Nature's offerings. "Those are plants and flowers, daughter of mine."

"Whatever." Her eyes gleamed when she looked up at him. "I hope you got some games. D'you have cable?"

"Nope."

"Daaady."

That made him laugh. "I don't have time to watch cable television."

"So what d'you do?"

"I do stuff on the net and I read. Ever hear of those things?"

She pushed some strands of hair behind her ears and slapped away a mosquito. "Jeez, Daddy, you're such a dinosaur."

"How about showing me some respect once in a while?" he asked, opening the door.

After she flung her bag on a chair, Kelleigh explored the house, which she hadn't visited since the first year he'd moved in. Xavier crashed on the sofa and closed his eyes.

"I hope you plan to cook," Kelleigh said, walking into the living room.

Xavier raised his eyelids and held back a yawn. "Don't tell me you don't know how."

She slid her hands into the back pockets of her jeans and watched her wriggling toes. "Mom never showed me how."

"Not to worry," he said, switching on the television. "I'll show you a thing or two before you leave. We can't have you growing up to be a woman with ten thumbs."

She didn't look too enthusiastic, but nodded and said, "Cool."

"You eat already?"

She nodded. "Yeah, but I'm a growing girl. I'll get something later."

"Not too close to bedtime, okay?"

"It never hurt me before and Mom lets me—"

"We play by my rules, okay?"

She rolled her eyes. "Fine."

"Leave your things in the room at the end of the passage and come get your first lesson in playing checkers."

She did the eye thing again. "We've only been playing that for like a hundred years."

"You can forget the rules of the past. You're a big girl now. I won't let you win anymore."

"Ha. We'll see who's the expert. Be right back."

She went to the kitchen, then the bedroom and came back wearing a tee-shirt with her jeans. He'd been relieved that he didn't have to give her another lecture about her dressing.

After she won one game to his three, Kelleigh went to the kitchen and came back with a soda. She sat on the floor and placed the bottle on the center table.

"You know that's not healthy, right?"

"Yeah, but like you used to tell Mom, let me live a little." She took a swig of the tangerine soda, smiling at him while she recapped the bottle to save the fizz.

"Right," he grumbled. "I hope you feel that way when your teeth start falling out."

"Daaaad, you're exaggerating. If it makes you happy, I won't drink the other one I brought with me."

She rubbed her hands together in preparation for the next game. Curious about her thoughts on her mother and their relationship, Xavier asked what he hoped sounded like a casual question. "You getting on any better with your mother?"

She lifted her shoulders and allowed them to fall. "Mom only remembers me when she gets miserable."

He felt his brows bunch together. "What you mean by that?"

"She's mostly okay." She looked at him through her lashes. "Until you come around."

Which made him question why Annette kept calling. "Your mom was concerned about you, which is why she asked me to talk to you."

Kelleigh grumbled and shook her head slowly. "You must be blind not to notice that she only wants to see you. She's not concerned about me."

"I wouldn't say that, but—"

"Come on, Dad, you know Mom's always studying or working. She never had time for me before, so why now that you're gone?" She hugged her knees and stared at her toes. "I know the divorce is coming through soon. I think that's what's bugging her."

Her comment on her mother's habits was correct, so it would be useless to deny the truth. She reached for the Kola Champagne, gulped some of it, and set the bottle down after a satisfied smack of the lips. "By the way, Daddy, you have a girlfriend yet?"

He couldn't help smiling; Kelleigh was full of surprises. "Why d'you want to know, and why would you dare ask me that?"

"I'm growing up you know, and I'd have to be blind not see how my friends' mothers looked at you when you used to take me to school."

He laughed, slumping on the sofa. "You know you're way too old for your own good?"

She bobbed her head, returning his grin. "Mom thinks so too. So does Auntie Babs."

"Can we forget my life and get back to the game?"

"Okay, but if you have a woman, I wanna know about her."

"Only if I know about any boyfriend you have, but I did say you were too young for that."

She screwed up her face. "Please. Some of my friends already have boyfriends."

Xavier paused while laying out the game pieces. "I just don't want to have to rip anybody's face off for messing with my daughter, okay?"

She nodded, then whispered. "What I told you the other day? It was the truth."

He was relieved that she was sensible enough to understand she was too young for that kind of intimacy. That would make him worry less, since he didn't have as much influence over her as when they'd lived together. He closed his eyes and thanked God she was a smart girl.

***

Saturday, March 26

Yolanda walked into the room behind Emile, who rushed to where Xavier sat behind the desk. Emile's arms lifted and fell and with his gaze, he followed the toe of his sneaker which he dragged back and forth on the tiles. After a moment, he scratched his ear.

Xavier got the feeling Emile had planned to hug him, until shyness prevented him. Xavier squeezed the boy's shoulder and pointed him toward the drums, chatting to put him at ease.

Yolanda moved to where the guitars hung, removed the one she liked, and went to stand by the window. She set up the stand, got her notes, and went straight to practicing. Apart from a mumbled hello, she said nothing.

Xavier didn't understand how she could practice in the same room as Emile, who still didn't realize that playing the drums required more skill than energy. He'd learn though; he had talent. All he needed was continued training, and regular practice.

Xavier wanted to give him a set of drums, but had to get that past Justine first, since she was the one who'd have to put up with the noise.

The door opened and Kelleigh poked her head inside. "Miss Delancy says there's someone who needs to speak with you out front."

"Thanks." His gaze swept over Emile and Yolanda. "Keep going guys. I'll be back in a few."

He left the room, passing Kelleigh in the doorway. She made no attempt to leave, holding on to the doorknob and looking around the room. A twinge of unease went through him, but he suppressed it. Nothing could happen by the time he got back.

But something did.

Kelleigh and Yolanda were yakking as though they'd known each other forever. Weren't girls supposed to be reserved when they met other girls in the same age-group? So much for what he knew.

Kelleigh was now strumming the guitar to a reggae beat he hadn't heard before and he wondered how she could concentrate on what her fingers were doing, when she was talking so much. It had been a while since he'd heard her play anything, which roused his guilt over neglecting her. He tuned out the girls' chatter and walked over to Emile, listening to his drum strokes. Without a doubt, he was improving.

Ill at ease, Xavier moved from behind Emile and strayed to the corridor outside, thinking kids these days made being an adult and a parent hard work.

While Kelleigh remained inside, Xavier didn't want to hang around Emile too much. God forbid that Kelleigh should find out about Emile before he was ready to tell her. He'd made up some ground he didn't want to lose. With all the talking going on between the girls, it was only wise to tell Kelleigh she had a brother before the weekend was over. The last thing he needed was a repeat performance from Yolanda along the lines of the one she'd put on for Emile a week ago.

He slipped into the room, dividing his attention between the girls and Emile. Seemed they had a mutual acquaintance named Tariq, which didn't surprise him. Kingston wasn't a large city and they didn't live that far apart. In a way, he was relieved that Kelleigh had taken to Yolanda. It would make things easier when he told her about Emile. He hid a grimace, wondering when he'd become a coward.

He stayed on edge until the lesson was over and even then, kept an ear tuned to their conversation. He didn't have the heart to deny Kelleigh her wish to come to the shop with him when she asked early that morning. He assumed she was also trying to make up for the time they had lost. Since his relationship with Annette deteriorated, Xavier spent little time at the house, but it hadn't occurred to him that he was robbing himself and Kelleigh.

When Justine appeared, she said hello, then smoothed a hand over her hair and fiddled with her handbag, the way she did when she was nervous. Xavier figured that the resemblance between them would tell her Kelleigh was his daughter. Or maybe she'd remember what Kelleigh looked like from the times he used to take her to tennis lessons.

Justine mumbled something to him, which he took to be a greeting, and quickly guided Emile and Yolanda out of the room and the shop, amid yells from Kelleigh and Yolanda that they'd link up soon.

He decided to phone Justine, but didn't admit even to himself the real reason he wanted to talk to her. Emile was the pretext he'd use to drag information out of Justine.

Later that evening, while Kelleigh had a shower, Xavier went to his room to do the same since she had promised to beat him in a Scrabble rematch when she was finished. He rang Justine, who said nothing after he identified himself. When he started to wonder if she'd ended the call, she spoke. "Uh, yeah. You want to speak to Emile?"

"I'm calling for you."

Silence again, then, "What...how can I help?"

"I want to see you tomorrow evening."

"Can't we talk on the phone?"

"No, I'd prefer if we do this face to face."

He pictured her frowning and smoothing her hair. When the humming in the line stretched without any words between them, Xavier spoke. "Meet me at Myra's at six thirty. You know where that is, right?"

"Yes, but I can't stay long. I have to prepare Emile for school tomorrow."

He'd never heard a weaker excuse. "Okay, it shouldn't take long. See you then."

Satisfaction curled his lips into a smile. He had Justine where he wanted her—unsure of herself and with no idea why he needed to meet with her. As much as he'd wanted to wring her neck over the past few weeks, he wouldn't do anything to hurt her.

He lay on the bed, hands flung over his head feeling for the locks he no longer wore. Sometimes he had thought she was as in love with his locks as she'd been with him. He moved his head in a negative motion while he laughed at himself. Those locks were as far in the past as his love affair with Justine. That's if she had ever loved him. Time and separation had eroded the confidence he'd had in her feelings for him. One thing he was sure of was the fact that he now made her nervous.

He turned his head to stare through the window at the shadows created by the Oleander bushes. Did he know what the heck he was doing? In any case, it was too late to go back now. Once he decided on a course of action, it was either do or die.

– 19 –

Justine & Xavier

Proverb: A nuh fi want a tongue mek cow nuh talk.
Meaning: There is usually more to a serious situation than meets the eye, which makes
   it prudent to keep one's own counsel.

Justine scanned the room, uneasy but resigned to waiting for Xavier to appear. The
muted light and the wicker chairs clustered around glass-topped tables made for a cozy
atmosphere, but she couldn't relax. She wanted to start their business, be done with it and
go home. What did he want that couldn't be discussed on the phone?

She looked at her watch, lifting the hair away from her nape at the same time. She was
beginning to feel hot. What had possessed her to leave her hair loose?

Because he likes it that way.

She quirked her lips, hearing Dionne's voice in her head. *Better get over yourself.*

He was five minutes late, which was out of character. Maybe he wasn't coming. Her
legs muscles bunched as she prepared to rise, and that's when he appeared.

The man sucked the air out of her lungs. Black pants and a loose-fitting black shirt
made him seem bigger and more powerful. Xavier had been appealing years ago, but

things had gotten worse, in that he now personified sex. Since his reappearance, he occupied too much of her thoughts. At the oddest moments, she caught herself thinking about making love with him. Her mind was stuck in a groove she couldn't climb out of, and that was alarming. She was older now and should have more control over her mind, but so much for that.

He sat, and surreptitiously, she breathed in his scent—a mixture of pine, jasmine, musk and another fragrance that eluded her. Shifting in the seat, Justine banished a picture of herself pressing kisses to his neck and shoulders while inhaling his scent. She breathed deeply, aware of what she was doing. She couldn't take him home, but could memorize his essence for later. Now she stared into his eyes, wondering what his life was like. An urgent need to know came over her. Was he still with Annette, existing as they had before the affair? Or had things changed?

"Justine," he said, reminding her of a time when her name was always a caress on his lips.

She nodded, acknowledging her name, but thinking how stupid she must look. She wanted to scrape her hair together, but would only call unnecessary attention to herself. He'd notice and think she was after him, so to compensate, she sat up straighter, and pulled the collar of her shirt together.

In contrast, he slouched lower in the seat and rested both hands along the chair arms, spreading his fingers over the surface of the wicker. She narrowed her eyes. If she didn't know better, Xavier was working his wiles on her. But no, that wasn't possible. Hadn't he behaved as though he hated her since they met again?

His fingers moved over the varnished surface of the chair and unwittingly, she thought of how he once roamed her body with his hands, confident of what his touch did to her. Her breath heaved past her lips in small gusts. *Come on, Justine, concentrate. That's not what you're here for!*

But he wasn't helping her in any way. Xavier ran his tongue over his bottom lip and settled himself more comfortably in the seat. Maybe she was going crazy or misunderstood the message he was sending.

She pulled in her stomach, reminding herself it was better to stay on the straight and narrow. Xavier had given her no reason to believe he thought of her as anything but the cowardly woman he accused her of being weeks ago. He startled her when he spoke. "What would you like to drink?"

"Fruit juice."

He stopped a passing waiter, who returned quickly with their drinks. He barely set it down before Justine took a gulp for want of something to do. Could Xavier hurry up with this cloak-and-dagger business and just get it over with?

"So what did you want to say to me?" she asked when she couldn't stand the silence any longer.

His eyes widened, as if he was guilty of something. "I wanted to make some firm arrangements concerning Emile."

She turned her head and wrinkled her brow. "Why couldn't we do this yesterday?"

"All the kids were there, remember? And you didn't stay long."

She sipped the tomato-red concoction and then slapped the glass on the table, sloshing the juice up against the rim. The delay was making her edgy, so she went directly to what was bugging her. "What exactly d'you want?"

His eyebrows rose, but he didn't remark on her tone. "I wanted to know whether you'd let Emile go out of town with me on a day trip and if you'd agree to letting him overnight with me, maybe in another month or so. Also, there's the matter of me contributing to his care."

She closed her eyes to prevent herself from answering right away. She didn't want him to think she was refusing without putting some thought into it. Though her first reaction was to tell him no, she didn't have a choice about sharing Emile, not with Xavier pushing this hard. Emile, of course, would be delighted at the prospect of having his father to himself. Why couldn't Xavier be one of those men who would have been happy to ignore Emile once he found out about him?

She was wasting time thinking that way, because she wouldn't have been attracted to that kind of man. Sipping more fruit punch, Justine delayed her answer while railing against her life. Why couldn't things be simple, like they were for other folks?

Dionne was running her business and raising well-adjusted kids. Kyra was helping Denton to run his garage and supporting her son, Demar, while he completed university on a football scholarship. Justine's life had turned out fine, but now she had the devil of a time just trying to stay ahead of this man who wanted her son. He'd never said anything remotely like that, but from the way he was looking at her, he expected her to say no to his request. Guilt made her want to fidget.

"Where d'you plan to take him?" she asked.

"The water park in Negril."

"Negril?"

"What's wrong?"

She knew her objection sounded foolish, but she made it anyway. "He's never been that far away."

"There's a first time for everything. You know I'll take good care of him."

"I know you will, but..." She stopped, reaching for a plausible objection.

His hand covered hers. "He'll be okay, and it's a great way for us to spend some time together, get to know each other."

Giving in to a sudden bout of anxiety, Justine let her gaze sweep the room. For a moment, she forgot she was no longer sneaking around with Xavier. She almost smiled, until she remembered the subject of their discussion.

"What if something happens?"

"Like what?" His thumb caressed her skin, leaving her incapable of thought.

She shrugged. "I don't know. Something that'll make him need me."

Laughing, Xavier squeezed her hand. "If you choose not to come, you'll be but a phone call away."

Her brows snapped up. "I'm invited?"

"I didn't intend for you to come, but until you feel confident I can take care of him, you might as well tag along."

She didn't like the sound of that. "I'm not trying to make him a mama's boy, it's just that—"

"Disaster might strike if you're not there to prevent it?"

Her mouth longed to turn up at the corners, even if he was being facetious at her expense. She swallowed that impulse. "I prefer to say a boy needs his mother."

"Fine then, I won't deny you that. I'll take you in another week or so."

"That might also mean taking Yolanda," she warned.

"That's fine," he said, smiling warmly at her.

She blinked and her mind went blank. Up to now, he hadn't put himself out to be pleasant. She grabbed a handful of hair and combed it over one shoulder. He watched her, but she couldn't read his eyes.

"About money for Emile, I'm doing okay, so—"

"This is not about you, Justine. It's about fulfilling my obligation to my son. If you wish, you can put the money into an account for his education."

"Fine, I'll do that."

She didn't like the hard edge to his words, but didn't see the value in arguing over a decision he'd already made.

After another sip of Lite Beer, he spun the bottle in slow circles. "So, Justine, how are you, really?"

A ball of thistle sat in her throat, stifling an audible response. Why did he need to know? Did he even care?

"Uh, I'm fine. Really."

Now she sounded like a naïve twenty-year-old, who didn't know whether she was coming or going.

He smiled, making her feel even worse.

"I mean I'm doing well. Living my life, you know."

His intense study made her nerves jump, and she wanted to bang her head against the table. Sweat beaded at her hairline and she willed them not to join forces and roll down her cheek. Xavier was looking at her as if he wanted something. She swiped at her brow, praying he wasn't thinking what she suspected was going on in his head.

Never mind that it might be what she thought she wanted or needed. No, she wasn't ready to travel that road again, even if he was looking at her as if he wanted to touch her with more than his gaze.

To avoid him, she stared at the wicker under the smoky glass and reminded herself how much she enjoyed her calm, ordered existence.

Angling her head to the side, she looked at the people around her talking, laughing and sharing drinks. Ordinary activity, same as she was doing, which shouldn't have her nerves short-circuiting.

Warmth spread over the back of her hand as his fingertips rasped against her skin. The guitar gives him calluses, she thought, conscious that his touch was igniting flames that needed to be quenched and only he knew how to extinguish the fires he was so good at starting.

Their gazes meshed and she recognized in his eyes shared memories that made heat lick over her skin. She drew her thighs together at the phantom sensation of his flesh sliding against hers.

She had to stop this.

Gently, she withdrew her hand. "This isn't a good idea."

His eyes questioned her. "Am I making you nervous?"

She cleared her throat. "I wouldn't put it quite like that. We shouldn't play games that will lead us into trouble."

"Who's playing?"

His lazy baritone rippled over her like a wave of cool breeze on heated skin. In her lap, she joined her hands, lest they did what they wanted to do, and reached for him, against her will. She closed her eyes, gathered her courage and spat her words. "You are. You're toying with me. I don't know why, but I'm not having any of what you're up to."

He smiled again, stealing her breath. "Trust me, the last thing I'd do is play with you."

She squirmed and then went still, determined not to lose her focus. "What is it you really want?"

His long fingers caressed the bottle, drawing her eyes. Her gaze collided with his, and she looked away, annoyed with herself. Suddenly, she was having withdrawal symptoms. Wherever she looked at him, she wanted to touch him and she couldn't, which made things worse.

"I'm trying to figure it out myself," he said.

His words shocked Justine, who stared at the table, gathering her scattered thoughts. How to kill any idea he might have about continuing their affair? The seconds ticked by with human chatter and the high-pitched clink of glasses intruding. Taking a deep breath, Justine asked him something sure to kill any amorous intentions he might have. "So where is your wife in all of this figuring?"

He rolled the bottle some more. A hint of a smile lifted his lips before he said, "Our divorce will be final in about two weeks."

Only fierce self-control stopped Justine from springing up and dashing off like a terrified rabbit.

***

Until he scared her half to death, Xavier didn't think about the impact his words would have had on Justine. Her wide eyes were full of sexual awareness and suspicion.

The moment he saw her again, he knew nothing had changed between them and now had the answer to the question that had occupied his mind since she reentered his life. She was definitely interested in him, but for how long?

That day in the shop, he'd felt her presence before he saw her, and his senses hadn't lied to him. Before she turned to face him, he'd known it was her and while he understood what he was letting himself in for, he had to know why she had turned her back on him. But Emile had appeared, sucking away his need to crucify Justine with questions, and turning his world ass backward.

Now that he had her to himself, he'd ask what had been on his mind for so long. "Why exactly did you leave me, Justine?"

Her fist closed around the oval pendant at her throat and she stared at him as if he had suggested they snort coke together. She made a rasping sound and grabbed the chair arms, making him think she'd spring up and run out of the bar. She didn't. Instead, she closed her eyes and massaged the teardrop pendant as one would handle worry beads. Knowing she was in the middle of a mini meltdown, he gave her time to compose herself. A few more people flowed into the bar and occupied tables around them.

When his gaze rested on Justine, she picked up a paper napkin, placed the glass on it and watched it absorb the water ring.

Gently, he said, "I'd like an answer."

"There were people depending on us."

"And I thought we had agonized over that and decided that our happiness was more important than trying to make other people happy."

She stared into the fruit juice. Easier, he supposed, than facing him. "I need to apologize for what I said the other day."

She looked him full in the face.

"About the woman you are."

Elbow on the table, he traced her cheekbone with his thumb. "I should have known you were too honorable to just leave."

She pushed her hair back and eased out of his reach. "At times, I think I might have eventually. You made me so—"

She cleared her throat and stared at him, as though trying to decipher his thoughts.

He picked up her hand, and folded it between his. "I made you so happy, maybe?"

She nodded.

He bit the inside of him mouth to stop himself from smiling. He could only image what it cost her to admit that. He released her hand and slumped in the chair, his eyes narrowed. Despite her confession, he wasn't satisfied.

The blender by the bar whirred above the customers' chatter, distracting him. He sipped more Lite Beer and scanned the room again, but when he looked at Justine, she still wasn't ready to face him. "Over the years, I've thought you never would have left."

"It's not—"

He shook his head. "It's not an accusation. I'm saying that based on who you are, it wasn't something you could have done. What happened to Yolanda gave you an out."

She laid both hands on the table and glared at him. "How dare you call me a coward."

"I never said that."

"But you implied it with that last remark."

"I'd be lying if I deny that I've thought it hundreds of times. But I also told myself that you were too decent a human being to put your happiness before your daughter's."

She bunched her hair and laid it over her other shoulder, twisting the ends to keep it together. How he wanted to...*concentrate!*

"There's something else I want to know."

"Okay."

"What have you gained from giving up on us? Did it eventually make you happy?"

She ran her hands down the front of her shirt and then studied her fingernails. "I gained peace of mind. I raised my children and learned to live with myself."

"Did you even think about how you hurt me?" he asked, unable to contain his resentment. "And d'you think it was any easier for me? I was prepared to sacrifice everything for you. For us."

She tugged the pendant so hard, it was a wonder the chain didn't break. She blinked several times and then latched on to the waiter, who passed too close carrying a loaded tray. Under the soft light, her eyes swam. "How can you ask me that?"

"Why wouldn't I ask? I never figured out how you could just walk away and leave me, leave us."

"I had no choice," she said, barely above a whisper. "It came down to you or them. I had to choose them. Milton had cancer, spent all our money being blackmailed by some man."

Staring at the table as though ashamed, she continued. "You don't know what it's like to think you're safe and protected, only to have the security blanket ripped away from you. D'you think I wanted to burden you with my financial problems? After Milton died, I was left with only my children, my personal savings and my pride."

He listened, unwilling to let her know her explanation had offered him new insight.

She continued, whispering so he had to lean forward to hear. "Milton's death was agonizing. How could I leave? Would you have wanted me, knowing I'd walked out on him in his illness, no matter that he was also unfaithful to me?"

She stared across the room, swallowing hard. When she looked at him, the vulnerability was gone, though her eyes were moist. "Besides, Yolanda would never have understood me turning her life upside down."

"The least you could have done was to have the courage to talk to me, Justine, but you took the coward's way out." When he could speak without shouting, he continued. "There's nothing you can say that will excuse the fact that you hid Emile from me."

She winced as if he'd hit her, and though he had apologized for calling her names, he couldn't stop hurling his fury at her. Her revelation had done nothing to soothe his disappointment and everything to rouse his anger. For so long, he had needed an outlet and though he had sworn not to do anything to hurt her, he couldn't stop the spite pouring out of his mouth. "Yes, Justine. When it comes down to bare bones, you hid my son, hoping you'd never lose face or have to admit that what you did was wrong."

Her eyes glittered and her nostrils widened, the way a cornered stray cat might react. She sobbed or hiccupped, he wasn't sure which. By the time he opened his mouth, she yanked her bag off the chair and ran out of the building.

He rose to follow her, grabbing the waiter by the shoulder. The startled man steadied the drinks on the tray he carried. Xavier shoved a five-hundred-dollar bill into his hand and spoke over his shoulder. "I'll be back in a minute."

In the parking lot he squinted, trying to locate Justine. She stood under a light to his right, digging in her handbag. She wiped her face on one sleeve and pulled something out of her bag. Despite her effort to get the car open, the door wouldn't budge. She stopped, dabbing her eyes.

A few strides placed him behind her. He slid a hand down her arm and took the key. When he turned her to face him, she sucked in a breath. He tipped her chin up with two fingers while she studied the fabric of his shirt. "I didn't mean to throw blame at you," he said.

He stroked the hair away from her forehead, weak to her tears. "I take that back. Of course, I wanted to blame you for everything, but I understand your reasons a little better now we've had a chance to talk."

She smiled through her tears. "You do?"

Using both thumbs, he wiped her tears. Then he nodded. "For years I didn't want to. I fed my anger and frustration, kept it alive."

He slid his hands into his pockets to keep them occupied. Her warmth and nearness were doing weird things to him. She wore something that reminded him of passion fruit, roses and vanilla. He exhaled and raised his head. "Seeing you in January brought back everything I tried to put behind me for such a long time."

He looked down at Justine, shocked when her palms came to rest on his chest. "I'm so sorry," she said.

He stepped away from her, hands still squashed in his pockets. Now he'd revealed too much. He didn't want her pity, but he did want her to understand how she'd hurt him and destroyed his trust.

While she stared at the space where he had left his shirt unbuttoned, the tip of her tongue slid out to wet her lips. He was a hundred percent sure Justine didn't realize what she was telling him subconsciously.

The wind picked up, cool and crisp.

Justine used both hands to comb her hair into some sort of order, her eyes never leaving his. He wasn't sure what she read in his expression, but didn't doubt that Justine wanted him as badly as he wanted her.

– 20 –

Sunday, March 27, 8:00 PM

Justine

Proverb: A nuh everything good fi eat, good fi talk.

Meaning: It's not necessary to make everything you know public knowledge, especially when the information can bring negative repercussions.

Justine cupped her hands around a mug of chamomile tea, while Miss Pauline sat across from her drinking mint tea.

Desperately in need of someone to talk to, Justine eyed the woman who had been with her for close to fifteen years. She'd taken care of Justine's home and helped raise Yolanda, spending time with her many evenings when Justine was occupied with Xavier. Now, she was Emile's caregiver and more like a grandmother than his blood relative.

That thought made Justine uncomfortable. Fact was, Hermine wasn't Emile's relative by blood, and Justine still hadn't told her differently.

The warmth of Miss Pauline's hand on hers startled Justine. The older woman's rough palm slid back and forth on Justine's skin as she spoke. "I know things not going well lately, but I been praying for yuh."

Justine clasped Miss Pauline's hand. "Thank you. Sometimes it seems like everything just turns upside down and there's no way of fixing them."

"Mi dear, time have a way of makin' everyt'ing fall into place." Miss Pauline withdrew her hand and turned the mug in slow circles. "I know yuh like to keep t'ings to yuhself, but the way Miss Yolanda carry on sometimes, I can't help hearing what's not my business."

She shot a glance at the doorway. "I know about Emile and I did suspect for a long time."

Thrown off balance by the meeting with Xavier and now Miss Pauline's confession, Justine wasn't sure what to say. She didn't get a chance to speak because her helper wasn't finished.

"I don't want to talk bad t'ings about di dead, but I know yuh had a hard time wid Mr. Milton and dat yuh did try to mek t'ings better. But mi dear, as yuh know, wha' gone bad a mornin' can't come good a evenin'."

She peered earnestly at Justine. "I'm a Christian woman and what yuh did was wrong, but God know yuh heart and I'm sure yuh know Him will forgive yuh if yuh ask Him. No matter how dark t'ings seem now, jus' trust and believe. Everyt'ing will work out."

Justine nodded, unable to say anything. Miss Pauline got up, touching Justine's shoulder. "Yuh should stop worryin' so much. Despite how yuh get him, Emile is a sweet bwoy and a gift from di man upstairs."

"I know," Justine whispered. She didn't have the will or the energy to say anything else. How Miss Pauline knew what was going on in her mind, Justine didn't know, but she was grateful for the woman's support.

After she settled Emile for the night, Justine wandered back to her bedroom and climbed into bed. She pointed the remote at the television, flipping through the channels. The Sunday night fare was sparse. She turned to Discovery Channel and settled in to watch the traditional practices of a tribe from Papua New Guinea. But she didn't stay absorbed in the program for long.

Xavier's pained expression—eyes troubled, mouth taut—intruded on her thoughts. Why had she believed he wouldn't suffer as much as she had? She had comforted herself often with the idea that he was a man and didn't feel as deeply. How foolish she had been.

Beyond any doubt, she had known he loved her. He hadn't told her often, but his willingness to turn his life on its ear for her had been enough evidence. They had talked incessantly about how they would tell their families and discussed coping measures for the fallout to come when her church community discovered their relationship. At least, she had talked endlessly about all the possibilities. He had soothed her fears and told her they would face everything one day at a time.

How ironic was it to meet her soul mate after she'd been married for ten years? She'd gone to an out-of-town conference for managers in the hospitality industry and he'd been playing with his band at the North Coast hotel where she was staying. Without planning to, they had consummated their relationship over that weekend and Xavier became such a fixture in her life that she became careless.

The issues connected to the night Yolanda fell ill remained a constant refrain in Justine's brain—fear that she would lose her only child, that God was punishing her for the sin of her addiction to Xavier McKellop, that her life would be over if Yolanda died.

Time should have healed her fears, but new ones replaced them—fear that God would take Emile from her; fear that one day her sin would be exposed; fear that Xavier would discover the child she neglected to tell him he had fathered.

She'd gone two out of three and hadn't fared all that badly. She now needed to lick the constant worry that Emile was only on loan to her. The Bible had much to say about children of adultery and every time her obsession led her to those specific passages, she fell into depression.

She sighed, twisting hair around her fingers. Maybe she was being melodramatic and needed to give her brain a rest. Only God knew how she hadn't suffered a mental breakdown. Dionne and Kyra had always been firmly in her corner and even when she didn't want to go on, or didn't think she could, they made sure she didn't give up. God bless them.

Xavier's words came back to her. *Our divorce will be final in two weeks.* If he'd pricked her after he said that, he wouldn't have found an ounce of blood running in her veins. She'd been frozen in place, except for her mind that refused to process what his words implied. He hadn't said anything further, and she had no right to think beyond what he said. Still, she wondered what reason he had to keep quiet about it for so long.

A sound came from the doorway, and Justine raised her head. Yolanda stood there, watching her. Justine waved her in. "Need something?"

Yolanda nodded and climbed on the end of the bed to sit on her heels, facing her mother. "You sure you're all right?"

Justine nodded. "I'm a bit tired, but I'll survive."

"What did Mr. McKay want?"

"To talk about spending time with Emile."

Playing with the laces on her sweat bottom, Yolanda looked sideways at Justine. "You sure that's all he wanted?"

Not wanting to give Yolanda any cause for alarm, Justine was casual with her response. "Uh-huh."

Yolanda changed position, pulling her knees to her chest and hugging them. "I wanted to ask you something about yesterday."

"Go on."

"Does Kelleigh know about Emile?"

Justine struggled not to fidget. "I don't think so."

Frowning slightly, Yolanda ran her fingers across her forehead. Justine wanted to hug her, but didn't move. It wasn't the right thing to do now. "It bothers you?"

Yolanda nodded and stretched her legs. "She's kinda cool, you know?"

Curious, Justine nodded. "So the two of you knew each other before yesterday?"

"Yeah, sometimes we hang out with the same people. She's a friend of one of Tariq's friends."

"Not a boyfriend?"

"Kinda."

"Does her dad know?"

"That's none of our business and I don't want you telling him." Yolanda brought her voice back down to a near-normal level. "If he finds out, she'll know I had something to do with it."

"You know I wouldn't do that."

"Sorry. Sometimes, when I think about my friends' parents and how they behave, I forget that you're actually kinda cool." She loosed her hair and retied it with the scrunchy, never taking her eyes off Justine. "D'you know if he's planning to tell her?"

Justine thought for a moment, unsure what Xavier planned to do. "I suspect he might, but I don't know how or when. That's the kind of man Xave-Mr. McKellop is. He likes things straightforward."

Yolanda folded her legs Indian style, making herself more comfortable. "I know I said the other day I wasn't happy about the whole thing but..." She wriggled her toes and smiled at Justine, which reminded her of when Yolanda was much younger. "You sure you guys aren't interested in getting back together?"

"We haven't talked about it." Justine let a few beats pass before she continued, "I said nothing would change in our family, but out of curiosity, would you have a problem with it?"

She shrugged. "I'm sorta getting used to the idea that Emile...you know. I dunno. It's still gonna feel weird, I guess."

"Both of us are mature adults, so we wouldn't rush into anything, and I did say we haven't discussed anything like that."

She met Yolanda's gaze squarely, letting her know she was serious. "I have you and Emile to think about, and you both come first. Understand?"

Yolanda scratched her scalp, grumbling. "Emile would be thrilled."

Justine edged forward to stroke Yolanda's hair. "I wouldn't do anything to make you unhappy."

"I know that, Mom."

Justine chucked her under the chin. "Even when you behave as if I hate you?"

Smiling, Yolanda spoke. "Yeah, even then, I know you love me."

"Come here, you," Justine said, holding her arms open.

Kneeling on the bed, Yolanda hugged her, and Justine hung on, grateful that although her misdeeds were exposed she still had her daughter's love. Xavier was right, she was too concerned about losing face.

Yolanda pulled back, sat on her heels, and stared at Justine, as though trying to make a decision.

"There's something I need to tell you."

"This sounds serious. Well?"

Yolanda clasped her hands together, before saying in a rush, "Uh, Mom, I do have a boyfriend and I want you to meet him."

Justine lowered her lids, sorting through her thoughts. "You're only fourteen, Landy. Why d'you—"

"I should have known you wouldn't understand," Yolanda said, shaking her head.

"All I'm saying is that—"

"Never mind. I don't know why I even told you anything." She stumbled backward off the bed. "All you care about is yourself."

"You know that's not true!"

Justine rose to follow her, but caught her foot in the rumpled sheet. She stumbled, righted herself and reached for Yolanda, who stood glowering in the doorway.

"Please, Landy. Let's talk about this."

"I don't see how it's gonna help. Just forget I said anything. I can't trust you anyway. Don't think I don't know you got the police to harass that boy after I asked you not to."

"Honey, I had to. Would you want to know he tried that with another girl and really hurt her?"

"The fact is, you broke your word."

"I didn't promise I wouldn't say anything. You're my first concern and I'll do anything to protect you, even if you don't understand my motives."

Yolanda stabbed Justine with a vicious glare. "I might have been your first concern in the past, but not anymore."

"Don't go there, Yolanda." Hands open, Justine pleaded with her. "You know that not true. Honey, let's—"

She reached for Yolanda, who slammed the door, uncaring or unaware that she almost mashed Justine's fingers.

Justine fell against the door, letting it support her weight. How was it possible to go from being allies to enemies in a few seconds?

She slid to the floor, arms folded on top of her knees. Eyes closed, she recalled Xavier's accusation, admitting he was right. Not only was she a coward; she was selfish and clueless about how to keep the people around her happy.

– 29 –

Xavier

Proverb: Young bud (bird) nuh know storm.
Meaning: The young consider themselves smart, but experience teaches wisdom.

God, how he wanted Justine.

Her closeness, while they stood by her car, was almost his undoing and her tears made him hurt as much as she did. Maybe worse. He hated seeing her unhappy, but what could he do? Until she let go of her guilt, nobody could help her. After so many years, she still clung to the past, punishing herself for things she couldn't change. He felt terrible about beating her over the head with his accusations, only to come full circle. Back to ground zero.

Was he willing to risk being hurt again? As far as he could tell, she had no ties to any other man and only seemed devoted to ensuring that her children were happy. Annette could take lessons from her.

He moved to the back verandah, staring into the garden while wondering how he'd tell Kelleigh about Emile. As tough as she acted, she was delicate, like the hummingbirds he watched each morning hovering over the peach blooms on the trumpet vine. Teens were resilient, but he also worried about what Annette would say when she found out. The last thing he needed was to have Kelleigh's thoughts poisoned.

She walked up behind him, neat in her school uniform, knapsack on her back. She'd turned up at the studio yesterday evening, distraught over an argument with her mother, who had refused to give permission for her to go on a day trip to Runaway Bay. She'd slammed into his office and flung herself on the chair across from his desk. "Daddy, you need to talk to Mom. Please."

She only called him that when she wanted something badly.

He dropped his pen and sat back. "What's wrong now?"

She threw both hands in the air and let them fall. "My class teacher has been planning this trip for months and Mom refuses to sign the permission slip."

"Did you two have another argument?"

She sighed and flicked her tie over her shoulder. "Yeah, I need some things and she won't get them for me."

"Like what?"

"Casual clothes." She smiled at him. "I'm a growing girl."

He wasn't fooled. "Is that all?"

She sighed. "She said if I didn't get my grades up in POB, she wouldn't let me go anywhere and she'd stop me from coming to your house."

"I'm sure she didn't say that last part, and what's POB?"

Kelleigh rolled her eyes. "Daddy, you're really a dinosaur. Principles of Business. And I did get my grades up. So, can I go?"

"I have to talk to your mother first. You know that."

He'd called Annette, only to realize that mother and daughter were engaged in a power struggle that had more to do with him than anything else. Annette preferred to have him come to see Kelleigh than to have her stay with him. Kelleigh wanted the opposite.

Custody of Kelleigh hadn't been an issue. It was understood that since he had moved out, Kelleigh would continue living with her, but that Kelleigh could stay with him whenever it was convenient.

Of course, Kelleigh coming to see him outraged Annette, but he reminded her that as his child, it was Kelleigh's right. Feeling ridiculous, he'd asked permission for her to overnight. Annette wasn't happy, but since he met her silly requirement, she had nothing to complain about.

After he hung up, he reminded Kelleigh that it was out-of-order to leave home with clothes to overnight—without permission—because of a disagreement with her mother. When he told her she couldn't always run away from her problems, she looked at him as if she had a question, but wasn't sure how to ask. She hadn't come up with her question since.

He bumped Kelleigh's shoulder and handed her the key to the truck. After securing the house, he slipped into the vehicle, where Kelleigh waited. "Sure you're not leaving anything?" he asked.

She slid him a glance that told him she was unsure of herself. "Just my pajamas, jeans and tee-shirt."

Leaving her things hinted that she wanted to spend more time with him. He didn't have a problem with that, but hoped she understood that discipline in his home would be a given.

"There's something I need to discuss with you," he said.

The suspicion in her eyes made him chuckle. "No, Kell, you didn't do anything this time."

She gripped the knapsack tight in her lap. "So what is it?"

"Like I said, nothing to worry about."

"Daddy." She drew the word out. "You can't back off after winding me up like this."

He pulled up at a stoplight and turned his head, smiling. "You're right. I shouldn't have mentioned it when I can't talk about the matter now."

"Matter?" She stared at him. "This sounds serious. You're sure I didn't do something?"

"Which begs the question, did you do something I should be concerned about?"

She slapped his arm. "'Course not. If I did, Mom would be in a total hurry to inform on me. Come on, Daddy. Tell me before I burst!"

He sighed. "I should have known better than to mention it."

She looked at her watch. "Yeah, but you have all of twenty minutes before the first bell rings."

"We're gonna need time to talk about this," he said, rubbing a thumb across his chin. "Tell you what. I'll tell your mother I'm picking you up after school and we'll go somewhere and talk, okay?"

She rolled her eyes and let out a dramatic sigh. "Fine, but you have to know I'm gonna be worried over this all day."

"Sorry, Baby girl. I shouldn't have said anything, but it's really nothing for you to worry about."

She folded her arms and peered at him. "You sure?"

He pulled off the street and into the school's driveway, mindful of the students in blue and white, heading in the same direction as the truck. Curbside, he allowed the engine to throttle. "I'm positive, Baby Girl. We'll talk this evening."

"Okay. Later then, Daddy."

"Later, honey." He kissed her cheek. "Love you."

"Love you too," she murmured as they hugged.

He watched her go, a half smile pulling at his lips. It wasn't too long ago that she smelled of baby powder. Now, she wore something flowery which reminded him that soon she would be a woman.

***

Though he told himself he wasn't nervous over the conversation to come, Xavier couldn't ignore the tension in his muscles. He wound his head in a circular motion, rolled his shoulders and left the bedroom, where he'd gone to change into a tee-shirt and sweat-pants.

Kelleigh waited for him in the living room, still wearing her uniform, minus the navy tie. When he entered the room, she swallowed fruit juice from a bottle and looked away from the television. "I thought you said you wouldn't be long."

"I've only been gone five minutes." He smiled. "I wonder where you come by all that impatience."

They smiled because it was a standing family joke that while he had the patience of Job, Annette couldn't bear to be kept waiting for anything.

Using the remote, she turned the television down. As she set the bottle on the center table, he sat beside her, unsure where to begin.

She tugged at her ponytail and met his gaze. "So, you gonna tell me what you couldn't tell me this morning, some time before I die of curiosity?"

He couldn't help smiling at her cheekiness. With the back of his hand, he touched her chin. "You're way too feisty, you know that?"

She did the eye-rolling thing. "Daaaad!"

"Okay, don't get uptight." He sighed, looking straight at her. "There will never be a good time to tell you this, but I don't want you to hear it from anyone else."

She nodded encouragement as though she could pull the words from him faster.

"The long and short of it is that you have a brother."

"A brother?" she squeaked, and her mouth fell open.

It wasn't a good time to smile, but he almost did because for the first time in ages Kelleigh was speechless.

"You mean like family?" she asked.

"Yeah. What other kind of brother would I mean?"

She drew her knapsack into her lap and pressed it to her chest. "Where this brother come from all of a sudden?"

"Some time ago, I had a relationship with someone else."

While she stared at the bag, Kelleigh swiped her bottom lip with her tongue. She tipped her head up after a moment. "What does this mean, Daddy?"

He shrugged. "I found out recently and didn't want you to hear it from anybody else, so I decided to tell you as soon as possible."

He couldn't read her expression and held himself stiffly, expecting something, but unsure of what that was. He hoped she didn't throw a tantrum because he wouldn't know how to cope, although she was probably entitled.

"Does Mom know?" she asked.

He shook his head. "No. I haven't told her."

She stared at him, eyes narrowed. "You plan to?"

"Yes."

"Why?"

"I owe it to her."

"I don't think you owe her anything." Mouth pulled into a pucker, she added, "She's only going to create a whole lot of drama over it."

"I'm doing it because of who I am." He touched her shoulder, and was gratified when she didn't pull away. "Fact is, it happened while I was married to her."

"Well, I don't think it's any of her business."

Staring at her, he said. "You know, sometimes you amaze me."

"What d'you mean?"

"I expected to get some drama from you, but you're dealing with it differently."

Her smile wasn't the usual unrestrained variety, but at least she wasn't shouting at him.

"Look at it this way, I can't do anything to change the fact that I have a brother, but don't think you're gonna get away without giving me all the juicy details."

He looked sideways at her, unsure she'd just said what he heard.

Seconds later, she laughed. "Okay, maybe I got a teensy bit carried away. I know I won't get *all* the details, but you know what I mean."

She bit the side of her lip and met his eyes, looking like a ten year old. "Will this change things between us, Daddy?"

For all her bravado, she was insecure. He cupped her cheek and reminded her of their private joke. "Of course not, you're still my favorite daughter."

"You sure you don't have another one out there somewhere?"

The uncertainty in her voice pained him, clogging his throat. "No, honey, you're still my only daughter."

Flinging the bag in the corner of the sofa, she turned to face him. "Am I gonna get to meet him?"

A few seconds passed before he caught up with the change in direction. Would he ever be able to keep up with this child?

"Can we cross that bridge later, Baby Girl?"

The pet name brought a smile to her face.

"You didn't expect me to ask?"

He put up both hands in surrender, left without words for the moment.

Her brows contracted and she squinted at the curtains as though trying to remember something. After a moment, she shook her head and focused on him, eyes alight with curiosity. "I want to meet him. Is he older or younger than I am? Boy, oh boy, Mom's gonna have a fit, but you know that already."

Eyes closed, Xavier felt relief spread through him. He didn't fool himself into thinking things were okay, knowing he had a fair amount of ground to cover with Kelleigh. He'd do the sensible thing and answer some of her questions now, to ease her curiosity and her mind. Annette would demand more from him and take careful handling. Almost divorced or not, she'd give him a hard time and then some.

$-$ 22 $-$

Thursday, March 31, 5:30 PM

Xavier

Proverb: Too much explanation bring exposure.
Meaning: In conversation, giving too much information can leave you vulnerable.

From the sofa, Annette gave Xavier a dirty look. "I should have known you'd get here quickly since she put you up to it."

Be patient, Xavier told himself. He settled on the opposite settee, hands clasped between his knees. "Come on Annette, you know I've always been fair to both of you."

She snorted. "Just a little more fair to Kelleigh all the time."

He decided not to pursue that argument. He couldn't win. "So what's this about you not sending her on that class trip?"

"It's a country outing, which is why I'm not willing to send her."

"But won't they be chaperoned?"

"Yes, but considering how wild she's gotten lately, I don't think—"

"She said you told her that making the trip depended on getting better grades."

Annettte messed with her hair and avoided looking at him. Her attention settled on the television droning in the corner. "I did say that, but—"

"You can't do that, Annette. If you tell her that going on the trip depends on her grades, then that's what you have to work with, but you can't say one thing and mean another."

She swung her legs to the floor and folded her arms. "I don't need you to tell me how to raise my daughter."

He was tempted to smile, but knew it would make her mad, so he cracked his knuckles and tried to come up with a suitable response. He couldn't think of anything that wouldn't make her angry, so he said what he was thinking. "Are you hearing yourself? She's going to hate you if you keep playing these games."

"And you're content to help her along."

"You know that's not true."

"That's how I see it."

Xavier sat back and ran both hands over his face. He was more tired than he realized. He held in a yawn, then spoke in what he hoped was a nonthreatening tone. "I'm asking you to rethink your decision. She really wants to go."

"Fine, but I hope you take responsibility when she gets pregnant."

"I won't ask how you got to pregnancy. If there are responsible adults with the group, there's so much and no more that can happen."

"It's clear you don't remember the things you did as a teenager." She pointed at him. "Speaking of which, you need to plan your schedule better if you're going to have Kelleigh over at your place."

"What happened?"

"She came back on Monday night, and said she waited until six-thirty, but you didn't show up."

He blinked, but said nothing. His daughter was crafty, but not as slick as she thought. Didn't it even cross Annette's mind that Kelleigh had spent the weekend with him and that he'd dropped her off on Sunday night?

"We probably got our wires crossed," he said. "Anyway, leave things to me. I'll make sure she behaves on this trip. You okay with that?"

Annette nodded, still unconvinced, if her narrow-eyed stare was anything to go by. It would have served Kelleigh right if she had said no. He rose from the couch. "Gimme a minute, I need to speak with Kell."

Annette picked up the book she had cast aside when he arrived. "Just remember if anything happens, this trip is your doing."

He stopped on his way out of the room. "D'you have any specific reason for thinking something might go wrong?"

"Not really. It's just her general attitude that worries me."

He stared at Annette, wondering for the thousandth time what he'd ever seen in her. Yes, she was still good-looking, beautiful, in fact, but her self-absorption drove him nuts. God forbid that Kelleigh grew up to be the same kind of woman as her mother. She'd drive some poor man mad.

He rapped on Kelleigh's door and entered when she yelled a welcome. In the center of the room he stopped; a quick study confirmed that she was still trying to keep her space tidy. She had books stacked on both sides of her desk and a folded pile of clothes on the bucket seat in the corner. Her dresser could have used some organization, but it was unrealistic to expect perfection.

She watched him from the bed, and he waited until she started fidgeting before he spoke. "Kell, you and I need to talk."

Her brows came close to meeting while she chewed a pencil.

He strolled around the room and stopped at the window, where he made out yellow hibiscus blooms in the fading rays of the sun. When he turned to face Kelleigh, her gaze danced away and settled on the desk. He sat beside her on the bed, leaning outward so he could see her properly.

"This time, about responsibility and trust."

She continued frowning while she fiddled with the pencil, waiting for whatever he planned to say.

"I'm talking about your Monday evening trick."

She went goggle-eyed and sat up straight to stare at him.

"Where did you go?"

She ran her fingers over the hem of her tee-shirt and wouldn't raise her head. When he was almost out of patience, she sighed and spoke to her knees. "I was over at Tasheka's house."

"Who?"

"A schoolmate."

"And what was so important that you had to lie about it so you could go?"

"It was just a group of us from my class. We had cake and ice cream after school." She spread her hands wide and her words turned plaintive. "It was her birthday, but if I told Mom, she wouldn't let me go. She never lets me go anywhere."

"She allows you to come visit me."

"You forget you had to fight her over that at first? Mom is difficult just because."

He took his turn sighing. "Be that as it may, you need to be honest. You can't lie to your parents and expect us to trust you. What you did shows you can't be trusted."

"Daddy!"

"Don't 'Daddy' me. What if something happened to you on the way home? And by the way, who took you back here?"

"Myron's mother," she said in a huff.

He massaged the frown lines on his forehead, disgusted with himself because he had no clue who her friends were. He really needed to spend more time with her. "And who is Myron?"

"He's in my class."

"You sure you're not lying to me?"

Her gaze jumped to his. "You see, because of how she treats me, I'm forced to lie and then this happens."

He slipped an arm around her shoulder. "Baby Girl, nobody forced you to lie."

"Well, I would have told the truth if I thought she'd let me go."

"Your mother has to feel she can trust you before she'll let you do certain things. Remember, you started acting up and she had to get me involved."

"No matter what I do, I can't win." She shook her head, ponytail swishing back and forth. "You gonna punish me?"

"Not this time. Just don't do anything like that again. You're straining my trust to the limit."

She nodded, but continued to worry the tail of her shirt. With the back of his hand, he lifted her chin. "You sure you don't have anything you want to tell me?"

"Like what?"

He shrugged. "I dunno. Some deep, dark secret you can share now that I'm in a not-so-bad mood."

Her giggle was overdone, but he ignored it as she poked him in the side and drew closer. "Everything's fine."

"Since you say so, I'll let things be." He hugged her, pressing a kiss to her forehead. "And remember, no more lying, okay?"

She nodded. "I promise."

"Good."

He left her and strolled to the living room where Annette was reading. He dropped into the sofa where he'd sat before. "I've spoken to her. Now there's something I have to tell you."

She lowered the novel and raised one eyebrow.

He saw no need to waffle and so went straight to the point. "I have a son."

She remained silent, then frowned. "Why you feel you had to tell me this?"

"I'm going to introduce Kelleigh to him sometime, so I thought you should know."

"How old is this boy?"

"Six."

She slapped the book shut. "So on top of cheating on me, you got a child?"

While Annette thought, he remained silent. Nothing he said would help his case or be acceptable.

She flipped the book to and fro, peeling back the pages with a snapping sound. She'd tear it if she used any more force. Eventually, she flung it aside.

"I bet you're with the slut who gave you that child."

"Annette, don't."

"Only a whore would sleep with someone's husband."

"I didn't tell you so you could throw insults."

"So why did you tell me? I didn't need to know that." She got up and walked around the sofa. "I hope your daughter won't feel cheated when you tell her what you've been doing."

"Kelleigh's young. She'll work through it and get over it."

"And how would you know?" She stopped in front of him, peering into his face. "You told her already, didn't you?"

He didn't have the chance to nod. She slapped him in the face, jerking his head sideways and sending pain lancing through his neck. By the time he blinked, she rammed him in the forehead with her fist.

For a moment, he couldn't see a thing. The woman packed a stiff wallop. He missed half her rant because of the ringing in his ear. When he could hear again, he absorbed the bitterness spewing from her lips. Then he got angry and stood, despite the throbbing above his eyes. She stepped back, but continued to hurl insults at Justine and him.

Kelleigh stepped into his line of sight, but by then the abuse became steam trapped under his skin, pushing him to the point of explosion.

"Just shut up!" The harshness of his tone shocked him and he lowered his voice. "You don't give a shit about anybody but yourself. Why should it surprise you that I'd tell Kelleigh first?"

Annette stared at him, an older but immature version of her daughter. Her fists came up and she hit him in the chest several times before she crumpled on the sofa, sobbing.

– 23 –

Justine

Proverb: A nuh so parson get him gown.
Meaning: Success doesn't come through wishing and hoping, but by hard work.

The muted light in the room, and the sensation of Xavier's skin kissing hers, heightened Justine's excitement. She closed her eyes and buried her lips in his shoulder to soften her cries. His passion matched hers; she threw her head back and...

"I'm glad you agreed to meet me to finish our discussion."

Xavier's voice dragged her from her fantasy, forcing Justine to squirm and dust her lap while she composed herself. "You didn't give me much of a choice," she said. "Those movie tickets for Yolanda and Emile guaranteed I couldn't say no. Especially since you told him first."

He ignored the accusation and let his gaze linger on her hair, lips and the valley between her breasts where the pearl pendant rested.

The murmur of voices around them increased as the bar filled with customers. They sat in a corner, where they had a view of the drafty room filled with heavy furniture. It could certainly do with a makeover to lighten the atmosphere, Justine thought.

Xavier picked up his ham and cheese sandwich and took a bite. After he swallowed, he met her eyes, a smile on his lips. "Well, I did want to distract them."

Afraid of his answer, she asked, "Why?"

Wishing she could stop herself, Justine glanced at her watch. Too much time remained until she was scheduled to pick up her children, and danger lurked at the table with this man who was once the center of her world.

"There are things we still need to talk about. Things I need to understand."

She lifted her shoulders, wishing he'd leave things as they stood. "I'm not sure what you mean."

"I think you do."

She used her fork to poke a French fry she had no intention of eating. "Why rehash all of this, Xavier. What's the point?"

"Ever hear about closure?" He drilled her with his eyes. "You didn't provide any."

"I still don't get the point."

"I need it before I can move on."

Her stomach convulsed as though she might vomit. She didn't want to hear what he was going to say next. To protect herself, she stepped in first. "I would have thought you moved on long ago."

"*You* might have moved on, but it's hard to close the door on something I don't understand. Seeing you again gave me the chance to settle our unfinished business."

Something invisible squeezed Justine's neck and it took all her strength to get her words out in the right sequence. "We don't have any unfinished business. We both went on with our lives and you did well, based on what I see."

He stabbed at a bunch of fries, which made her wince. He laid down the fork, his movements restrained. "What about the stuff you can't see, Justine?"

Staring at the skin below his open collar, Justine decided she'd rather think about what she could see. In seconds, she changed her mind. She was becoming obsessed with the thought of getting back in bed with Xavier. Not good. She sighed, unwilling to go where he was leading. "You know, you haven't said exactly what you want from me. I don't think you've even decided."

His hand slid over hers and clasped her wrist. A pulse beat in her throat and she made a fist. If he touched the inside of her wrist, he'd feel the blood surging through her veins.

"That's what you think. I know exactly what I want from you."

His thumb wound over the back of her hand, warming her skin. Did he know what he was doing to her? His intense gaze did not hint at triumph, but was more questioning, as though seeking knowledge.

He turned her hand over, stroking the inside of her wrist, setting her nerves on edge and shooting heat to her armpit. A fire spread in her chest, along with panic. She had to unscramble her thoughts, otherwise she'd say yes to whatever he had on his mind. After being strong for so long, she couldn't let down her guard. Did he expect her to believe all was forgiven? And how could she be sure he wasn't playing with her?

He'd never been a man given to playing games, but now he was making her wait to see what he wanted or needed from her. He could think again if he believed she'd get careless because he was laying on the charm.

She glanced around the room, searching, and longing to pull her hand from his. At the same time, she didn't want to be separated from him.

All the stools at the high, wooden bar were taken. The slow, jazzy music had grown louder, so had the conversations around them. The evening crowd was in high gear.

Xavier tightened his grip, forcing her to look at him. Frightened, she met his eyes. "What you're doing is dangerous," she whispered. "Maybe you should just lay your cards on the table."

"I want you."

Blood thrummed though her head. She stared at him, speechless. When she got her brain and her lips to cooperate, she asked, "Just like that?"

"You know as well as I do what's happening between us."

She shook her head. "Doesn't mean we have to do anything about it. We're sensible adults."

He released her hand. "That's the problem with you. You don't do anything on impulse. Always the sensible thing."

"Are you suggesting I forget everything and jump into bed with you?"

Despite the annoyance darkening his eyes, he smiled. "Nothing like that. I'd prefer that you know what you're doing *before* you jump into bed with me."

She licked her lips. It was the wrong thing to do. Their gazes locked. Her breath wafted through her open lips. He was going to kiss her. Then someone laughed, and she remembered where they were. She cleared her throat, pressed the handbag on her lap and avoided his eyes. They must have looked like two lovesick teens, staring at each other like that. Dionne and Kyra would have a field day with it if she told them. She blinked, drew a deep breath, and good sense reasserted itself. "Are you saying you've forgiven me for what I did to you?"

He didn't answer.

Satisfied, she smirked. "I thought so."

Two vertical lines appeared between his eyebrows. "What d'you mean by that?"

"You might think you want to continue from where we left off, but there are things to consider."

"Sure. I'd like to hear you name them."

"First of all, how can you be in a relationship with someone you hate?"

He smiled again, that lifting of the lips that wasn't exactly amusement. "I don't hate you."

She didn't question why her heart was leaping about in her chest. "Well, sometimes, you certainly look at me as if you do."

For a moment, he looked uncomfortable. "It's a matter of self-preservation."

A sense of loss pressed down on her, forcing tears into her eyes. She didn't want to think about what he must have seen as the ultimate betrayal. Turning her head, she followed the movement of one of the waiters.

Her thoughts shifted and blood raced through her veins, pounding to a joyous tune. *He didn't hate her.*

When she realized he was studying her, she crashed to Earth. No matter what he said, they had some major hurdles to cross. She didn't trust him, or more to the point, wasn't sure he could see what she had done objectively. Until she was sure where she stood, she wasn't going to put her heart at risk.

Her gaze settled on the plate of uneaten Fish and Chips. Even if she wanted to start over with Xavier, hadn't she promised Yolanda that nothing was going to change?

***

After hugging Xavier around the waist, Emile bounced to the car and got in the back seat. Xavier climbed into his truck and waited for them to drive out of the parking lot. He had followed Justine to the theatre because he promised Emile he'd be there when the movie ended. At the end of the street, Xavier indicated he was turning left. He tooted the horn and waved.

Through the half-open window, Emile called, "Bye, Daddy!"

His yell was enough to stun Justine.

"Jeez," Yolanda said. "You think you could shout any louder?"

"So how was the movie?" Justine asked.

Glaring over her shoulder, Yolanda said, "It was okay, when the radio that's now sitting behind us wasn't going nonstop."

Emile poked his shoulder between the seats and spoke into Justine's ear. "She just annoyed 'cause she did want to forget about me and chat with her friends."

Justine stilled Emile with a disapproving look and then slid Yolanda a glance that said she needed information.

"It was only a bunch of us from school."

"Are you're sure that's who it was?"

"Yes, Mom, it was just me and my girlfriends."

"How come they found out so fast you'd be there?"

"Some of my friends do actually get to go out you know, and you're forgetting that you told me last night." Yolanda shook her head. "I called Kim when I found out, okay?"

"Sorry, babes, I forgot."

Yolanda wedged herself sideways with her shoulder pressing into the seat. "Where did you and Mr. McKay go and what did you talk about anyway?"

Though she hesitated, Justine didn't see the harm in answering. An open conversation would help their ceasefire along. After a discussion early that morning on parental responsibility, she'd gotten Yolanda to understand why she'd pursued the near-rape incident with the police. The boy hadn't been picked up, but working through Yolanda's network of friends, an officer had contacted him and warned him about his risky behavior.

While she picked her words, Justine kept her attention on the road. "We went to Tony's and we talked about Emile."

It's only a half lie, she told herself. Leaning sideways, she prodded Emile with her shoulder. "And how often do I have to tell you to stop squeezing yourself between the seats? Sit back and put on the seatbelt."

He muttered, but did as she told him. "So what did you say about me?"

"None of your business," Justine said without missing a beat.

"But Mommeeee!"

"Our conversation was private and that's final."

They drove is silence for a few minutes and Emile waited until she got the green at the stoplight before bombarding her again. "Mommy, I have a question."

"Go ahead, hon."

"I still don't understand why I have a different Daddy from Landy."

Justine shot Yolanda an accusing glance while she worked out what to say. Nothing came to mind, so she asked a question of her own. "Why d'you keep asking the same things?'

"'Cause I don't understand, and you told me not to be afraid to ask questions."

"Not the same ones all the time."

"Okay, I have another one then."

"Ask it," she said, meeting his eyes in the mirror.

"When I asked Mr. McKay—my dad if he really wasn't Landy's daddy, he said no, but he told me he was a daddy already. His daughter is almost the same age as Landy. He said I might have seen her at the studio. Her name is Kelleigh."

Justine exchanged a glance with Yolanda, who had her head against the seat, listening to Emile.

"I guess I have another sister, huh?" He leaned as far forward as the seatbelt allowed, and grabbed Justine's seat. "When am I gonna meet her?"

Justine disguised her gasp with a cough. Though she had been adamant about not wanting to wreck Xavier's home life, she hadn't thought about how Xavier and Emile's meeting would affect Kelleigh. Knowing Xavier, he would want the two kids to know each other. She hoped Kelleigh was a lot less difficult to handle than Yolanda. Otherwise, Xavier's life would be hell.

"Hey," Emile shocked Justine's eardrums once more. "Wouldn't it be cool if Daddy came to live with us? Then Landy could have a daddy too."

– 24 –

Saturday, April 9

Xavier

Proverb: Better fi ride a donkey weh carry yuh, dan a horse weh throw yuh.
Meaning: It's wiser to go slow and steady rather than rushing into possible disaster.

His thigh slid between Justine's, igniting the nerve endings in his privates. He suspected the same thing was happening to her, if the quick breaths she took was anything to go by. He murmured in her ear. "This was something we never did. Dinner and dancing."

It wasn't something they'd had the luxury to do as cheaters. She pressed her hands to his chest, putting distance between them. He let her, but continued to inhale the vanilla fragrance rising from her hair. The aroma had intensified as her body heat climbed. Her smell was doing strange and yet familiar things to his body.

Justine was a peculiar woman, with ideas he couldn't fathom, however hard he tried. At dinner, she picked at the Curried Shrimp, and barely ate anything. Maybe she was nervous or perhaps, she was still on her guilt trip, thinking she shouldn't be with him. Her sleeveless black dress was modest. Only a hint of cleavage showed and her jewelry consisted of a pearl choker and matching earrings. The three faux pearl buttons above her waist distracted him all evening. It took little effort to remember her full, rounded breasts and their sensitivity to his slightest touch.

He'd avoided staring directly at her in an attempt not to frighten her. She startled easily, as though she expected him to attack her—not physically, but with words. He'd given up trying to put her at ease when she'd almost knocked over the glass because he touched her wrist. They both knew the magnetism was still there between them; he just needed to convince her to give it a chance. Her questions during their last date exasperated him, but he needed patience to win her confidence.

His thighs continued to brush hers, taking him back seven years, a dangerous place to be, but he couldn't help himself. He brushed her earlobe with his lips. A moan escaped her throat and lodged in his ear, bringing back the memory of the insatiable desire and madness that marked their relationship. He kissed her ear again. This time she stopped and stared up at him.

Under the dim lights, couples swirled around them, propelled by the slow rhythm of an eighties love song. Xavier was barely aware of anything but Justine. The tip of her tongue emerged to wet her lip. He followed the movement with his eyes, bending toward her.

Briefly, the music stopped.

He grabbed her wrist and wound through the crush of bodies to the cool of the verandah surrounding the building. There, he hugged her. "Woman, what are you doing to me?"

"I could ask you the same thing," she said, close to his neck.

In the muted glow from the wall lamps, he smiled. "I don't think either of us knows what the heck we're doing."

"That dangerous," she said.

He stepped back and leaned against the wooden railing, facing her. "True."

He took her hand and pulled her between his thighs, kissing her eyelids and murmuring to bring comfort and ease the lines of concern between her brows. She opened her eyes. "When did you say your divorce becomes final?"

"Any day now."

Though he'd been talking to her on and off for the past couple of weeks, he'd avoided personal questions, fearing she'd clam up and backpedal on him. He confined himself to conversations about Emile and fielded her shy probing to do with his life and music in the intervening years. Here was an opening he could use. He kissed her, a chaste reflection of the passion building inside him. "You seeing anybody?"

She shook her head. "You?"

"No."

"So what's stopping us?" he asked.

She hid her face, forehead pressed to his shoulder. "We're not the same people."

He lifted her chin to see into her eyes. "Yes and no."

Frowning, she asked. "What does that mean?"

"We've grown and changed, but at heart, I don't think we're that different."

She stepped out of his embrace, hugging herself. "There's no point in lying to our-selves. I can't run into something with you until I know exactly where you stand. You deny hating me, but I know you're lying. You must have wanted to kill me for what I did."

"I'm not gonna deny it, Justine, but I have a much better understanding of why you walked away.

Her raised eyebrows gave away her surprise. "You do?"

He pulled her to him by the arms. "I've been trying to tell you that for a while now. You are who you are, so right this minute, you're holding back, perhaps thinking you don't deserve happiness."

A soft intake of breath and an exhale fell between them.

"Yes, I know that's how you think. I worked that out from what you've told me." He kissed her forehead. "I don't mind taking things slow. See where they go. What about you?"

She swallowed, and her breath huffed out. "I guess that would be okay."

He kissed her, teasing and tasting at the same time. She opened to him, responding to the slow surge of his tongue inside her mouth. His hands wove into her hair, loosening her bun and sending soft strands cascading down her back. The friction of her tongue against his aroused him, but he didn't pull away. He wanted her to know what she had the power to do to him after all this time. She eased closer and he deepened their kiss. She slid her arms around him, whimpering in her throat. At the strong pull of his lower body toward hers, he lightened the kiss and stepped back. This was no place to get carried away.

Gently, he turned Justine so her back was to his chest and continued to hold her, kissing her neck. The vanilla from her hair was a source of comfort.

Her ribs rose and fell in a rapid cadence below his hands. The pulse at her neck beat against his mouth. He wrapped his hands around her waist and kept his mouth to himself. Like him, she needed a chance to take her temperature down a few notches.

"There's one thing we should think about," she murmured, turning sideways to lean into him.

"What's that?"

"Our children. What are we going to tell them?"

"Shouldn't we discuss that when we know where we're going?"

Smiling, he kissed her cheek. "I'm convinced that if you don't have something to worry about, you don't know what to do with yourself."

"You're not exactly right. It's just that I see complications before they arise."

He turned her to face him, and allowed himself the luxury of running his palms over her satiny skin. "I suggest we enjoy this time around. You don't have a husband. Soon, I won't have a wife. Let's relax and rediscover each other. Deal?"

She tugged at the ends of her hair, before nodding. "Deal."

His thumbs stroked her cheek and their gazes caught again. Xavier felt he was sharing much of his thoughts without saying anything to Justine. He read the doubt in her eyes, and sought to convince her that he wouldn't hurt or let her down.

Another couple walked onto the patio and though it was dark, Justine inched away as if she didn't want to be seen with him.

"Something wrong?"

She shook her head, but he sensed she was no longer comfortable. "Time to go," he said, taking her arm.

They didn't speak much on the way to her house, but from time to time he glanced at her, smiling for no particular reason. Justine always had the power to lift his spirit, simply by being close to him. He patted her hands, which lay clasped in her lap. Though she tried to appear calm, her twitching fingers revealed her nervousness.

How long would it take before she got out of the comfortable groove she'd fallen into? He'd have a heck of a time getting Justine to believe that anything good would come of a relationship between them. The one thing he had going for him was Emile's existence. That definitely gave him an in, and even if she was inclined to part ways with him, his connection to Emile would preclude that. *God bless that child.* Despite Justine's resistance, Emile would bring him closer to her.

In her driveway, he let her out of the vehicle, waited while she got the grille open and walked with her to the door. It took her a few seconds to get the door open. Moving slowly, she wrapped both arms around her waist and looked up at him. "Thanks, I enjoyed this evening."

"So did I," he said, letting his gaze stray to the doorway, where a sliver of light came from the living room. The kids in bed yet?"

She shook her head. "Emile's probably still watching television. He said he wanted to wait up for me, but that was just an excuse."

"I won't come in."

She chuckled, pushing hair away from her face. "I appreciate it. It'll only take him longer to settle down to sleep."

He touched her shoulders, unable to keep his hands off her. In her ear, he whispered, "I want to kiss you again."

She tipped her head up, sending hair floating around her shoulders. Using both hands, she did something to her hair that made it into a bun. Then she gripped his shoulders and let her fingers slide down his arms.

His lips moved against hers in a slow caress. She breathed out, fanning his face with warm air. He deepened the kiss, reminding himself of what was promised to him if he could get her to forget her fears. As blood flowed to his groin, Xavier warned himself to let Justine go before his control slipped away. After all, they were standing outside the doorway, where any of her children could push the door open and see them.

She protested in her throat when he tried to pull away. One final stroke of his tongue across hers and he released her. A second later, he pressed his lips to hers again. "Talk to you in the morning."

He went to stand outside the grillework while she put on the padlock and closed it.

"Hug Emile for me," he said over his shoulder on the way to the gate. "And get inside."

She ignored him, watching from the doorway while he drove away. Sure, he wanted her to be safe, but it also felt good to know she cared enough to wait until he left before she locked up for the night. That was Justine, nothing, if not caring, which was more than he could say about Annette. All the years he'd wasted on her should have been spent with Justine.

The night air washed his face in a cool wave, while he thought about the intervening years. He'd given up traveling with the band because Kelleigh needed him, and he hadn't regretted it. Spending more time at home allowed him to do a better job of supervising her, and setting up the studio facilitated his love for teaching.

He realized he had talent in that direction through teaching Kelleigh how to play several instruments. Pity he hadn't had the chance to do the same for Emile earlier. The familiar anger threatened to settle on him, but he pushed it away in favor of staying in the present.

Still, a twinge of disquiet pierced him. He'd be walking a hard road from here, with no guarantee that Justine wouldn't devastate him as she had last time.

– 25 –

Sunday, April 10

Justine

Proverb: Brick pon brick build house.
Meaning: Achieve your goals by taking small steps.

After the heat Xavier stirred in her blood and flesh, Justine expected sleep to elude her, but that wasn't the case. She overslept, and woke to find the sun painting lines across her face. Thank God Miss Pauline was in residence this weekend, otherwise Emile would have dragged her out of bed at dawn to fix breakfast. That woman was a godsend.

Justine rolled out of the reach of the sun's rays and lay studying the ceiling, hands supporting her head. She smiled, remembering the brush of Xavier's lips and the swell of his arousal. She wasn't doing so badly for a forty-three-year-old woman. But Xavier was involved, so why had she expected things to be any different? They'd never been able to get enough of each other. How well she remembered her sense of panic whenever she woke in his arms to discover that she'd overslept when she should have been home.

She'd worried more about Yolanda being deprived of her company than about her husband. By then, Milton had alienated her through absorption with his problems and had sunk into depression in the months before he died.

She tried to shut the door on those memories, but they refused to stay at bay. Already her mind had dredged up a picture of Milton's drawn face, his weight sucked away by cancer cells. By the time she'd overheard him talking about his health with Warren, his blackmailer, he was too far gone for help. Not that there was any time or money left for treatment after that long stint paying out money to Warren.

She grimaced, thinking about what life might have been like if things had turned out differently. She and Kyra still wondered how they came out of that situation minus HIV, considering Warren's bisexual lifestyle. Kyra had kicked him to the curb and moved on with her life.

While Justine and Kyra waited for the results of their HIV/AIDS test they survived days filled with worry and had come through that experience buoyed by desperate prayers and Dionne's insistence that everything would work out fine.

Justine needed to discuss this latest decision with her girls. Dionne wouldn't hesitate to tell her if she was heading in the wrong direction. Kyra would support any move that made Justine happy. Talk about friends for the journey. She had two of the best.

***

Dionne waved her fork around, the wedge of Potato Pudding in danger of landing on the table. "There's nothing like the love of a good man," she said. "You look a lot livelier since the last time I saw you."

"Who said anything about love?" Justine asked.

Dionne gave her one of those looks that told her she was being ridiculous, so Justine kept quiet.

"I don't know who you're trying to fool," Dionne said. "You never stopped loving that man. It's about time you admit it to yourself."

To prevent an unnecessary argument she couldn't win, Justine chewed on the crust of the pudding Kyra had served them. The coconut flakes and potent white rum reminded Justine why she didn't eat most of the goodies Kyra baked. One, she was sure to leave packing more weight than she arrived with and two, she'd be half drunk by the time she got behind the wheel.

They'd agreed to meet at Kyra's because Denton had gone to the garage in the middle of the afternoon to do a rush job for a client. More to the point, Denton and Kyra had no children between them, so their home guaranteed the women's conversations wouldn't be overheard.

Through the sheer curtains, Justine gazed into the backyard. The leaves on the Ackee tree stirred in the wind, the unopened bell-like fruit shrouded in pink and yellow cocoons. Justine poked at the pudding, suddenly shy about sharing her thoughts. Then she made up her mind. If she couldn't share her feelings with her friends of umpteen years, who could she talk to? Before responding, she sipped lemonade. "I'm not saying yea or nay, but I'm afraid he'll do the same thing I did to him."

By glancing at her watch, Justine avoided the incredulous eye rolls she was sure Dionne and Kyra were exchanging.

"You're making me think Music Man is immature and spiteful." Dionne swallowed lemonade from a tumbler before she continued. "You're also telling us you think he's into playing games."

"He said he isn't."

Dionne's eyebrows did an elevator lift. "Oh, so you asked him that?"

Justine stabbed the pudding to avoid answering.

Dionne laughed, a tinkling sound that set Justine's nerves on edge.

"You're like a spoiled little girl starved for attention and craving reassurance. There are no guarantees in life, Justine. Enjoy the moment and plan for the things you can control. The other stuff you just take as they come." She stared at Justine, wearing her tough-as-nails expression. "Just remember, mi not going to pet and powder you if you chase him off for no good reason and then start acting like some lovesick teenager who ca'an make up her mind. You need to grow up."

Nettled, Justine snapped. "I'm just not sure I want to put myself out there at this point in my life, and what d'you mean I need to grow up? That was uncalled for."

"Really?" Dionne pointed at her. "Sometimes you should step back and look at yourself. After the train wreck you caused, you should be glad Music Man is talking to you, much less giving you the time of day."

"We knew he'd find out one day," Kyra added in a gentle tone. After fleeting eye contact with Dionne, Kyra continued speaking. "We stood behind you because that's what friends do. You have a chance to make things right, to be happy. You should make the most of it."

Dionne sighed. "What Kay's trying to say is that you need to get over yourself, stop bleating about the past and get on with your life."

Justine couldn't put a name to the emotion that held her in its grip. In a strangled voice she asked, "What if things don't work out?"

"You move on, of course," Kyra said, "but you'd be a fool to let X-man escape a second time."

Justine couldn't help laughing. "X-man? Are you four or forty plus?"

Kyra returned the grin. "Well, at the rate you're going, he's gonna need some superpower to get past your defenses."

If only Kyra knew. It wouldn't take much effort for Justine's resistance to crumble. She feared that Xavier wouldn't have to look at her twice before she fell into bed with him. That would take their relationship to its former level and beyond.

She had no clue how to approach a situation in which they were free to be together. Not that Xavier was at that point yet because he still had the divorce pending. What would his wife think if she knew there was another woman waiting to take her place? Worse, a woman who had a child with her husband?

Justine doubted she'd be able to put her life back together if she parted from Xavier again. Though unsettled, she pushed her worries aside. As Yolanda told her so often, she needed to listen to her own advice. "Ninety-nine percent of the things we worry about never happen," she murmured.

Now if she could only believe her words.

CHAPTER ONE

–26 –

Tuesday, April 12

Xavier

Proverb: Finger never say 'look here', him say 'look yonder'.
Meaning: People don't usually point out their own faults.

Xavier massaged the space between his eyes, while his breath left him in an audible tide. Annette sat in one sofa and Kelleigh sat in the other. Mother and daughter glared at each other in a silent showdown.

"This is getting old," he said. "Why is it suddenly impossible for the two of you to get along in the same space?"

"She's just totally out of hand, has no manners and wants to do her own thing."

He pinned his daughter with a hard stare. "D'you remember our discussion?"

She pressed her lips together, nodded and folded her arms tighter across her chest.

"So if you understand what I said, why did you do what you did yesterday?"

She sighed and looked down at her legs.

"Well?"

"It was my friend's birthday. We were over at her house eating pizza." She jerked her chin in her mother's direction. "She said I couldn't go."

Another birthday? He turned toward Annette, but she avoided his gaze. "Any particular reason you didn't want her to go?"

"She has a wild bunch of friends and some of them smoke ganja. I just don't—"

"That's not true," Kelleigh said, getting to her feet, her face twisted in outrage. "You said you smelled it when you drove up, but—"

Xavier silenced Kelleigh with a hard look. "That's not how we raised you, okay? You don't jump up and scream at your mother."

"Sorry," she mumbled, and sat poking at the carpet with her big toe.

He hated distressing her like this, but wouldn't excuse her for disrespecting her mother. His gaze skipped to Annette and he didn't have to wonder how mother and daughter had grown apart.

While they'd been bickering in a marriage gone bad, Kelleigh had developed into a young woman who needed to be handled as such. Treating her like a child would yield the same results every time.

Annette leaned forward, nostrils flared, finger stabbing the air. "Apart from that, she has a boyfriend I don't like."

"She doesn't like anybody, least of all, my friends," Kelleigh shot back.

"Is it possible for my ears to catch a break here?" Xavier asked, frowning. "Annette, how did you know where to find her?"

"When she wasn't home by six, I called her phone. That's when she told me where she was."

Kelleigh hunched over the cushion she'd pulled into her lap and continued to pout.

"And what's this about a boyfriend? Didn't I say you were too young for that?"

"You said I was too young for sex. You didn't mention boyfriends."

"Keep being a smartass and I won't let you out of the house until you're so old no man will look at you."

Kelleigh looked at the ceiling, as if to say he was no better than her mother. He stretched his legs and deliberately took on a relaxed pose. He wouldn't get anything out of Kelleigh otherwise.

"So, who is this boy?"

When Kelleigh squished her lips together and looked at him like that, she reminded him too much of Annette. He tilted his head slightly to encourage her to talk to him. She sighed, before speaking through her teeth. "Myron. His name is Myron."

He'd heard the name before. It had to be the last time Annette had complained about Kelleigh's friends.

"And how close are you with this boy?"

"Daddy!"

He sat up. "Look, your mother has concerns. So do I. We wouldn't be asking these questions if we didn't care."

Kelleigh flexed her fingers and turned accusing eyes on her mother. "The problem is, she doesn't realize I'm not twelve anymore, and you're taking her side."

"Kell, I'm trying hard to see things from your angle, but you're not giving me any reason to believe you're mature enough for me to trust you." He included Annette with a glance. "From what your mother tells me, you're up to your usual tricks."

"But—"

He pointed at Kelleigh. "Stop."

"But Daddy—"

"Stop. Right. Now."

He didn't see how it was possible for Kelleigh's lip to jut any further, but it did. She picked at the ripped-by-design portion of her jeans.

"This is the second time in two weeks your mother is complaining about the same thing. That's unacceptable. I think your mother will agree that a month's lockdown should be enough time for you to think about your behavior." He met her eyes, unimpressed by her cold stare. "In that month, you can forget about staying over with me."

Kelleigh attempted to speak, but didn't while tears spilled and ran down her cheeks. She wiped her face on her shirt, sniffed, and continued playing with the torn jeans material.

"D'you understand?" he asked.

"Yes, Dad," she said, emphasizing each word. "I understand perfectly. You're taking that witch's side against me." She stood. "Now I hate you just as much as I hate her."

She rushed out of the living room, sobbing. He expected her to slam her bedroom door, but was surprised when she didn't. Not knowing what to do, he looked at Annette who seemed unperturbed by their daughter's outburst.

"She'll get over it," Annette said with a wave. "She's told me she hates me often enough. I bet she's beginning to believe it."

How could she be so cool after that? Teenagers were prone to melodrama; he saw enough of it with the ones he gave music lessons, but this child was his and her outburst made him uncomfortable. Kelleigh had never told him she hated him, not even when she was hurt and confused by his moving out of the house. She'd hugged him long and hard on the day he left. He'd expected a tantrum, but she'd only embraced him and stood on the verandah, watching him go with tears in her eyes. He'd almost decided to stay, but knew it would be pointless. He and Annette were too far gone in their separate lives to take another crack at their marriage.

He agonized over the pain Kelleigh had to be feeling. She'd convinced herself her parents hated her and that she hated them. He wanted to comfort her, but had to maintain a united front with Annette, although it pained him.

Annette drew her legs up and pushed her hair behind one ear. "So, what d'you plan to do about that boy, Myron?"

Tired of her hands-off attitude, he snapped, "Maybe if you'd take an interest in Kelleigh, I wouldn't have to be around here so often trying to apply some discipline."

"I hope that *bastard* you have isn't making you forget your responsibility to your *legitimate* child."

"And I hope you realize the term *bastard* was taken off the law books on this island in the seventies."

"I couldn't care less. All I want to know is how you plan to help me manage Kelleigh."

"You don't have to worry about that. You're totally clueless where she's concerned anyway."

Annette pulled herself upright. "Don't you dare act sanctimonious with me. I'm all Kelleigh has now that you've moved out. I don't understand how you expect to be a father when you're not around."

"Countless men do it, Annette. You won't be the first or last woman to go through a divorce."

"And I suppose I also won't be the first or last woman to know after the fact that my husband cheated on me."

"Don't start acting as if you even care. It doesn't suit you and I know better."

It occurred to Xavier that they kept rehashing the same argument over their marriage, parental responsibility and now his situation with Justine and Emile. He returned to the argument when Annette's voice climbed to a near shriek.

"You're a fine one to talk. If you gave a shit about Kelleigh or me, you'd be home, where you belong."

He rose from the sofa. "This is stupid and it's leading nowhere. I'll drop by to see Kelleigh in another couple of days."

"Don't bother to inconvenience yourself," She said, staring somewhere over his shoulder. "It's not as if I need you."

On his way to the door, he paused. "I'm not doing it for you. Despite what you think, my daughter needs me and I'm prepared to be a parent to her. I wish you'd take your head out of your ass long enough to realize she also needs her mother."

She flung her ever-present book at him, but it missed and hit the door. With a curl of the lips intended to convey his disgust, he shut the front door between them. Her next words stopped him and it took him several seconds to work out what she'd said. *Just wait, I'm gonna fix you, that bitch and the bastard you got!*

The night air crept over his skin in a cold caress. He drew a deep breath and got into the truck. Annette was good at making threats, but there was so much and no more she could do. Kingston was just big enough that there was hardly a chance she could know Justine or Emile.

The thought that Kelleigh and Yolanda moved in the same circles gave him a twinge of discomfort. He pulled away from the sidewalk, reassuring himself that Annette was so far removed from Kelleigh's activities that he was connecting dots that didn't exist.

– 27 –

Justine

Proverb: Man a plan and God a wipe out.
Meaning: Human beings make plans, but what God ordains will be done.

Justine purred low in her throat as their tongues meshed, swirled and held. Gently, she suckled, not wanting the kiss to end. The shirt fell from her shoulders in a whisper and settled around her elbows. Xavier groaned into her mouth, maneuvering her arms until he removed the silk shirt.

His fingers roamed back and forth over the silky material of her bra. Back arched, Justine pressed into his hands, greedy for his continued teasing. His lips roamed her neck and shoulders, heating her skin wherever they went. His tongue glided into her ear, and she shivered, but the tremors had nothing to do with being cold. Electric shocks tormented the secret places on her body that Xavier had known intimately.

Eager to let her fingers roam once familiar territory, Justine pushed the shirt off Xavier's shoulders. In the dim light, they stumbled to the bed. He fell against her, removing her skirt and panties, exploring her body with hot kisses and fleeting passes with his callused fingertips. While Xavier prepared himself for their lovemaking, Justine reacquainted herself with the ridges and hollows that characterized his body.

She exhaled his name when he sank inside her. Eyes closed, she clung to him, unwilling to stop their frenzied coupling for fear they'd somehow be forced to end this consummation. He matched her recklessness, uttering guttural cries. She pressed her nails into his skin when he held back, as he used to do, for fear of hurting her. Then, in preparation for the inevitable, she wrapped herself around him.

Keening cries came from her throat while she strained against him, and at the summit of her climax, Justine released something between a sob and a yell. Heart racing, Xavier met her frantic rhythm, intensifying her climax as he reached his peak.

Heart hammering, Xavier collapsed next to her, his hands and lips soothing and caressing. She kissed and licked the sweat from his skin, burying her nose in his damp flesh, savoring what had been denied her for the thousands of days she'd been separated from this man who meant the world to her.

This evening's date had come to an unexpected, but satisfactory end.

Breathing through his mouth, Xavier said, "I feel like I've been on a fast."

"Me too," she wheezed, lifting tangled hair from her forehead.

Xavier made himself more comfortable and pulled Justine into his arms. Nuzzling her neck, he whispered, "I've missed you."

Through her tears, she smiled. "Not as much as I've missed you."

With one thumb, he wiped the moisture from her cheeks. "We've wasted so much time," he said.

She sighed against his mouth. "But at least you understand why I did what I did. It was best for both of us."

"Let's agree to disagree," he said, sweeping an arm over her thigh.

Goose bumps licked her skin, as if her body had never forgotten what his touch did to her. He traced the stretch marks on her lower belly, and her hips lifted in response but she didn't want him focused on her imperfection. She gripped his wrist and opened her mouth to object, but Xavier had other plans. Rolling her onto her back, he nudged her lips apart and filled her mouth, stifling her protest.

Their lovemaking was slow, sweet, deliberate, bringing tears to her eyes and delicious heat to her nerve endings. At the height of their passion, she clung to him mindlessly, her limbs fused to his.

After they returned to the confines of the bed, Justine pressed tiny kisses to Xavier's mouth, unmindful of anything but him.

The distant dinging of the clock marked the hour, reminding Justine that she needed to be elsewhere soon. She smiled. "I can't believe I'd let something like this happen at my age."

He pulled her to him, hooking an arm around her neck. "You make it sound like you're dead or I'm a toad."

She rolled her head toward him. "Neither, but I've spent so much time being sensible, it's kind of second nature."

"Well then, it's time to live a little and act on your impulses."

"That's hard to do when you have kids."

Her words were a reminder that she had the luxury of staying with Xavier, if she chose. It was the Easter weekend, and Miss Pauline had gone home for the holidays. Yolanda and Emile were at Dionne's house for a sleepover with her kids. Though Justine had dropped off Yolanda and Emile after a fried fish dinner, Dionne had no doubt stuffed them with spiced bun and cheese sandwiches, washed down with milk. Their children loved that Eastertime snack before bed.

Justine yawned and snuggled against Xavier's chest, wondering if they were okay. Swallowing a smile, she reminded herself that Dionne would call if anything went wrong. Yolanda had no choice but to behave because Dionne was an indulgent, yet firm caretaker.

Xavier's deep intake of breath, and the rasp of his hair against her cheek, jogged Justine from her thoughts.

"Didn't you ever want to tell me?" he asked.

"Tell you what?" she said, to give herself time to think because she knew what he meant.

She glanced around the room, and rose to pick up a tee-shirt resting at the foot of the bed. After she covered herself, she pulled the sheet over their legs and leaned against the headboard.

He'd had the room redecorated; beige drapes hung at the window, complementing the bed sheet's copper, tan and brown highlights. He'd replaced the dresser and chest-of-drawers too. The winged single-cushion sofa was also new and matched the rich colors of the comforter.

Examination complete, Justine ran a hand over Xavier's chest avoiding eye contact. He stroked her leg. "So, you gonna answer me?"

"I couldn't have told you, so what was the point of thinking about it?"

He drew himself up on his elbows, the creases between his eyebrows apparent. "You mean to tell me you never wondered what I'd say or do if you told me about Emile?"

"Okay, so I did think about it a few times."

His steady gaze told her he suspected she was lying.

"All right, a few thousand times."

"So what kept you from doing something about it?"

"I'm sure you've asked me that already in a different way." Justine brushed the tips of her fingers along her hairline, avoiding his eyes. "Why d'you keep doing this?"

"I'm still trying to work through how and why you did what you did. The sensible part of me understands, but deep inside, I'm not satisfied with your explanation."

With her fingers now busy twisting her hair, Justine snapped, "I don't want to talk about this now."

He sat up. "You know, the years haven't changed you much. You still prefer to hide from the things you don't want to face."

"That's unfair!"

"But it's the truth."

"And what did I hide from before?" She asked, angling her head to peer into his face.

"The fact that your marriage was stifling you, the fact that you felt guilty all the time, the fact that you loved me."

She lay still and then sighed. "I suppose."

"After Milton died didn't you feel you could have contacted me?"

Pain wadded in her throat and she could barely squeeze out a response. "I told you, I didn't want to break up your family and it was too late. You would have been angry."

"It would never have been too late for me to know I have a son."

Justine gulped, dislodging the blockage that kept her from speaking. "I know and I'm sorry."

"I accept that, but I can't help wondering if you're sorry you never told me or you're sorry I found out."

She turned her head away to hide the hurt that radiated like a physical ache through her chest. How could he even think that way after making love to her as if he cared? "How can you say that?"

"Let's face it, you would have been quite okay if I hadn't seen Emile." The now familiar lines appeared between his brows again. "What I can't figure out is how come I never saw you before. You bought the guitar there and I adjusted it each time it came back."

She shrugged. "Yolanda came in each trip. That last time though, I figured your saleswoman would probably tear out of there screaming, so I took it into the shop myself."

A smile curved Xavier's lips. "I only brought out the guitar because I wanted to see the picky customer who kept finding fault with it. I should have known it was a teenage girl."

Justine matched his smile and touched his cheek.

"I'm glad I came to look," he said.

"I'm glad you did too," Justine whispered, startled by her words.

He touched her chin, before flipping his legs off the bed and heading for the bathroom.

She wished she was as confident in her nakedness. The first time she'd made love with him, she'd been as concerned, wondering what he thought of her body and if he'd been satisfied. The all-consuming passion between them had put her fears to rest soon after, but now her insecurity returned to plague her. She hadn't gained any weight, but she was seven years more mature.

The bed dipped under Xavier's weight, and his hand crept across her stomach. He pulled her close, lacing their fingers. "Are you gonna promise me you'll try to work through things differently if or when problems crop up between us?"

"I can't change who I am, but I'll try."

"I think you deserve a reward for that," he said, teasing her thighs apart.

"How old are you again?" She said in his ear. "Shouldn't we take things slow? I'm—"

"Come on, Justine, like I said, live a little. I might be worn out tomorrow, but help me make the most of tonight."

"Okay," she whispered as his circled her navel. Tracing a line down his back, she told herself to relax, further persuaded by the ease with which his caresses had her ready for lovemaking again.

Lashes lowered, she longed to enjoy the moment without overthinking everything. But the pessimism that was ingrained in her psyche whispered that she had to cover all her bases because life was seldom straightforward and things never went the way she expected.

– 28 –

Saturday, April 30, 2:55 PM

Xavier

Proverb: Bad family better dan (than) empty pigsty.

Meaning: Family members can be aggravating, but it's better to have them than to be alone.

Xavier stared at his son across the room, but his mind was on his daughter. He'd be lying to himself if he didn't admit how concerned he was about Kelleigh. He'd spoken with her on the phone several times this week and had last seen her on Thursday. Though she had answered his questions about how she was doing, she wasn't the least bit interested in talking to him. She looked and sounded depressed.

He was now sure the decision to stop her from coming over had been too harsh. She had to be bored out of her mind staying home all day on the weekend. He couldn't look to Annette for guidance on what to do because he doubted she'd be objective. Perhaps he should have spoken to Justine. She'd probably know what was up with Kelleigh, since Yolanda had as much rebelliousness going on.

Now, for reasons he didn't understand, his worry had tripled overnight and for the first time since he found out Emile was his, Xavier couldn't wait to end their lesson. Yolanda had finished hers and was doing what intrigued her most, studying the guitars in the showroom out front.

He tapped a pencil against the desk, heard Emile stumble over a few strokes, but was too distracted to correct him. Lorraine, the shop attendant, appeared in the doorway. The deep lines on both sides of her puckered mouth screamed disapproval. "You're not answering the extension."

She'd worked for him more than two years and he'd ignored the fact that she sometimes treated him as if she owned him. Since Justine had started coming to the shop, Lorraine had been giving him attitude, but he ignored her behavior since he'd never given her any indication that he was interested in anything outside of a professional relationship. She hung on to the doorknob. "Your wife is on the line."

If he wasn't so taken up with his thoughts, her words would have irritated him. She'd always referred to Annette by name before this. Something had gotten into her, and that thing was jealousy over Emile and Justine. He hadn't told her about Emile. It wasn't any part of her business, but only a self-absorbed person wouldn't see how much the boy resembled Xavier. He sat up, took his feet off the edge of the desk, and dismissed her with a wave. "Thanks."

He rested the phone between his ear and shoulder, watching Emile, who continued to tap out a rhythm while his tongue worried the corner of his mouth.

"What's up?"

Annette screeched his name and babbled words he didn't understand.

Something intangible swelled in his throat and he gripped the phone tighter. "Annette, slow down. You're not making sense."

Her voice came down marginally. "Kelleigh," she wailed. "She's not in her room."

Xavier rested his forehead in his hand, ignored the pounding in his chest and tried to make sense of Annette's words. "You're saying she's not at home?"

"She was here last night. She ate dinner at six o' clock, then she went to her room."

"And you didn't check on her after that?"

"No." Annette sniffled.

"Did she have breakfast?"

"I...No."

"Did you see her anytime today?"

Now she was crying. "No."

"So you have no idea when she might have disappeared." *And he hadn't bothered to call last night.*

"She's grounded. She's not supposed to go anywhere."

Xavier ignored the retort that came to mind. "Have you called any of her friends?"

"I don't know their numbers," she wailed.

He massaged his forehead where it started to throb. "D'you know where any of them live?"

She moaned his name. "How could she do this? Doesn't she know I'll worry? What if something happens to her?"

Gently, he said, "Come on, Annette. Try to hold it together. I'll pick you up and we'll go to the police. Then we can go check with her friends."

If we can find them, he added silently, unwilling to give way to rising panic.

"Okay, but come quick."

"I will," he said, feeling sorry for her.

How did Annette expect to keep tabs on Kelleigh if she didn't even have telephone numbers for her closest friends? He sucked his bottom lip into his mouth, knowing he had to take some blame. He didn't know much about Kelleigh's friends either. He'd used the excuse of estrangement from Annette to distance himself from his daughter's life. He'd gone from one extreme to the other. Before he opened the business full-time, he used to spend a lot more time with Kelleigh, taking her to whatever lessons or extracurricular activities she liked.

Annette and he should have recognized that Kelleigh needed them more than ever. She'd been crying out for their attention, but they were too busy fighting each other to notice. Now, she'd forced them to focus on her.

The last time they were together as a family, Kelleigh tried to talk to him and he'd shut her up because of his annoyance. At fifteen, she was all kinds of vulnerable. Too many times on the news, there were reports of teens who'd been raped and killed. He prayed that wouldn't happen to Kelleigh. She *had* to be safe.

He closed his eyes, willing his thoughts to settle. Why think about the worst that could happen? She was probably safe with friends.

Only a few more minutes to go before Justine picked up Emile.

His senses told him Justine was near before he saw her and the combined fragrance of vanilla and musk alerted him to her arrival. He raised his head and there she was in the doorway, caressing him with her eyes, in the same way he was thinking about her. His belly warmed, but he took no pleasure in it. He turned to face her, but couldn't hide his anxiety.

She came to his side, her face a mask of concern. "Xavier?"

Lorraine appeared behind Justine, hovering.

"Yes, Lorraine?"

She licked her lips and wouldn't look him full in the face. "I was just checking if you needed anything."

He put aside irritation and decided to talk to her later about her behavior. "I'm fine, thanks. Would you cancel my other lessons for the afternoon?"

"Okay." Reluctantly, she left, drawing the door up close, but not shutting it completely.

Justine touched his shoulder. "Something wrong?"

He nodded. "I gotta go. Kelleigh's disappeared. Seems she ran away some time between last night and this afternoon."

Justine touched his cheek, then pulled her hand back, as though she had done something forbidden. "I hope she's okay." She looked behind her before speaking again. "As you know, I've been having some trouble with Yolanda too. They're at that stage—boyfriends, peer pressure, you know how it is."

He nodded again and called to Emile. "Time to stop, Em."

"Awww, can't I play a little longer?"

"Not today, I have an emergency. Gotta leave now."

"Can't you just listen to this piece?" Emile asked, shoulders slumped.

"No, Emile," Justine said, "he has to go. Now."

Her words got the desired response. Emile got up, put his sticks in his knapsack and shuffled toward Justine. He hung on to her waist and spoke to Xavier. "You gonna come see me tomorrow?"

"I'm not sure yet."

Emile's mouth pulled down at the corners and his head lowered further. Xavier pulled him forward to sit on his leg. "I—something's come up that I need to take care of, but I'll come if I can, okay?"

"All right."

Xavier didn't feel like smiling, but did to appease Emile. "You know I'll call, right?"

"Yes, but if you come, that would be better."

"I'm gonna try hard, okay?"

Emile rubbed the toes of his sneakers together and sighed. "Sure."

He didn't look pleased, but that was the best offer Xavier could make for now. Justine's dark eyes reflected his worry. Despite the weight on his spirit, one corner of his mouth curled up.

If Justine could make things right by sheer force of will, that's what she'd do. Her support buoyed him, and he prayed he'd bring Kelleigh home safe before the day ended.

– 29 –

Saturday, April 30, 3:30 PM

Justine

Proverb: Ackee love fat, okra love salt.
Meaning: To each man his own taste.

Justine did her best to hide her distaste. "Your mother knows you wear an earring?"

The young man nodded. "She cool wid it."

Justine winced and flashed Yolanda a sharp look. What was she thinking? Apart from being too young for a boyfriend, Yolanda's taste couldn't be trusted. While Justine didn't want to give Yolanda the impression that she wanted to choose her friends, this young man was the limit.

He'd turned up shortly after they got home, banging on the postbox, only stopping short of yelling when Justine went out on the verandah to ask what he wanted. After Yolanda ran outside and said she knew him, Justine had gone back to her office to finish an article. Soon after, Yolanda asked Justine to come to the living room.

Justine pretended not to notice when Yolanda dragged the baseball cap off his head and dropped it in his lap. His torn, oversized jeans and baggy tee-shirt hid an emaciated body. At least his eyes were clear, which meant he probably wasn't snorting anything, not that that precluded a hundred other unsavory activities he could be involved in.

At times like these, Justine regretted Milton's passing. Yolanda needed a strong hand. Once more, Justine cursed her absorption and lax attitude over the years, but hoped she'd passed on enough of her values to help her teenager make wise decisions.

The affection with which Yolanda looked at Neil disturbed Justine. At almost fifteen, Yolanda had no business looking at any boy like that. Justine hadn't been allowed to have a boyfriend at that age and her mother would have put a quick end to any such notion.

Justine forced herself to move, folding her hands in her lap. Her stillness was unnatural and from Yolanda's expression, she'd guessed how Justine felt. Her daughter's face settled into lines she hoped had disappeared for good. Yolanda slipped a hand into Neil's.

So she planned to be defiant, did she? And for what? Surely, she was scraping the bottom of the barrel to have come up with this specimen. Sighing, Justine remembered that their last argument had to do with this boyfriend. If Dionne could hear her thoughts, she'd say Justine was a tight-ass and she'd be right. Holding back a smile, Justine mumbled, "She'd have a fit if Fiona brought home this bit of riffraff. "

But Fiona wasn't even thirteen, so Dionne didn't have the same worries about teenage pregnancy just yet. All the same, kids nowadays did get way ahead of themselves.

Yolanda stood, jerking Justine from her mental wanderings.

"Come." Yolanda tugged Neil's hand until he got up, jamming the cap down so far on his face he couldn't possibly see anything.

Idiot.

"Where are you going?" Justine asked.

"I'm just taking Neil to the bus stop."

"Awright, Mrs. Charles."

Neil waved, and Justine squeezed her face into something she hoped resembled a smile. From Yolanda's sour expression, Justine hadn't been successful in fooling her.

When they left, Justine stared at the ceiling, thinking. At times like these, she was tempted to blame herself for everything that went wrong in their lives, but knew she had to be objective. Maybe reasoning with Yolanda would help. What did she see in that thug-in-waiting? Did he have any functional brain cells? She couldn't tell by the few words he'd said. Hopefully, with time and wisdom, Yolanda would lose the attraction she had for Neil. That day couldn't come soon enough.

The sofa sank and Emile chirped in her ear. "Mom, is what wrong with Landy again?"

She turned her head, inhaling a combination of cocoa butter, sunshine and sweat. "Speak properly."

"She almost knocked me over on her way outside. And who's that boy?"

"Her friend," Justine said.

"He's cool," Emile said, switching on the television.

"Why? What's so special about him?"

"I love his sneakers. They're maaaad."

"They're about the only thing about him that's cool," she mumbled.

"You don't like him?"

"I need to think about that some more."

Emile stared at her, remote in hand. "Now I know what's wrong with Landy. You made her mad."

"She's been mad about everything for a while, you know that."

Emile scratched his ear and looked at her the way Xavier did when she said something he refused to understand. "But she was getting better. Now she's gonna start being mean to me again."

"Come on. You're exaggerating."

"You'll see when she starts screaming at you."

Justine hugged him and kissed his temple. "You worry too much. Everything will be fine."

The slamming of the door contradicted her statement. Emile switched off the television and slid off the couch. "Going to my room."

Yolanda walked into the living room and sat on the couch beside Justine. "So why don't you like Neil?"

"Who said I didn't like him?"

"Your face looked as if he crawled out of a manhole and made everything stink."

"I didn't think any such thing. He just untidy and you know I don't approve of men wearing earrings."

"You know it's hip."

"It might be, for you and his mother, but I don't like it."

Yolanda sighed. "Mom, can't you make an effort for my sake?'

She raised both hands in surrender. "Fine, but it's not like my opinion is going to change."

Yolanda turned to face Justine, shaking her head. "See, you've made up your mind about him already."

"It's not that I've made up my mind, but the boy isn't giving me anything to work with."

Yolanda took a breath, ready to launch into an argument. It gave Justine pause. Maybe, Yolanda had a point. Sure, Neil looked like thug material, but Justine had to keep an open mind and be practical. A life which included Xavier lay ahead and she would prefer if Yolanda could get along with him. Still, she had to speak her conscience. "You know how I feel about men who wear their pants hanging below their butt with their underwear showing, and the earring says something about him that I don't—"

"So you're going to get stuck on his earring without trying to get past what's on the outside?" She got off the sofa to walk back and forth, the wide legs of her jeans flapping around her feet. "You really should think about taking some of your own advice. You keep telling me not to judge people." Here she mimicked Justine. "Because you can't tell what their situation is and what makes them behave the way they do."

She sat, hands on her knees. "Despite what you think, he's a nice guy, and I like him."

"I'm not going to tell you not to see him. I still think you're way too young for a relationship, but I'm sure you'll find a way to be with him anyhow."

"And?"

"I'd like you to think about why you're seeing him and whether he's the right guy for you."

Yolanda pushed the hair away from her forehead and smiled grudgingly. "I didn't say I was going to marry him."

Despite her discomfort, Justine laughed. "I never said you were going to either."

She patted the seat, and Yolanda settled closer to her.

"Tell you what, if you like him that much I'll give him a chance despite what I think. Can you live with that?"

Yolanda nodded and gave Justine a smile guaranteed to make her say yes to anything. "You're the best."

"I know, that's why I'm your mother."

Justine hugged Yolanda, thankful that she'd avoided another blowout. While she had her attention, Justine decided to press her advantage. "I want you to promise me something."

"What's that?"

Breathing deeply, Justine wondered why she'd never spoken to Yolanda seriously about sex. Sure, she'd provided books, but she hadn't taken the time to have a discussion. She traced one of her daughter's eyebrows before cupping her cheek. "I know I've told you you're too young to have sex and I mean that, but when the time comes, would you at least think about how it can change your life, and maybe talk to Kyra or Dionne if you feel you can't talk to me?"

Yolanda looked at her as if she'd lost her mind. "Auntie Dee would just kill me, okay?"

"What I'm trying to say is that it's okay to say no. And it's definitely not okay for anybody to pressure you into doing anything you don't want to do."

"I know, Mom. After what happened the other day, I'm more careful about the company I keep."

"Always knew you were your mother's child."

They chuckled and Yolanda headed for the kitchen, where Miss Pauline was preparing Gungo Peas soup.

Yolanda's mention of the near rape fixed Justine's mind on Xavier and Kelleigh. A glance at the clock confirmed that more than an hour had passed since they left the studio, but it was much too early to call him. No way did she want to intrude on his family time. He'd be by Annette's side, helping her face the stress, bewilderment and fear that would have come with Kelleigh's disappearance.

Xavier and Justine seemed to be living parallel lives. They'd both had partners unsuited to them and now their daughters had turned out to be troubled teens. Thank goodness Yolanda had come home safe and wiser for her experience.

Justine prayed that wherever Kelleigh had gone, she wouldn't be hurt. She didn't deserve that, and her father could certainly stand to catch a break after the emotional whirlwind he'd gone through since discovering Emile.

And what about Annette? Doesn't she deserve a break too? Maybe this crisis will bring them together and heal their relationship.

Blindsided by that thought, Justine forgot Xavier's divorce was all but final. She picked up the phone off the side table, couldn't remember who she planned to call, then gently replaced it in the cradle.

– *30* –

Xavier

Proverb: If you 'crape (scrape) gourdy (gourd), you find wormhole.
Meaning: If you look for faults, you will find them.

He stood inside Kelleigh's room, surrounded by a sea of tangerine. Even the chair in the corner wore a slipcover in the same delicate shade of orange. From the seat, a familiar item winked at him. He dug into the pile of books and clothing spilling over the chair arms, fingers tangling in an electric cord. Clumsy with haste, he snagged the high-end phone, snug inside its shocking-pink skin lined with faux-diamonds. Another one of Annette's misguided indulgences.

Fear and relief mingled in a nauseating tide; fear that Kelleigh was somewhere in Kingston without any means of contacting her family and relief that she hadn't been ignoring his calls. The display indicated a dozen missed calls. He'd called at least eight times. He was about to scroll through the numbers when the phone buzzed. The LCD indicated 'TRICIA' was calling.

"Yes, can I help you?"

"Sorry, wrong number."

"This is Kelleigh's dad." Thinking quickly, Xavier improvised. "She left her phone at home."

"Really?" The high-pitched voice conveyed suspicion. "Kelleigh *never* goes anywhere without that phone."

Which means she forgot it in her haste to leave.

"Well, she did this time. You're Tricia right?"

"Uhuh."

"I'll let her know you called. Matter of fact, I might call you back in a few."

"Why?"

Now the girl sounded more suspicious, and he felt like a pervert. Should he be honest and tell her Kelleigh had run away? A few seconds of thought convinced him otherwise. He didn't want to advertise that his daughter was missing unless it was necessary. And Kelleigh would want to save face with her friends if she hadn't told them her plans.

"Never mind, I'll ask her to call."

Annette walked up behind him, sniffling. "What are you doing? Our daughter is missing and you're on the phone?"

Xavier swallowed the first words that came to his mouth and held up the cellular unit. "Recognize this?"

Guilt seeped into Annette's eyes. "H-how was I supposed to know she left her phone?"

"Did you even think to call the number?"

She looked into his eyes as if she'd find the answer to his question there.

"I...she hardly ever..."

Struggling to keep his tone even, Xavier gripped her shoulder and turned her toward the door. "Wait for me in the living room. I'll be there in a minute."

He sat on the edge of the bed, unable to ignore the sinking in his gut. The comforter was rumpled, but the bed hadn't been slept in. Kelleigh normally kicked the sheets all over the place while asleep. If she left last evening, where had she spent the night? Annette's complaints about some boy beat against his forehead.

What was his name?

Martin? Marcus?

Moving down the list of phone contacts, Xavier left the bedroom.

Annette sat on the couch, supporting her forehead with one hand. She raised her head, eyes brimming with tears.

"Come," he said, taking her hand.

She stood, hugging him around the waist, letting her tears wet his shirt. He rubbed her back and pecked her forehead. "We have to go," he murmured.

He waited while she picked up her handbag and secured the front door. The yard still hadn't been cut and the blooms from the young Poui trees had created a blanket of yellow on the lawn, but that was the least of his problems. Too much time had already gone by since Kelleigh left home.

On the way to the station, he tried to piece together the happenings from the previous evening. He didn't discover a lot more than what Annette told him earlier, except that they had quarreled again. This time, over some friend who had visited.

"You do realize you could have avoided embarrassing her in front of her classmate."

"Grounded means grounded, Xavier."

"I agree, but you could have waited 'til the girl left."

"You always take her side, and—"

"It's not a matter of taking sides. What I'm saying is that you could have handled the matter differently. You know she's very sensitive. Anyway, now is not the time for this. What's that child's name?"

"Tasheka, and since you're such a model parent, maybe it would be better if you took her."

The stoplight changed, so he couldn't see Annette's expression to determine whether she was serious or just being cantankerous.

"Trust me, I've thought about it," he said.

Annette opened her bag, but didn't make any attempt to take anything out of it. "Since I'm such an unfit mother, when we find her, we should discuss it."

"Nobody said you were unfit."

"But you keep implying it."

"No matter what I say, you're going to twist it, so just forget it. We'll talk about this when we find Kelleigh."

Sobbing, she got tissue out of her bag and blew into it.

Xavier ignored her since he wasn't in any mood to put up with one of her drama queen episodes, and she was halfway there already.

In the parking lot at the police station, he searched the phone for Tasheka's number. After learning that she hadn't seen Kelleigh since Friday, and evading the girl's questions, he helped Annette out of the van, keeping an arm around her as they entered the one-story building. The phone buzzed in his pocket. He pulled it out and looked at it while it continued humming. He was in no mood to satisfy Tasheka's curiosity. She'd get the message and stop calling.

At the counter, an officer invited them inside, listened to their story and assigned another officer to take their report. A policewoman asked what felt like a million questions, half of which they couldn't answer, to Xavier's shame. At the end of the interview, she requested a recent picture of Kelleigh.

Annette turned to him, eyes still swimming. He got out his wallet, and removed a head shot from the last set of school pictures. He skimmed the photo before handing it over, letting his thumb rest against Kelleigh's cheek. *Jesus, let her be safe.*

Outside the police station, he gave Annette his hanky. "Would you prefer to go home or do you want to come with me while I try to track down her friends?"

She blew her nose and mumbled. "I want to go home."

She probably wanted to be there in case Kelleigh showed up, but experience told him she was too lazy to go searching. He shook his head, and told himself to stop being so hard on her. They were in this together. "Fine. I'll do the rounds."

Just as he didn't know Kelleigh's friends, Xavier couldn't say who Annette's friends were. She was such a self-contained woman that he doubted she had any friends other than people she studied with, and her associates from work. It struck him that she could say the same about him. In recent times, he accepted the fact that he'd isolated himself without realizing it. His parents and siblings all lived overseas and they only exchanged occasional phone calls.

He'd never invited any of the band members home, when they were an active group. Nor had Annette ever gone with him to the North Coast when the group was playing on the hotel circuit. And without either of them knowing it was going to happen, one such trip to Ocho Rios was where he'd first made love to Justine. But now was not the time to rehash how their affair had started.

After he took Annette home, he sat in the living room going through Kelleigh's phone and calling down the list of names he'd given to the police as those who might be her closest friends. The policewoman had stared at Annette and him, as though they were a hopeless pair. And they were.

The time for pride was past, but he felt like a fool each time one of Kelleigh's friends said they hadn't seen her. He also doubted whether a couple of them were telling the truth. A few times he demanded to speak to their parents, who shared his concern, but said they hadn't seen Kelleigh.

Annette curled up in the sofa across from him, eyes fixed on the television while her tea went cold. She wasn't watching the set, and he didn't have the heart to ask if she couldn't think of anything that would help him find Kelleigh.

He rubbed his eyes and let his head rest on the back of the sofa. A scene from one the many standoffs they'd had played behind his eyelids. He sat up, forcing himself to concentrate harder. "What was the name of that boy you said was Kell's boyfriend?"

"I can't remember," Annette said, still staring at the screen.

"Work with me, Annette. We were sitting right here when you complained about him. I asked Kell his name and she told us."

He got up, pacing the edges of the room and shifting his gaze from the family portraits lining the walls. It didn't prevent him seeing in his mind's eye how Kelleigh had progressed from precocious toddler to a sweet-natured—if demanding—preteen and to the point she was at now. He wished he knew when everything had changed.

He thought back, picturing Kelleigh seething on the sofa because Annette told him she had a boyfriend. What was the damn boy's name? He sat again, paying close attention to the names going by on the phone's LCD screen, sure Kell had mentioned a name starting with M. But the listing in her phone only yielded up Martine and Mikheala in addition to the names he'd seen earlier.

Sighing, he continued down the contacts. The boy's name had to be in there somewhere. Desperation had a hold on him by the time he got to Patrick, Peter and Phil. Then he hit, Richard, Robert and Ron. Everything inside him said he had the right name. His memory kicked in and clear as a bell, he heard Kelleigh say 'Myron'.

He used his phone to make the call and used the 'private' function just in case Kelleigh was with Myron. A husky voice answered the number just as Xavier decided he was going to find Myron and kill him, whether or not he'd seen Kelleigh.

"Who dis?"

Damn waster.

"Myron, where's my daughter?"

Silence.

"Either you let me speak with your mother or I'm going to get the police to shake the information out of you." Hoping the boy wasn't a quick thinker, he asked, "What's it going to be?"

"Hold on," came the gruff response.

Xavier prayed his gamble would pay a bonus. With the fear many teenage boys had of the police, he figured Myron would have caved in at the thought of being interrogated and possibly manhandled.

After a brief discussion with a timid-sounding woman, Xavier told Annette he'd be back and sped toward Duhaney Park, a lower-middle-class Kingston community. While he drove, he considered what he could have done differently and acknowledged that Annette and he would have made better parents if they'd concentrated more on their family life.

Both of them had left Kelleigh to do what she pleased, within reason, and now they were seeing the result of their inertia. His daughter wasn't beyond help. He just needed to be a father to her. The fact that she needed attention couldn't be any clearer than if she'd decided to jump from the top of a building.

And the fact that you keep having the same thoughts means you should get off your ass and do something before it's too late.

His promise to Kelleigh that she could come over sank him in guilt. He'd yanked that away, knowing she looked forward to being with him. He'd also forgotten he asked Justine to let him take Emile to the water park in Negril. Good thing he hadn't mentioned it to Emile. He relaxed his shoulders and quit trying to strangle the steering wheel. *What kind of father can I be to Emile if I've done such a piss-poor job with Kelleigh and can't even keep things straight in my head?*

At six-thirty, he pulled up in front of a drab, white house with a peaked roof set behind a picket fence. A pearl-white Honda Civic hatchback was parked close to the sidewalk.

Xavier rapped on the mailbox that hung on the gate and waited. A mouse-like woman called him inside and invited him to sit on a set of ratty verandah chairs.

Xavier declined to sit, knowing how intimidating he was, standing so far above her. She stuttered her way through their conversation, while a sulky boy he took to be Myron came and stood in the doorway.

"You Myron?"

He nodded, and Xavier wanted to shake him and ask where he'd left his manners. Instead of indulging himself, Xavier went directly to what was important. "When was the last time you saw Kelleigh?"

Myron leaned against the doorjamb, insolence in his stance. "Thursday."

His answer was quick, but he didn't look at Xavier.

"Has she talked to you on the phone since then?"

He hesitated over his answer. "She call me yesterday in di evenin'."

But Xavier already knew that as he'd gone through her call history. Pity he didn't have a way to find out what they'd talked about. This boy, with his boxers on display, didn't impress him. What the hell did Kelleigh see in this waster?

Xavier couldn't say how he knew Myron was lying, but was sure the boy had knowledge of Kelleigh's whereabouts. He'd have a thing or two to say to both of them when he found her.

The boy came close to jumping out of his clothes when Xavier sidestepped his mother and gripped him by the collar. "You're going to be very sorry if I find out you know where my daughter is."

Myron's gaze was defiant, but fear clouded his eyes.

While his mother sputtered her outrage, Xavier banged their gate shut and got in the truck, fending off panic. Night was coming, and with it an insistent clawing in his gut, for he had no idea if Kelleigh was safe. The optimist in him wanted to believe she'd be okay, but the untold danger on the streets of Kingston had him terrified.

Instead of going home, Xavier circled the block and parked the Tundra around the corner from Myron's house.

– 39 –

Saturday, April 30, 6:40 PM

Justine

Proverb: 'Yes, yes' never carry man over mountain.
Meaning: In difficult situations, offer solutions rather than mere talk.

Justine typed the last sentence and sent the article to print. Another job done, and one more to go. She lifted the paper from the printer and moved to the love seat to edit. The house phone at her elbow rang. A glance at the display identified the caller. "Hey, Dionne, what's up?"

"Just checking on you. Didn't see you earlier today."

"I couldn't come to you. Had to take Emile to the dentist after drumming."

"So, things are going well with Music Man?"

"I can't complain. We're taking things slow this time around."

"So you come to your senses, eh, and admit you're still crazy in love?"

Chuckling, Justine dropped the paper and pen in her lap. "I never could hide anything from you, eh?"

"Nope. I've got a good nose in the happily-ever-after department."

They laughed, and Justine took a deep breath. She kept her voice low, just in case either of her children burst into the room. "You're right. I'm just as mad about him now as I was then, but I have to be careful. He…I don't think he's forgiven me."

"Why d'you say that?"

"Well, he hasn't said he loves me."

A burst of raucous laughter from Dionne stiffened Justine's spine.

"What the heck are you laughing about?"

"You think the man is a damn fool? After you walked away without a word, you expect him to give you his heart for you to stab him in it again?"

Justine protested in her throat, unable to find words to defend herself.

"How is it possible to get to your age without having some handle on reality? Apart from the fact that it's way too soon for Music Man to mention your name and love in the same sentence, have *you* told him you still love him?"

Justine grunted.

"I didn't think so." Dionne sighed. "After all these years, I still don't understand the way your mind works. Have you stopped to think that maybe he's waiting for you to wake up and tell him what he needs to hear? In case you didn't hear me the first time, *remember the man gave you everything and you let him down.*"

"That's what I mean. I don't think he's gonna tell me he loves me, until he hears it from me."

"Can you blame him?"

Sighing, Justine said no.

"You're a bright woman, so wrap your head around this: when you're ready to commit to him, Xavier will know. Meantime, enjoy what you have together. I'm keeping my fingers crossed that you'll have a happy ending this time."

"Me too."

Justine dropped the phone in her lap, staring at the monitor across the room. Would she ever be ready to share her feelings with Xavier? What if she told him she wanted forever with him and he rejected her or backed out as she had seven years ago? She wouldn't survive that.

Maybe she'd take Dionne's advice, which was what Xavier had also suggested. She'd deprived herself of happiness long enough. What did she have to lose if she had an affair with him? Nothing, except maybe her heart and her sanity.

She relaxed, remembering their lovemaking a week ago. Seven years was a long time to abstain. The experience had reawakened her yearning for him and the need for sex. *And at my age too.* What she wouldn't do to make love with him again, but he had major problems. How could she have forgotten?

She looked at the wall clock before picking up the handset. Hardly taking a breath, she waited for Xavier to answer his cell phone. "I was calling to see if anything's changed with Kelleigh. Is she okay?"

"I still don't know."

Justine played with the teardrop pendant at her neck. "How long has it been now?"

"A whole day at six o' clock."

"I don't know what to say. The stress you must be feeling. Anything I can do to help?"

"No, hon, but I'm glad you called."

"It's the least I can do. How are you holding up?"

"I'll be okay. Annette is a mess though. We've told the police and talked to a few of Kelleigh's friends, but nothing so far."

Swallowing hard, Justine thought back to when Yolanda had done the same thing. She pressed the phone to her ear when Xavier spoke again.

"I'm keeping my hopes up that we'll find Kell soon."

"Me too. I'll touch base with you in another hour or so, okay?"

"Yeah, thanks. Talk to you."

The sheet of paper crackled under Justine's hand when she got to her feet. Hoping she was making the right move, she left the phone in the seat and went to Yolanda's room. She knocked at the door and slipped inside at Yolanda's call.

Justine ignored the piles of books and paper. She talked nonstop to Yolanda about keeping her room clean, but as soon as her daughter obliged her by tidying up on Saturday mornings, the mess came right back. But at least Yolanda was home.

Justine eased down beside her on the bed. "What you reading?"

Yolanda removed her earphones and showed Justine the front cover of a literature book. "We're supposed to read a couple of chapters for homework."

She raised her head, eyes filled with concern. "You all right, Mom?"

"Why d'you ask?"

Yolanda bounced up to sit cross-legged, pulling her tee-shirt down. "You're looking at me all funny."

Justine allowed her smile to widen. "I'm just thinking what a wonderful daughter you are."

"Now I know something's wrong."

Despite the anxiety knotting Justine's stomach, she chuckled. "Have I told you lately how much I love you? And that I'm glad you're my daughter?"

Yolanda rolled her eyes and snickered. "Not lately, but I think I know all that."

Justine gripped Yolanda's hand in hers. "Promise me something else?"

The laughter left Yolanda's face. "What?"

"That no matter what, even when you think I don't understand what you're going through, you'll talk to me before you do something drastic?"

Her eyebrows rose, but seconds later she nodded. "I used to feel you didn't listen to me, but I don't feel that way now."

"I'm glad." Justine hugged Yolanda, while whispering in her ear. "I love you so much."

Yolanda turned her head away, blinking rapidly. Justine didn't want to embarrass her so she pretended not to notice. Yolanda inhaled noisily, before she spoke again. "Did something happen?"

Cupping her cheek, Justine nodded. "Mr. McKay's daughter is missing."

"Really?"

"Yes, since last night."

"Oh." Yolanda's fingers crept to the tie at the front of her sweatpants. She knotted and unknotted it, her concentration intense. Justine waited because it was obvious Yolanda knew something.

Justine slipped her arm around Yolanda's shoulders. "Mr. McKay said Kelleigh's mom is falling apart."

Yolanda opened her mouth and a wash of air preceded her words. "She thinks her mother doesn't care about her."

Justine didn't ask how Yolanda knew that. Instead of asking, Justine stayed still, waiting for what Yolanda would say next.

"She's so cool, I really like her you know?"

Justine squeezed her shoulder, but didn't interrupt.

"And I wouldn't want anything to happen to her." She picked up the laces, and flipped them back and forth. "I'm not a hundred percent sure, but I think Myron might know where she is. Yesterday evening, when we were at Tariq's house, he was talking to Angie and he said something about Kelleigh keeping a low profile. I didn't hear anything else though. He started whispering after that."

"Thanks, honey, I'm sure that will help."

Justine stood, but didn't move because Yolanda grabbed her wrist. "You can't let her know I told, okay? My friends will think I'm an informer."

"'Course not." Justine smoothed her hair. "Thanks for trusting me, and for doing the right thing. You're a good friend, and her parents will be so relieved."

Justine hurried back to her office and sank behind the desk to dial Xavier's number. "Xave? I was just talking to Yolanda, and based on something she overheard yesterday, she thinks a boy named Myron might know where Kelleigh is."

His breath hissed in her ear, and she imagined him rubbing a hand over his face.

"Thanks. That boy really wants me to wring his damn neck." He muttered a curse word and then spoke in an urgent tone. "Gotta go, Justine. I'll call you back."

Mystified, and wondering what had come up, Justine hung up the phone.

– 32 –

Saturday, April 30, 7:20

Xavier

Proverb: Before beard hang low yuh shave it.
Meaning: Taking a situation in hand prevents it from getting worse.

The battered Mitsubishi Galant passed Xavier at the corner where he went to buy a handful of sweets. He followed the car with his eyes, the same way he did for every vehicle that drove past. He didn't need the candy, but thought he looked suspicious idling on the corner. The vendor eyed him as though she suspected he was up to no good. Were the positions reversed, he'd be wary too. She'd been watching him trying to outwalk his anxiety for the last forty minutes.

The Mitsubishi pulled up at the curb in front of Myron's house. A moment later, two people wearing dark hoodies left the building and sped across the pavement into the vehicle. Though Xavier wanted to be sure one of them was his daughter before he accosted the pair, he crossed the avenue and got into the truck, still parked on the side road. He switched on the engine, crept to the intersection and drove off when the taillights on the white Galant got to the next corner.

He followed them, winding through the community, trying not to get too close. He didn't want to frighten them, but had a hard time talking himself out of overtaking the car. He'd be in serious trouble if he threw his fists into those boys' faces, especially if Kelleigh wasn't with them. But his gut told him Kelleigh was in the backseat, oversize sweatshirt or not. He imagined the police telling him he should have known better than to attack a group of teenagers without provocation.

I doubt they'd do anything different if their child went missing.

The car pulled up at another house and this time the driver, as well as the passengers, got out of the vehicle. The gravelly voice of a local deejay pumped out of the one-story building, poisoning the air with obscene lyrics. The group of three entered the house, looking over their shoulders.

Xavier pulled up a few yards behind them, hit the sidewalk and strode to the rusted metal gate protecting the property. In the lull before the next track shattered the night air, Xavier picked up a stone and banged the gate. The driver of the car appeared in the doorway. "What you want?"

"My daughter."

The wanna-be gangster looked behind him, frowning. "A who dis man want?" he asked of someone Xavier couldn't see.

Myron came to investigate. At the sight of Xavier, he quailed.

Quelling the urge to rip the gate off the hinges, Xavier called, "Kell!"

He hoped she wouldn't make him have to go inside after her. He called again, unable to keep the impatience out of his voice.

Kelleigh appeared in the doorway, hands swaddled in her pockets. Her hair was a mess and she looked all of ten years old in windbreaker, giant tee-shirt, and jeans. She hunched, head drooping between her shoulders. Her tired eyes sought his and she looked as if she wanted to cry.

He had never loved her more.

He beckoned for her to come to him. She stood still for a moment, said something to Myron and then hesitantly walked toward Xavier. She opened the gate and stood before him on the sidewalk. Under the streetlight, he caught the sheen of tears in her eyes. Holding both arms out to her, he said, "Come."

She walked into his embrace, unquestioning. He hugged her, sucking in the lemony scent coming from her hair, protective of her frail body. Then he got mad at whoever had encouraged her to do such a reckless thing. Holding her away from him, he asked. "Are you okay, Baby Girl?"

She nodded, hand clamped over her mouth as if to stop herself from bawling. As he led her away from the house, his arm around her shoulder, she turned as though searching for someone. Myron stood inside the property watching them.

Xavier pointed at him. "Don't even think about calling my daughter."

"Daddy—"

"Not here," he said.

When they sat in the van, he got out the phone and rang her mother. "Annette, Kelleigh's okay. She's with me."

Annette demanded to speak with Kelleigh, but he put her off. It made sense to delay a possible shouting match until he got Kelleigh home. "We'll be there soon," he said and rang off.

He needed an explanation from Kelleigh before they got there, because he couldn't defend her if he didn't know what was going on in her head. He squeezed her shoulder. "You sure you're okay?"

Kelleigh nodded and sniffled into her sleeve. "I'm fine, Daddy."

Realizing that the boy hadn't left the gate, Xavier threw a glare behind him as he drove away. He pulled into a shopping mall near the community and parked, watching people going in and out of the nearby supermarket. Gripping the wheel, he let a few beats pass before he said anything. "I'm not sure what's going on with you, but I'd really like to understand what made you do a stupid thing like that."

"Mom and I had another argument. I told her I was gonna run away and she said to go ahead, see if she cared."

"You know your mother. She didn't mean it."

"Then why say it?" she yelled, dragging a hand across her nose. "She makes me feel as if I don't count for anything. Like I don't matter."

Xavier wanted to bang his head against the wheel. How could he get through to mother and daughter? After he thought for a moment, a spark of an idea came to him from a conversation with Annette earlier in the day. He wasn't sure how he would manage his love life with a fifteen-year-old in his space, but her well-being came before anything else. "Would you like to stay with me for a while?"

"You mean that, Daddy?"

"I wouldn't want anything worse to happen, nor do I want you running off again. Speaking of which, where were you?"

"I stayed with Myron last night."

He glared at her in the light from the street lamp. "You're not telling me you slept with that boy?"

She gripped his shirt. "No, Daddy, nothing like that. I stayed in Lisa's room. She's his sister."

"And his mother knew?"

"Yeah, she likes me."

And she didn't say a word about Kelleigh being inside her house. He pictured the mousy woman with zero personality. Of course, she'd fall in with anything her son wanted.

"D'you know she can get into trouble for something like that?"

She gaped at him. "How?"

"The police can charge her with aiding a minor to run away from home. That's the law. Plus, she misled me by not telling me you were in that house."

"But she was only helping me."

"But not thinking about how distraught your parents must have been. A sensible adult would have made a phone call."

"She didn't mean any harm."

"I'm sure she didn't, but that's not the point. And what is that place that boy took you to? It looks like a crack house."

She stared at her nails as if he hadn't spoken.

"D'you know what can happen to you in a house where there's no parental supervision and a bunch of horny teenage boys?"

She opened her mouth, but he raised a hand to keep her quiet. "I know you're not going to try and tell me there was a responsible adult inside that house. Point is, you could have been raped or worse."

He let his words sink in before he spoke again. "By the way, considering that you're turning into a cunning, slippery female, how do I know you're telling the truth about anything that's happened since you left home?"

Kelleigh breathed deeply and shook her head. "Daddy, you know I don't lie to you."

"You just don't tell me stuff you think I shouldn't know."

"Mom never listens to me, and she doesn't believe a word I say, so why would I even bother telling her anything?"

"Are you sure there's nothing you can do to try to get along better with her?"

She spread her hands. "I do try, but Mom doesn't care about anything but her job and her books. She doesn't understand me or even know I'm there half the time. How many times have I told you that?" She looked him in the eyes. "And isn't that part of why you left?"

It was his turn to sigh. "You think maybe some distance between the two of you might change things?"

She shook her head. "Mom just isn't interested in me. I told you, she's more concerned about getting you back."

Again, he was saddened that Kelleigh knew she wasn't at the top of her mother's priority list and to make things worse, he couldn't tell her otherwise, since he also didn't understand Annette. He wondered what Justine would say, given the circumstances.

The cell phone pulsed in his pocket. He smiled when he looked at the display. As though his thoughts had summoned her, Justine was calling. "Anything yet, Xave?"

"Yeah, I found her. She's okay."

"Thank goodness. Guess you guys can sleep easy tonight. I won't keep you. Talk to you tomorrow."

"Thanks for checking on us."

"You know it's no bother."

"Take care." He squinted in the dark, thinking how uncertain Justine sounded. Something wasn't right. He wanted to ask what was going on with her, but couldn't with Kelleigh sitting beside him.

She jabbed him in the side when he put the phone away. "You really like her, don't you?"

He got Kelleigh's cellular out of the dashboard and handed it to her, frowning. "You know Justine?"

"Daddy, I'm not deaf or blind or stupid. That's Yolanda's mom. Plus, you just called her name."

"Could be another Justine," he said, feeling like he'd been caught in wrongdoing.

"Mmm-hmm," she said slowly.

He got the truck moving and kept his eyes on the asphalt, uncomfortable with where the conversation was heading. "Just remember you're not out of trouble yet. You still have a lot of explaining to do."

She sank in her seat, chewing her nail and throwing him sideway glances. Twenty minutes later, he pulled into their yard and parked the truck. "We have to lay some ground rules for when you're at my place. We'll talk about that later. When we get inside, let me do the talking, otherwise your mother won't hear of you staying with me."

He hated sounding like he was in cahoots with Kelleigh, but didn't have a better way to manage the coming confrontation. God help both of them if Annette decided to obstruct him. Maybe he shouldn't have said anything to Kelleigh before discussing his plans with her mother, but what choice did he have under the circumstances?

− 33 −

Saturday, April 30, 8:00 PM

Justine

Proverb: If yuh don' tek (take) it, yuh don' have it.
Meaning: Fight for what you want or your dreams will slip away.

After her conversation with Xavier, Justine wanted to look in on Yolanda, if only for the sake of her peace of mind. Yolanda would think she was being a nuisance and might ask if Justine thought running away from home was communicable. Instead of giving in to her urge, Justine edited the lifestyle article once more.

The need for reassurance shot clean out of Justine's mind when her cell phone pinged and she picked it up. She had an e-mail, which was curious. Nobody ever sent e-mail to her phone account. The message was from annettemckay@mail.digitech.com. Justine made the connection immediately and took several deep breaths before she wheeled closer to the desk and opened the message.

Your bastard son won't hold Xavier. He belongs at home with his family. If u have any shame or a conscience, get out of our lives. Find your own man.

Despite the cool evening, warmth rippled under Justine's skin. She wiped her forehead, pushing away the hairs that had come loose from her ponytail. Her stomach fluttered and she licked her lips. Maybe the message was a mistake. But no, the e-mail address had to belong to Xavier's wife.

How did she get my phone e-mail address? I don't even remember it.

A chill replaced the heat, spreading downward from her face to her limbs. Her hands curled into fists and she hunched over the desk as if it would lessen her shame. Shame over being caught in the same situation she thought she had left behind; shame that she'd been found out, and obviously, Xavier's wife knew about Emile.

She got up, walked to the window, her throat aching. She should have known this would happen. What good could come of what had been a bad situation from the beginning? Fighting tears, she stared at the dark carpet of grass outside the window. An aching lump sat in her throat, but she refused to let the tears come. What good would it do to cry? She circled the office wishing for a magical solution, knowing that was, at best, childish.

When she'd decided to leave Milton, she and Xavier had reveled in their commitment to each other and relaxed their strict stance on contraceptives. She realized she was pregnant only after she changed her mind about starting over with Xavier, but not for a minute did she think about an abortion. Personal belief and religious conviction prevented her from terminating the pregnancy and more than anything else, she wanted Xavier's baby, especially since she couldn't have him.

Justine dropped into the seat to read the text again, but this time tears of outrage flooded her eyes. How dare Annette send this to her?

She's perfectly entitled. I really have no standing in Xavier's life, other than what happened last week, which was clearly a mistake. And how on earth did Annette find time to send me a message after what's happened with Kelleigh?

Head between her hands, Justine stared at the desk. She couldn't tell Xavier. That would be too humiliating, but what else could she do?

Pushing away her thoughts, she decided to see what Emile was doing.

He sat in the living room, sedated by the television, despite having a book open on the sofa beside him. Reading wasn't yet one of his favorite things to do. She slid onto the couch, needing to hug his sturdy little body. A hug from him always put things in proper perspective and made her feel a thousand times better. Hand around his shoulder, she tipped Emile's head up to kiss his temple. "What's on now?"

"Phineas and Ferb," he said, gaze still stuck to the screen.

"Want a snack?" Justine asked, needing something to do.

Emile turned his head. "How come? You always say nothing but tea after dark."

The wall clock drew Justine's eyes and she rubbed his head. "It's also past your bedtime, hon."

"Can we call, Daddy?" Emile asked. "We still don't know if he's gonna come over tomorrow."

"Now might be a bad time."

Xavier would be in the middle of his family reunion. The thought made Justine weepy. Emile calling Xavier daddy had the same effect. She didn't know when she'd get used to that.

Emile's shoulders sagged under her hand. "Awww."

"Tell you what," she said. "I'll make you a cup of Milo while you go change into your PJ's. Meet me back here and after that, I'll lie down with you. We'll call your dad in the morning, okay?"

He nodded and switched off the television. "D'you think he'll get to come tomorrow?"

"I'm not sure, but he's come ever since you started spending Sunday afternoons together, right?" Emile nodded while she spoke, but Justine wondered if she was talking out of turn. "I'm sure if he can, he will."

Emile dragged himself to the edge of the sofa and stood in front of her, scratching his ear. "You think he loves me?"

Where had that come from? She bobbed her head. "I'm sure he does. That's what daddies do."

The miniature trucks and buses that kept popping up after Xavier's visits, plus the time he spent with Emile over the last few weeks told Justine everything she needed to know. Problem was, how would Xavier fit Emile into his life alongside what was happening at home now? A progress report about his divorce proceedings would have been reassuring to have right now.

As she entered the kitchen, Justine wondered if she was destined to be happy. Any sum including Justine and Xavier always equaled disaster. Just as she was starting to think they might actually have a chance, family obligations came between them, just as before. *But that's a normal part of life.*

The electric kettle whistled within a few minutes and Justine prepared the promised cup of Milo, spooning in condensed milk and topping it with a sprinkling of nutmeg. She placed the cup on the side table near the sofa, setting the saucer on top to keep the drink warm. Five minutes after that, Emile still hadn't returned. Leaning back, she called down the corridor. "Emile! Your Milo is getting cold."

When he didn't respond, Justine went to his room. He wasn't there, but he'd thrown off the clothes he had worn earlier. They lay in a pile on the chair in the corner. Puzzled, Justine left his room, knocked on Yolanda's door and opened it.

From the bed, Yolanda spoke over her shoulder. "If it's Emile, you're not welcome. If it's Mom, weren't you here just a while ago?"

"I thought Emile was with you."

"Haven't seen him," Yolanda rolled to face Justine, her attention on the phone in her hands. She tacked on a snide smile. "He might be in his favorite place."

A peek around the half-open bathroom door confirmed that Emile wasn't in there. Justine shook her head, chuckling over Yolanda's quip. Justine should have gone straight to her office. Emile liked to sit at her desk and spin in the seat. Sometimes, she let him use her desktop computer for his games, since Yolanda wouldn't let him near the hand-me-down laptop Justine had given her when she bought a new one.

Justine pushed the office door and the last traces of her smile vanished. Emile sat at her desk, talking on the phone.

"No, she doesn't."

He ran a finger over the spiral edge of her notebook, head tilted to one side. "But she said if—"

Mouth open, Justine moved toward Emile, hoping he wasn't talking to Xavier. The queasiness in her stomach told her otherwise.

Emile's brows moved toward each other, then settled in their normal position. "So we can talk again in the morn—"

His eyes went marble wide when he saw Justine standing in front of the desk. Then he looked at the phone as if it had turned into a snake. From where she stood, Justine heard a shriek. Heart pumping against her ribcage, she grabbed the handset. "...drop dead and give us a frigging break!"

Justine broke the connection and dropped the phone on the desk. She stared at Emile, afraid to ask what he'd heard. She guessed he took a detour to steal a call to his father, and that Annette had somehow got hold of Xavier's phone.

Justine wanted to pick Emile up and squeeze him to her breast the way she used to do when he was much younger, but he was too heavy and wouldn't want to be treated like a baby. His lips trembled and he rolled his eyes, trying not to cry.

What did that witch say to my baby?

He shuffled to her, feet shrouded in gray bunny slippers. His arms crept around her waist. "Mommy, who's a home wrecker and what is a bastard?"

Cupping his cheeks, Justine knelt before Emile. She met his eyes, trying to convey positive energy she didn't feel. "None of those words apply to us, honey."

He dragged one hand across his nose. "So why did that woman call us those names?"

"Maybe she's hurting and—"

Emile's screwed his face into a moue, reminding her of Yolanda when she was displeased. "I'm gonna call Daddy back. We didn't finish talking and that woman—"

Gripping both his shoulders, Justine held Emile so he couldn't get away from her. "I don't think that's a good idea."

"Why?"

"It just isn't," Justine said, trying to keep her voice even.

What was Xavier thinking to let Annette abuse her child? Emile started to protest, but the phone rang. He wriggled closer, stretched across the desk and picked up the cordless phone. "Daddy?"

Emile squinted at Justine while she prayed that whatever Xavier said would help him forget Annette's words. With the phone squished to his ear, he walked around the desk, heading for Justine's chair.

She wanted to interrupt, but thought it best to wait until the conversation ended. Something hit the desk, startling Justine. The phone skated over the papers and clattered to the tiles. Emile fell into the seat with tears wetting his cheeks. "He doesn't want to come."

Justine picked up the phone, certain that wasn't the case, but afraid of what she'd hear. "Hello?"

Xavier sounded urgent. "Justine, let me talk to Emile."

A glance at Emile confirmed that he was beyond upset. She shook her head and sighed. "I don't think he wants to talk to you."

The heaviness to Xavier's breathing told Justine he wasn't in a good place.

"Okay," he said, "but tell him I will definitely see him tomorrow, okay?"

"I will."

"Take it easy," she said after a moment.

"Yeah, if that's possible."

She couldn't ignore the bitter tinge to his voice, but had her own problems to work through. She laid the phone on the desk and stood over Emile. "Hon, apart from the fact that you disobeyed me and called your father, you're behaving like a spoilsport."

"You didn't say I couldn't call him."

"I told you this wasn't a good time."

Emile sank lower in the chair and refused to look at her.

"You have to understand that your father has some problems and he's doing the best he can."

Emile said nothing, but continued to cry, which made Justine want to howl. She choked out a few more words, despite her frustration. "He said he'll see you tomorrow."

With anger twisting his features, Emile shouted, "I don't care."

He ran past her and a moment later, a door slammed.

I don't have to ask where he learned that.

Justine walked around the desk and collapsed in the seat, trying to make sense of the last hour. Emile was mostly obedient, so why did he have to disobey her this time? Now he was hurting, and there was nothing she could do that would make him feel better.

She didn't even know where she stood with Xavier. His wife had her cell number, which Justine used for business and so couldn't turn off indefinitely. Annette seemed prepared to hold on to Xavier. If he decided to stay, there was nothing Justine could do about it, but what if Annette got it in her mind to do worse than send insulting messages?

It's nothing more than you deserve.

Though she knew the voice came from within—the same judgmental one that had held her in its grip for what seemed liked forever—Justine pressed her palms to her ears and closed her eyes.

Too disheartened to fight, she let the tears come.

– 34 –

Saturday, April 30, 8:00 PM

Xavier

Proverb: When coco (cocoa) ripe, 'im mus bus.
Meaning: It's easy to identify someone's intentions by their actions.

Annette waited for them in the living room, looking much better than she had earlier in the evening. She'd even put on some lipstick. Xavier encouraged Kelleigh to sit in the sofa opposite him. Once she settled there, he addressed Annette. "I guess you called off the search with the police."

Annette sniffed and nodded. "I was embarrassed to say she was staying with friends, and I didn't know."

Xavier willed Kelleigh not to say anything and was pleased when she held her silence and kept her face blank.

"Why would you do something like this?" Annette asked.

Kelleigh pulled the windbreaker closer and studied her knees. "I told you I was going to leave, and you said I should."

"So if I told you to go jump off the causeway, you'd do that too?"

Anger sparked in Kelleigh's eyes, but she didn't respond to Annette's taunt.

"Of course you don't care that you had me worried or that I haven't had a peaceful moment all day."

"Then why didn't you look for me?" Kelleigh snapped. "Why send Daddy if you care so much?"

"I had to stay here in case you came home."

"Right. That's what you told yourself so you could sit at home and do nothing."

"Be careful you don't get in more hot water than you're in already."

Kelleigh flashed Xavier a silent, but desperate signal that forced him to intervene. "Annette, maybe it would give you some breathing room if Kelleigh stayed with me for a few days."

"Who told you I needed any breathing room?" Annette looked back and forth between them. "And why would she need to stay with you?"

"We discussed this today, Annette. Why would you want to continue living in a situation where the two of you are fighting every day?"

"She's my child, she's supposed to stay with me and I don't want you mixing her up with your bastard."

Kelleigh's mouth hung open and she blinked as though she'd heard an obscene word.

Xavier sat forward. "I'm going to pretend you didn't use that word again, and I'm going to assume you know better than to say something like that in front of our daughter."

"I don't care what you say. That boy is a bastard, d'you hear me?" She sat forward, shaking. "A frigging bastard and nothing is gonna change that!"

It took Xavier a few seconds to get his mouth working, and when he looked at Kelleigh, her jaw still hung slack. "Kell, give me a few minutes with your mother. Please."

Annette flipped her wrist toward Kelleigh. "She might as well stay. There's nothing you're gonna say to me that she can't hear."

"Very well then. I know you're angry because I have a son, but nothing is going to make him go away. All you're doing is showing our daughter that you're childish and spiteful."

Annette stood, breathing hard. "How dare you? I'm supposed to live with what you did?"

He stood to stare her in the face. "In case you've forgotten, we're almost divorced."

She stood akimbo and smiled, a spiteful grimace. "There's still time for me to change my mind and contest the divorce."

Xavier didn't acknowledge that bit of rubbish with a response. His silence didn't bother Annette, who continued ranting. "And if you think Kelleigh's leaving this house, you're making a sad mistake."

From the corner of his eyes, Xavier saw Kelleigh hug her legs and lower her head. He kept his voice even, not wanting to provoke Annette further. "I don't know what you've been smoking, but you're the one who's gonna have to think again if you believe I'm leaving her here with you."

"You can't take my daughter without my permission."

"I'm her father and since you can't ensure she's safe, there's no reason she shouldn't be with me where I can keep an eye on her."

"I'm calling the police to tell them you're kidnapping her."

"Go right ahead. Kelleigh, get your things. We're leaving."

She hurried to her room before he finished speaking.

"Two can play," Annette said as she crossed to the sofa and picked up the phone.

Xavier couldn't have cared any less who she was calling. The vein throbbing at his temple threatened to burst. He'd had enough of chasing all over the place this evening and then having to pander to Annette's stupidity. Her threat didn't faze him; she'd pressured him in so many ways over the past few months, her tactics were becoming old.

His cell phone rumbled at his waist. He got it out of the case and checked the screen, frowning. Justine was calling again. He walked to the kitchen, hoping nothing was wrong. He could handle so much and no more in one evening. "Yeah, Justine."

"It's Emile. Mommy said you were working out some stuff." Here, his voice dipped. "Did the problem get fixed yet?"

"Not quite, I'm still working on it."

"What about tomorrow?" Emile sounded plaintive, which made Xavier feel worse. "Does that mean you won't come?"

"You know I'll try hard to be there, don't you?"

"Yes, but what if..."

Emile had run out of steam, and despite his weariness, Xavier smiled. Where was Justine? Usually, she hovered over Emile while they talked on the telephone and stopped him when she thought he was asking too many questions, as if she thought Xavier would mind. He leaned against the sink, rubbing his eyes. "Does your mother know you're on the phone with me?"

"No she doesn't, but she said if—"

Someone yanked the phone from his hand. Xavier's head jerked up when Annette streaked out of the kitchen, yelling into the instrument.

Is she losing her mind?

Fear and fury combined to make Xavier careless. He caught Annette in the living room, grabbing her arm. She slapped him with her free hand and ran toward her bedroom, shouting into the phone. With his shoulder, he prevented her from slamming the door in his face and grunted when his foot got squeezed in the doorway. He shoved the door open, and Annette stumbled backward. She fell on the bed, screaming. "Bastard! Why don't you and your home wrecker of a mother drop dead and give us a frigging break!"

The seconds passed in slow motion while she pulled back her arm and hurled the phone at him. Xavier was too stunned to do anything but moan when it hit him on the collarbone. The pain kept him stock-still for agonizing seconds before he could get his mouth to form any words.

By then, disappointment and disbelief stole his anger. Only God knew what Kelleigh was thinking about her mother's outbursts and the way they were both behaving. His words, when they came, were matter-of-fact. "You're a fucking Jezebel. I don't know what the hell you think you're doing, but there's no way you and I are getting back together. What kind of woman would say what you just did to a child? I can't even figure out how I made the mistake of marrying you."

Annette flounced toward the bathroom, smirking. When she got to the door, she spoke over her shoulder. "Careful you don't come running back to me when *Justine* refuses to have anything to do with you."

What the hell? How did she know about Justine?

He wanted to shake the facts out of Annette, but didn't waste his time. She wouldn't tell him anything. One thing was obvious; she'd done something he was going to regret.

He got the phone off the carpet, groaning when the movement set off the ache below his neck. A call to Justine yielded no results. Emile didn't want to talk to him and who could blame the boy? His track record as a father wasn't impressive. He could only pray that as of now, he'd do right by both his children, Annette permitting.

He grimaced at that thought, knowing it was a copout. He'd do anything to build a strong connection with his son and strengthen the bond he had with his daughter.

***

Kelleigh's mood improved once they left the house and Annette's disapproving silence. *She's in too good a mood if you ask me.* But what the heck, she deserved a little peace and stability.

A cool wind blew through the cab and Kelleigh closed the window. The drop in temperature told him it was getting late. God, he needed some rest. His exhaustion reminded him that he was at the wrong end of forty.

"I've been wondering about a couple of things," Kelleigh said.

"Like what?" Xavier asked, letting loose a yawn.

"Have you been out with Auntie Jay yet?"

In the darkness, he nodded, catching himself too late to do anything else. He hoped she'd stop with the questions, but knowing Kelleigh she had more curiosity than was healthy for one person.

"So you guys have something going?"

He kept the smile off his face and met Kelleigh's inquisitive gaze. "Child, mind your own business."

She giggled, without a care that she wasn't yet out of trouble. "I haven't met my brother formally, but I've been adding some numbers."

He spared her a glance while they waited at the stoplight. "What numbers?"

"Will you be honest and tell me if I'm right?"

He shrugged. "Maybe."

She poked him in the side. "Daddy!"

"Like I said, maybe."

"Okay, so I saw you at the studio with Landy's brother a few weeks ago, and I couldn't help noticing that he looks a *lot* like my daddy."

Xavier stepped on the gas harder than he planned and the Tundra raced forward. That was exactly what he feared when he'd taken her to the store at her insistence. Not that he'd had a choice.

Kelleigh peeled the seat belt away from her chest and studied him. "The woman who came to collect that little boy is also Landy's mother. Soooo..."

"Since Math was never your strongest subject, your numbers could be wrong."

She shook her head. "I think my numbers add up just fine. You see, my father didn't raise a fool."

He struggled not to laugh, but amusement won.

Wearing a satisfied smile, she said, "I'm thinking that based on my daddy sounding all lovey-dovey on the phone, he has the hots for that little boy's mother, who also happens to be called Justine."

He swallowed a curse when he went lead-footed again. Kelleigh laughed and tugged at the seatbelt. "You're gonna give us whiplash if you keep doing that."

He wasn't sure he liked his fifteen-year-old being up in his business, but couldn't help being proud that she was no slouch. "I'm not going to confirm or deny anything. You're too smart for your own good. And what d'you know about 'lovey-dovey'?"

"Your voice went soft and gooey. I know lovey-dovey when I hear it."

"That just tells me I need to watch you like a hawk so you don't get into anything you shouldn't."

She rolled her eyes. "Come on, Dad. If I know so much, why would I do anything to get into the kind of trouble you're talking about?"

"That's what I'd like to know."

Xavier relaxed, enjoying the breeze flowing in through his window and thinking he had Kelleigh where he wanted her.

She poked him in the shoulder when they approached the parking space outside his townhouse. "Since I'm staying with you, can I go with you next time you visit my brother?"

He parked the truck before saying anything else out of fear that he'd plow over the sidewalk and into the flowerbed. Still stuck between apprehension and horror, he mumbled. "That's not a good idea."

"Why? All you need to do is ask his mother if I can come over." She leaned across the seat and folded her arm through his. "Yolanda and I are getting tight, so I'm sure she won't mind. Plus, if you tell her I'm staying with you—"

"You have this all worked out, don't you?"

"Oh, yeah."

He wondered how the two girls found time to get so friendly since they attended different schools, but he had a bigger worry. How would Justine react to his request? She'd probably have a meltdown, fuelled by one of her guilt trips. One thing was certain, he'd have to ask, otherwise Kelleigh would nag him to death and there was no way he was letting her out of his sight after what she'd done yesterday.

Seeing Emile was a must—if only to reassure him that things would be okay—but it also meant Xavier was between two families, a challenging place for any man.

He waited until they were inside the house before he got to the heart of his concern. "You want to tell me what's going on with that boy before I go and beat it out of him myself?"

Kelleigh stared at him, lips glued shut, as if her life depended on maintaining her silence.

Long after he thought she wasn't going to speak, she gulped and stuck her hands back inside her pockets. "Daddy, there's nothing 'going on' on as you put it. I know you said I can't have a boyfriend, but I really like Myron and wish you'd give him a chance."

Xavier barely stopped himself from rolling his eyes. The young people he taught were definitely rubbing off on him. He held in a yawn and avoided Kelleigh's doe eyes. "Look, since you like him so much, I'll consider talking to him some time."

He held up one hand when an ecstatic grin spread across her face. "But not in the next few weeks; maybe not in the next year either."

Her slumped shoulders and watery eyes made him want to hug her. Instead, he squeezed her shoulder. "Trust me when I say I'll feel better laying some ground rules for the two of you when I can be in the same room as him without wanting to rip his head off his damn neck."

"Daddy!"

"You can Daddy me all you want. You've taken about ten years off my life by disappearing the way you did. And he's a damn liar. He told me he hadn't seen you, when all the time he was hiding you. Believe me, I'm not going to forget this for a while."

Her pleased expression slid away and she looked at her feet.

Trying not to come across as a total hard-ass, Xavier patted her shoulder. "Sorry, Baby Girl, but that's all I can offer for now. Be glad what's-his-name is not in hospital suffering from the beating I would have put on him if it wasn't for the fact that I found you when I did."

"Daddy!"

Her round eyes and gaping mouth reined in his growing annoyance. "Just don't do anything like that again. Next time, you won't get off so lightly."

Kelleigh launched herself at him, squeezing him to her chest. "I love you, Daddy."

"Love you too, Baby Girl."

He stroked her back, remembering Annette's earlier comment about Justine rejecting him. Sighing, he put aside the anxiety now plaguing him. No sense buying additional trouble when he already had more than enough to go around.

– 35 –

Sunday, May 1, 2:30 PM

Justine

Proverb: Nuh leggo (let go) door fi hold post.
Meaning: Don't give up something certain for what is uncertain.

Justine longed for a private conversation with Xavier, but it wasn't going to happen any time soon. He glanced at her, but she kept her face blank. Let him wonder what she was thinking. His sharp gaze followed the movement of her hand, and she stopped tugging her hair. At this rate, she'd have a bald patch by the time he left. She let her hands fall to her lap, but her knees wouldn't stay still. She wanted the visit to be over, but that also wasn't going to happen in the next few minutes. Xavier's children were having too much fun.

Emile sat between Kelleigh and Xavier, wearing a smile as wide as the room.

"Gimme a few minutes," Yolanda said as she left the room with her cell phone pressed to her ear. One of her friends from school had called about homework, but Justine expected her to return the moment she finished.

From the conversation between Kelleigh and Yolanda, Justine guessed that the two girls had talked sometime before Xavier came over. Justine was beyond surprised that they liked each other. Didn't Yolanda have reservations about Xavier, and shouldn't Kelleigh be resentful over sharing her father? But who knew with teenage girls. They were as unpredictable as the transport system in Kingston that everybody complained about.

A tic Justine had never felt before tortured her right eye. She wiggled her butt in the settee for want of something to do, other than rip out her hair. She'd tried to get out of today's visit but hadn't seen a way after Xavier explained how eager Kelleigh was to meet Emile properly.

She hadn't told him what had been happening since she got up this morning. He had enough stress without her adding to his problems. She'd changed her mind a hundred times about talking to him, but figured telling him was the right thing to do, though she was tempted to keep her silence. She sighed, wondering when she'd get a chance to talk to him.

On the seat next to her, the phone buzzed and pinged. She picked it up and unlocked the display. Another text from Annette. Didn't she have anything else to do? Without reading the message, Justine deleted it. It could only be another round of insults.

When she looked up, Xavier was watching her. He had to be wondering who was texting her so often. The current message was the fifth one since they arrived. Justine had served dinner, thinking it would be easier if Kelleigh and Emile got to know each other over a meal. The traditional Sunday fare of French Fried Chicken with Rice and Peas and vegetables had gone over well. Miss Pauline had helped Justine prepare dinner, but had gone to her room after a formal introduction to Xavier, who she'd seen in passing several times. Justine suspected she was giving them space, and was grateful.

The phone had interrupted them several times and when Justine checked the messages after a trip to the fridge, she couldn't ignore the curiosity Xavier didn't try to hide.

Hoping her unease wasn't obvious, Justine shifted her gaze to Kelleigh. While she didn't exactly look like Emile, they shared similar features. The shape of Xavier's forehead and chin were apparent, as well as his toffee-tinted skin. Kelleigh had lustrous curls tamed in a ponytail and she was tall, but nowhere as sturdy as Emile.

She'd been cautious with Justine at first, but got over her shyness, thanks to Emile's boatload of questions at dinner. It was clear she adored her dad. She'd stuck close to him, with a hand on his arm until Emile inserted himself between them. Justine had wondered if bodily contact was Kelleigh's way of declaring ownership of her father, but killed the thought after Xavier introduced them and they sat down to eat.

As though she sensed Justine's scrutiny, Kelleigh raised her head. Justine's first impulse was to shift her gaze, but instead pinned a smile to her mouth. To her surprise and not for the first time, Kelleigh offered her a genuine smile. Justine was too wound up to do anything but blink. Now the girl would think her a few cards short of a full deck. Justine relaxed her grip on the arm of the sofa. "Uh, would you like something to drink? We've got some fruit juice left over from dinner." She stole a glance at Xavier. "We also have soda."

Kelleigh also looked at him. "Thanks. I'll have fruit juice."

Justine smiled, thinking Xavier had done well in helping Kelleigh make wise choices. She needed to stop letting her kids wheedle her into buying things that weren't good for them.

"It's okay, Mom," Yolanda said, returning to the room and laying a hand on Justine's shoulder. "We'll get it."

Angling her head toward Kelleigh as she went by, Yolanda said, "Come."

Justine occupied her fingers with her hair, watching the two girls bounce toward the kitchen. It took Emile thirty seconds to decide he wouldn't be left out. He trailed them into the kitchen.

From where she sat, Justine couldn't see the kids, but winced at the slamming of the fridge door. A burst of laughter followed moments later. She stopped torturing her scalp with her nails, when Xavier spoke. "I know this is hard on you, but you want to tell me what you're so worried about?"

She was halfway to shaking her head when she remembered her decision to talk to him. "Give me a minute."

Casual-like, she wandered toward the kitchen. The girls' voices had faded and as she thought, they had gone into the backyard. Their indistinct words told her they were some distance away. A shriek came from Emile. Laughter followed, and Justine's heart fluttered back into place.

She sat next to Xavier and opened the first message she'd received that morning. She handed him the phone and in her mind recited the message she now knew word for word.

Xavier doesn't belong to you, so don't get comfortable. He'll be back home soon.

He drew a prolonged breath and closed his fist around the phone.

"I deleted some of them, but there's more," she said, moving closer and taking the cell from him to display the list of messages. She handed the phone back, staying close enough to bask in the joy of being near him, but with some space between them so their children wouldn't wonder about their closeness when they came back inside.

He said nothing until he finished reading, but took her hand. "I hope you're not buying into any of this. Like I told you, our divorce is almost final."

"I know, but she doesn't plan to give you up."

With her gaze, Justine caressed Xavier, imagining the stubble on his cheek chafing her skin. "Where does that leave you?" she asked.

Xavier winced as he turned his head. He loosed her hand and touched his collarbone. "Don't you mean us?"

Justine didn't answer, but scanned the cream drapes, the set-of-three paintings and the blood-red Anthurium blooms in a vase across the room.

Xavier's breath fanned her cheek in a sigh as delicate as the touch of a feather. "You're such a damn coward. Don't you ever fight for anything? Doesn't what we have mean anything to you?"

Feeling as if he'd hit her, Justine swung her head to look at him. "I fight for things when I'm entitled to them. Other than a child between us and some sex that was probably a mistake, what do we have, Xavier?"

A pair of lines formed between his brows and as she watched, he withdrew from her, leaving her cold.

Oh God! Why didn't she think before she rammed her foot down her throat?

Now, he looked as if he wanted to slap her silly. He licked his lips and stared at his hands, folded between his knees. "I'm such a damn fool."

Fearing she knew what he meant, Justine studied his motionless fingers, saying nothing.

"Only a numbskull would do what I've done. I walked into the same situation, without realizing that you haven't grown up or let go of your guilt trips."

"Don't even go there—"

"Shut the fuck up. You don't know what it means to commit to anybody but yourself and your crusade to be a martyr." He laughed—a sound rife with bitterness—and spread his hands. "I might be older, but I sure as hell am not wiser."

A deep silence fell over the room like a shroud on a coffin. Justine wanted to move, but couldn't. Inside, she screamed. *This can't be happening!*

Her mouth refused to cooperate with the distress signals from her brain ordering her to say something to soothe Xavier's hurt. Sure he'd been offensive, but wasn't that what she deserved for rolling over without a fight and saying the first thing that came to mind?

His voice was a whip cracking the stillness. "You know what? Forget I said anything about us trying a second time and while you're at it, forget what happened between us last Saturday. The only thing that matters is Emile."

Her eyes stung, but before she could give in to her pain, Emile ran into the room, panting and pointing to his father. "The policeman outside wants to talk to you."

If Xavier felt Justine's probing gaze, he didn't acknowledge it. He stood and put a hand on Emile's shoulder. "What policeman?"

"The one that said he came 'cause of Kelleigh."

Xavier hurried to the front door and turned to Emile, who trotted behind him. "Stay with your mother."

"Awww."

"You heard me."

Emile plunked himself in the largest sofa and folded his arms across his chest.

"Where are Kelleigh and Yol—?"

The two girls appeared, looking like Justine felt, and as though by prior agreement, they sat on either side of Emile. Kelleigh picked at the threads hanging off the designer slashes on her jeans.

Unsure of what to say, Justine went with instinct. "Kelleigh, you want to tell me what just happened?"

She curled her body forward, speaking to her sneakers. "My mother's cousin is outside. She sent him."

Icy heat wrapped Justine's throat. *How does that woman know where I live?*

She held back fear and satisfied her need for information. "Why?"

Kelleigh shrugged and mumbled. "I'm staying with Daddy for now. She...uh...she..."

Justine closed her eyes, sighed and wished she was one of those women who was super-competent and knew what to do in awkward situations like this. Miss Pauline would encourage Justine to do what came naturally, but what if Kelleigh blamed her for all this? And wasn't Xavier coming back?

Justine went through the door, closed it behind her and approached Xavier where he stood by the gate. An unmarked Toyota was parked on the street, with a man still inside. The one who stood on the sidewalk shifted from foot to foot, rubbing the back of his neck while listening to Xavier.

"...her to use you to aggravate me?"

"She has a legitimate complaint."

"Give me a break." Xavier spread both hands. "How long have you known me?"

The man's gaze shifted to Justine. "That's beside the point."

"Bullshit."

Despite knowing she was invading a private conversation, Justine stood beside Xavier, who ran his fingers back and forth over his brows. She touched his arm. "Would the two of you like to sit on the verandah instead of standing in the sun?"

"Thanks, but that's not necessary. Dennis and I will be finished in five minutes."

Justine refused to move, since she had no idea what would happen next. Didn't Emile say this man was a police officer?

Xavier turned her toward the house by the shoulders. "It's okay. Really. I'll be there in a few minutes."

She stared at him, wanting to protest, but not sure why.

Gently, he shoved her. "Go on."

One last look at the bald stranger and Justine left them. She didn't pull the grille shut, nor did she close the front door. She sat close to the doorway, keeping the men in view. The children remained where she left them, watching television, but Kelleigh's anxiety was obvious in the questioning look she shot Justine.

She shrugged. "Your dad says he'll be finished shortly."

Kelleigh nodded and went back to staring at the television. Justine lifted a shoulder in response to Yolanda's silent question. She didn't know what was going on either. Soon, Emile came and sat beside her, trying to see what his father was doing in the yard.

Xavier walked toward the carport, head down, hands in his pockets. Justine's desire for everything to be right in his world was an intense ache that made her want to hug him, but there was no way she could do that. Not after his words to her and not with a trio of curious children watching.

Xavier stood in the doorway, jangling the coins in his pockets. "Kell, we should go."

She opened her mouth, but changed her mind and rose. "Okay."

When she stood beside him, Xavier slid his arm around her shoulder. "Emile, I'm sorry, but we have to leave, okay? I'll call you."

Running his slippers back and forth on the tiles, Emile asked, "When?"

"How about later?"

"Okay."

"It was fun being here, Mrs. Charles," Kelleigh said, offering a twitch of the lips that passed for a smile.

Poor kid. "It was nice meeting you. I hope you come again."

"Me too."

She avoided saying good-bye to Xavier. Maybe she'd call him later.

If he'll talk to you.

The downward slant to Xavier's lips was the only hint that he was under stress and Justine was all too aware of how she had contributed. As though she was a stranger he'd made eye contact with on the street, he said, "I'm sorry about all of this. It won't happen again."

As tears pricked her eyes, Justine couldn't help thinking how much his words sounded like good-bye.

– 36 –

Xavier

Proverb: Marriage have teeth and him bite very hot.
Meaning: A marriage can become a source of pain.

"I'm clueless about why you need to involve Babs in our family business," Annette said, lifting her chin in her sister's direction.

Truer words have never been said, Xavier thought. Clueless described his wife perfectly. Odd that he still thought of her as such. Habit, he supposed. Shifting his gaze to Barbara, he spoke. "I asked her to come here to try and make you see sense."

Annette rolled her eyes. "And why is Dennis here?"

"Since you decided to involve him in your attempt to embarrass me, I thought it would be okay, and in case you've forgotten, these people are your family."

After glancing at Kelleigh, who sat at his side, Annette put on her stubborn face.

He'd waited two days before confronting Annette because he had to work around Barbara and Dennis's schedule. He also had to get over the fury Annette and Justine had aroused in him.

"I'm sorry if you feel I've gone over the edge, but I don't know what else to do." Xavier glanced at the group sitting around the living room. "You signed the divorce papers and knew the end was coming, so I don't understand the things you've done, especially over the past few days. I asked Babs to speak with you because she's someone we both respect, but that—"

"You're damn out of order to do that."

"You didn't leave me any choice."

"Well maybe if you were prepared to spend—"

"Prepared to spend what? More time going around in circles, like we're doing now? I've moved on. All you have to do—"

Annette glared at him, her complexion darkening. "Don't tell me what I *have* to do!"

Xavier's control slipped away on a riptide of anger. He stood, shooting arrows at her with his eyes. "What you *have* to do is stop making silly excuses to get me over here every other day."

Annette rose and faced him. "You're in such a goddamn hurry to get rid of me, you don't even have time for your daughter."

"You're a fine one to talk. When was the last time you spent an hour with your nose outside a book or without the television on?"

"Don't you dare act as if I'm the only one at fault here. Matter of fact, I plan to set everything straight."

She rushed out of the room, leaving them in silence.

Kelleigh rubbed her forehead, and Xavier dropped into the seat, squeezing her shoulder and thinking he couldn't be so lucky that Annette would give in to the inevitable. But this wouldn't be the first time she'd find a way to do something silly to spite them both.

"I'm sorry, Baby Girl," he said in Kelleigh's ear.

She nodded, flicking her school tie with a finger. He touched her chin, disheartened by the sorrow and resignation mirrored in her eyes.

Barbara and Dennis wore the same helpless expression. They'd tried reasoning with Annette, but the meeting had broken down after a few minutes. Eyes closed, he wished to be anywhere else but in this living room trapped in a situation that shouldn't have gotten to this stage.

Something hit him in the chest, and he opened his eyes. Annette pressed a sheet of paper to his shirt, which he grabbed by reflex. She cut her eyes at him and backed away. "I won't contest the divorce, but I've filed for sole custody of my daughter."

She spun away, her dress swirling around her knees.

When the bedroom door slammed, Barbara spoke. "I'm sorry. I didn't see that coming."

While he scanned the paper Annette had shoved at him, Xavier massaged his forehead and let his body go slack. "If I know Annette, this isn't the end. I really hoped you would have gotten through to her."

Barbara looked at Xavier and then at Kelleigh as if weighing her thoughts before she spoke. "Trust me, she understands that it's over. Sometimes the familiarity and comfort of having someone around blinds us to the fact that a relationship isn't working."

Against his will, Xavier smiled. "Which of you is the social worker again?"

Barbara returned his smile. "Annette is too close to what's happening. Social worker or not, in your personal life, it's hard to separate good sense from feelings."

"I guess."

"So what's gonna happen with Kelleigh?" Dennis asked.

Xavier ran a hand over his face, gathering his thoughts. He'd forgotten Dennis was in the room.

"I can't believe Annette went back on her word. We agreed that custody wouldn't be an issue. Kelleigh would stay here and I'd visit and have her over whenever she likes." He clasped her hand. "With what's been happening over the past few months, I think it's best for her to stay at my place for a while."

He squeezed Kelleigh's hand. "Hon, can you give us a few minutes."

She didn't look enthusiastic, but got up. "Sure. I'll get a few more things from my room."

He waited until the door closed before picking up the thread of the conversation, but Dennis spoke first. "Considering the filing, Annette's gonna have a problem with you taking Kelleigh. That's why—"

"That's part of the reason I invited you here," Xavier said. "Annette cannot disrupt my life whenever she likes, using Kelleigh as an excuse. Until I'm sure they can get along in the same space, I'm not leaving Kelleigh here."

"Annette *is* her mother," Barbara said gently, her locks shifting around her shoulders.

"Yeah, and I'm over here way too often trying to prevent them from fighting each other."

Xavier sighed. "Babs, you know she'll listen to you. I have no intention of taking Kelleigh away from her mother, unless that's what she wants."

He walked around the room, sifting his thoughts. From the whatnot, he picked up a picture of Kelleigh. Her wide, toothless smile took him back to the time when he still believed he could mend his marriage. He rested the picture next to one that captured all three of them, and came back to sit near Barbara. "Can you at least get her to back off for now? Kelleigh needs some space to forget the constant bickering."

Babs got to her feet, her shift brushing the floor. "I'll do my best."

"That's all I'm asking." Xavier picked up the paper he'd dropped in the seat, waiting for relief to grip him, but he was empty. Perhaps because he was wound too tight and refused to let himself think about Justine and their situation. Why waste the time? And it would be easier if he didn't think about how stupid he'd been to let her back into his heart. He closed the door on his emotions and focused on Dennis's narrow face.

"Since you guys are so close, I'm gonna ask you to encourage her not to pull anything like she did on Sunday. I'm in a sticky situation right now and can't handle the stress."

"Woman trouble, eh?"

"You can call it that."

"Things will work out. I'll do what I can. Annette is depressed and thinks she still needs you."

"Can you do me a favor? Check in with her every couple of days? When her temper wears off, she gets—"

"Weird? Devious?" Dennis shook his head slowly, an admission of his cousin's flaws.

"Yeah. I don't want her to be alone with too much time to fill."

"Don't worry, I'll keep an eye on her."

When Kelleigh walked in, carrying a knapsack, Xavier got to his feet and clapped Dennis on the shoulder, hoping he wouldn't have to go to Annette's bedroom before he left. As though he'd telegraphed his thought to her, Barbara walked into the living room, rubbing one side of her forehead.

"Annette okay?" he asked.

Babs sighed. "Yes. I told her I'd stay over since Dave is out of town at a seminar, but she says she'll be okay."

Xavier wished Annette would let her sister stay, but couldn't tell her what to do. Not that she'd listen to him.

"Is she okay with me taking Kelleigh for the next few days?"

Babs nodded, looking as tired as he felt.

"Thanks, I really appreciate your help."

"You know it's no problem." She hugged him and when she stepped back, patted the side of his face. The wrinkles around her eyes deepened when she smiled. "Be happy."

He nodded and turned away. Happiness was something that eluded him at every turn. He guided Kelleigh to the door, hoping everything she'd witnessed between him and Annette wouldn't sour her views on romance. Then he remembered that boy, Myron. She still had lots of time on her side.

Inside the truck, Xavier asked whether she'd gotten homework.

"Is there ever a time when I don't?"

He brushed her face with his knuckles. "Have I told you you're way too cheeky?"

"Only several hundred times already."

She laughed and in the falling darkness, he realized how much she looked like her mother. Feeling something close to regret, Xavier reminded himself that he'd tried to rekindle their former closeness. After Justine, he'd thrown himself into winning Annette as in the early days, but her preoccupation with work and study made it hard to compete. All that was in the past. Soon, Kelleigh would be all that connected them.

The buzzing of the cell phone at his waist cut into his thoughts. A glance at it told him Emile had tracked him down. He smiled and put the phone to his ear, wondering how Justine was coping with the hefty bills Emile had to be racking up by calling from the landline to the cell phone.

"Daddy? How come you're not at home yet?"

"I had to do something, but I'm on the way now."

"You and Kelleigh?"

"Uh-huh."

"Can I talk to her?"

"Sure." Xavier gave Kelleigh the phone.

Eyes on the road, Xavier listened to the one-sided conversation. His two children could talk the ear off anyone who cared to listen. Holding back laughter, he wondered what that said about their parents.

Kelleigh poked him on the arm with the phone.

He put it to his ear. "Yes, Emile."

"Hold a minute," the boy said before launching into a muffled conversation. He came on the line again, speaking loudly. "Mommy wants to talk to you. She said so today, but now she's gonna wait 'til Saturday."

"That's okay," he said and told Emile goodbye. Putting off things was typical of Justine. Didn't matter though, he'd made it clear they were finished. Still, he wondered what the hell she wanted.

It wasn't like he gave a shit, but that didn't stop him from smelling the vanilla in her hair and the buttery stuff she used on her skin. If he closed his eyes, he could also smell...

A horn blast behind them forced his mind back to the congested road. A packed bus swerved in front of him and changed lanes again, to a chorus of horns.

On impulse, Xavier stroked Kelleigh's cheek. "You know you mean the world to me, don't you?"

She leaned toward him, trapping his hand between her head and shoulder. "Mmm-hmm."

"And don't you forget it, Baby Girl."

She giggled, rubbing her cheek against the back of his hand.

Rubbing absently at the still-tender spot on his collarbone where Annette had hit him, Xavier reminded himself that Kelleigh and Emile were his priority. He had nothing left over for Justine or any other woman.

– 37 –

Saturday, May 7, 1:55 PM

Justine

Proverb: Clothes cover up character.

Meaning: You can't tell what someone is capable of doing, judging by appearance.

Emile stood on the sidewalk knocking his sticks together and marking time.

"Mom!" He stretched the word to two syllables. "Can you hurry?"

"Can I at least switch off the engine before I get out?" Justine flicked a wrist at him. "You don't need me anyway. I'll be inside in two minutes."

He dashed off before she finished speaking, yelling over his shoulder. "Okay."

She gripped the wheel, staring at her fingers. She had to face Xavier sometime and she'd already waited too long. Yolanda touched her shoulder. "Mom, you sure you're okay?"

"I'm fine." Justine nodded and forced a smile. "You go ahead."

Yolanda made a show of checking that her knapsack was securely zipped before turning sideways to face Justine. "Uh, I know I've been a horror, but I really don't mind you and Mr. McKay...you know...I know you like each other and everything, so..."

Justine wanted to hug Yolanda, but patted her hand instead. "It's okay, hon. I don't think we—never mind. It's time for your lesson. We can talk about this later, okay?"

Yolanda nodded and got out of the car. She removed her guitar from the trunk and crossed the sidewalk to the door. Justine wrapped her fingers around the wheel again as if it was her last hope of survival in a shipwreck. She was only too aware that the more time she allowed to go by, the more it would look as if she was avoiding Xavier. Not that he cared. He'd made it plain enough that he didn't give a damn.

Well he did, until you messed things up again.

Sighing, she got out of the vehicle to face the heat, which blanketed her on the sidewalk. She spared a glance for the people walking past and locked the vehicle via remote, on the way inside. She wished she could press a button in the same way and make everything go right in her life.

She greeted the saleswoman, who turned her head away as though Justine had some contagious disease. Justine went past with her chin held high; the silly witch probably still had her panties in a bunch over Xavier. Funny how you could get used to anything if you were exposed to it long enough.

Following the sound of the guitar, Justine walked to the second room Xavier used for his students. She rapped on the door, opened it and stopped. Xavier was playing the guitar. He raised his head, and she could have sworn he almost smiled at her. He nodded without losing a beat and when he finished, he gave Yolanda the guitar. "That's what I want to hear, you playing with more confidence."

Brows wrinkled, Yolanda asked, "You think I can manage that rhythm?"

"I know you can," Xavier said.

Yolanda sat and began to imitate the piece Xavier had played. The sound wasn't as fluid, but her satisfied smile said she was pleased with her effort. Justine looked at the coral polish on her toes, pained by the obvious pleasure Xavier's approval brought her daughter. At times like these, the void Milton had left was obvious.

Justine's gaze went to Emile who sat behind the drums. The tip of his tongue prodded his lip, while he tapped out a beat that told her he was improving.

Reminding herself that she was interrupting their session, she focused on Xavier, whose face was a blank mask. Her heart quailed, but she cleared her throat and looked at both Emile and Yolanda again before she murmured, "Can I talk to you later?"

He waited so long to answer, she thought he'd refuse. Then he nodded. "Sure."

"When I come to pick up the kids," she said, backing toward the door.

Outside the doorway, she straightened her spine and went past the woman out front. Through the plate glass she spotted Kelleigh about to enter. Kelleigh glanced over her shoulder before she smiled and said, "Hi, Mrs. Charles."

"You're good?" Justine asked.

Kelleigh fiddled with the strap on the knapsack she carried and nodded. "Yeah."

A well-dressed woman walked up behind Kelleigh and scanned Justine from hair to feet before she approached the counter.

The resemblance between the woman and Kelleigh was obvious, so Justine knew who she was without an introduction. While Justine's heart shriveled, the sales attendant smiled and chatted with Kelleigh's mother.

Hypocrite. Yakking it up with Annette as if she didn't want Xavier too. The thought got Justine moving. "Take care," she mumbled.

Kelleigh nodded. "You too."

While forcing herself to walk at a moderate pace, Justine sorted through her thoughts. Annette didn't seem like the type who would do the things she'd done already. Yelling at a child and sending endless texts was something an unstable person would do. The woman who walked into the store looked like someone Justine would keep company with.

But looks were deceiving. Justine knew that better than anyone. No matter what was going on with her, she'd always behaved as if things were normal. She'd gotten through her first separation from Xavier moving by rote from one day to another. Only her friends had recognized that she'd been existing on automatic pilot.

She got in the car and headed to Kyra's house, where Dionne was also meeting them for their henfest, as her husband, Clay would say. Justine had thought about making an excuse to stay away, but figured it would be easier to forget what had happened between Xavier and her if she stayed occupied.

She parked close to the sidewalk behind Dionne's car, got her handbag and stepped on the grass verge. A white Lexus with chrome rims rolled up and stopped behind Justine's car, blocking the driveway. The door opened and Annette got out.

Justine's stomach clenched around the late breakfast she'd eaten, and her breath ran short. She moistened her lip while giving herself a pep talk. She had the advantage; if she needed help, her friends were but a shout away. She just had to get through whatever was coming now.

The sun glared down, raising perspiration in her armpits. She hung her bag over her shoulder and glanced toward the house, before addressing Annette, who stopped a few steps away. "Why are you following me?"

Annette pushed hair behind her ears and studied Justine as though she was something her dog had vomited. "Because I wanted to talk to you."

"You saw me at the shop. You could have spoken to me there."

"That wasn't convenient."

"I don't know why you'd want to talk to me, but I don't believe—"

"I don't care what you believe," Annette said, "What I know is that you're the conniving bitch who's been seeing my husband and now you're trying—"

"Please." Justine shook her head. "Xavier and I don't have a relationship."

"That's probably because he came to his senses and now sees you for the slut you are."

Justine's hands rolled into fists, and she spoke through her teeth. "Who the hell you think you're talking to like that?"

"You thought your little bastard would hold him, but of course, that didn't go like you planned."

"Just get the hell away from me, before I have to call the police."

Justine's skin prickled with embarrassment. A man across the street was clipping a Hibiscus hedge and watching them. The snipping of the clippers slowed and almost stopped. When Justine looked at him, his hands faltered on the garden scissors and he stared into the bush.

"You have a nerve to threaten me," Annette yelled, shaking a finger in Justine's face.

"Justine, what's going on out there?" Dionne opened the grille and walked toward them, with Kyra following close behind.

"You ruined my life!" Annette continued, "Slept with my husband, had this bastard and now you're trying to take Xavier too."

"Get a grip," Justine said, "If you were treating him right, Xavier wouldn't have had time to be sleeping with anybody else."

Annette shouted in Justine's face. "Bitch!"

Stepping back, Justine asked, "Why don't you go home and take care of your business, instead of harassing me?"

A slap jerked Justine's head sideways.

"Whore! That's for sleeping with my husband."

The blow pushed Justine off balance and she scrambled not to fall. For what seemed like ages, Justine couldn't see anything, but felt the blood pounding through her head. Before she righted herself, Annette hit her again. "That's for ruining my family life, and this—"

Annette didn't land the third blow because Dionne grabbed her arm and pulled her away.

Justine ignored the throbbing around her eye, planted her feet on the grass and slapped Annette across the mouth. "That's for being such a bitch. And this—"

She raised her arm again, but Dionne inserted herself between them. "Justine. No!"

Her panicked cry brought Justine back to reality and she picked up her handbag and let herself be pulled toward the house. Kyra examined the side of Justine's face, muttering. "Senseless cow."

They went to the kitchen, where Justine sat picturing the altercation. As her mother used to say, what never happen' in a year, happen' in a day. Justine had never been in a fistfight in her life.

That's not quite accurate.

She dropped her bag on the floor, cringing as she shoved aside the memory of the few instances when she'd tussled with Milton, who'd slapped her a time or two.

Kyra left the room and returned with a towel. She got ice from the freezer and instructed Justine to hold the makeshift icepack to her eye. After she put a glass of water in front of Justine, Kyra pulled out a chair and dropped into it. "What the hell just happened?"

Justine rested her elbow on the table, supporting her forehead. "I dropped off the kids with Xavier. She followed me here."

An engine started, and Justine slumped in response. "I hope that stupid woman just goes home."

A moment later, Dionne walked in and sat with them. "I swear that woman is mad as shad. Justine, you better watch yourself. She sounds serious as hell, making threats and everything. I suggest you get Xavier to deal with her."

Kyra moved her head in a sharp nod. "Right."

"I had to threaten to kick her into next year before she'd leave, but she swear blind she gonna have it out with you."

Justine shook her head. "I just can't win. If I'm with Xavier, I have problems. I decide to give him up and I still have problems."

"When did the give-him-up part happen?" Dionne asked, snagging Justine's water and wiping sweat from her forehead.

"After she sent someone to my house about Kelleigh and she's been texting me."

"So what does that have to do with Xavier? The decision to give him up, I mean."

"A relationship between us won't work." Justine cupped a hand to the side of her head and stared at Dionne. "I can't believe this is real, that I just hit Xavier's wife."

Dionne and Kyra did some silent communication, before Dionne got up and went to the fridge. She brought back a jug of water, refilled the glass and sat glaring at Justine. "Your problem is that you need to get over yourself. Dat woman nearly clobber you into the ground and you worried about hitting her back?"

"You shoulda wake sooner and land two more blows to even things up," Kyra added.

Their reasoning, and the ridiculous nature of the dispute with Annette, lifted Justine's spirit. She stopped smiling when the muscles around her eye protested. "How I became friends with two hooligans, I don't know."

"All is fair in love and war," Dionne said. "You love this man. It's your business if you let him get away again. I'm done preaching and parting fights."

"You need to put that damn woman in her place," Kyra said. "If you don't, she'll keep stalking you and you'll never be rid of her."

Justine pressed the towel to her face and took a deep drag of air. The Chicken Foot soup bubbling on the stove reminded her of a time long past, when life was simple and other people made decisions for her.

In the last week she couldn't make up her mind about approaching Xavier. She knew she had to talk to him if she hoped to salvage their budding romance, but after the way he'd looked at her last Sunday, she needed a sensible plan of attack. Of course, it would have helped if she knew what she wanted.

Come on, Justine. After all this time you know what you want. Why is it so hard for you to admit you want what you couldn't allow yourself to have seven years ago?

Her problem had always been following through, as it was now. She'd been lying to herself, thinking she didn't know exactly what she needed, despite the hurdles she had to cross.

* * *

Justine entered the studio, regretting the bowl of soup she'd had at Kyra's. It sat like lead in her stomach.

"Daddy's in the back," Kelleigh said, peering at Justine as though she wanted to ask her something, but wasn't brave enough.

Emile and Yolanda continued playing their instruments, ignoring Justine. She was now used to them wringing every moment from the time Xavier gave them. She cracked a smile at Kelleigh, but didn't think she fooled the girl, who continued to study her, while picking out a tune on a keyboard.

Justine had loosed her ponytail and combed her hair to frame her face. Anybody with live brain cells would wonder why she chose to wear her hair down in the bone-melting heat outside.

At the door to Xavier's office, she wondered whether this was the right time to approach him. She decided—battered face or not—now was as good a time as any other to talk to him. She'd already waited too long. She prayed the wide arm of her glasses would help hide what Kyra and Dionne had disguised with foundation and powder.

Xavier looked up from the computer when she walked into the room, forgetting to knock first.

She pointed at the door. "Sorry, I—"

He waved her toward a seat. "It's okay. What can I do for you?"

She sat, keeping the left side of her face turned away from him. This was the first time she'd been inside his office space. One side of the room held a sofa, an end table and the huge mahogany desk that separated him from her. The other half had a worktable running along one wall and instruments she assumed had been left for repair. When she looked at him, he was watching her, his eyes revealing nothing.

"I meant to speak to you, uh, after Sunday."

"And you waited a whole week?"

She tried not to flinch, telling herself she deserved that bit of sarcasm. She pushed her hair back, and felt herself slipping into fighting mode. "You can be intimidating, you know."

"And you're a coward."

"Whatever. I still wanted to—"

"What happened to your face?"

She licked her lip and angled her injured cheek farther away from him. "What d'you mean?"

He got up and came around the desk, which made Justine want to move out of his reach. Light as a butterfly's wings, his fingers brushed the hair away from her face. "I have to wonder what's come over you when you leave with a ponytail and come back wearing makeup, glasses and have your hair down. Either you're trying to put some moves on me or you ran into some trouble."

He lifted her chin, looked at her skin and spoke softly. "Knowing what I do, I'd guess trouble found you."

His nearness was doing things to her that she had no business feeling. Did he understand what he was doing to her by behaving as if he cared about her wellbeing?

He sat in the second visitor chair, still focused on her face. "You going to tell me what happened, or you going to force me to play detective?"

"Uh, I was over at Kyra's house and I fell in her—"

"Don't insult my intelligence. Kelleigh is with Yolanda and Emile. Her mother got here just as you were leaving. Annette was coming to see me, but she barely said hello and raced out of here like a cat with its tail on fire." His stare intensified, making her want to squirm. "Now you turn up trying not to look as if you've been attacked and then decide to lie to me."

"What was I supposed to do? Run over here and complain to you that she hit me?" Justine twisted her fingers together, muttering. "She's probably going to complain to you anyway that I hit her."

She couldn't be sure, but thought Xavier smiled. He got up and gently tugged her hand. "C'mere."

She let him pull her up to stand with her chest pressed to his. She closed her eyes and buried her nose in the warmth of his neck. Musk and man; how she'd missed that intoxicating combination. She sniffed to get rid of the tears burning her eyes and nose. Being this close to him made her feel that everything was going to be all right, but she knew their problems couldn't be solved with a hug.

He murmured in her ear. "Tell me what happened."

She did and then begged him to do nothing. "I'll handle it myself," she said.

Shaking his head slowly, he asked, "What am I going to do with you, Justine?"

He lifted the glasses from her nose and laid them on the desk, studying the area around her eye. His breath washed over her skin, and her stomach scrunched up and quivered in response. Without her permission, her chin tipped up and she closed her eyes. Xavier's lips brushed hers in answer to her unspoken request. Heaven lasted only a few seconds before he withdrew from her, clearing his throat. He made her sit, and went to his seat behind the desk.

While she struggled to get her breathing back to normal, he played with a flat pick, staring at it as if it would disappear if he didn't keep an eye on it. Her nerves were stretched taut by the time he spoke. "I assume you came here because you wanted to make up with me."

She nodded, unable to deny that was what she wanted.

He set his jaw and lifted his gaze to hers. "I'm not about to let you lead me down the same path as before to leave me hanging."

"I didn't—"

He got up, throwing the pick on the desk, next to her glasses. "Nothing you say is going to convince me that you're prepared to stand behind any promise you make." He looked at her again, allowing her to see his pain. "You made promises to me that you broke, and frankly, you've done nothing to convince me you won't do the same thing again."

She attempted to speak, but he came to her side and placed a finger over her lips. "Here's the deal. From now on, you're going to have to prove yourself to me. I know this is going to be a tough one, but I'd like Emile to spend the rest of this weekend with me."

Justine frowned. "But how—"

"If it makes you feel any better, Kelleigh's staying with me."

"He's never been away from me a whole night. What if—"

"I'm sure you can find a hundred reasons why he can't stay with me, so why don't we ask him how he feels about it?"

Now he was being unfair. Of course, Emile would be ecstatic. Justine wanted to deny his request, but she'd never have believed getting back on his good side would have been this easy. She thought of a dozen reasons why Emile shouldn't overnight. Then she thought about how much a chance at happiness with Xavier meant to her.

Xavier's closed expression said he believed her answer would be no. She shut her eyes, let her breath out and then whispered, "Okay."

– 38 –

Saturday, May 7, 9:30 PM

Xavier

Proverb: Stone a river bottom nuh know sunhot.

Meaning: You cannot relate to someone's choices and experiences if you haven't been in their situation.

Though his eyelids drooped, Emile refused to admit he was tired. "You sure I have to go to bed now?"

Xavier tapped him under the chin. "We'll still be here tomorrow, so it's okay to get some sleep now."

Emile yawned and scooted to the edge of the sofa to stand. "G'night Kelleigh."

She looked up from the laptop and smiled at him. "See you in the morning, little man."

Emile giggled and dragged the back of his hands across his eyes. Xavier guided him out of the living room to the bathroom. While Emile brushed his teeth, Xavier leaned against the doorjamb, watching.

"Can you lie down with me for a little bit?" Emile asked when he got in bed.

Xavier nodded, suddenly uncomfortable, although this was the sort of thing he'd wanted to do for Emile since he knew he had a son. He switched off the overhead light, but left the lamp burning on the bedside table.

"Sometimes, Mommy stays with me until I fall asleep," Emile explained while he spun one thumb around the other.

"There's nothing wrong with that," Xavier said, folding both hands under his head.

Emile curled on his side, with one fist under his cheek. "Can I come back next week?"

Xavier chuckled. "You ever hear about living in the moment?"

"What that mean?"

"Enjoy the time you have now and don't worry about tomorrow."

"Mommy says people have to make plans." His words slowed and he yawned.

"I agree, but it's also fun to enjoy what you have right now. I'll talk to your mother about you staying again, okay?"

Emile nodded, blinked a couple of times and fell asleep.

For no reason he could explain, tears filled Xavier's eyes. That hadn't happened in more years than he could remember. He rolled on his side, watching his son. Emile had insisted he wanted to sleep with Xavier, although the sofa could have done double duty as a rollout bed. Xavier understood that like him, Emile wanted to cram as much activity as possible into the limited time they had together.

Xavier picked up Emile's hand. Even at six-plus, his fingers were long and the nails square at the tips like his. His gaze shifted to Emile's face, where his lashes rested against baby-smooth skin. Xavier smiled; though Emile resembled Justine, so much of himself was reflected in the boy. Nobody could question their familial connection when they were in the same space.

That thought brought tears to his eyes again. How could Justine have thought she was doing the right thing by not telling him about Emile? He'd never get a sensible reason out of her, other than her wish not to ruin his family, but he knew it was more than that. She wouldn't admit it to herself, but she didn't want to share Emile. Letting him into Emile's life would have meant uprooting her comfortable and secure world.

His skin went hot and resentment stirred the longer he looked at Emile. He forced himself to change the direction of his thoughts. Things could have been worse. Had they not met by accident, he wouldn't have found out about Emile and Justine would never have told Emile about him.

He ran a finger down Emile's arm, kissed his forehead and sat up. When he got to the door, he stood staring at Emile, who hadn't moved. From their interaction during the evening, he learned that Justine had never had a man in her life, at least not one she took home. Nor did Emile have any sort of father figure besides her friends' husbands or the fathers of his classmates.

Justine was something else. She'd called Emile during the evening with the excuse that she was checking to see if his sinuses were acting up and whether he needed antihistamine. She had serious attachment issues, but Xavier didn't discount her feelings. She had been the center of Emile's world until recently.

Even now, Xavier wasn't sure how he felt about her. On an emotional level, he still loved her, but on a rational level, he held back, expecting that despite what she said, she'd let him down again.

Rolling his shoulders to get the kink out of his neck, Xavier suspended his thoughts and went back to the living room.

Kelleigh shifted the laptop on her legs and looked up at him. "You all right, Pops?"

He nodded. "Just thinking."

He lay down, angling his head so he could see the television, where a sitcom was in progress. He watched for a few minutes until he missed the tapping of Kelleigh's fingers on the keyboard. He looked across at her where she sat without moving, the lamp forming a halo around her hair.

"What?" he said.

"I dunno, I guess I'm just worried about you. I thought you'd be happier to have Emile over."

"I am, but I've got a lot on my mind."

"Like what?" Kelleigh put the laptop aside and unfolded her legs.

"You. Me. Him."

She removed the band from her hair and canted her head toward him. "What d'you mean?"

"Things are too up in the air with you, and then there's Emile."

Pushing the hair away from her face, she studied him for a moment. "Are you thinking about me staying here?"

Xavier nodded. "Despite what I told Dennis, I'd prefer to have you here with me."

Her brilliant smile rewarded him, but he acknowledged that it would be challenging to get her mother to change her stance on custody. He also had to talk to Annette about her fight with Justine. What she was thinking when she hit Justine was beyond him. No sane man he knew would try something like that with another man.

He'd talk to Annette in the morning and set her straight.

– 39 –

Sunday, May 8, 4:30 PM

Justine

Proverb: Tek (take) sleep and mark death.
Meaning: Use one situation to gauge what might happen in other circumstances.

"Yah!" Emile jumped and kicked the hedge, sending a shudder through the leaves of the Gold Duranta lining the fence.

Yolanda looked up from her phone and shook her head. "I told you he'd long to come back for the Battle of the Bushes."

Justine wiped the counter, keeping her eyes on Emile who had moved on to jabbing the Ixora with half of an old mop stick. Thank goodness it wasn't in bloom. Where he got the energy she didn't know. They'd had dinner a half-hour ago and he could hardly wait to go outside. She let him have his way to take his mind off when next he'd get to spend a weekend with Xavier. That was all he talked about over dinner.

She hadn't gotten a chance to talk to Xavier because he didn't stay long, but he had assured her that Emile had been well-behaved. He kissed her cheek before he left, and she had murmured that she still needed to talk to him. He sized her up for a moment before nodding and pressing his lips to hers for a second.

"Take that!" Emile's shout and wide slashes at the Rose bush yanked her away from that interlude.

"Remember that's off limits," Justine yelled. "Maybe you should come inside now."

"There's nothing to do in there." He faced the window, waving the make-believe sword. "This is more fun."

"Only ten minutes more. Then you have to shower."

"Okay." He spun away, running from side to side making zooming noises, his hands spread wide.

She turned and caught Yolanda looking at her as if she had a question.

"What is it?" Justine asked.

"D'you ever do anything except worry about us?"

Justine glanced at the window. "Of course, I do."

Yolanda's fingers raced over the phone's dial pad, texting. She laid the phone down and raised her head, trying not to smile. "Like what?"

"Well...I work." She shrugged, smiling. "I chauffer you kids all over the place and sometimes I read, but you know all that."

"See! We both know you don't have a life." Cupping her cheek in one hand, Yolanda looked sideways at Justine. "I don't think you stopped worrying about Emile the entire night. If I didn't force you to play Chinese Checkers, you'd have driven me bananas roaming the house, like some demented ghost."

Chuckling, Justine sat across from Yolanda, who winced when she looked at the side of her mother's face. She hadn't asked any further questions after Justine made up a story about knocking her head against the cupboard in Kyra's kitchen, but Justine had seen the doubt in her eyes.

"Worrying is part of what parents do," Justine said. "You'll know what I'm talking about when you have children."

The phone pinged and Yolanda picked it up. "Ya know, with all the trouble I've given you, I'm not so sure I'm gonna have any kids."

"Well at least you admit you've been nothing but trouble over the past few years."

"Don't get carried away." Yolanda sent another text and sat back. "I'm just saying that maybe you deserve a break."

Justine stared at her, mouth half open. "What happened to you? Let me feel your forehead to see if you have a fever or something."

Yolanda giggled while checking the cell for new messages. "I'm just thinking how much you've given up for us, you know?" She lifted one shoulder in a shrug. "Auntie Dionne and Auntie Kay both have husbands, and you don't. You just have us."

Justine ran her palm over the back of Yolanda's hand where it rested on the table. "You and Emile are everything I need."

Yolanda smiled, but it wasn't a joyful gesture. "Mr. McKay makes you happy. I see it when he's around."

Justine's eyes watered and she lowered her head. "I do have feelings for him, but as I told you—"

"No!"

Emile's scream sent a jolt through Justine, who exchanged a wide-eyed stare with Yolanda. Justine swung sideways in the chair, raking Yolanda's skin in her haste to see what had happened to Emile. She tried to right herself, but crashed to the floor with the chair. Her head, arm and hip banged against the tile, but no pain registered. She sprang up and grabbed the edge of the sink. Emile wasn't in her line of sight. Her eyes met Yolanda's and panic reflected from her daughter's face.

They ran for the door at the same time, jostling each other to get outside. The backyard was empty, except for Emile's sandals, abandoned on the lawn.

"Emile!"

They raced around the side of the house and into the front yard, where the metal gate hung open. A white car peeled toward the corner and swung onto the major road. Justine ran to the corner, screaming Emile's name, fearing she'd lose sight of the Lexus. It swung on both sides of the roadway before careening around another corner.

Justine surprised herself by bursting into tears. Yolanda put her arms around Justine's shoulders and spoke in a shaky voice. "You think the person in that car took Emile?"

Justine nodded, unable to hold in the sobs raking her throat. She turned back the way she'd come and winced, realizing she had nothing on her feet. Bits of gravel and road grit dug into her soles. Despite that, Justine ran toward the house, not stopping until she stood in the living room with the phone to her ear.

Panting hard and stuffing her hair back into a knot, Justine waited for Xavier to answer his cell phone. When he didn't, tears flooded her eyes again. She dashed the sweat from her forehead with an unsteady hand and tried the number a second time.

He didn't answer.

With tremors racking her hands and body, she dialed his home number, from the pad beside the phone. Emile had insisted that she didn't move it though he knew the numbers. Thank God she'd listened to him.

Ignoring the emptiness in her belly, Justine waited. Kelleigh answered, but Justine couldn't say a word. Grief tore through her and when Yolanda squeezed her shoulder, Justine gave her the phone. She talked for a moment, before Justine shook off her sluggishness and held on to Yolanda's arm when she called Xavier's name. "Let me talk to him."

"Justine? Tell me exactly what happened."

"Annette took Emile," Justine said. Her voice sounded as if it was coming from some faraway place inside her. "She has my baby."

Silence met her announcement. When he spoke, his words came slowly, as if he was reluctant to speak them. "Are you sure?"

"Yes." She wanted to curse and shriek at him, but what good would that do? Taking a deep breath, she said. "It was a white Lexus with fancy rims. I remember them from yesterday."

Yolanda listened, pressing her fingers to the corners of her eyes, trying not to cry. Justine had no such inhibition.

The low rumble of Xavier's voice lent comfort and an illusion of stability to a world that had spun off its orbit. "Hang on, Justine. I'll be there in a few minutes."

Justine didn't answer. Everything had fallen apart, just as she knew it would one day. Emile was torn from her, just as she expected. What she hadn't anticipated was him being kidnapped by the woman she had sinned against in conceiving him.

Everything that had happened since Xavier found out about Emile's existence had wound its way to this day and this specific incident. She didn't know what had triggered Annette's actions, but that didn't matter. The disaster Justine had been expecting since Emile's birth had come to pass just when she'd allowed herself to stop obsessing about his wellbeing. Last night she'd been restless simply because she missed him. Today was a whole other matter.

She sank on the sofa, unsure what to do. Should she call the police or wait for Xavier to come? Her brain fogged over and she jerked when Yolanda sat next to her. Tears ran off Yolanda's chin and fell onto her jeans shorts. Justine held Yolanda as close as she could. She didn't know how things could be all right until they found Emile, but she murmured to Yolanda. "Don't worry. He'll be okay."

As she smoothed Yolanda's hair, Justine prayed. *Lord, please don't take my baby.* She didn't want to be presumptuous, but couldn't help thinking she'd done more than enough penance over the years. She'd almost lost her daughter, given up the soul mate she'd found too late, and she'd lost her husband.

But Emile had made up for everything. Though Xavier had come back into her life, she couldn't imagine going on without his child.

Please, God! Keep my baby safe.

Pain stabbed her left elbow and hip, but she kept stroking Yolanda's hair. She'd think about everything else after Emile was back with them.

But what if that woman hurt him? What if he didn't come back?

Shaking her head, Justine stilled her thoughts and continued to rock Yolanda, waiting for Xavier to come.

Emile would come home.

Any other scenario was too painful to imagine.

– 40 –

Sunday, May 8, 4:40 PM

Xavier

Proverb: Beautiful woman, beautiful trouble.
Meaning: A beautiful woman comes with many complications.

Xavier was in two minds as to whether to go straight to Justine or the house where he used to live with Annette. Would she take Emile there? He doubted it. He didn't even want to think she'd taken Emile, but Justine had been certain it was her.

Annette must have lost her damn mind.

He ignored the glare though the windscreen, pushed the buttons on his cell phone, and then pressed it to his ear. Annette's home phone rang unanswered. He tried her cellular, but it went straight to voice mail.

"Did Mom really do this?" Kelleigh asked from the passenger seat.

Her voice startled him as he'd forgotten she was in the van. He shot across the intersection, foot heavy on the gas, trying to beat the red light. When the truck bumped on the uneven road, he lifted his foot, slowing the vehicle. "Justine says she did, and her description of the car was right."

Kelleigh looked like she'd start crying inside a minute. It occurred to him that the females around him always seemed to be crying. Not a good sign where he was concerned.

"Are you sure I should go over there with you?" she asked.

"I don't have a choice. I'm not leaving you alone when I don't know what's happening with Annette."

Kelleigh dragged the sleeve of her tee-shirt across her face and turned her head toward the window. She'd seen the houses on that stretch at least a hundred times, so he assumed she didn't want him seeing her tears.

He let a few minutes go by before touching her shoulder. "Don't worry. Just pray Emile is okay."

He gave her his phone. "Dial Uncle Dennis's number. It's in the contacts."

He could have done it himself, but wanted to concentrate on getting them safely to Justine's house, as well as keep Kelleigh occupied. She didn't need to be thinking about taking blame for her mother's behavior.

Earlier in the day, he left Kelleigh and Emile at home and went to see Annette. Their meeting

hadn't gone well. She accused him of trying to turn Kelleigh against her and insisted that he bring her home immediately. When he refused, she swore she'd call the police.

He left the house feeling unsettled, but prepared for the fight to come. Never in a decade would he have expected her to do something this crazy. Considering what she did for a living, she should have a better handle on her problems than most people.

Kelleigh nudged his arm and handed him the cellular. He wedged it to his ear. "Dennis, I need your help. Annette's taken my son from his home and she's not answering any of her phones."

"What the hell you just say?"

"You heard me. I'm on the way to see his mother, but I need you to contact Annette. She has to bring Emile home. You tell her I said she'd better not hurt him if she knows what's good for her."

"Threats won't solve anything." Dennis let out his breath on a groan. "Why would Annette do something this stupid?"

Xavier glanced at Kelleigh, who tugged at the frayed pattern on her jeans. He didn't doubt she was listening. He reworded what he started to say. "I spoke to her about Kelleigh today. You and I will talk later. Please do what you can to get her to—"

Dennis rushed to reassure him. "Don't kill yourself worrying. Annette has a temper, and she can be spiteful, but she's not vicious. I'll find her."

"Thanks, man," Xavier said.

His thoughts tumbled over each other, threatening to bring on a headache. Should he call Annette's sister? After a few seconds, he threw that idea aside. Better to wait and see how things went before alarming Babs. Just for something to do, he called Annette's numbers again. Nothing. "Kell, would you ring your mother from your cell and see if she answers?"

She lifted her body sideways and got the phone out of her jeans. She dialed and shook her head almost immediately. "It went to voice mail."

He cursed under his breath, gripping the wheel as if his life depended on keeping hold of it. He had no clue what he was going to say to Justine, but that didn't matter. She needed him more than she ever had, and he'd be there for her.

"Dad!" Kelleigh pointed to the windshield.

Xavier twisted the wheel hard to the left to avoid hitting the car in front of him. The truck screeched and he swung into the right lane only to be greeted by an extended honking from the vehicle he'd obstructed.

"Damn lunatic!" The driver shouted as he whizzed past.

"Shut the hell up." Xaiver groused, but his heart wasn't in it.

Five minutes later, they sat in Justine's driveway.

"I'll stay here," Kelleigh said, huddling in the seat.

Xavier opened his mouth to tell her not to be silly, but figured she thought this crisis was somehow her fault. He too felt responsible for Annette's actions. Maybe he'd stated his wishes prematurely, but there was no ideal time to talk about their daughter or Annette's attack on Justine yesterday. It also didn't make sense allotting blame now. He had to keep his head screwed on tight. Justine would be going nuts and Emile had to be frightened out of his mind.

Xavier put his foot on the asphalt, but Kelleigh made no move to get out. "Come on, Kell," he said, "Don't do this to me. I'm sure Justine can't hold you responsible for this."

"I just can't," she said, moving her head from side to side.

He had no idea what to do and was relieved when Justine came to the doorway, holding on to the door frame. She looked from him to the open door and then walked toward the truck.

When she stood beside it, she put one hand in his, rested the other on the inside of the door and leaned down to Kelleigh's eye level. "Hey there, Landy's inside. You can go in."

Kelleigh said something Xavier didn't hear. Justine squeezed his hand, still speaking to Kelleigh. "I don't mind. Really. And it would make me feel better."

Kelleigh got out and hurried past, with her head held down.

He locked the truck, keeping Justine's hand folded in his but trying to delay the moment he had to look directly at her. He'd know then that she blamed him for Emile's disappearance. He got her out of the sun and examined her face. She'd been crying, even now, her eyes watered. He brushed away the hairs that had worked their way from the knot at the back of her neck. The bruise around her eye was an unwelcome reminder of what Annette was capable of doing.

"I don't know what to say." He spread both hands before resting them on her shoulders. Afraid of her answer, he asked, "Did you call the police?"

She shook her head. "I was waiting for you to get here. I called, but when I got the station, I-I hung up, 'cause of Annette. I don't know what to do. Am I losing it?"

He stroked her cheek and kissed her forehead. "No, you're not crazy. I called Dennis, the guy who was here when Kelleigh came with me. He's a policeman."

"What is he going to do? Didn't she send him to make mischief?"

"He's Annette's cousin—"

"He's only going to try and—"

He gripped her shoulders. "Hear me out, Justine. He is her cousin, but he's also a good man. He's going to help us find Annette. I'm calling him again, okay?"

When he got his phone out, Justine walked into the house. He followed her inside, dialing while she moved around the living room, as if searching for something she'd misplaced. Dennis answered, and Xavier tried to control his mounting anxiety. "You found her?"

"Not yet. She's not answering me either and she isn't at home. I'm on my way to a make a few more checks."

Pained by Justine's anxious stare, Xavier made a decision. "I'm sorry, but if we don't hear something within fifteen minutes, I'm going to file a formal report. I know you're doing all you can, but this is a criminal matter. Annette can't—"

He couldn't continue, and was relieved when Dennis filled the gap.

"I understand. I'll do my best. I'll ring you in twenty minutes, whether I find her or not. We'll take things from there."

Xavier didn't remark on the fact that Dennis had given himself more time to maneuver.

"Thanks."

Xavier sat, supporting his forehead with one hand, plagued by worry. Annette was a mother, which had to count for something. Rubbing his temples, Xavier wondered where Kelleigh had gone but supposed she was with Yolanda. Time passed and the only intrusion was the ticking clock. He didn't realize Justine had left until her footsteps sounded on the tiles.

"Where's Kelleigh?" he asked.

"In Yolanda's room. They're okay. I know she's hurting too, so I let her know that I don't blame her for any of this."

Xavier exhaled heavily, thankful that somehow Justine found the will to be kind to the child of the woman who had taken hers. She sat, sliding her hand across his back. "D'you have any idea why she'd take him?"

Unable to look at her, he murmured to the tiles. "This morning I spoke to her about custody of Kelleigh."

"What did she say?"

"That she'd fight me. She already filed for custody."

Laying a hand on her breast, Justine sputtered then gathered her thoughts. "Does she think taking my son is going to help settle where Kelleigh lives?"

Xavier spoke low in his throat. "As senseless as this is going to sound, she blames you for our problems."

"Why? Weren't you getting a divorce when we met again?"

He nodded. "Yeah, but it's easier to blame someone else than to admit she's half the reason our marriage fell apart. I could choose to do the same thing, but I know there were times I failed her and also times when I could have tried harder to make things work."

Justine pressed her hands to her eyes, her mouth turned down at both corners and her shoulders drooped. She personified despair. Her grief pained him and he too felt as if someone had stolen something invaluable from him. He fought a creeping apprehension. The longer Annette was silent, the more spiteful and willful she'd become. The years had taught him that.

Emile was sheltered and used to a loving environment. He wouldn't know what had hit him. Annette couldn't have found a more cruel way of hurting them all in one blow.

"Sorry doesn't cut it, but I can't tell you how bad I feel," he murmured.

For a while, she said nothing. Then she whispered, "His hands always remind me of yours." She cleared her throat and spoke louder. "He did everything early. Smiled. Crawled. Sat up. He even had baby teeth before I expected them."

Eyes closed, he listened to all high points he'd missed in his son's life. How ironic was it that his soon-to-be ex-wife was the reason he now had a fuller picture of Emile's earliest years?

"He went to preschool before he was three." Justine said. "Every time I looked at him, I wondered about you. Did he look like you when you were a boy? Did he act like you did?"

Xavier didn't think she was talking to him, but he answered anyway. "He does. I have pictures somewhere."

"He'd love to see those," she said, so quietly he wasn't sure what he'd heard at first.

She hunched, head in her hands, elbows propped on her knees. He put an arm around her and touched his forehead to hers when her tears wet the skin on the back of his wrist. He needed to go searching for Annette, but didn't want to leave Justine. Something tangerine-scented drifted from her hair. Distracted, he drew a deep breath, helpless do to anything for the moment, but wait.

The phone at his waist buzzed. He got it out, flicking it open with his thumb. He frowned at the display, which read *Private*. The blood pounded through his head and he drew a deep breath. "Annette?"

"I wonder how you feel now that I have your little bastard child?"

"You frigging mad or what?"

Justine jerked sideways, her gaze fastened to his face.

"You have no right to take Kelleigh."

"I haven't taken her, Annette. You agreed days ago that she could stay with me for a while." He got up to escape Justine's mounting anxiety. "I don't have time for this! What did you do with Emile? D'you know you can be locked up for kidnapping?"

Justine scrambled to her feet and grabbed his arm. "Let me talk to her."

He shook his head.

"Well, now you know what it feels like to lose your child."

"Come on, Annette. You sound like a mad woman. Tell me where to collect Emile and I'll ignore the fact that you've done something that could land you in Bellevue. After you tell me what I want to know, we can talk about Kelleigh. You better pray Justine doesn't press charges."

"You have a damn nerve defending that slut. I'm going to file assault charges against that bitch for what she did to my face."

"Assualt charges my ass! Where can I pick up Emile? Dennis and I will meet you, and you better not be messing me around."

"Bring Kelleigh with you and we'll settle this once and for all."

He gave in, sure the top of his head was about to explode. "Whatever. Where are you?"

"You think I'm stupid? I'm not telling you. I'll call Dennis. He'll pick you up. Make sure you bring Kelleigh."

Justine's nails dug into his arm through his shirt. If not for that, he'd think he was having a nightmare, but this was real, with the potential to turn disastrous. "Don't worry, I'm coming," he said.

"I'm coming with you," Justine said, blinking back tears that wouldn't stop flowing.

He gripped her shoulders and shook her gently. "No. What you're going to do is call Dionne and Kyra. Have one of them come over and keep you company. Kelleigh and I will bring Emile home."

She shook her head. "I have to come."

He tightened his grip on her. "No, you don't. I'll take care of this."

She closed the space between them and grabbed his shirt. "Please, Xavier. I'll stay in the van."

"Think for a minute, Justine. Kelleigh's mother wants to see her. Who's gonna stay with Yolanda?"

"I'll get Kyra to come over." Her shoulders heaved and her breath shortened to gasps. She wasn't far from a breakdown. "Please, I can't stay here doing nothing."

She let her forehead touch his chest, and he held her tight, disturbed by the heat coming off her skin. Going against what he knew to be good sense, he relented. "Okay, I'll take you. Call Kyra and have her come now."

She nodded, sucking air into her mouth. He wanted to tell her everything would be okay, but he would have been lying. His instincts told him Annette wouldn't hurt Emile, but he couldn't be sure. She wasn't the same woman he'd married.

The muscles in his shoulders tensed and knotted. If Annette had already done the unthinkable, wasn't it possible she'd do worse?

− 49 −

Sunday, May 8, 5:00 PM

Justine

Proverb: God sit high, but him look low.
Meaning: God rules the heavens, but also takes care of mankind.

Justine met Xavier's eyes in the rearview mirror. In them, she read guilt and sorrow, but was too eaten up by her own sense of loss to comfort him. She hoped he could read her as well as she understood him. She didn't blame him for Annette's deeds.

The air-conditioning cooled her skin, but her eyes burned. Her head drooped on the back of the seat and she closed her eyes. *Please God, let him be all right.* That mantra continued to beat in her head, closing off everything else.

She didn't have to worry about Yolanda. Both Dionne and Kyra had showed up on her doorstep minutes after her call. The two women shooed the three of them out the door with assurances that they'd stay with Yolanda as long as necessary.

Kelleigh sat low in the front passenger seat, hands clasped in her lap. From time to time, Xavier glanced at her.

Although the van was tinted, Xavier and Justine agreed it was better if she traveled in the back. He had begged her to remain in the vehicle and let him negotiate with Annette.

Although unsure that she wouldn't go back on what she told him and do whatever was necessary when the time came, Justine had given him her word.

She sat forward when the Corolla before them slowed and stopped by the curb. Xavier parked behind Dennis, in line with a driveway that led to a narrow, two-story house. A mango tree grew close to one side of the building, shielding it from the sun. The wine-red roof, and closed shutters in the same color, reminded Justine of dried blood. Nothing moved behind the windows on the first floor. Justine didn't know where they were, having sat in a vacuum during the ten-minute ride.

"Are you sure she's here?" Justine asked.

Her voice was rusty, as though she hadn't used it in ages.

Xavier nodded. "This is where she told Dennis to come."

Gripping the seat, Justine sat forward. "What now?"

"Dennis, Kelleigh and I go inside. You wait here."

She opened her mouth to protest, but Xavier touched her hand. "I know this is hard, but sit tight. I'll get him back, okay? Remember you promised me."

Letting her breath out through her lips, Justine nodded.

Xavier squeezed Kelleigh's shoulder. "You ready?"

She nodded and opened the door while Xavier brushed his knuckles over Justine's injured cheek. "Soon come."

Gripping both sides of the seat in front of her, Justine watched them. Dennis opened the gate and got on the phone when he stepped inside the yard. He spoke into it while walking around the side of the house, with Xavier and Kelleigh close behind.

Feeling trapped in the vehicle and chilled by the air-conditioning Justine got out, looking at her watch. Only half-an-hour had passed since Emile disappeared, yet it seemed a lifetime had whipped by. She paced the width of the driveway, wanting to go inside the property to see what was happening, but she'd promised. The evening sun did nothing to warm her skin or her empty insides.

She cocked one ear, sure she'd heard voices. Facing the truck, she thought for a moment. What if she left it and somebody stole it? That was quite possible though the neighborhood seemed decent enough and nobody would blame her, given the circumstances. She turned toward the house, muttering. "To hell with it."

She opened the gate, ran across the grass and kept to the wall until she came to a verandah at the back. A dusty washing machine and a patio chair occupied one corner. The grille and door were half open. She stepped onto the verandah and stopped to listen.

Dennis was speaking, but she couldn't understand all his words. He sounded as if he was pleading. "...only make things worse."

Annette yelled, her speech garbled.

"Daddy, I want to go home," Emile cried.

Justine's hand jerked, banging the grille shut behind her. The voices stopped and in the next few seconds noise exploded in the room.

A scream from Kelleigh. "Mommy, no!"

A pained yelp. "Annette!"

A shocked cry from Dennis. "Jesus!"

Sobbing from Emile.

Justine yanked the door wider and in an instant, assessed what had happened. The scene resembled one from a movie set. Annette stood at an angle from Justine, gaping at Xavier and holding a dripping knife.

Blood ran from Xavier's elbow, staining his shirt. Dennis looked at Xavier's arm, sighed and shook his head.

Emile cowered beside Kelleigh, who stood with her back to the door. "I want my Mommy," he said, sniffling.

"Shut up," Annette screamed, facing Xavier and her cousin. She shifted her gaze to Xavier. "I didn't mean to do that."

"Fine, then get rid of the knife," Xavier said.

Dennis moved toward Annette, his hand outstretched. "Give it to me before you hurt anybody else."

With one palm pressed to her forehead, Annette stuck out her arm. "I don't know why...I'm sorry."

Dennis took the kitchen knife by the handle and met Justine's eyes over Annette's shoulder. He shook his head.

Justine ignored his warning and grabbed Emile. He struggled to get away until she called his name. Sobbing, he flung both arms around her waist and pressed his face to her shirt.

Annette rushed forward, her hands fisted. Justine held Emile tighter, swinging him around so he was out of Annette's reach. Absently, Justine noticed that the only evidence of their run-in was Annette's swollen lips.

"What are you doing here?" Annette asked.

"Mommy, don't!" Kelleigh grabbed Annette and pulled her backward. Pinning her flailing arms to her sides, Dennis helped restrain Annette.

Justine covered Emile's ears, expecting abuse from Annette, but she only asked a question. "Why did you have to come back into his life? We would have—"

"Come on, Annette," Xavier said, his voice low. "You and I were finished before Justine came back into the picture. It's time to stop pretending there's anything left between us and get on with your life. I need to see a doctor. We'll talk after that."

Annette moaned and dropped on the sofa, crying. Dennis sat with her, holding on to her arm. She tried to dislodge his hand, but he wouldn't let go. "I'm taking Xavier to the hospital and dropping you off at Babs's house."

"I want to go to my own home."

"Don't try my patience," Dennis said. "One more word out of you and I'm taking you to the lockup tonight on assault charges."

"You can say anything you like, but—"

Dennis tugged Annette's arm and spoke close to her ear. "I'm speaking to you as an officer of the law and not your cousin. If you refuse to cooperate, I'll make sure you have at least a few days in lockup where you can think about what you've done. You hear me?"

She stared at the opposite wall and refused to answer.

"Did you hear me?"

"Yes, and you don't need to tear my arm off."

"Consider yourself lucky. Losing a limb would be a small return for all the trouble you've caused today. Where are the keys for this house?"

Annette pulled a key ring from her skirt and gave it to Dennis without looking at him.

Pressing his shirt over the cut, Xavier crossed the room to stand beside Justine. The white undershirt he wore also had bloodstains.

"Are you going to be okay?" she asked, feeling useless.

"Yeah. Can you drive the truck?"

She nodded and caught Kelleigh watching her. Smoothing a hand over Emile's hair, Justine asked, "You want me to keep Kelleigh until you get your hand looked at?"

He nodded. "Thanks."

Xavier hugged Kelleigh with his good arm. "You'll be okay until I come back?"

Kelleigh nodded. "Yeah."

"Xave?"

He looked at Justine over Kelleigh's head.

"You should keep your hand up, to slow the bleeding."

He let Kelleigh go and followed Justine's advice, holding his hand upright.

Justine moved toward the door, taking Emile with her. She wondered whether she'd be able to let him go to school tomorrow, trembling at the thought of having him out of her sight. Kelleigh walked behind them, turning back when her mother called her name.

Dennis got Annette off the couch, speaking to her so no one else could hear his words. Kelleigh moved slowly toward her mother and stood before her. Annette put her arms around Kelleigh, crying into her shoulder. "I'm sorry, baby."

Kelleigh stood with both hands hanging at her sides. Sighing, Justine turned away, taking Emile with her. Inside the truck, he put on the slippers Justine had brought with her.

Nobody said anything on the drive home. Emile sat in the front seat, while Kelleigh slouched in the back, staring out the window. At home, Yolanda, Kyra and Dionne kissed and petted Emile, who didn't mind the attention and told them what had happened in minute detail. After her friends left, Justine sat on the toilet lid helping Emile with his shower.

When he got out of the tub, she dried him gently, as she had when he was a baby. He stood still, touched her cheek and then examined his fingers. "You're crying, Mommy."

She bobbed her head, unable to speak.

"It's okay," he said, stroking her cheek. "She didn't hurt me."

"Are you sure?"

"She only hit me once, when I was crying." He ducked his head as though embarrassed. "She said big boys don't cry for their Mommies and I was to shut up."

Squeezing him to her inside the towel, Justine said. "It's okay for you to cry if you want to, even if you're a big boy."

Wondering whether she should put him through his experience again, she asked, "How did she get you into the car?"

"I saw her talking with Daddy at the shop yesterday. She told me Daddy sent her to get me. When I said I couldn't go without my sandals, she told me to shut up and pushed me inside."

"But hon, remember what I told you about never going anywhere with strangers?"

Emile shook his head. "She's not a stranger. She told me she's Kelleigh's mommy."

Knowing she couldn't win this argument, Justine changed tack. "Why did she cut your father?"

"She didn't mean it. Daddy was trying to get me away from her, so she waved the knife to keep him from taking me and it cut him."

Justine was sure there was more to it than that, but sent him to his room to put on fresh clothes. She went back to the living room and found Kelleigh sitting where she'd left her. The television was on, but though Kelleigh looked at the screen, Justine knew she wasn't watching.

In the kitchen, Yolanda rattled around, preparing a snack.

Justine sat in the small settee, trying to put words together. She fixed the hair at her nape that had come undone. "You know none of this is your fault right?"

Kelleigh nodded, but her closed expression and slumped shoulders said she thought otherwise.

"Sometimes adults aren't sure what they want and it can be confusing for everybody."

"I know," she said. "Mom is a good example. She doesn't really want Daddy, but she doesn't want to live without him either. Kinda the way she feels about me."

"I'm sure she loves you."

"Yeah, but she doesn't know what to do with me when I'm around."

Justine didn't understand why Kelleigh chose to take her into her confidence, but recognized that she needed someone impartial to listen to her thoughts.

"Give it time. Things have a way of working out and people do change." Justine checked that Yolanda was still occupied in the kitchen before she continued speaking. "Your father and I, uh, we never meant to hurt your mother. We didn't meet again until a few months ago."

"I know."

Justine wasn't sure what else she knew, but now wasn't the time to ask. Yolanda came into the living room, carrying a tray. She gave Kelleigh a bowl of ice cream and Jello, set another dish on the center table and went back to the kitchen. When she returned, she dropped into the seat beside Kelleigh and handed her a spoon.

"Thanks." Kelleigh ate a scoop of the pistachio ice cream before placing the bowl on the table. She shifted on the cushion and twisted her fingers together. After a glance at Yolanda, she cleared her throat. "I don't mind if you and my dad get together."

They exchanged another look and Yolanda smothered a smile, sucking on the spoon. "I don't think she's going to listen to you. My mother takes a lotta convincing. I told her I wouldn't mind either, but she doesn't believe me."

Justine opened her mouth to protest, but stayed quiet in the face of the eye rolls and giggling going on across the center table.

Yolanda poked Kelleigh with her elbow. "Having you as a sister would be pretty cool."

Justine's face went hot at the thought of the two girls discussing her business, when she didn't even know whether she was coming or going. "Don't get carried away guys. Xavier and I aren't…"

She didn't finish. Yolanda said something to Kelleigh that made her crack another smile. Emile hung over the back of the sofa. "Where's my ice cream?'

"In the fridge," Yolanda answered.

A moment later, Emile wriggled between Kelleigh and Yolanda, who made room for him. He ate the ice cream with his usual appetite, giving no hint that he'd been in danger a short while ago. Justine gave thanks for his safe return, unable to take her eyes off him.

Meanwhile, the two girls continued to watch her, as if they knew something she didn't.

– 42 –

Sunday, May 8, 7:00 PM

Xavier

Proverb: Di best o' field must have weed.
Meaning: The best of people or situations come with flaws.

"That should be it," the doctor said, squinting behind his glasses. He laid the scissors down and removed his gloves. "Give me a moment."

He left the room and returned with a sheet of paper, which he shoved at Xavier. "Antibiotics and pain meds. You want to fill this tonight."

"Thanks," Xavier said and got to his feet. On his way out of the tiny treatment room, he folded the prescription and slipped it into his shirt pocket. He glanced across the corridor at the roomful of people still waiting to see a doctor. Thank God that was over for him. A text from Dennis five minutes ago confirmed that he was waiting in the parking lot. He rang Kelleigh, who answered, sounding breathless.

"Daddy, everything all right?"

"Yeah, I got some stitches. Nothing to worry about."

"Good. You coming soon then?"

"Yeah, give me another twenty minutes or so."

"All right." A few seconds passed, then she whispered, "Love you, Daddy."

He smiled. "Love you too, Baby Girl."

He stood on the verandah, scanning the asphalted lot for Dennis's Corolla. When he found it, he held his arm at an angle to take the pressure off it and got into the car.

"I guess you'll be okay," Dennis said, swinging onto the roadway.

"Yeah. It could have been worse. The knife missed the main artery."

Dennis sighed. "I don't even know what Annette was thinking. This is so way out as to be unbelievable."

Xavier couldn't help the edge to his voice when he spoke. "Is it?"

A horn blared ahead of them, which made Xavier wonder at the number of people on the road at that time on a Sunday evening. Dennis waited for the traffic to move before he asked, "What d'you mean?"

"You must be the only one who hasn't noticed that Annette has changed, yet the two of you are so close."

He nodded. "She has changed, but this is just weird."

"I'm not sure she meant to cut me, but what the hell was she doing with a knife? And to hold Emile like that at knifepoint? I'm surprised he didn't piss his pants. I don't even want to think about what could have happened if she'd cut anybody else."

"You mean Emile or Justine." Though Dennis's words sounded like a question, it was more of a statement. "You're not thinking about pressing charges?"

"Would it solve anything?"

Dennis shook his head. "What you gonna do about her?"

As they went past a row of jerked chicken vendors on the side of the road, the smoky aroma made Xavier's stomach grumble. He hadn't eaten since early afternoon. He forced himself to focus on the conversation.

"Question is, what are *you* going to do? She'll listen to you. You better convince her to get counseling."

"How am I going to get her to do that?" Dennis asked, glancing at him.

"I don't know, but if you don't, I *will* press charges. If only to let her know she can't run around acting like a mad woman."

Dennis slowed as they approached the next stoplight. "Would you really do that?"

Trying to find a comfortable position for his hand, Xavier asked, "What would you do if you had a partner who knows your relationship is over, but is hanging on out of spite?"

"Annette thinks things can still work between both of you. Maybe—"

Xavier shook his head. "Look, she signed the divorce papers because she knows as well as I do that it's too late for us. I'm a convenience that Annette is used to having around. She's forgotten what a relationship is about and I've gone down that road and stayed there too long with no cooperation from her. I'm done, and she needs to move on."

Rubbing his hand over his smooth head, Dennis yawned. A moment later he spoke. "That's easier said than done, but anyway, I'll do the best I can."

"Another thing. Whose house is that and how did she get the keys?"

"It belongs to one of her co-workers. She said something about it being up for sale. I suspect she told the owner she wanted to have a look at it."

Annette had no intention of buying another house and it wasn't her style anyhow, which made Xavier think she'd planned her actions with care, using the property as a convenience. "I wonder what the owner would think about what she's done today."

Dennis didn't answer and Xavier decided to let the argument go; his brain could use the rest.

A few chains from another group of chicken vendors, Dennis swung the car into the parking lot of an all-night pharmacy. "Where's your prescription?"

Xavier handed it to him with some cash, and settled his head against the seat. While waiting to see the doctor, he'd gone back to the time spent with Justine earlier in the evening.

Despite her faults, nobody could say she wasn't a good mother. Her care and concern for her children was always evident. Hell, she even had enough compassion to spare for his daughter, though it had to be painful to look at Kelleigh.

His thoughts strayed to the subject he'd been avoiding since he left for the hospital. Did Annette intend to harm Emile? He didn't know. All he knew was that when she held on to Emile and started waving the knife around, he couldn't risk losing the child who had renewed his interest in being a father.

Shame settled on him. Sure, he loved Kelleigh, but he'd been marking time living day by day. And then came Emile, a vivid splash of color on the drab canvas of his life, and how could he deny that Justine had made him interested in love again? Plus, she'd always stirred his desire for sex.

Did he have the time or energy to take a chance on Justine again? He sighed, admitting he was a coward, like Justine. She seemed to have put her life on hold, just as he had.

Her main issues seemed to be sharing Emile's love and the uncertainty surrounding Annette. His only fear was that she would disappoint him, but it was stupid to waste more time when what he wanted was in front of him. All he had to do was leave the past where it belonged and accept what Justine was offering.

Dennis's return brought Xavier's mind back to the brightly-lit parking lot. He picked up the paper bag Dennis threw in his lap and opened it. "Thanks."

Suddenly tired and sleepy, and knowing he'd be a fool to attempt driving tonight, Xavier said, "I'll leave the truck at Justine's place and get a ride home with you."

"No problem."

They pulled into Justine's driveway and parked. She'd left the light on in the carport, where her car was locked in. A smile pulled at Xavier's lips when he imagined having the lights left on for him. That was the kind of considerate thing Justine would do.

"I'll be out soon," he said.

Dennis nodded, fiddling with the radio dial. "Take your time."

When Xavier got out of the car, Justine was at the entrance and had the padlock open. She'd changed into a shift that clung to her curves. She let him in and took his right arm, her gazed fixed on the bandage on his other arm. "Will it be okay?"

He nodded. "Yeah."

"Will you be able to play, I mean?"

Despite feeling as if he would fall at any moment, Xavier pulled her closer, kissing her temple as they entered the living room. "Yes, in a few weeks, I'll be as good as new."

"That's a relief," she said, through swollen lips. Her eyes were red, but her gaze reflected relief and affection. She examined him as closely as he was watching her. Then she smiled, splayed her fingers across his back and rested her head on his chest. Pleased that she'd cast aside her usual restraint, Xavier dropped a kiss on her forehead.

"Where are the kids?" he asked.

"In Emile's room. The girls are playing some kind of video game with him."

"I called Kell on my way here. She'll probably be out any minute now." He stepped back, holding on to Justine's arms. "You know we need to talk, right?"

She nodded, keeping her eyes on his shirt. "Can I ask you something?"

"Sure."

"What are you going to do about Annette?"

He let his arms drop and stepped away. "Does where we go from here depend on my answer?"

She dipped her head and folded her arms around her body. Her voice was low, forcing him to concentrate. "I'm afraid, Xavier. I've always been cautious, a coward as you say, but I want to..."

Never in a million years would he have expected her to admit so openly what he had accused her of so often in the past. He missed what she said after that, but was too preoccupied to be irritated by his inattentiveness.

"...with you, but what if—?"

A slamming door and high-pitched giggles stopped Justine. Kelleigh and Yolanda came down the passage and entered the living room. Emile ran behind them, bolting to Xavier's side. "I was worried about your arm, but Mommy said the doctor would fix it up."

Xavier squeezed his shoulder. "Yeah, he did a good job. I got stitches and all."

Emile's eyes opened as wide as twenty dollar coins. "Can I see?"

"Yeah, but you have to wait until the bandage comes off."

"Oh," Emile said, staring at the bulky dressing.

A few more seconds' worth of staring at Emile reassured Xavier that the child would be okay. Still, he couldn't resist making sure. "You all right, Little Man? From today, I mean."

He waved both arms. "I've never been kidnapped before. I'm gonna tell everybody about it in school tomorrow."

Silence filled the room. The two teenagers looked at both Xavier and Justine. Yolanda burst out laughing, while Kelleigh lowered her head and allowed a pained smile to slip out. When he looked at Justine, Xavier confirmed that she wore the same horrified expression he did.

"Uh, hon," Justine beckoned for Emile to come to her. "That's not exactly something you can talk about with your friends. Besides, Annette didn't mean you any harm."

Emile's mouth dropped open. "But she said she'd slap me silly if I didn't shut up."

"I know, but it would be best not to talk about it, okay?"

From Emile's puzzled expression, it was clear he didn't understand the logic behind Justine's request, but he nodded and let a few seconds pass before asking, "I can't even tell Kevin?"

Slowly, Justine shook her head. "It's better if we keep it in the family."

Emile put both hands on his hips. "What about Miss Pauline? Can I tell her when she comes back in the morning?"

Xavier didn't hear Justine's response and wasn't sure what she meant by family, but the sound of it pleased him. Seeing their children together provided a snapshot of what life with Justine might be like. "Time to go, Kell," he said, realizing that Dennis had been waiting a while now. "I'll call you, Emile."

Kelleigh said her good-byes, rubbed Emile's head and left the house. Justine followed Xavier out the door with Emile trailing behind. Xavier stood beside Justine, his arm around her waist.

"Can I leave the truck here until tomorrow?" Xavier asked.

"Sure. How's Kelleigh getting to school?"

He hadn't thought about that, but improvised without stopping to think. "I'm sure I can arrange something."

"Don't worry about it," Justine said. "If you don't mind, I can pick her up. Her school isn't far from Landy's."

"Okay, I'll talk to her and confirm with you when I get home." He brushed her lips with his. "Thanks for everything."

She touched his cheek. "I'm just glad you're okay and that we got Emile back. Go get some rest."

He kissed her again, whispering against her lips. "We'll talk soon." To Emile he said, "You're a brave boy. Take care of Mommy, okay?"

Emile stood straighter and hugged Justine's waist. "Okay, I will."

As they drove away, Xavier closed his eyes, aware that he had several critical issues that needed to be settled.

***

On the way to the kitchen to take his pain medication, Xavier passed Kelleigh in the living room. The television was on, but she was busy with the cell phone, her fingers moving over the keypad. He drank water, staring out the back window, his mind occupied by Justine.

Kelleigh laughed, and he smiled in response. He'd gotten used to having her around again and here he was contemplating another change in his life.

He strolled back into the living room to stand in front of the sofa. "You do remember you have school tomorrow?"

"But Daddy, it's just after nine."

"And time for you to be in bed."

She turned off the television and stood, rolling her eyes. He ignored her snit and hugged her, smiling into her hair. "I did tell you about the ground rules you'd have to live by while you're here."

"Fine, but you're such a killjoy."

He chuckled. "Yeah, but I'm only doing it because I care and it's what's best for you."

"I know. By the way, who owns that house where Mom took Emile?"

"It's a long story, but nothing for you to worry about."

In front of her bedroom door, Kelleigh stopped him with a hand to his arm. "You remember what we were talking about earlier?"

He nodded and waited while she decided what she needed to say. "I didn't ask what you're going do about Mommy, but I still can't believe she did that. I know she wouldn't hurt me, but it makes me nervous just thinking about what she might do if she gets really upset." Kelleigh leaned against the wall and tipped her head back to look at him. "And what you gonna do about Auntie Jay?"

He was caught flatfooted, but hid his surprise. He should have known she'd broadside him with her concerns. He rubbed his forehead, acknowledging this as the third time he'd been asked the same question today. Stroking her cheek, he said, "Don't worry too much, okay? Things will work out."

"I hope so." She hugged him around the waist. "Just don't take too long to figure things out. Auntie Jay really likes you, but I don't think any sane woman would put up with what happened today, and remember you're not getting any younger."

"Are you saying Justine's sanity is in question?"

Despite his straight face, Kelleigh smirked. "I'm not saying another word. I might get in trouble."

Hiding a smile, he ruffled her hair. "Have I told you yet today that you're way too cheeky?"

"Naw, this is the first time." She laughed and slipped inside the bedroom to switch on the light. "G'nite, Daddy."

"Remember Justine is picking you up at seven, so go straight to bed."

She rolled her eyes again. "Right away, Captain Killjoy."

When he lay in bed with his arm propped on a pillow, trying to ignore the drumbeat inside, Xavier rehashed the day's events—Justine's panic, but her willingness to let him take the lead, her disobedience overtaking good sense, her concern for him and Kelleigh, her helpfulness in the face of his temporary handicap.

He smiled in the darkness.

When she put her fears aside, Justine was a wonderful ally and one hell of a woman.

– 43 –

Tuesday, May 10, 5:00 PM

Xavier

Proverb: Want all, lose all.

    Meaning: When you become too greedy, you lose everything.

"Why didn't you bring Kelleigh?" Annette asked.

Xavier chose to ignore her demanding tone. He wanted to leave quickly, minus any drama. "She's with her study group," he said.

"Are you sure?"

"Yeah, I spoke with her friend's mother and I'm picking her up after I leave here."

"So when are you bringing her home?"

He scratched his brow, wondering if Annette understood the seriousness of what she'd done and how it affected their situation.

"As soon as I think you're stable," he said, resting his elbow on the chair carefully so as not to put any pressure on the stitches in his arm.

"Are you serious?" She turned toward Dennis, who came into the living room carrying a bottle of Red Stripe Beer.

"Do I look like I've lost my mind?" she asked.

"Sometimes I have to wonder," Dennis said, and sat in the small sofa. He rested the beer on the center table and wiped his palm on his jeans. "I agree with Xavier on this. If Kelleigh was my daughter, I wouldn't let her back in this house until you proved to me that you're in your right mind."

"Well, she *is* my daughter and—"

Dennis held up one hand to stop Annette. "And you're in no position to demand anything. Since you weren't convinced when I spoke to you on Sunday night, I asked Xavier to come here this evening and outline the way things are going to be."

Annette folded her hands in her lap and let a blank expression cover her face. In Xavier's mind, the white wraparound dress that fell to her ankles reflected her empty life.

"You may feel you've been wronged, but you crossed a line when you took Emile," Xavier said.

Annette didn't respond, but by the way she held herself, Xavier guessed she didn't feel any differently about the circumstances now than she did on Sunday. He didn't give a hoot about her feelings, but did want her to realize he was serious.

"I'd like to know how you got Justine's telephone number and e-mail address, and how you know where she lives."

Annette continued wearing her poker face while running one hand over the chair arm. A multi-hued flash of light grabbed his attention; Annette still wore her engagement ring and wedding band. That was, of course, her choice and nothing to do with him.

Dennis sat forward and touched his cousin's arm. "I'm not sure you realize that what you did is illegal. That's stalking. Now, how did you come by that kind of personal information?"

She crossed her arms and mumbled into her chest. "I have a friend who works for the phone company."

Xavier scratched his ear, wondering whether Annette was telling the truth. God help Lorraine Delancy if he found out she'd had anything to do with this. A few minutes went by before he said what was on his mind. "I could insist that you tell us who this 'friend' is, but I won't. What I *am* going to insist on, is that you see a therapist."

She drew her head back and cut her eyes at him as if he was the one with his mental faculties in question.

"Don't look at me like that," he said. "I'm not doing this out of spite. I want to be sure you can take care of my daughter and that you're working on all that anger and bitterness that has you doing irrational things that make me doubt your sanity."

"But—"

"Here's the deal. Either you go to therapy or I'm reporting what you did to the police. We'll see what happens to your custody application after you're charged with a criminal offense."

Annette turned toward Dennis. "You goin' to let him do that to me?"

Dennis shook his head. "You did this to yourself. You're damn lucky he hasn't made a report already, especially since you gave us your word on Sunday."

Annette moved to the edge of the seat, clasping her hands. "I didn't mean to hurt anybody. It happened because you took Kelleigh and—"

"Don't start that again. I'm beginning to think you have quicksilver in your brain." Xavier got up, pacing in front of the settee. He stopped where she sat. "It's decision time. The way I see it, you have only one option, and don't think I won't be making sure you follow through."

They stared at each other for several moments, while Xavier wondered where the woman he married had gone. With a tiny shake of the head, he acknowledged that he too had changed. He just wasn't sure whether for better or worse. He quieted his thoughts when Annette spoke.

"Fine, I'll make an appointment tomorrow."

He sat, staring deep into her eyes. Despite what her clear gaze told him, something in his psyche warned that Annette was showing him what she figured he wanted to see. He buried the thought and told himself it was important for her to understand exactly where he stood now; he could analyze everything else later.

"Further to that," he said, "you don't contact Justine or Emile again. Ever. They have nothing to do with us. You do anything to hurt either of them and I'll make you wish you had died and gone to hell. D'you understand me?"

She acknowledged him with a nod.

"Good. Kelleigh will call you later."

After giving Dennis a grateful nod, Xavier got to his feet and left the house where he'd spent most of his manhood. He drove away, aware that a new chapter of his life was about to unfold and that he held Justine and their children's future in his hands.

— 44 —

Saturday, May 28

Justine

Proverb: Love and cough can never hide.
Meaning: Someone in love is as obvious as a cough.

"Mom, just go," Yolanda said, giving Kelleigh a sidelong glance.

"Yeah, we'll be okay. Really." Kelleigh nodded encouragement to Justine, who watched Emile hopping from foot to foot.

He wore swimming trunks and a tee-shirt with the water park's logo that Xavier had bought him in the gift shop. Emile tugged at Yolanda's blouse, pointing to where a man was handing out rubber tubing. "I want to go on that ride next."

"Soon," Yolanda said, pleading with Xavier silently. "If Mom would just go."

Xavier dropped an arm over Justine's shoulder. "They'll be fine until we get back. We'll only be away for an hour or so and there are lifeguards assigned to all the rides."

"And remember, the sooner you go away." Emile waved both hands at them. "The sooner you can come back."

His gesture made Justine laugh, since he was only interested in getting on the next ride and enjoying himself with them out of the way.

"Okay, guys," Justine said. "Remember to call us if you need anything. Are you sure you have enough money?"

Both girls nodded, showed their teeth in pseudo-smiles and waved good-bye. Emile stamped his foot and yelled in a two-syllable, sing-song voice. "Mom!"

Justine raised both hands in a gesture of surrender. "Okay, I'm going. Later, guys."

"Bye, Mommy and Daddy! See you later!" Emile waved madly before dragging Yolanda and Kelleigh in the opposite direction.

Xavier chuckled, gently turning Justine toward the parking lot. She looked over her shoulder while their children disappeared in the crowd of people seeking thrills on the water slides.

"You need to learn how to relax," Xavier said, when they sat inside his truck.

"It's just that Emile—"

"Will be well-taken care of by his sisters."

"The water park—"

"Has an army of lifeguards who know how to do their job."

"The girls—"

"Are growing older every day and need to be trusted to be responsible, and they're crazy about Emile, okay?"

"You mean Kelleigh is crazy about Emile," Justine mumbled, unwilling to be pacified.

Xavier squeezed her leg. "Come on, Yolanda loves him. You know that."

"Yeah, I know." She sighed and stared through the windscreen, admitting she was beaten.

"You need to learn to relax. As they say, take a chill pill."

"Right." With her gaze, she followed the coastal road they were now traveling.

He touched her chin. "I'm serious. Promise me you'll try to enjoy our time together without obsessing about the kids."

The affectionate light in his eyes reminded Justine how much she had longed to see that exact reaction from him. She ran the back of her hand under his chin, grateful that he had overlooked her weakness and stupidity and given her another chance. She unsnapped the seatbelt and kissed his cheek. "I promise."

"Good girl," he said, giving her leg another squeeze.

While planning their one-day trip to Negril, they all agreed that while the kids were at the water park, Xavier and she would spend some time at a nearby all-inclusive hotel using day passes. The two weeks during which they organized the outing gave Justine and Xavier a chance to reconnect. The two families also got to know each other better.

After lunch and a stroll through the hotel property, Justine urged Xavier down to the strip of coastline that was part of the Seven-Mile-Beach. Eyes closed, and face turned up to the sun, Justine dug her toes in the powdery white sand. Xavier carried her sandals swinging from his fingers. Dressed as they were in casual gear, they would look like a regular couple out for a stroll, but Justine knew there was much more to their private interlude.

He took her hand, humming *You are the Sunshine of My Life*—something he used to do in the old days. Tears rushed to her eyes, forcing her to turn her head aside. When Xavier squeezed her hand, she met his gaze embarrassed by the tears trailing down her cheeks.

She hoped none of the tourists lying on the row of beach chairs noticed she was crying.

He led her away from the shore and pulled her into the shade of a coconut tree, holding her close. "You're remembering that walk we took on the beach and that other night when we made love for the first time."

She nodded as their mad coupling on the sand came to mind in vivid color, making her want him now. They weren't free then and she'd agonized over their actions.

He kissed her forehead. "It's time to release the past, Tina. It's gone. We can never make what we did right, but we can move on from here knowing that we'll be doing things differently this time."

She couldn't say a word if she tried. Joy swelled inside her, stealing her voice and bringing more tears to her eyes. She sobbed into his shoulder, unable to explain what was happening to her.

His divorce was final more than two weeks ago, and since that time, she assumed—by his actions—that he still wanted to be with her. Before the divorce, she'd hardly dared to pray for what she desired more than anything in life, but now that both of them were free, all she wanted was to be with Xavier.

He held her away, frowning. From his pocket, he pulled a hanky and dabbed her face. "Come on now, Justine. You're going to make people think I've been abusing you."

She smiled through her tears and kissed his chin. "Never."

"Then stop crying, woman."

"I can't help it! I'm just..."

He pressed his forehead to hers and wiped away a tear with this thumb. "Happy?"

She cupped both sides of his head and whispered in his ear. "You're the only man who's ever made me feel whole. Contented. Happy. I love you so much."

His eyes turned moist and he touched his lips to hers again. "I love you too. You know that. I've always loved you."

"And yet, for so long I thought you hated me."

"I explained that to you. Self-preservation. I don't think I'd have survived you cutting out on me again. One day I'll explain what you leaving without a word did to me, but not today. Today, I just want to be with you."

His words started her tears again.

"Come on, babes, you're gonna make me start crying in a minute."

That made her giggle. "Really? A tough guy like you?"

"You don't seem to realize that I can be a tough guy with everybody else but you."

She moved to one side, sure she'd seen a bench behind him. Gripping his hand, she walked to the cement seat and pulled him down beside her. He laid her sandals on the edge of the bench.

"There's something I want to know." She licked her lips, not sure she should even ask the question dying to fall from her lips. At his raised eyebrows and quick nod, she asked, "Did cutting your hair have anything to do with me?"

He stared out to sea, studying the rolling waves capped by white foam. He sat still for such a long while, she wondered if he'd forgotten the question, and when she tried pulling her hand out of his, he held on tight.

"Six months after you walked away, I decided to wipe every trace of you from my life. The hair was first to go because you were so fascinated with my locks." He turned his head toward her. "So yes, cutting them off had everything to do with you."

She ran her thumb back and forth over his skin, saddened by his confession. "I thought so."

For several minutes, they sat without touching. Then Justine moved closer and nudged his arm up and over her shoulder. She held on to his fingers and turned her head to kiss his palm.

Her eyes went liquid again, forcing her to tip her head backward to prevent the tears from falling. "Xave, just so you know. There hasn't been a day in these seven years that I haven't thought about you. I wanted to contact you so many times, but..." She shrugged. "I just couldn't face you with what I'd done. I couldn't wreck your family or tell Emile. Yolanda. And I still haven't told Emile's grandmother, which I have to do. Some time.

"When Milton died, it was simpler to go on as if things were normal." She took a deep breath and let it out slowly. "Dionne and Kyra said it would backfire on me, and they were right."

"Your friends are smart women. One day you should introduce me to them properly."

"Don't worry, they're dying to meet you *properly* too."

"I'm sure we can arrange that."

Xavier moved his lips lightly against hers until her lashes fluttered down. He made her wait and when his tongue slid into her mouth, she purred deep in her throat. The sweet invasion brought back the memory of his lovemaking nearly a month ago.

His fingers skimmed the front of her shirt, setting her nerve endings alight. Justine pulled her thighs together and the wind's caress reminded her they were on a beach. She broke the kiss, giggling. "What is it with you, me and beaches?"

"Dunno, but we're a tad too old to be caught and charged for getting on bad in a public place."

"I agree with you there."

"So, woman of my dreams." He faced her, letting his arm rest along the back of the bench. "I haven't got a ring yet, but when are you gonna marry me and my daughter?"

Her mouth opened, but no sound came out. She wrapped her ponytail around her hand and tried again. "Whenever you care to have me and my daughter and our son."

"How does as soon as possible sound?"

"Sounds like paradise to me, Mr. McKellop."

The wash of the sea, the sand between her toes, and Xavier's company was all Justine needed now. The children came to mind and a moment later, Annette, along with the fear Justine still held that retribution would come because of her relationship with Xavier.

"You never did say how you dealt with Annette, and after what happened with her, I still worry about Emile."

"She's in therapy. It was that or face charges. Trust me. You won't have to worry about her."

"Okay. Have you thought about where we're going to live?"

"Somewhere new, I think. Both our homes have too much history. We need to make new memories in our own space."

"I like the sound of that. You know Emile will want all kinds of details, like when we're gonna be together as a family and where we'll be living."

"I wonder where he came by that need-to-know-now disorder." Xavier laughed, a carefree sound that put a smile on her face.

"And what will—"

He put a finger to her lips. "Tina, stop. We'll have the devil of a time keeping track of two teenagers with hormones running wild and one kid who wants to experience everything today. If you don't slow down, you'll stress yourself to death before we even start the journey."

He removed the cell phone from his waist and looked at it. Smiling, he put the instrument to his ear. "I didn't expect to hear from you lot so soon. You guys ready?"

He listened for a bit before his smile graduated to a grin. "No, we won't stay gone for the rest of the day and no, you can't come back to Negril next week."

Justine didn't have to ask which of their children was on the phone. When Xavier hung up, she rested a hand on his thigh. "Are you sure you know what you're getting yourself into?"

He tickled the back of her neck and then stroked her ponytail. "Anywhere you are is where I want to be. Plus, Emile is a wonderful bonus that makes us complete."

She pressed both hands to his chest, studying his facial features. The wind blew her hair against his skin, and while he tried in vain to neaten her ponytail, she gazed at him, unashamed of her open adoration. "Xavier McKellop, one day I hope to find the words to tell you how much you mean to me."

"And I'll never stop trying to find the right ones to tell you how much I love you," he murmured against her lips.

That promise was enough for Justine.

Absolution

Wednesday, June 1

Xavier has a damn nerve. He bloody well knows I don't belong here.

Annette studied her nails before she continued scanning the room.

The cobalt-blue blinds hid the afternoon sun from her eyes and sealed her in a cozy space dominated by a mahogany desk, plush furniture and a floor-to-ceiling bookshelf crammed with reference books.

She studied the rings on her left hand. So many memories were contained in those pieces of platinum and baguette diamonds. How Xavier expected her to just get on with her life after seventeen years of marriage, she didn't know. He'd taken twenty years of her life and left her to start over with that bitch and the bastard they'd gotten between them.

Movement from the other side of the desk reminded Annette she wasn't in the room alone. Majorie Dacres watched her. Having to see a therapist was laughable, not to mention humiliating. She, a social worker and not just any social worker. The human psyche was her area of specialization; the path she'd chosen for her career. She almost had a Master's, for heaven's sake.

Pity you didn't do such a great job with your family.

She banished that thought. Studying had eaten up most of her adult life, but the results were worth the sacrifices she'd made. She was one of Jamaica's eminent consultants in the Social Services, her specialty being children and family life. The irony of being inside the office of a family life minister as a patient didn't escape her.

Annette's skin crawled again and a tide of heat washed upward from her chest to scald her face. The only reason she was here was because Xavier insisted he'd press charges if she didn't see a therapist. Never mind the fact that she'd explained why she cut him and that she hadn't meant to do it.

The only good thing that came out of that disaster was that her daughter Kelleigh was now coming around. The nervous looks she sometimes threw at Annette disturbed her, but they'd been at odds for so long it was no wonder her fifteen year old couldn't appreciate the mother-daughter bond that was a natural part of life.

The therapist shifted in her chair and folded her hands on the desk. "Mrs. McKellop, why are you here?"

Annette made the dumpy woman wait while she thought about what to say. Her blue-white hair was at odds with her unlined face and plump body. She looked more like forty than the sixty-odd-year-old grandmother Annette knew her to be.

Ms. Dacres cleared her throat. "Mrs. McKellop?"

Glancing at her watch, Annette sat erect in the seat that was more sofa than patient's chair. She smoothed the skirt of her business suit and looked to the woman's left, latching on to the pearl earring that clung to her earlobe.

"My husband insisted that I come." She studied the toes of her leather pumps. "There was an incident."

"So you came under duress."

Gritting her teeth, Annette answered, "Yes."

A smile entered the woman's voice. "As you know, there shouldn't be any embarrassment about seeing a therapist, but as professionals, we know there's a stigma attached."

Her chair squeaked and she moved something on the desk before speaking again. "It's clear you're feeling some resistance, but if you're going to be seeing me, it makes sense for us not to waste each other's time. Can we start with the incident that brought you here?"

Annette stared at the woman. Who the hell did she think she was to believe that a pep talk was what she needed? And that she was so weak-minded, she'd spill her guts at the first invitation. She probably knew more about the human mind and therapy than the old dinosaur across the desk.

Her anger stirred again. She didn't understand what Xavier thought would come out of his ridiculous stipulation that she go into therapy, but she knew one thing. Divorced from her or not, he wouldn't have a moment's happiness with that bitch and the bastard he'd gotten during their marriage.

Damn cheat!

While Annette twisted the rings on her finger, her gaze fell on a globe depicting a scene outside a country house. A strong desire to hurl it across the room swept over her. Wrecking the glass figurine would satisfy the anger twisting and tumbling in her belly. If only for the moment.

She skimmed the office with her eyes, working out what to stay to satisfy the woman in front of her and occupy the half hour that stretched before them. She traced the stitches on the leather case in her lap, while her thoughts wrapped around Xavier. If he believed he could leave her and their daughter behind like old newspaper, he could just think again.

Meet the Author

National Bestselling Author, J.L. Campbell, writes contemporary, paranormal, and sweet romance, romantic suspense, inspirational and women's fiction, thrillers, as well as new and young adult novels.

Campbell, who hails from Jamaica, has penned nearly fifty books. She is a certified editor, and book coach. When she's not writing, Campbell adds to her extensive collection of photos detailing Jamaica's beauty.

Connect with her on social media: https://sociatap.com/JL_Campbell

Or visit her on the internet at www.jlcampbellwrites.com

Other Books by J.L. Campbell

Savor the taste of tropical living by sampling the Island Adventure Romance series, which currently has five exciting, stand-alone stories that feature feisty women and determined men. Then have your fill of contemporary and sweet romance, new adult, young adult, thrillers, and women's fiction titles.

Romantic Suspense (Island Adventure Series)

Anya's Wish

Chasing Anya

Contraband

Taming Celeste

Grudge

Hardware

Lady Guardians: Bankrolled

King of Evanston (Kings of the Castle)

Knight of Paradise Island (Knights of the Castle)

Queen of Kingston (Queens of the Castle)

Operation Ivory (Promise Me A Miracle)

Hidden Enemy (Evanescence)

New Adult

Perfection

Fixation

Persuasion

Women's Fiction

A Baker's Dozen-13 Steps to Distraction (novella)

Dissolution

Distraction

Retribution

Absolution

The Thick of Things

The Heart of Things

The Pain of Things

Inspirational Fiction

DNA

Sacrifice

Dominic's Pride

Inspirational Non-Fiction

Vision: Aligning With God's Purpose For Your Life

Young Adult

Christine's Odyssey

Saving Sam

Short Story Collections

Don't Get Mad...Get Even (free)

Don't Get Mad...Get Even: Kicked to the Kerb

Contemporary Romance

The Short GameThe Long Game

The Spice of Life

The Blind Shot

The Spice of Life

Rory

Zorra

Contemporary Romance (Sweet Holiday Series)

The Vet's Christmas Pet

The Vet's Valentine GiftThe Vet's Secret Wish

Sold!

Cupid's Gift

Blindsided

Daycare Santa

Paranormal Romance

Phantasm

Thriller

Flames of Wrath

Murder by the Book

www.ingramcontent.com/pod-product-compliance
Lightning Source LLC
Chambersburg PA
CBHW020949260626
47169CB00006B/1888